PRAISE FOR P

PRAISE FOR *BROKEN PRINCE*

"If you want a movie like experience that'll give you so much and leave you hankering for more, you've got to read this!!"—Suzanne, *Tied Up In Romance*

"This book had it all. Great writing, awesome characters, high school drama, sexual tension of the charts, angst all wrapped up into an addictive package."—*Schmexy Girl Book Blog*

"... a dynamic story that was full of hilarious moments, gut wrenching events, provocative moments and a deviously angsty story line."—Miranda, *Red Cheek Reads*

"This book was cracktastic and totally addicting."—*Kimberlyfaye Reads*

"...this is one book that will have you turning the page with fervour and relishing every second."—Kelly, *Perusing Princesses*

"If you're looking for a book with a deliciously cruel and interesting cast of character, look no further. This is for you." - Rowena, *Book Binge*

TWISTED
PALACE

erin watt

ALSO BY ERIN WATT

Paper Princess
Broken Prince
Twisted Palace

COPYRIGHT

Copyright © 2016 by Erin Watt
Cover Design by Meljean Brook
ISBN: 978-1682305065

ACKNOWLEDGMENTS

WHEN WE STARTED WRITING *PAPER Princess* in the fall of 2015, we wrote it for each other. We traded the chapters back and forth via email. The words flew onto the page.

As much as we loved the project, however, we never imagined it would resonate with so many readers all over the world. We're so very thankful for how you readers have embraced these stories. You've given these characters life.

We also need to thank Margo, who sat and listened to our outline and gave us early feedback.

Early readers Jessica Clare, Michelle Kannan, Meljean Brook, and Jennifer L. Armentrout, who gave invaluable critique.

Our publicist Nina, for handling all the publicity for this project. We know it's been a mountain of work!

We'd be lost without Natasha and Nicole, our assistants, who help make sure we're on task every day.

And of course, we are forever indebted to all the bloggers, reviewers and readers who took the time to read, review and rave over this book. Your support and feedback makes this whole process worthwhile!

*To the readers who fell in love with this series.
You made these stories come alive in a manner we never
anticipated. Thank you.*

CHAPTER 1

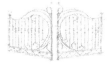

REED

"Where were you between eight p.m. and eleven p.m. tonight?"

"How long were you sleeping with your father's girlfriend?"

"Why did you kill her, Reed? Did she make you mad? Threaten to out the affair to your dad?"

I've watched enough cop shows to know that you keep your mouth shut when you're in a police interrogation room. Either that, or you just utter the four magic words—*I want my lawyer*.

Which is exactly what I've been doing for the past hour.

If I were a minor, these assholes wouldn't dream of questioning me without a parent or an attorney present. But I'm eighteen, so I guess they think I'm fair game. Or maybe that I'm stupid enough to answer their leading questions without my lawyer.

Detectives Cousins and Schmidt don't seem to care about my last name. For some reason, I find that kind of refreshing. I've gotten a free pass my entire life because I'm a Royal. If I get in trouble at school, Dad writes a check and my sins are forgotten. For as long as I can remember, girls have lined up to hop into bed with me so they can tell all their friends they bagged a Royal.

Not that I want girls lining up for me. There's only one girl I care about these days—Ella Harper. And it absolutely kills me that she had to watch me get dragged out of the house in handcuffs.

Brooke Davidson is dead.

I still can't wrap my head around it. My father's platinum-blonde, gold-digging girlfriend was very much alive when I left the penthouse earlier.

But I'm not telling these detectives that. I'm not an idiot. They'll twist everything I say.

Frustrated with my silence, Cousins slams both his hands on the metal table between us.

"Answer me, you little shit!"

Under the table, my fists start to curl. I force my fingers to relax. This is the last place I should lose my temper.

His partner, a quiet woman named Teresa Schmidt, shoots him a warning look. "Reed," she says in a soft voice, "we can't help you unless you cooperate. And we want to help you here."

I arch a brow. Really? Good cop/bad cop? I guess they've watched the same TV shows that I have.

"Guys," I say carelessly, "I'm starting to wonder if you have hearing issues or something." Smirking, I cross my arms over my chest. "I've already asked for my lawyer, which means you're supposed to wait until he arrives to ask questions."

"We can ask you questions," Schmidt says, "and you can answer them. There's no law against that. You can also volunteer information. For instance, we can move this process along if you explain things like why you have blood on your shirt."

I resist the urge to clamp a hand against my side. "I'll wait until Halston Grier gets here, but thanks for your input."

Silence falls over the small room.

Cousins is visibly grinding his molars. Schmidt just sighs. Then both detectives scrape back their chairs and leave the room without another word.

Royal - 1

Police - 0.

Except, even though they've clearly given up on me, they still take their sweet-ass time granting my request. For the next hour, I sit alone in the room, wondering how the hell my life got to this point. I'm not a saint and have never claimed to be one. I've gotten into my share of fights. I'm ruthless when I need to be.

But...I'm not this guy. The guy who gets dragged out of his own house in handcuffs. The guy who has to watch fear fill his girlfriend's eyes as he's hauled into the back of a police cruiser.

By the time the door swings open again, claustrophobia has set in, spurring me to be ruder than I should.

"Took you long enough," I snap at my father's lawyer.

The fifty-something gray-haired man is dressed in a suit, despite the late hour. He gives me a rueful smile. "Well. Looks like somebody is in high spirits."

"Where's Dad?" I demand, peering past Grier's shoulder.

"He's in the waiting room. He can't be in here."

"Why not?"

Grier shuts the door and walks over to the table. He sets his briefcase on it and unbuckles the gold snaps. "Because there are no restrictions against parents testifying against their children. Testimonial privilege extends only to spouses."

For the first time since I was arrested, I feel queasy. Testifying? This isn't going to go to *court*, is it? How far are these cops planning on taking this bullshit?

"Reed, take a breath."

My stomach twists. Damn it. I hate that I revealed even a trace of helplessness in front of this man. I don't show weakness. Ever. The only person I've ever been able to lower my guard around is Ella. That girl has the power to smash through my barriers and actually *see* me. The real me, and not the cold, callous ass that the rest of the world sees.

Grier pulls out a yellow legal pad and a gold fountain pen. He settles in the chair across from mine.

"I'm going to make this go away," he promises. "But first I need to know what we're dealing with here. From what I've managed to squeeze out of the officers in charge of the investigation, there's security footage of you entering the O'Halloran penthouse at eight forty-five tonight. That same footage shows you leaving about twenty minutes later."

My gaze darts around the room, searching for cameras or recording equipment. There's no mirror in here, so I don't think there's anyone watching us from some shadowy second room. Or at least I hope not.

"Everything we say in here is between us," Grier assures me when he notices my wary expression. "They can't record us. Lawyer/client privileges and all that."

I release a slow breath. "Yeah. I was at the penthouse earlier.

But I didn't fucking kill her."

Grier nods. "All right." He jots something down on his notepad. "Let's go back even earlier. I want you to start from the beginning. Tell me about you and Brooke Davidson. No detail is too small. I need to know everything."

I swallow a sigh. Awesome. *This* is going to be fun.

CHAPTER 2

ELLA

THE ROYAL BOYS HAVE ROOMS in the south wing, whereas their dad's suites are on the other side of the mansion, so I hook a right at the top of the stairs and hurry across the gleaming hardwood toward Easton's door. He doesn't answer at my soft knock. I swear, that boy could sleep through a hurricane. I knock a bit louder. When I hear nothing, I push the door open to find Easton sprawled facedown on the bed.

I march over and shake his shoulder. He moans something.

I shake him again, panic bubbling in my throat. How is he still sound asleep? How had he slept through all the commotion that just happened downstairs?

"Easton!" I burst out. "Wake up!"

"What is it?" he grumbles, one eyelid slitting open. "Shit, is it time to go to practice?"

He rolls all the way over, pulling the blankets with him and revealing a lot more skin than I need to see. On the floor I find a pair of discarded sweatpants and toss them on the bed. They land on his head.

"Get up," I beg.

"Why?"

"Because the sky is falling!"

He blinks groggily. "Huh?"

"Shit's bad!" I yell, then force myself to take a deep breath, trying to calm down. It doesn't work. "Just meet me in Reed's room, okay?" I snap.

He must hear the uncontrollable anxiety in my voice, because he tumbles out of bed without delay. I see another flash of bare skin before I duck out the door.

Rather than go to Reed's room, I sprint across the wide hallway toward my own bedroom. This house is ridiculously large, ridiculously beautiful, but everyone inside of it is so messed up. Including me.

I guess I really am a Royal.

But no, I'm really not. The man downstairs is a glaring reminder of that. Steve O'Halloran. My not-so-dead father.

A wave of emotion sweeps over me, threatening to buckle my knees and send me into a bout of hysterics. I feel terrible about just leaving him down there. I didn't even introduce myself before spinning on my heel and running upstairs. Granted, Callum Royal did the same thing. He was so racked with concern for Reed that he simply blurted out, "I can't deal with this right now. Steve, wait here for me," Despite my guilt, I push Steve into a tiny box in the back of my mind and slap a steel lid on top. I can't think about him right now. My focus needs to be on Reed.

In my room, I waste no time sliding my backpack out from under my huge bed. I always keep it in a place where I can easily access it. I unzip the pack and sigh in relief when I see the leather wallet that holds the monthly cash payments I get from Callum.

When I first moved here, Callum promised to pay me ten thousand dollars a month as long as I didn't try to run. As much as I hated the Royal mansion at the beginning, it wasn't long before I grew to love it. These days, I can't imagine living anywhere else—I'd stay even if I didn't have the cash incentive. But because of my years of living without any cash—and my generally suspicious nature—I never told Callum to stop.

Now I'm eternally grateful for that incentive. There's enough money in my bag to sustain me for months, probably longer.

I shoulder the backpack and then hurry toward Reed's door at the same time Easton emerges into the hall. His dark hair is sticking up in a hundred different directions, but at least he's got pants on now.

"What the fuck is going on?" he demands as he follows me into his older brother's bedroom.

I throw open the doors of Reed's walk-in closet, my gaze frantically darting around the large space. I find what I'm looking for on a low shelf in the back.

"Ella?" Easton prompts.

I don't answer him. He frowns as he watches me drag a navy-blue suitcase across the cream-colored carpet.

"Ella! Damn it, will you just talk to me?"

The frown turns into wide-eyed gawking when I start throwing stuff into the suitcase. Some T-shirts, Reed's favorite green hoodie, jeans, a couple of wife-beaters. What else would he need… Um, boxers, socks, a belt—

"Why are you packing Reed's clothes?" Easton is

practically shouting at me now, and his sharp tone snaps me out of my panic.

The worn gray T-shirt in my hands falls to the carpet. My heartbeat accelerates as the gravity of the situation hits me again.

"Reed was arrested for killing Brooke," I blurt out. "Your dad's at the police station with him."

Easton's jaw drops. "What the hell?" he exclaims. And then, "The cops came when we were at dinner?"

"No, after we got back from D.C."

Everyone minus Reed had gone to D.C. for dinner earlier. That's how the Royals roll. They're so loaded that Callum has multiple private planes at his disposal. It probably helps that he owns a company that designs airplanes, but it's still ridiculously surreal. The fact that we took a plane from North Carolina to D.C. tonight—to go for *dinner*—is crazy-rich. Reed stayed behind because his side hurt.

He'd been stabbed at the docks the other night and claimed that his pain meds made him too woozy to go with us.

But he hadn't been too woozy to go see Brooke...

God. What had he *done* tonight?

"It happened about ten minutes ago," I add weakly. "Didn't you hear your dad screaming at the detective?"

"I didn't hear a goddamn thing. I...ah..." Shame flickers in his blue eyes. "I kinda pounded a mickey of vodka when I was at Wade's tonight. Came home and crashed right afterward."

I don't even have the energy to lecture him about his drinking. Easton's addiction issues are serious, but Reed's *murder* issues are a million times more urgent at the moment.

I curl my fingers into a fist. If Reed were here right now, I'd punch him—both for lying to me and for getting hauled away by the police.

Easton finally breaks the stunned silence. "Do you think he did it?"

"No." But as confident as I sound, inwardly I'm shaken up.

When I got back from dinner, I saw that Reed's stitches were pulled and he had blood on his stomach. I keep those incriminating tidbits from Easton, though. I trust him, but he's hardly ever sober. I need to protect Reed first and foremost, and who knows what might come out of Easton's mouth when he's drunk or high.

Swallowing hard, I refocus on that task—protecting Reed. I hurriedly toss a few more items of clothing into the suitcase and zip it up.

"You haven't told me why you're packing," Easton says in frustration.

"In case we need to run."

"Us?"

"Me and Reed." I bolt to my feet and race over to Reed's dresser to raid his sock drawer. "I want to be prepared just in case, okay?"

That's the one thing I excel at—being prepared to run. I don't know if it'll come down to that. Maybe Reed and Callum will stroll through the front doors and announce, "All fixed! Charges were dropped!" Maybe Reed will be denied bail or bond or whatever the hell it's called, and won't come home at all.

But in the event that neither of those things happens, I want to be ready to skip town in a heartbeat. My backpack is always stocked with everything I need, but Reed's not a planner like I am. He's impulsive. Doesn't always think before he acts—

Before he kills?

I shove the horrible thought aside. No. Reed couldn't have done what they're accusing him of.

"What are you guys yelling about?" a sleepy voice comes from Reed's doorway. "We can hear you all the way down the hall."

The sixteen-year-old Royal twins step into the room. Each one is wearing a blanket around his waist. Does no one in this family believe in pajamas?

"Reed offed Brooke," Easton tells his brothers.

"Easton!" I say in outrage.

"What? I'm not supposed to tell my brothers that our other brother just got arrested for murder?"

Sawyer and Sebastian both hiss out a breath.

"Are you serious?" Sawyer demands.

"The cops just took him away," I whisper.

Easton looks a bit queasy. "And I'm just saying, they wouldn't have done that if they didn't have some kind of evidence against him. Maybe it's about the…" He draws a circle in front of his stomach.

The twins blink in bewilderment.

"What? The baby?" Seb asks. "Why would Reed care about Brooke's demon spawn?"

Crap. I forgot that the twins weren't in the loop. They know that Brooke was pregnant—we were all there for that horrible announcement—but they're in the dark about Brooke's other claim.

"Brooke was threatening to say that Reed was the father of the kid," I admit.

Two sets of identical blue eyes widen.

"He wasn't," I say firmly. "He only slept with her a couple times, and that was more than six months ago. She wasn't that far along."

"Whatever." Seb shrugs. "So you're saying Reed knocked up Dad's child bride and then offed her because he doesn't want to have a little Reed running around?"

"It wasn't his!" I yell.

"Then it's really Dad's?" Sawyer says slowly.

I hesitate. "I don't think so."

"Why not?"

"Because…"

Ugh. The secrets in this house could fill half the ocean. But I'm done with holding any of them back. It hasn't done us any good.

"He had a vasectomy."

Seb narrows his eyes. "Dad told you this?"

I nod. "He said he did it after you guys were born because your mom wanted more kids and couldn't have them because of some medical condition."

The twins look at each other again, communicating silently.

Easton rubs his chin. "Mom always wanted a girl. She talked about it a lot, said a girl would've softened us up." His lips twitch. "But I don't think girls make me soft in any way."

Frustration jams in my throat. Of course Easton's going somewhere sexual. He always does.

Sawyer smothers a laugh behind his hand while Seb grins openly. "So let's assume that Reed and Dad are both telling the truth—who's the baby daddy then?"

"Maybe there isn't one?" Easton suggests.

"There has to be," I say. Both Reed and Callum never

doubted Brooke's pregnancy claim, so it had to be true.

"Not necessarily," Easton counters. "She could've been lying. Maybe her plan was to fake a miscarriage after Dad married her."

"Sick, but possible." Seb is nodding, clearly on board with this idea.

"Why don't you think Reed killed her?" Easton asks me, his blue eyes flickering with curiosity.

"Why do you believe he's capable of that?" I shoot back.

He shrugs and looks at the twins instead of me. "If she was threatening the family, maybe he is. Maybe they got into an argument and there was an accident. There's lots of explanations."

The sick feeling in my stomach threatens to erupt. The image Easton is casually painting is…possible. Reed's stitches were ripped out. He had blood on him. What if he…

"No," I choke out. "He didn't do it. And I don't want us to even talk about it anymore. He's innocent. End of story."

"Then why are you getting ready to skip town?"

Easton's quiet question hangs in the bedroom. I swallow a moan of agony and rub my eyes with both hands. He's right. A part of me has already decided that Reed could be guilty. Isn't that why I have his suitcase and my backpack all ready to go?

The silence drags on, until it's finally broken by the unmistakable sound of footsteps somewhere below us. Since the Royals don't have live-in staff, the boys instantly tense up at the signs of life downstairs.

"Was that the front door?" Seb asks.

"Are they back?" Sawyer demands.

I bite my lip. "No, that wasn't the front door. That was…"

My throat closes up again. God. I forgot about Steve. How could I forget about him, damn it?

"That's what?" Easton pushes.

"Steve," I confess.

They all stare at me.

"Steve's downstairs. He showed up at the door just as Reed was taken away."

"Steve," Easton echoes, slightly dazed. "Uncle Steve?"

Sebastian makes a croaky sound. "*Dead* Uncle Steve?"

I grit my teeth. "He's not dead. He looks like Tom Hanks from *Castaway*, though. Minus the volleyball."

"Holy shit."

When Easton starts for the door, I grab his wrist and try to haul him back. I don't have the strength for that, but the contact gives him pause.

He tilts his head to study me for a second. "You don't want to go down there and talk to him? This is your *dad*, Ella."

My panic returns in full force. "No. He's just a guy who knocked up my mom. I can't deal with him right now. I…" I gulp again. "I don't think he realizes I'm his daughter."

"You didn't tell him?" Sawyer exclaims.

I slowly shake my head. "Can one of you go downstairs and…I don't know…take him to a guest room or something?"

"I'll do it," Seb instantly replies.

"I'm coming with you," his brother pipes up. "I've gotta see this."

As the twins race for the door, I quickly call out to them. "Guys, don't say anything about me. Seriously, I'm not ready for that. Let's wait until Callum gets home."

The twins exchange another one of those glances where a

whole conversation takes place in a second.

"Sure," says Seb, and then they're gone, galloping down the stairs to greet their not-dead uncle.

Easton steps closer to me. His gaze lands on the suitcase near the closet, then locks onto my face. In a heartbeat, he grabs my hand and laces his fingers through mine. "You're not running, little sis. You have to know it's a stupid idea."

I stare at our entwined fingers. "I'm a runner, East."

"No. You're a fighter."

"I can fight for other people. Like my mom or Reed or you, but…I'm not good with conflict at my door." I chew harder on my bottom lip. "Why is Steve here? He's supposed to be *dead*. And how could they arrest Reed?" My voice trembles wildly. "What if he actually goes to jail for this?"

"He won't." His hand tightens on mine. "Reed's going to be back, Ella. Dad will take care of everything."

"What if he can't?"

"He will."

But what if he can't?

CHAPTER 3

ELLA

AFTER A SLEEPLESS NIGHT, I find myself in the sitting room that overlooks the front courtyard. There's a plush bench tucked beneath the enormous expanse of windows that make up the front of the house. I throw myself onto the cushion, fixing my gaze on the circular driveway beyond the windowpane. My phone is in my lap, but it hasn't made a peep all night or morning. Not a phone call, not a text. Nothing.

My imagination is running wild, conjuring up all kinds of scenarios. He's in a cell. He's in an interrogation room. His wrists and ankles are shackled. He's being beaten by a cop for not answering questions. Does he have to stay in jail until the trial? I don't know how this whole arrest, charge, trial thing works.

What I do know is that the longer Reed and Callum are gone, the lower my spirits sink.

"Good morning."

I nearly fall off the bench at the sound of the unfamiliar male voice. For a second I think that someone broke into the house, or that maybe the detectives are back to do a search. But when I glance at the door, I find Steve O'Halloran standing there.

The beard's shaved off and he's dressed in a pair of slacks and a polo shirt, looking a lot less like a homeless person and a lot more like the students' fathers you see around Astor Park, the private school the Royals and I attend.

"Ella, right?" There's a hesitant smile on his face.

I nod abruptly and place my phone facedown as I turn back to the window. I don't know how to act around him.

Last night, I hid in my bedroom while Easton and the twins took care of Steve. I don't know what story they told him about me, but it's obvious he has no recollection of me or the letter he received from my mom before he left on the hang-gliding trip where he supposedly died.

Easton stopped by before he went to bed and informed me that Steve was in the green guest room. I didn't even know there was a green guest room or where it was located.

A crippling sense of anxiety makes me want to run and hide. I *am* hiding. But he found me anyway, and facing my father is more intimidating than beating back a hundred mean girls at school.

"Well. Ella. I'm a tad confused."

I startle at the nearness of his voice. Looking over my shoulder again, I find him standing only a couple feet away.

I dig my heels into the cushion of the bench, forcing myself not to move. He's just a man. Two legs, two arms. Just a man who got a letter from a dying woman about a long-lost daughter, and instead of tracking that woman and that child down, he went on an adventure. That kind of man.

"Did you hear me?" He sounds even more bewildered now, as if he can't figure out if I'm ignoring him, or just hard of hearing.

I cast a desperate glance toward the door. Where's Easton? And why isn't Reed home yet? What if he never comes home?

I almost choke on the raw panic that burns my throat. "I heard you," I finally mutter.

Steve moves even closer. I can smell whatever soap or shampoo he used this morning. "I'm not sure what I expected when I got out of that taxi last night, but..." His tone becomes wry. "It sure as hell wasn't this. From what East told me, I gather Reed was arrested?"

My head jerks in another nod. And for some reason, it bugs me to hear him call Easton "East." The nickname feels wrong leaving the mouth of a stranger.

He's not a stranger. He's known them since they were born.

I gulp. Yeah, I guess he has. I guess if anyone is a stranger to the Royals, it's me and not Steve O'Halloran. I think Callum once told me that Steve is the godfather to all the boys.

"But nobody has thought to explain to me who *you* are. I know I've been gone for a while, but the Royal household has been a bachelor residence for years."

A chill flies up my spine. No. God, no. I can't have this conversation right now. But Steve's light blue eyes are probing my face. He's waiting for an answer, and I know I have to give him *something*.

"I'm Callum's ward."

"Callum's ward," he echoes in disbelief.

"Yes."

"Who are your parents? Friends of Callum's? Do I know

them?" he wonders, half to himself.

Panic jolts through me, but luckily I don't have to answer, because I suddenly glimpse a black Town Car pulling into the driveway.

They're back!

I lunge off the bench and make it to the parlor in two seconds flat. A weary Callum and an equally tired Reed trudge inside, but both stop in their tracks when they spot me.

Reed turns. His vivid blue eyes slowly find mine and lock on.

My heart stutters, then careens into a gallop. Without a word, I launch myself at him.

He catches me, one strong hand burying itself in my hair and the other wrapping around my waist. I cling to him, mashing myself chest to chest, thigh to thigh, as if I can keep him safe with this simple embrace.

"Are you okay?" I whisper against his left pec.

"I'm fine." His voice is low, gruff.

Tears sting my eyes. "I was scared."

"I know." His breath wafts over my ear. "It's going to be okay. I promise. Let's go upstairs and I'll explain everything."

"No, you won't," Callum says tersely, overhearing Reed's promise. "No talking to anyone unless you want to make Ella a witness."

A witness? Oh God. The police are talking to *witnesses* and Reed is trying to tell me everything is *okay*?

Another set of footsteps echoes behind us. Reed releases me, and his eyes widen at the tall, blond man who enters the foyer.

"Uncle Steve?" he blurts out.

"Reed." Steve nods in greeting.

Callum spins toward my father. "Steve, Christ, I forgot you

showed up. I was thinking I'd dreamt the damn thing." His gaze swings between Steve and me. "Did you two meet?"

I nod vigorously and try to convey with wide eyes that I don't want the whole daddy/daughter thing coming out. Callum's brow furrows, but his attention is dragged away when Steve says, "We were just getting acquainted when you arrived. And no, you didn't dream it. I survived."

The two men eye each other for a moment. Then they both step forward, meet halfway, and exchange a manly hug that includes several good-natured back slaps.

"Damn, it's good to be home," Steve tells his old friend.

"How are you even here?" Callum shoots back, looking dismayed. "Where the hell have you been the last nine months?" In a voice that's half angry, half awed, he adds, "I spent five million dollars on a search and rescue effort."

"It's a long story," Steve admits. "Why don't we go sit down somewhere and I'll fill you in—"

A pounding of feet on the stairs interrupts him. The three youngest Royal brothers appear on the second-floor landing, their blue-eyed gazes instantly homing in on Reed.

"Told you he'd be back!" Easton crows as he takes the steps two at a time. He has a serious case of bedhead and he's wearing nothing but boxers, but that doesn't stop him from dragging Reed in for a quick hug. "You okay, bro?"

"Fine," Reed grunts.

Sawyer and Sebastian round out the group, focusing on their father. "What happened at the police station?" Sawyer demands.

"What's going to happen now?" Seb chimes in.

Callum sighs. "I got a friend out of bed—a judge I know—

and he came down this morning to set bail for Reed. I need to deliver Reed's passport to the clerk of court tomorrow morning. In the meantime, we wait. You might have to stay here a while longer, Steve," he informs my father. "Your place is currently being held as a crime scene."

"Why? Did someone finally off my beloved wife?" Steve asks in a dry voice.

I jerk in surprise. Steve's wife, Dinah, is a terrible, venomous woman, but I can't believe he's joking about someone killing her.

Callum can't believe it either, because he responds in a sharp voice. "Hardly something to joke about, Steve. But no, it's Brooke who died. And Reed here is being falsely accused of having a hand in that death."

Reed's fingers tighten through mine.

"Brooke?" Steve's eyebrows soar up to his hairline. "How did that happen?"

"Head injury," Reed says coolly. "And no, I didn't do it."

Callum glares at his son.

"What?" Reed growls. "Those are facts and I'm not afraid of the facts. I went there last night after a phone call from Brooke. You were all gone and I felt okay, so I went. We argued. I left. When I left, she was unhappy but alive. That's the story."

What about your stitches? I want to scream. *What about the blood I saw on your waist when I came home from dinner?*

The words stick in my throat, making me cough violently. Everyone stares at me for a moment, before Easton finally speaks.

"Okay, if that's the story, I'm on board."

Reed's expression darkens. "It's not a story—it's the truth."

Easton nods. "Like I said, totally on board, bro." His gaze travels to the newcomer in our midst. "I'd way rather hear

Uncle Steve's story, anyway. Coming back from the dead? That's badass."

"Yeah, he wouldn't tell us a thing last night," Sebastian grumbles, glancing at his dad. "He wanted to wait for you."

Callum lets out another sigh. "Why don't we go into the kitchen? I could use a cup of coffee. The coffee at the police station gave me heartburn."

We all follow the head of the Royal household into the massive, modern kitchen that I fell in love with the moment I moved in. As Callum walks over to the coffeemaker, the rest of us gather at the table. We all sit down as if this is just any other normal Sunday, not the Sunday after Reed was arrested for murder and a dead man walked out of the ocean to our front door.

It's so surreal. I can't make sense of this. Any of it.

In the chair beside mine, Reed rests a hand on my thigh, although I'm not sure if it's to comfort me or himself. Or maybe he's comforting us both.

After he's settled in his seat, Easton gets right down to business. "So are you finally gonna tell us why aren't you dead?" he asks my father.

Steve smiles faintly. "I still can't tell if you're happy or sad about that fact."

Neither, I almost blurt out. I manage to tamp down the response at the last second, but it's the truth. Steve's reappearance is more confusing than anything. And maybe a bit terrifying.

"Happy," the twins reply in unison.

"Obvs," Easton agrees.

"How are you alive?" Reed, this time. His voice is sharp,

and his hand moves soothingly over my thigh, as if he knows how on edge I am.

Steve leans back in his chair. "I don't know what Dinah's told you, if anything, about our little trip."

"You went hang-gliding and both harnesses failed," Callum says as he joins us at the table. He sets a cup of coffee in front of Steve, then sits down and sips his own cup. "Dinah was able to deploy her emergency 'chute. You dropped into the ocean. I spent four weeks searching for your body."

A crooked grin pops up on Steve's face. "And only five million, you said. Did you cheap out on me, old man?"

Callum doesn't find this amusing. His expression grows as stony as the face of a cliff. "Why didn't you come straight home after you'd been rescued? It's been nine months, for Pete's sake."

Steve runs a shaky hand over his jaw. "Because I didn't get rescued until a few days ago."

"What?" Callum looks startled. "So where the hell were you for all those months?"

"I don't know if it was the illness or malnourishment, but I can't remember everything. I washed up on shore on Tavi—a tiny island about two hundred miles east of Tonga. I was severely dehydrated and in and out of consciousness for weeks. The natives took care of me, and I would have returned earlier except the only way off the island was via a fishing boat that comes around twice a year to trade with the islanders."

Your dad is talking, my brain tells me. I search his face for traces of myself and find nothing except our shared eye color. Other than that, I have my mother's features, her body type, her hair. I'm the younger, blue-eyed version of Maggie Harper, but she must've made no impression on Steve because he shows no signs of recognition.

"Apparently the islanders harvest a particular seagull egg that is sold as a delicacy in Asia. The fishing boat took me to Tonga where I then begged my way back to Sydney." He takes a sip of his coffee before making the understatement of the century. "It's a miracle I'm alive."

"When did you get to Sydney?" Sebastian asks.

My dad purses his lips in thought. "I don't remember. I want to say three days ago?"

Callum balks. "And you didn't think to call and tell us you were alive?"

"I had some matters to take care of," Steve says tightly. "I knew that if I called, you'd be on the first plane out, and I didn't want to be distracted from my search for answers."

"Answers?" Reed echoes, his tone sharper than before.

"I went to find the guide who led the hang-gliding expedition, and track down my things. I'd left behind my passport, a wallet, clothes."

"Did you find the guide?" Easton's caught up in the story, too. We all are.

"No. The tour guide had been missing for months. Once I hit that dead end, I went to the American embassy and they shipped me home. I came directly here from the airport."

"It's a good thing you didn't go home," Callum says grimly. "Or you might've been arrested, too."

"Where's my wife?" Steve asks, sounding wary. "Dinah and Brooke are attached at the hip."

"Dinah's still in Paris."

"What were they doing there?"

"She and Brooke were shopping," Callum pauses. "For the wedding."

Steve snorts. "What schmuck got suckered in for that?"

"This one." Callum points to himself.

"You're kidding."

"She was pregnant. I thought it was mine."

"But you had the vas—" Steve cuts himself off and quickly looks around the table to see if anyone had caught his slip.

"The vasectomy?" Easton finishes.

Callum's eyes cut to me before shifting back to his son. "You know about that?"

"I told them." I jut my chin. "There are too many stupid secrets in this house."

"I agree," Steve declares. He turns to pin those familiar blue eyes on me. "Callum," he says without taking his gaze off mine. "Now that I've answered all your questions, perhaps you can respond to one of mine. Who is this delightful young woman?"

Reed's hand tightens over my thigh. The knot in my stomach feels like a block of cement now, but at some point, the truth had to come out. Might as well be now.

"Don't you recognize me?" I ask, smiling weakly. "I'm your daughter."

CHAPTER 4

ELLA

I DON'T THINK STEVE O'HALLORAN is a man who's caught off guard too often. Pure shock stiffens his body and floods his expression.

"My…" He trails off, turning to Callum for…assistance? Support? I'm not sure.

But for a man who so casually asked if someone had "offed" his wife, he doesn't seem equipped to handle the less dramatic revelation that he's sitting at the same table as his kid.

"Daughter," Callum finishes gently.

Steve blinks in rapid succession.

"Do you remember the letter you received before you and Dinah left for your trip?" Callum asks.

Steve slowly shakes his head. "A letter… From whom?"

"From Ella's mother."

"Maggie," I say, my voice hoarse. Thinking about my mom always makes my heart ache. "You met her eighteen years ago when you were on shore leave. You two…uh…"

"Hooked up. Knocked boots. Did the horizontal mamba," Easton supplies.

"Ella's mother got pregnant." Callum takes over before his son says the million inappropriate things we all see dangling at the end of his tongue. "She tried to track you down during the pregnancy but was unsuccessful. When she was diagnosed with cancer, she sent a letter to your old base, hoping they'd find a way to get it to you. And they did. You received the letter nine months ago, right before you left."

Steve is blinking again. After a few seconds, his eyes focus and he stares intently at me. Curious. Pleased.

I squirm in my chair, which causes Reed to stroke my leg in reassurance. He knows I don't like to be the center of attention, and right now everyone in the room is looking at me.

"You're Maggie's daughter," Steve says, his tone a mixture of wonder and interest. "She passed away?"

I nod, because the lump in my throat is too big to speak around.

"You're…my daughter." The words come out slowly, as if he's testing their flavor.

"Yep," I manage to get out.

"Wow. Well. Okay." He rakes a hand through his long hair. "I…" A wry smile touches his lips. "I guess we have a lot to talk about, huh?"

A spark of panic ignites my belly. I'm not ready for this. I don't know what to say to this man or how to behave around him. The Royals might have known Steve for years, but he's a stranger to me.

"I guess so," I mumble, staring down at my hands.

Callum takes pity on me by suggesting, "But that can wait until later. After you're settled."

Steve glances over at his old friend. "I assume you'll let me stay here until the police release my penthouse?"

"Of course."

My anxiety intensifies. Can't he check into a hotel or something? Yes, the Royal mansion is huge, but the thought of living in the same house as my presumed-dead father makes me nervous.

But why? Why aren't I throwing my arms around this man and thanking God he's alive? Why aren't I ecstatic at the idea of getting to know him?

Because he's a stranger.

That's the only answer that makes sense right now. I don't know Steve O'Halloran, and I'm not good at letting new people in. I spent my entire childhood moving from one place to another, trying not to get close to anyone because I knew that Mom would just pack us up again and then I'd have to say goodbye.

When I came to Bayview, I didn't plan on forming any real bonds. Somehow, I wound up with a best friend, a boyfriend, surrogate brothers whom I adore, and a man—Callum—who, as screwed up as he is, has become a father figure to me.

I don't know where Steve fits in. And I'm not ready to figure it out yet.

"That will give Ella and me time to get to know each other on her own turf," Steve is saying, and I realize he's smiling at me.

I muster up a smile in return. "Cool beans."

Cool beans?

Reed pinches my thigh teasingly, and I turn to see him fighting a laugh. Yeah. Maybe Steve isn't the only one who's in shock right now.

Luckily, the discussion soon turns toward Atlantic Aviation, Callum and Steve's business. I notice that Steve doesn't seem interested in the minute details—just a project that the two refer to in vague terms. Callum once said they do a lot of work for the government. Eventually, the two men excuse themselves and duck into Callum's study to go over the company's last quarterly report.

Alone with the boys, I search their faces for signs that they're as freaked out by all this as I am.

"This is weird, right?" I blurt out when nobody says anything. "I mean, he just came back from the *dead*."

Easton shrugs. "Told you Uncle Steve was a baller."

Sawyer snickers.

I shoot a worried look at Reed. "Am I going to have to move in with him and Dinah?"

That sobers up the kitchen.

"No way," Reed says immediately. Low and firm. "My dad is your guardian."

"But Steve is my father. If he wants me to live with him, then I'd have to go."

"No. Way."

"Not happening," Easton agrees. Even the twins are nodding emphatically.

Warmth unfurls in my chest. Sometimes I still can't believe that we all hated each other when I first got here. Reed was determined to destroy me. His brothers alternately taunted or ignored me. I fantasized about running away on a daily basis.

And now I can't imagine not having the Royals in my life.

Another wave of anxiety churns in my stomach as I remember where Reed spent the night. There's a very real chance he *won't* be in my life anymore, not if the police really believe he killed Brooke.

"Let's go upstairs," I say in a shaky voice. "I want you to tell me everything that happened at the station."

Reed nods and gets up without a word. When Easton rises, too, Reed holds up a hand. "I'll fill you in later. Let me talk to Ella first."

Easton probably sees the panic etched into my face, because for the first time ever, he actually does what he's told.

I lace my fingers through Reed's as we climb the back staircase to the second floor. Once we're alone in my room, he wastes no time locking the door and yanking me into his arms.

His mouth lands on mine before I can blink. The kiss is hot, desperate, and all tongue. I thought I was too exhausted to feel anything other than, well, exhaustion, but my entire body tightens and aches as Reed's skilled lips tease me to the edge of oblivion.

I groan in protest when he breaks away, which makes him chuckle. "I thought we were going to talk," he reminds me.

"You're the one who kissed me," I grumble. "How am I supposed to concentrate on talking when your tongue is in my mouth?"

He pulls me onto the bed. A second later, we're curled up on our sides facing each other, our legs twined together.

"Were you scared?" I whisper.

His gorgeous face softens. "Not really."

"You were arrested for murder," I say in anguish. "*I* would be scared."

"I didn't kill anyone, Ella." He reaches out and strokes my cheek with his fingertips. "I swear to you, Brooke was alive when I left the penthouse."

"I believe you."

And I do. Reed isn't a killer. He's got flaws, lots of flaws, but he could never, ever take someone's life.

"Why didn't you tell me that you went over there?" I ask in a hurt voice. "What did Brooke say to you? And the blood on your side…"

"I pulled my stitches. I wasn't lying about that. Must've happened on the drive home, because I wasn't bleeding when I was over there. And I didn't tell you because I was high on pain meds when you got back, and then we started fooling around…" He sighs. "I got distracted. And honestly, the whole thing didn't even seem important. I was going to say something in the morning."

There's nothing but sincerity on his face, in his voice.

I lean into his palm, which is still cupped over my cheek. "Did she want money from you?"

"Yup," he says flatly. "She was freaking that Dad scheduled a paternity test. She wanted to make a deal—if I signed over my trust fund to her, she'd take the cash and split. We'd never have to see her again."

"And you said no?"

"Hell yeah I said no. I wasn't going to pay that woman a dime. The DNA test would've shown that her baby wasn't mine *or* Dad's. I figured we just had to wait it out for a few more days." His blue eyes darken. "I didn't think she'd fucking get herself killed."

"Do you think it was an accident?" I'm grasping at straws, but I honestly don't understand how any of this happened. Brooke is—was—awful, but none of us wanted her dead.

Gone, maybe. But not dead.

Or at least I didn't.

"I have no clue," Reed answers. "I wouldn't be surprised if Brooke had enemies we don't know about. She could've pissed off someone bad enough that they decided to bash her head in."

I wince.

"Sorry," he murmurs hastily.

I sit up and rub my tired eyes. "What evidence do the cops have?"

"Video footage of me entering and leaving the building," he admits. "And something else, too."

"What?"

"I don't know. They're not telling us yet. Dad's lawyer says that's normal—they're still trying to build their case against me."

I feel sick again. "They don't have a case. They *can't*." My lungs seize up, making it hard to breathe. "You can't go to jail, Reed."

"I won't."

"You don't know that!" I jump off the bed. "Let's just go. Right now. You and me. I already packed your bag."

Reed bolts up in shock. "Ella—"

"I mean it," I interrupt. "I've got my fake ID and ten grand in cash. You've got a fake ID too, right?"

"Ella—"

"We could create a new life somewhere," I say desperately. "I'll get a job waitressing, you can work construction."

"And then what?" His voice is gentle, and so is his touch as he gets up and tugs me toward him. "Live in hiding for the rest of our lives? Look over our shoulders all the time worrying that the cops will find us and haul me away?"

I bite my lip. Hard.

"I'm a Royal, baby. I don't run. I fight." Steel hardens his eyes. "I didn't kill anyone, and I'm not going to prison for something I didn't do. I promise you."

Why does everyone always feel the need to make promises? Don't they know that promises always get broken?

Reed squeezes my shoulder. "These trumped-up charges will go away. Dad's lawyers aren't going to let—"

A high-pitched shriek cuts him off.

We both spin toward the door, but the scream didn't come from the second floor. It came from downstairs.

Reed and I fly out of my room, reaching the second-floor landing at the same time as Easton.

"What the hell was that?" Easton demands.

That was Dinah O'Halloran, I realize when I peer over the balcony railing. Steve's wife is standing in the middle of the parlor below us, her face whiter than a sheet, one hand raised in the air as she gapes at her not-dead husband.

"What's going on here?" she's shouting in horror. "How are you *here*?!"

My father's mild voice wafts up the stairs. "Hello to you, too, Dinah. It's wonderful to see you."

"You're…you're…" She's stuttering. "You're dead! You *died*!"

"Sorry to disappoint, but no, I'm very much alive."

Footsteps echo, and then Callum appears beside Steve. "Dinah," he says tightly. "I was going to call you."

"Then why didn't you?" she roars, teetering on her five-inch heels. "You didn't think to pick up the phone sooner to let me know that *my husband is alive*?"

As much as I dislike Dinah, I kind of feel bad for her. She's so obviously stunned and confused by this, and I don't blame her. She just walked in and saw a ghost.

"What are you doing here?" Steve asks his wife, and something about his blasé tone rubs me the wrong way.

I get that Dinah is a bitch, but can't he at least hug her or something? She's his *wife*.

"I came to see Callum." Dinah won't stop blinking, as if she can't figure out if Steve is actually there or if she's hallucinating. "The police…they left a message on my phone. They said my penthouse—" She hastily corrects herself, "Our penthouse… they said it's a crime scene."

I wish I could see Steve's expression, but his back is to the stairs. I only have Dinah's expressions to gauge his, and it's clear that whatever she's seeing on his face is making her extremely uneasy.

"They told me Brooke is dead."

"That seems to be the case," Callum confirms.

"How?" Dinah wails, her voice shaking wildly. "What happened to her?"

"We don't know yet—"

"Bullshit! The detective said they detained a suspect for questioning."

Reed and I slowly edge away from the railing, but it's too late. Dinah has spotted us. Sharp green eyes laser into us, and she releases a cry of outrage.

"It's him, isn't it! Reed did this to her!"

Callum steps forward, entering my line of sight. His shoulders are like two granite slabs, rigid and unyielding. "Reed had nothing to do with it."

"She was having his baby! He had *everything* to do with it!"

I flinch.

"C'mon," Reed mutters, reaching for my hand. "We don't need to listen to this."

But we do. That's *all* we're going to be listening to once the news of Brooke's death gets out. Soon everyone is going to know about Reed and Brooke's affair. Everyone's going to know that she was pregnant, that he went over to the penthouse that night, that he was interrogated and charged with her murder.

Once the story breaks, the vultures are going to circle. The pitchforks will come out, and Dinah O'Halloran will be leading the charge.

I suck air into my lungs, hoping to calm myself, but it doesn't work. My hands are shaking. My heart is beating too fast, each *thump-thump* vibrating with fear that I feel straight to my bones.

"I can't lose you," I whisper.

"You won't."

He pulls me away from the landing and draws me into his arms. Easton disappears into his room as I press my face tight against Reed's muscled chest.

"Everything will be okay," he says gruffly, his fingers sliding through my hair.

I feel his heartbeat against my cheek, and it's steadier than mine. Strong and even. He's not afraid.

And if Reed, the guy who was just arrested, isn't afraid, then I need to take his lead. I need to borrow his strength and conviction, and allow myself to believe that maybe, for the first time in my screwed up life, everything *will* be okay.

CHAPTER 5

REED

"THINK WORD'S ALREADY SPREAD, BRO," Easton mutters under his breath.

I shove my shit into my locker before surveying the room. Usually chatter and jokes are tossed around the locker room during our early morning practice, but everyone is quiet today. A number of eyes slide away, not willing to meet mine. My gaze ends on Wade, who winks and gives me the thumbs up. I'm not sure what that means, but I appreciate the support. I return the gesture with a brief nod.

Beside him, our left tackle, Liam Hunter, stares at me. I give him a nod of acknowledgement, too, just to piss him off. Maybe he'll come at me and we can work out some of our aggression on the tile floor. I lift my hands to motion for him to come forward, but then the lawyer's admonition rings in my ears.

"No fighting. No detention. No bad behavior." Dad had stood next to Grier outside the police station, glowering as the lawyer reeled off instructions. "One wrong step and the prosecutor will be all over it. You have that assault charge for whupping that kid's butt at your school last year."

I had to bite a hole through my tongue to keep from defending myself. Grier knows why I beat that boy's face into a pulp, but I'd never hurt a woman.

Though if there ever was a woman who needed hurting, it was Brooke Davidson. I hadn't killed her, but I'm sure as hell not sorry she's dead.

"You shouldn't be here," a low, angry voice says from behind me.

I pluck the athletic tape out of my gym bag before turning to face Ronald Richmond. "That so?" I say easily, taking a seat on the padded metal bench in front of my locker.

"Coach kicked Brian Mauss off because he accidentally hit his girlfriend."

I roll my eyes. "As in her face accidentally fell onto his fist and she sported a shiner for three weeks and all her homecoming pictures had to be digitally altered? That accident?"

Beside me, Easton snorts. I finish wrapping my hands and toss East the tape.

Ronnie scowls. "About as accidental as you offing your dad's trashy girlfriend."

"Well, then you'll want to tuck away Brian the Abuser's invite, because I didn't kill anyone." I give him my friendliest smile.

Ronnie juts his weak chin. "That's not what Delacorte is saying."

"Daniel's not around to talk about shit." My dad had that rapist asshole shipped off to a juvenile military prison.

"I'm not talking about Daniel," my teammate sneers. "Judge Delacorte was over having drinks with my dad yesterday and he said the case against you is open and shut. Video shows you went into the apartment. Video shows you leaving. Hope you like getting it up the ass, Royal."

Easton starts to rise. I clamp a hand around his wrist and drag him down. Around us, the team looks uneasy, some of them whispering to each other.

"Judge Delacorte's dirty as hell," I answer coldly. He tried to bribe my dad to prevent Daniel from being punished. It hadn't worked, so I guess now he's coming after me to stick it to my father.

"Maybe you don't belong here." Liam Hunter's quiet voice slices through the room.

We all swivel toward him in surprise. Hunter's not much for talking; he's all about action on the field. He doesn't run with our crowd, despite the numerous invitations that I know come his way. He keeps to himself. The only person I've seen him hang around with is Wade, but then again, everyone gets along with Wade.

I quirk an eyebrow toward my friend, who responds with a small shrug. He's as clueless as I am about Hunter's thoughts.

"You got a problem with me, Hunter? Say it."

This time when Easton pushes to his feet, I don't stop him. As for me, I remain seated. As much as I like to solve my arguments with a fist, the lawyer's warning sits like a weight on my shoulders.

"We want to win the State Championship," Hunter points out. "And that means no distractions. You're a distraction. Even if you didn't do it, there's still going to be a lot of negative attention."

Even if I didn't do it? It's a big step from beating some kid's face in for trying to smear my mother to actually killing someone, but the entire locker room appears to be making that leap today.

"Thanks for your support," East says sarcastically.

Wade decides to step in. "Reed's a hothead. No offense, brother," he says to me.

"None taken." There's no point in pretending I don't like a little physical violence. But just because I like to punch a few people in the face doesn't make me a killer. "But since I didn't do it, then this will all go away."

"In the meantime, there's going to be a circus around here." Ronnie decides to pick up Hunter's train of thought and stupidly run with it. "We'll constantly be asked questions about it when the focus should be on football. This is the last year for half of us starters. Is this the way we want to go out?"

More than a few of my teammates are nodding in agreement. Status is everything to a lot of these kids, and graduating with a football championship under their belts will give them some serious bragging rights.

But I never imagined that they'd hang me up by my nuts just so they can win a damn game.

I slowly unclench my fingers. *No violence*, I remind myself. *None.*

Sensing my patience is strained to the limit, Wade gets up. "Ronnie, we have all of a dozen reporters who cover our games, and most of them ride our jocks so hard, I don't even need to get laid after the last whistle. Besides, Reed's one of our best defensive players. Without him, I'm gonna need to score five, maybe six touchdowns, and I don't wanna work that hard." He turns to Hunter. "I hear what you're saying, but Reed's not gonna be a distraction, are you, man?"

I shake my head curtly. "No, I'm here to play football, nothing else."

"Hope so," the big man says.

And then it hits me, what Hunter's really concerned about. He's a scholarship student at Astor and needs a free ride for college. He's worried my drama is going to scare colleges away.

"Scouts are still gonna come to the game to see you, Hunter," I reassure him.

He looks doubtful, but Wade pipes up in support. "No doubt. They're all salivating over you. Plus, the more wins, the better you look, right?"

That seems to satisfy Hunter, because he doesn't voice another objection.

"See?" Wade says cheerfully. "'S'all good. So let's just go practice our nuts off and compare notes about who we're all taking to Winter Formal next month."

One of our wide receivers snickers. "Seriously, Carlisle? What, are we a bunch of chicks now?"

With that, the mood in the locker room lightens.

"This is bullshit," Ronnie snaps. "He shouldn't freaking be here."

Or maybe it doesn't.

I stifle a sigh.

At Ronnie's unhappy glare, East slaps his chest. "C'mon, Richmond, let's do a few Oklahoma drills. Maybe if you can put me on my ass once, you won't worry so much about the press."

Ronnie flushes. The Oklahoma drill requires one player to take on another while the teammates huddle around in a circle. East hardly ever loses, and certainly never to Ronnie.

"Fuck you, Easton. That's the problem with you Royals. You think violence solves everything."

My brother takes a step forward. "It's football. It's supposed to be violent."

"Gotcha. So killing a woman you don't like is just natural for you guys, huh?" An ugly smile twists his mouth. "I guess that's why your mother killed herself. She was tired of dealing with psychos."

The thin thread of my self-control snaps as a red haze washes over my eyes. This piece of crap can say whatever he wants about me, but to drag my mother into this?

Oh. Hell. No.

I'm on him in a heartbeat, one fist slamming into his jaw as we both crash to the floor. Shouts break out all around us. Hands reach out and grab my collar and the back of my shirt, but nobody is able to haul me off him.

I hear a sickening crack. Primal satisfaction rushes through me when blood spurt out of Ronnie's nostrils. I broke his nose and I don't give a shit. I get one more blow in, a jab to his chin, before I'm suddenly wrenched away.

"Royal! Where's your fucking head!"

Instantly, the anger in my gut is sucked away and replaced by a knot of anxiety. Coach is the one who pulled me to my feet, and now he's standing there, his face red and his eyes glittering with fury.

"Come with me," he growls, bunching his fist into the bottom of my practice jersey.

The locker room is as silent as a church. Ronnie is staggering to his feet and wiping his bloody nose. The other players are staring at me in apprehension. Before Coach drags me through the doorway, I catch a glimpse of East's uneasy expression, Wade's frustrated one, Hunter's resigned one.

Shame churns inside me. Damn it. Here I am, trying to prove to these guys that Royals don't answer every minor bit of bullshit with a fist, and what do I do? I bring out the fists.

Fuck.

CHAPTER 6

ELLA

WORD OF REED'S ARREST SPREADS like a prairie fire. While working the register at the bakery, I can hear the aborted whispers and feel the weight of covert stares. The Royal name is mentioned frequently. One fashionable elderly lady who comes in every Monday for a blueberry scone and a cup of Earl Grey tea point-blank asks me, "Are you that Royal ward?"

"Yes." I swipe her heavy platinum card and hand it back.

She presses her pink-painted lips together. "Doesn't seem like a good environment for a young lady."

"It's the best home I've ever had." My cheeks burn, part embarrassment and part indignation.

For all their faults—and the Royals have many—my statement is entirely truthful. I've never had it better. For the first seventeen years of my life, I lived with my flighty mother, one foot in the gutter, one hand reaching for the sky. At any given moment, I wasn't sure we'd have enough to eat during the day and a roof over our heads at night.

"You seem like a nice girl." The lady sniffs, her whole

demeanor saying that she's reserving judgment on that comment.

I know what she's thinking—I might be a nice girl, but I live with those evil Royals and one of them is on the front page of the *Bayview News* as a potential suspect in the death of Brooke Davidson. Not many people know who Brooke is, other than she was the sometime companion of Callum Royal. But everyone knows the Royals. They're the biggest employer in Bayview, if not the state.

"Thanks. I'll bring out your stuff when it's ready." I dismiss her with a polite smile and turn to the next patron, a younger professional woman who's clearly torn between wanting to hear the gossip and wanting to make whatever early morning appointment she's all dressed up for.

At the wave of my hand for her card, she makes the quick decision that she can't be late. Good call, lady.

The line moves on, and so do the comments, some hushed, some intentionally carrying across the small café. I ignore them all. So does my boss, Lucy, although her ignorance stems from busyness rather than deliberate indifference.

"Weird morning, isn't it?" Lucy says as I'm hanging up my apron on the back hook. She's elbows-deep in flour.

"Why do you say that?" I feign ignorance.

From the racks of cooling baked goods, I pluck an extra muffin and donut for Reed. If it were me, I wouldn't be able to eat a bite, but that boy seems to have a stomach of steel. Apparently being accused of murder doesn't faze him one bit.

Lucy shrugs. "Vibe seems off. Everyone's quiet this morning."

"It's Monday," I say, and that reply seems to satisfy her.

After all my goodies are packed away, I sling my backpack over my shoulder and make the short walk to Astor Park. It's hard to believe that only a few months have passed since I started school here. Time flies when you're fighting bullies and falling in love.

Only Easton is waiting for me on the front steps when I arrive from the bakery. I frown, because usually Reed is with him, but my man is nowhere to be seen. It's clear by the acre of space around Easton that the Astor Park kids are all up-to-date on their daily news. Any other day and this gorgeous boy would be surrounded by girls.

"What'd you bring me, sis?" Easton jogs over to snatch the white pastry box from my hands.

"Donuts, muffins." I look around again. "Where's Reed?"

Easton doesn't look up from his examination of the goodie box, so I can't make out his expression. I do notice that his shoulders tense up a little. "Talking to Coach," is all he says.

"Oh. Okay. Like, a meeting or something?"

"Or something."

I narrow my eyes. "What aren't you telling me?"

Before he can respond, Val comes strolling over to us.

"Hey, girl!" She flings an arm around my shoulder. Either she hasn't read the papers yet or doesn't care. I'm hoping it's the latter.

"Hey, Val." As I greet her, I don't miss the relief on Easton's face. He's definitely keeping something from me.

Val's gaze falls to the box in Easton's hand. "Tell me you have something for me," she begs.

"Chocolate chip muffin." I smile wryly as she grabs the muffin and takes a huge bite. "Bad morning?"

"You have no idea. Jordan's alarm went off at five this morning and she slept through Katy Perry's "Rise" for five repeats. I officially hate Katy Perry and Jordan."

"That's what makes you hate Jordan?" In the chronicles of mean girls, Jordan Carrington might be the patron saint. There are so many things to hate her for other than her music taste.

Val laughs. "Among other things. Anyway, you're a goddess. And a trooper, because your morning must be a million times worse than mine."

I frown at her. "What do you mean?"

She raises one eyebrow, which gives her already pixie-like face an even more elfish look. "I mean, Reed beating up Ronald Richmond at practice. Everyone's talking about it and it only happened an hour ago."

My jaw drops. Then I spin around to glare at Easton. "Reed beat someone up? Why didn't you tell me?"

He smiles around a mouthful of pastry, and I'm force to wait until he swallows before I get a reply. "Because it's no biggie, okay? Richmond was running his mouth and Reed put a stop to it. He didn't even get suspended or anything. Coach just gave him a warning—"

I'm already marching to the front doors. I can't believe Reed got into a fight and Easton didn't tell me about it!

"Wait up," Val calls out.

I stop to let her catch up to me, then take off at a brisk pace again. Maybe I can intercept Reed before he goes to his first class. I know he can handle himself in a fight, but I want to see him with my own two eyes and make sure he's okay.

"I saw the paper this morning," Val says in a quiet voice as she keeps up with my breakneck strides. "My aunt and uncle were talking about it. Things are bad in the Royal palace, huh?"

"Badder than bad," I admit.

We're halfway to the senior wing when the first bell chimes. Crap. I skid to a stop, torn between hurrying forward to find Reed and making it to class on time. Val solves the dilemma by touching my arm.

"If he's already in class, his teacher won't let you go in and talk to him," she points out.

She's right. My shoulders sag as I turn back in the opposite direction. Again, Val keeps up with me.

"Ella."

I keep walking.

"Ella. Come on. Wait." She grabs my arm again, and there's concern etched into her face as she studies me. "He didn't kill anyone."

I can't even begin to explain how relieved I am to hear her say that. My own doubts about Reed's innocence have been gnawing at my insides ever since he got arrested. I hate myself for even entertaining those thoughts, but every time I close my eyes, I remember his torn stitches. The blood. The fact that he went to the penthouse without telling me.

"Of course he didn't," I force myself to say.

Her gaze sharpens. "Then why do you look so worried?"

"I'm not worried." I hope my firm tone is convincing. I think it is, because her features relax. "It's just...everything is such a mess right now, Val. Reed's arrest, Steve showing up—"

"What?" she exclaims.

It takes me a second to remember that I haven't even told her about my father yet. I didn't want to say it over text, and there wasn't a single opportunity to call Val yesterday because of all the chaos in the house.

"Yeah. Steve's back. Surprise—he's not dead, after all."

Val looks a bit dazed. "You're joking, right?"

"Nope." Before I can elaborate, the second bell rings. This is the one that warns us we have one minute to get to class—or else. "I'll explain everything at lunch, okay?"

She nods slowly, the stunned expression never leaving her face. We part ways at the next hallway, and I head for my first class.

Within three seconds of sitting down at my desk for first period, I discover that Val isn't the only one who's seen the morning paper. When the teacher turns her back on the class for a moment, some douche leans past two desks to shout-whisper, "You can come live at my house, Ella, if you're scared of being murdered in your bed."

I ignore him.

"Or maybe that's what turns your type on."

When I first arrived at Astor Park, I learned pretty fast that most of the kids here aren't worth my time or effort. This campus is so gorgeous with its lush green lawns and tall brick buildings. It looks picture perfect, but it's filled with the unhappiest, least secure teens I've ever had the misfortune of meeting.

I swivel in my chair, lean across Bitsy Hamilton's desk, and stare directly into the douche's muddy green eyes. "What's your name?"

He blinks. "What?"

"Your name," I repeat impatiently. "What is it?"

Bitsy raises a hand to hide a smirk.

The douche's face twists into an indignant sneer. "Aspen," he replies tightly.

"Aspen? For real?" What a dumb-ass name.

Bitsy's laughter is barely being contained at this point. "It's Aspen, for real," she chokes out.

"Jesus, okay. Here's the deal, *Aspen*. I've dealt with more in my short life than you'll ever experience, so all the idiotic insults you can come up with only make you look pathetic. I don't give a rat's ass what you think of me. Actually, if you don't step back and rethink your decision to even look in my direction, I'll make it my sole goal for the rest of this semester to drive you literally insane. I'll stuff week-old seafood in your locker. I'll destroy your homework. I'll tell each and every girl in this place that you have gonorrhea. I'll have pictures of you wearing girl's undies made up and distributed in giant full-color prints around school." I smile coldly at him. "Do you want that to happen to you?"

Aspen's face turns as white as the snowy town he was named after. "I was just joking," he mumbles.

"Your jokes suck. Hope you have a job with your daddy waiting, because I can't imagine your little brain making it through college." Then I spin around and face the front of the room.

AT LUNCH, OUR TABLE IS subdued. I fill Val in about Steve's sudden reappearance, but we don't get a chance to discuss how shaken up I am about it, because Reed, Easton, and Wade join us instead of sitting at the football table.

That's the first sign that something is wrong. I mean, Reed's been charged with murder, so life is *very* wrong in general, but the fact that he's not sitting with his teammates tells me that things are worse than I thought.

"You really didn't get in trouble for fighting at school?" I murmur to him as he settles in the seat next to mine.

He shakes his head. "Got a warning." Then his expression grows tortured. "But you know it's gonna get back to Dad and my lawyer. They won't like it."

I don't like it, but I paste on an encouraging smile because I know he's already under enough stress as it is. It's just…

I love Reed, I really do, but his temper is his own worst enemy. If he can't get himself under control, things could get a million times worse for him.

Across the table, Val moves her kale salad around her plate. Her gaze keeps darting toward Wade and then back to her plate. Wade is doing the same thing—sneaking peeks at Val before focusing intently on his burger.

They're making obvious efforts not to look at each other, and for some reason that cheers me up. It's nice to see that I'm not the only one in a state of pure misery.

Immediately, guilt gets the better of me, because if Val's studiously avoiding Wade and he's too embarrassed to meet her eyes, then something bad must have happened. I make a mental note to ask Val about it when we're alone.

"So," Wade says when the silence becomes unbearably long. "Who's excited about Winter Formal?"

Nobody answers.

"Really? No one?" He slides a pointed look to Val. "What about you, Carrington? Got a date?"

She gives him a stony glare. "I'm not going."

The table goes quiet again. Val picks at her salad with the

same half-hearted energy I'm using to pick at my chicken.

"Not hungry?" Reed asks gruffly.

"I don't have much of an appetite," I admit.

"You worried?" he murmurs.

"A little." More like a lot, but I tamp down the truth and paste on another smile.

I think Reed sees through it, because he leans over and kisses me. I let him distract me with his mouth because it feels good, but deep down I know that kisses are a temporary fix.

Pulling back, I tell him that. "You can't kiss the worry out of me."

His hand roams up my side to settle right under my breast. His thumb brushes the bottom curve, sending shivers through me. I stare into his blue eyes, full of wicked promise, and decide, okay, maybe he *can* kiss the worry out of me.

I move a few strands of his silky hair away from his face, wishing we were alone and he could turn his unspoken promises into a reality. His hands tug me forward so he can kiss me again. This time, I open my mouth and let his tongue sweep inside.

"Not while I'm eating," Easton groans. "You're ruining my appetite."

"I don't think that's remotely possible," Val says.

I smile against Reed's mouth and then settle back in my seat.

"Well, *I'm* getting turned on. Anyone want to make a trip to the bathroom with me?" Wade asks cheerfully.

Val's mouth stays firmly shut.

"Everything's going to be fine," Reed tells me. "Except Easton's stomach maybe. He might need medical attention after inhaling all those carbs." He gestures to the mountain of pasta on Easton's plate.

"I'm a nervous eater," his brother replies.

I make an attempt to follow Reed's lead and lighten the mood. "What was your excuse last week when you ate an entire batch of cookies?"

"That was just me being hungry. Besides, they were cookies. Who needs an excuse to eat cookies?"

"I feel like that's a sexual question," Wade chimes in. "And the correct answer is, no one ever needs an excuse to eat cookies."

"You do need permission, though," Val says tersely, focusing her gaze on Wade for the first time since he sat down. "And if your mouth is all over someone else's cookies, then other bakers aren't going to be interested in offering you their cookies."

Then she gets up from the table and stomps off.

"Hey!" Wade shouts after her. "I only had those other cookies that one time and only because the baker I wanted to get the cookies from was closed!"

He shoots up from his seat and hustles after Val, leaving Easton, Reed, and me staring after them.

"I have a feeling they aren't talking about cookies," Easton remarks.

No kidding. And as much as I hate seeing Val upset, I can't help but envy her problems.

Relationship issues are a lot easier to manage when you're not worrying that your boyfriend might go to prison.

CHAPTER 7

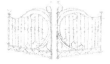

REED

THE MOMENT I WALK THROUGH the front door, my dad pokes his head into the parlor and jerks a finger in my direction. "I need you in my study. Now."

Ella and I exchange a wary look. It doesn't take a rocket scientist to figure out that word of my fight with Richmond got back to Dad. Damn it. I was hoping to tell him myself.

"Should I come with you?" Ella asks with a grimace.

After a beat, I shake my head. "Nah. Go upstairs and do some homework or something. This won't be fun." When she hesitates, I give her a gentle nudge. "Go. I'll be up soon."

I wait in the parlor until she disappears upstairs, then release the unhappy sigh that's been jammed in my chest all day long. School sucked ass today, and not just because I broke a teammate's nose. The whispers and stares got to me. Normally I don't give a crap what my classmates think of me, but today the tension in the air was almost suffocating.

Everyone wonders if I killed Brooke. Most believe it. Even some of my own teammates. Hell, sometimes I think

Ella might believe it, too. She hasn't said that, but at lunch I caught her staring at me when she thought I wasn't looking. She had this expression on her face. I can't even describe it. Not quite doubt, but apprehension maybe. A flicker of sadness, too.

I told myself that she was just freaked out about everything, but a part of me wonders if *she* wonders. If she keeps looking at me like that because she's trying to figure out if she's dating a killer or some shit.

"Reed."

Dad's sharp voice spurs me to motion. I march down the hall to his study, and my mood sinks even lower when I spot Grier behind the commanding desk. Dad is sitting on the nearby armchair.

"What's wrong?" I ask instantly.

"Do you really need to ask?" Dad's expression is dark and menacing. "I got a phone call from the headmaster earlier. He told me all about your little temper tantrum in the locker room."

I bristle. "It wasn't a temper tantrum. Richmond was saying shit about Mom."

For once, the mention of my mother doesn't cause my dad to soften. "I don't care if he was insulting Jesus Christ himself— you can't fight at school, Reed! Not anymore, and especially not when you're facing a second-degree murder charge!"

Equal parts shame and anger weigh on my gut. My dad's face is red, his fists clenched together at his sides, but through the haze of anger in his eyes, I catch a glimpse of something even worse—disappointment.

I can't remember the last time I cared whether or not my father was disappointed in me. But…I kind of care right now.

"Sit down, Reed." The request comes from Grier, who has his trusty gold pen poised over his legal pad. "There are a few things we need to go over."

Reluctantly, I walk over to one of the padded chairs and sit down. My dad stiffly lowers himself into the other chair.

"We'll discuss the fighting in a moment," Grier says. "First, you need to tell me why your DNA was found under Brooke's fingernails."

Shock slams into me. "What?"

"I spoke to the assistant district attorney today, as well the detectives in charge of the investigation. They were waiting for DNA testing to be conducted before they divulged any details to us. But the results are back, and believe me, they were eager to share them." Grier's face becomes grave. "Skin cells were found in the fingernail scrapings they took from Brooke. DNA matches yours."

"How did they get my DNA?" I demand. "I didn't provide a sample."

"They have it from the last arrest."

I wince. *Last arrest.* That sounds bad. "They can do that?"

"Once you're in the system, you're there forever." Grier shuffles a few papers while Dad looks on grimly. "We're going to go over your night, step by step, second by second. Don't leave anything out. If you passed gas, I want to know about it. What did you do after you went to see Brooke?"

"I came home."

"Right after?"

"Yes."

Grier's features sharpen. "Are you sure about that?"

I furrow my brow. "I...think so?"

"Wrong answer. The security footage has you arriving an hour later."

"Arriving where?"

"Here," he snaps, looking annoyed. "Your home has video surveillance, Reed, or have you forgotten?"

I glance at my father, who nods grimly. "We checked the tapes when you were at school," he tells me. "The cameras show you coming home at ten p.m."

"A full hour after you left the O'Halloran penthouse," Grier points out.

I scan my brain again, trying to remember that night. "I drove around the city a bit," I say slowly. "I was still pissed about that whole conversation with Brooke. I wanted to calm myself down before I—"

"No," my dad interrupts.

"No what?" I'm so fucking confused right now.

"You don't say stuff like that, you hear me? You cannot insinuate, even between us, that you were in a state that required 'calming down' that night. You fought with Brooke, but it was no big deal," Dad says firmly. "You were calm when you went there and calm when you left."

Frustration knots inside me. "What does it matter if I drove around for an hour or three or ten?" I burst out. "*Their* tapes show me leaving the penthouse twenty minutes after I got there. So what if I didn't get home until an hour later?"

"They're going to subpoena your security footage," Grier tells my father, as if I hadn't even spoken. "It's only a matter of time."

"Again, what does it matter?" I press.

Grier points the pen at me. "It matters because you lied. If you lie once on the stand, they will crucify you there."

"The stand? I'm going to have to testify?" A whirlwind of emotions forms one giant lump in my stomach. I've been telling myself all along that the police will find the real killer during the investigation, but it looks like they think *I'm* the real killer.

"The detectives noticed you touched your waist a few times and that bloodstains on your shirt developed throughout the interrogation."

"Fuck," I mutter. It feels like a rope just got wrapped around my neck.

"How did that happen?" Grier pushes.

"I don't know. Maybe when I was driving? Or I reached for something?"

"And this injury was the one you sustained how?"

I don't have to be a lawyer to know that my next admission is going to sound bad. "I got stabbed on the docks."

"And you were down there why?"

"Fighting," I mumble under my breath.

"What was that?"

"Fighting. I was fighting."

"You were fighting?" he repeats.

"There's no law against fighting." One of the guys I fight at the docks is the son of an assistant AG. He claims that if we all agree to participate, we aren't doing anything wrong. Wanting to get hit by someone else isn't a prosecutable offense.

But I guess it can be evidence of someone who's violent and possibly murderous.

"And no exchange of money? I have a Franklin Deutmeyer, otherwise known as Fat Deuce, who says that Easton Royal places bets with him for football games. You telling me he never bets on your fights?" Grier doesn't wait for my lie. "We interviewed Justin Markowitz, who says that there is plenty of money exchanged."

It doesn't sound like he needs a response, and I'm right, because Grier barrels forward like he's ready to give the closing argument to put me away.

"You fight for money. You fight because it makes you feel good. You put a kid in the hospital for no good reason—"

I do interrupt this time. "He insulted my mother."

"Like this Richmond boy whose nose you broke today? He also insulted your mother?"

"Yes," I say tightly.

"And what about Brooke? Did she insult your mother, too?"

"What are you saying?" my father growls.

"I'm saying your son has a temper," Grier snaps. "You so much as breathe on his dead mother's grave—"

Dad flinches.

"—and he loses control." Grier tosses his pen on the desk and glares at me. "The DA has a real hard-on for this case. I don't know why. They've got unsolved crimes up the wazoo, murders that happen regularly from the drug trade, bookies like Fat Deuce running around taking money from kids, but they like this case and they like you as the one who did it. Our investigators did a little digging and there are rumors that Dinah O'Halloran may have had a relationship with DA Pat Marolt."

This time it's Dad who curses. "Goddammit."

The rope gets tighter.

"They're going to interview every single one of your classmates. If you've had problems with any of them, you'd better tell me about it now."

"You're supposed to be one of the best lawyers in the state," Dad says testily.

"You're asking me to perform a miracle," Grier snaps back.

"No," I interrupt. "We're asking you to find out the truth. Because while I don't mind taking a free shot to my jaw, I do care about going to prison for something I didn't do. I'm an asshole, for sure. But I don't hit women, and I sure as shit would never kill one."

Dad steps close and lays a hand on my shoulder. "You win this case, Grier. I don't care what else you have on your desk. Nothing else matters until Reed's free of this."

The *or else* is implied.

Grier's mouth thins, but he doesn't object. Instead, he rises, tucks all his papers away, and says, "I'll get to work."

"What should we be doing while the investigation continues?" Dad asks, seeing Grier to the door.

I'm stuck in the chair, wondering how in the hell my life has come to this. I look down at my hands. Did I kill her? Did I dream leaving the penthouse? Am I suffering some weird memory lapse?

"Put on a happy face, act normally, and pretend you're not guilty."

"I'm *not* guilty," I growl.

Grier pauses in the hall. "The DA needs means, motive, and opportunity to prove the crime. Brooke struck her head on the fireplace with enough force to cause her brain to shear from the spinal cord. You're big and strong and like to punch people around. They have you on tape within the golden period. And they have motive. Oh, and Ella Harper?"

I tense up. "What about her?"

"Stay away from her," Grier says flatly. "She's your biggest weakness."

CHAPTER 8

ELLA

R𝐄𝐄𝐃 𝐈𝐒 𝐖𝐀𝐈𝐓𝐈𝐍𝐆 𝐅𝐎𝐑 𝐌𝐄 on the front steps when I get to school. This time Easton is the one who's missing, but I'm kind of grateful to be alone with Reed, especially after last night. His meeting with Callum and Grier left him sullen and close-mouthed, and it was the first night in a long time that he didn't sleep in my bedroom. I didn't beg him to stay, but I did push him to talk.

From the little he told me, I guess the lawyer is worried about Reed's fighting and the fact that he was unaccounted for during the hour he left the penthouse to the time he got back to the Royal mansion.

That part, I don't really get. So what if he didn't go home right away? It doesn't mean he was doing anything suspicious, especially since the cops know he left the penthouse twenty minutes after he got there.

Still, if it bugs Grier and Callum this much, then it must be important. So it's the first thing I bring up once I kiss Reed hello.

"I still don't get why that hour you were driving around means anything."

His eyes darken, which, combined with his untucked dress shirt and unbuttoned blue blazer, gives him a bad-boy vibe. I was never drawn to the bad-boy type before I met Reed, but in him I find it kind of irresistible.

"It doesn't mean anything," he mutters.

"Then why is the lawyer so worried about it?"

Reed shrugs. "I don't know. But I don't want *you* to worry about it, okay?"

"I can't not worry." I hesitate, not wanting to bring up this idea again because I know it makes him mad, but I can't help myself. "We still have time to run," I plead, then look around to make sure nobody is lurking near us. I lower my voice to a whisper. "I don't want to sit here and wait for you to be locked up."

His eyes lose that hard glint. "Baby. It's not going to happen."

"How do you know that?" A helpless feeling washes over me. "I've already lost the only other person who meant something to me. I don't want to lose you, too."

Sighing, Reed pulls me into his arms and kisses my forehead. "You're not going to lose me."

His mouth travels lower and finds mine, and he slips his tongue between my lips, taking my breath away, making my knees a little weak. I grab onto his biceps so I don't fall over.

"You're the strongest person I know," he whispers against my lips. "So be strong for me, okay? We're not running. We're going to stay and fight."

Before I can respond, a car engine snags my attention. I

turn around in time to see a police cruiser pulling into the huge drive in front of the main building.

Both Reed and I stiffen.

"Are they here for you?" I ask anxiously.

His dark expression is back, blue eyes fixed on the cruiser. "I don't know." His face only gets cloudier when a stocky man with a bald head gets out of the driver's side. "Shit."

"You know him?" I hiss.

Reed nods. "Detective Cousins. He's one of the cops who interviewed me."

Oh God. This can't be good.

Sure enough, Cousins marches over the second he spots us on the steps. "Mr. Royal," he says coolly.

"Detective," Reed answers, equally cool.

There's a tense moment of silence before the detective turns his sharp gaze on me.

"Ella O'Halloran, I presume?"

"Harper," I bite out.

He actually rolls his eyes, which I find a bit rude. "Well, Ms. *Harper*. You're actually the first person on my list this morning."

I scowl at him. "Your list of what?"

"Witnesses." Cousins looks kind of smug as he smiles at me. "The headmaster is allowing me to conduct interviews in his office this morning. If you'd follow me, please…"

I stay put. Callum already warned me something like this could happen, so I'm prepared for it. "Sorry, but that's not happening. My guardian needs to be present for any and all interviews." I smile back, also smug. "So does my lawyer."

The detective narrows his eyes. "I see. So that's how we're going to play it." He nods curtly. "Then I guess I'll be in touch with your guardian."

With that, he brushes past us and disappears through the front doors.

Once he's gone, my confident façade drops and I instantly look at Reed. "He's interviewing people today? *Who?*"

"I don't know," he says grimly.

"Oh my God, Reed, this is bad. This is really bad."

"It'll be fine." But his tone lacks its usual confidence. "Come on. We should get to class. Text me if you have any problems today, okay?"

"Why would I have any problems?" I ask warily.

His answer is cryptic. "Natives are restless."

This entire conversation—and Detective Cousins just showing up out of the blue—didn't do a thing to ease my worries, and I think Reed knows it, but he still puts on a smile and walks me to class as if everything is A-OK. After a quick kiss, he takes off in the other direction. I can't shake my concern. It falls over me like a heavy blanket, and by the time I walk into my chemistry class and settle in my usual seat next to Easton, despair is leaking out of every pore of my body.

"What's wrong?" Easton asks immediately.

I lean in to hiss in his ear. "The cops are here to interview people about Reed."

Easton is unfazed. "Nobody around here even knew about Reed and Brooke," he whispers back. "The interviews will turn up nothing."

I peek around to make sure nobody is listening. "But everyone in school knows about his fights." Another thought occurs to me. "And Savannah knows about the Dinah thing."

He frowns. "That has nothing to do with Brooke."

"No, but they might be able to twist it around." I wring my hands together as my anxiety returns, even worse than before. "If they find out that Dinah was blackmailing Reed's brother, they might come up with some crazy theory that Reed went to the penthouse looking for *Dinah* and killed Brooke instead."

It's a ridiculous thought, but it's just plausible enough that Easton actually looks worried. "Shit."

"If they talk to Savannah, do you think she'd say anything?"

He slowly shakes his head. "I...don't think so?"

That's not good enough for me. Not in the slightest. "We have English with her next period. I'll talk to her."

"And what? Threaten to break her legs if she squeals?" His smile is weak and forced.

"No, but I'll make sure she knows how important it is not to bring up the Gideon and Dinah thing."

"Sav hates the Royals," he says in a tired voice. "I'm not sure anything you say to her is going to convince her to keep her mouth shut."

"Maybe not, but I'm still going to try."

AFTER CHEM, I RACE TO the second floor to try to intercept Savannah Montgomery before she reaches our English classroom.

Gideon's ex-girlfriend is the most contradictory person I've ever met. She was the one who gave me a tour of Astor Park Prep when I started here, and although she was kind of bitchy that day, she also offered a lot of unsolicited advice about how to survive this school. And even though she kept her distance and didn't talk to me much in class, she still took the time to warn me about Daniel Delacorte, and then she helped me and Val get revenge on the creep.

So I guess she's an ally?

Honestly, I don't really know. She's hard to read on a good day, and impossible to read every other day.

Today falls into the unreadable category. She frowns when she sees me loitering outside the door, but she does say "Hey" in a voice that lacks hostility.

"Can we talk for a minute?" I ask quietly.

Suspicion flickers in her eyes. "Why?"

I will up some patience. "Because we need to talk."

"Class is starting."

"Mr. Winston is ten minutes late every day and you know it. We have time." I plead at her with my eyes. "Please?"

After a beat, she nods. "Fine. But make it fast."

We walk silently down the hall toward a bank of lockers that's squished into its own little corridor. Once we're alone, I don't waste any time.

"The police are here today interviewing some of Reed's friends and classmates."

She doesn't look at all surprised. "Yeah, I know. I already got a summons to Beringer's office. I'm talking to them at lunch." She rolls her eyes. "They wanted to pull me out of class and I was, like, fuck that. I'm not falling behind just because some Royal killed his daddy's girlfriend."

I flinch as if she's slapped me. "Reed didn't kill anyone," I say between clenched teeth.

Savannah shrugs. "Don't care if he did. I never liked Brooke."

I furrow my brow. Did Savannah even know Brooke? I'm confused for a second, until I realize that Sav *did* know her. She referred to Brooke as an "extra" the day she gave me the Astor Park tour, and she'd dated Gideon for a year, so she must have run into Brooke at the house on a bunch of occasions.

"That woman was garbage," she adds. "Gold-digger with a capital G."

"Either way, Reed didn't kill her."

She arches a perfectly shaped eyebrow. "Is that what you want me to tell the cops?"

I swallow my frustration. "You can tell them whatever you like, because he didn't do it. I wanted to talk to you about the other thing."

"What other thing?"

I shoot a glance at the main hall. It's empty. "The Gideon and Dinah thing."

According to Reed, Dinah broke into Gid's phone and stole nude pictures that he and Savannah had exchanged. With that ammo, she's holding a statutory rape charge over his head, because Savannah was only fifteen at the time, while Gideon was eighteen.

At the sound of Gideon's name, Savannah's wary expression transforms into one of pure malice. "You mean that thing where my boyfriend screwed a trashy cougar?" she snaps.

"Yeah, and that the trashy cougar is blackmailing him with pictures *you* sent him," I snap back.

This time it's her turn to flinch. "Are you saying it's *my* fault Gid is in this mess? Because it's not! *He's* the cheater. *He's* the one who hooked up with that awful woman, and it's *his* fault she became obsessed with him and stole his phone. All I did was send pics to my boyfriend, Ella!"

I see myself losing control of the conversation, so I hastily put on a calm, non-threatening tone. "I'm not blaming you at all," I promise. "All I'm saying is that you're involved in this whether you want to be or not. Gideon could get in a lot of trouble if the cops find out about Dinah and the pictures."

Savannah doesn't answer.

"I know you hate him, but I also know you don't want to see him go to jail. And telling the detectives about it will only make them try to somehow use that information against Reed." I glare at her. "And Reed's innocent." Or at least I think he is.

She stays quiet for a long time. So long that I don't think I've gotten through to her. But then she lets out a heavy breath and nods.

"Fine. I'll keep my mouth shut."

Relief swamps me, but Savannah doesn't even give me the chance to thank her. She just walks away without another word.

CHAPTER 9

ELLA

I DON'T SEE SAVANNAH AGAIN for the rest of the day. Normally I wouldn't think twice about that since we don't have any afternoon classes together, but the paranoia is getting to me. She was supposed to speak to the detective at lunch. I was hoping she would track me down afterward and tell me about the interview, but she didn't, and I don't even catch a glimpse of her in the halls during the second half of the day.

At lunch, though, Val confessed that the detectives left a message with her parents this morning asking for permission to interview her. I guess her aunt and uncle are like Callum, because they insisted on being present for Val and Jordan's interviews.

Yup, Jordan. Apparently she's on Cousins' list, too. Which is very, very disturbing, because I know Jordan's only going to have terrible things to say about Reed.

I'm not sure who the cops even spoke to today, other than Savannah. I'm dreading my own interview, but hopefully Callum can delay it for as long as possible. Maybe until these detectives do their stupid job and find the real killer.

If there's a real killer…

A silent scream forms in my throat, causing me to stop in the middle of the parking lot. I hate these thoughts that keep popping into my head. I *hate* that I'm still having doubts about Reed. He insists he didn't kill Brooke. He swears he didn't.

So why can't I one-hundred-percent believe him?

"The parking lot is for cars, little sis, not people."

I spin around to find Easton grinning at me. He gives me a little nudge forward, adding, "Poor Lauren's been trying to pull out of that space for about, oh, two minutes?"

My gaze shifts to the red BMW with its engine running. Sure enough, Lauren Donovan is waving at me, a slightly apologetic look on her face, as if she's the one inconveniencing me and not the other way around.

I wave in apology at the twins' girlfriend and hurriedly step out of the way. "I spaced out," I tell Easton.

"Still worried about the interviews?"

"Yeah. But I did speak to Savannah and she promised she wouldn't say anything about the Gideon stuff."

Easton nods. "That's good, at least."

"Yeah."

"Ella," Reed's voice comes from behind us. "Ride home with me?"

I turn as he strides into the parking lot with Sebastian at his side. Again, my paranoia kicks in. "What happened? Don't you have practice?"

He shakes his head. "East does, but I'm excused. Dad just texted and ordered me to come directly home."

Fear pricks my spine. "Why? What's going on?"

"I don't know." Reed looks frustrated. "All he said was that it's important. And he already cleared it with Coach."

His face is hard, which means he's worried. I'm learning that Reed gets mean when he feels backed into a corner, and this corner filled with police, investigators, and prison has to feel like the smallest, loneliest corner in the world.

"Does he want me there, too?" I ask warily.

"No. But I do." Reed glances at his youngest brother. "Seb, you cool driving Ella's car back?"

Sebastian nods. "No prob."

I toss him the keys, then watch as he heads for my convertible while Easton jogs off to football practice. Reed and I climb into his Range Rover, but I'm not sure why he asked me to ride with him, because he doesn't say a single word for the first five minutes of the drive.

I stare out the window, chewing on my thumbnail. Silent Reed is tough for me to deal with. It reminds me too much of when I first moved in with the Royals. All I received from Reed were glares and cutting remarks, which was a huge difference from what I was used to. Mom was slightly—okay, *really*—irresponsible, but she was always cheerful and never kept her emotions in check. I was the one who did that.

"Say it," Reed suddenly barks.

I'm startled. "Say what?"

"Whatever it is you're obsessing about. I can hear you thinking, and if you bite any harder on your finger, it's gonna come off."

Chagrined, I look down at the teeth marks on the side of my thumb. Rubbing the redness away, I say, "I didn't think you noticed."

He answers in a low, gruff tone. "I notice everything about you, baby."

"I'm worried. You keep telling me not to be, but it's only getting worse" I admit. "At school, it's easy to see the enemy. To categorize people into helpful or unhelpful, for you or against you. This thing just seems so big."

So *scary*, but I keep that to myself. Reed doesn't need to hear my fears. He'd take them on his shoulders and try to carry them along with all the other baggage that's weighing him down.

"It's all going to get taken care of," he says, his capable hands guiding the SUV down the long paved driveway toward the Royal house. "Because I didn't do it."

"Then who did?"

"Maybe the kid's father? Brooke was probably shaking down as many marks as she could that night. I wasn't the only idiot who—" He stops abruptly.

I'm glad he does, because I don't like thinking of Reed having sex with anyone else, even if it was before me. God, it'd be so nice if he was a virgin.

"You should be a virgin," I inform him.

He lets out a surprised laugh. "That's what's got you all wound up?"

"No, but think about how many problems would be solved by that. You wouldn't have this thing with Brooke. The girls at school wouldn't be drooling all over you."

"If I was a virgin, all those girls at school would be trying to get in my pants so they could say they were the first to climb Mount Reed." He grins as he pulls to a stop around the side of the house.

The Royals have an entire parking area in the courtyard

with special brick pavers set into a spiral pattern that leads into a garage that stores all their vehicles. Except no one likes to use the garage. Usually the courtyard is filled with the black Rovers or Easton's cherry-red pickup.

"Girls aren't like that," I say as I get out of the SUV and reach in for my backpack. "They wouldn't compete to deflower you."

Reed's hand is there first. He pulls the bag out of my grip with a smirk. "Girls are exactly like that. Why do you think Jordan's after you all the time? You're competition, babe. Doesn't matter what you've got downstairs, most people are competitive as shit. And the kids at Astor? They're the worst of the lot. If I was a virgin, that'd be one more contest for someone to win."

"If you say so."

He comes around the front of the Rover and drapes an arm around my shoulder. Dipping low so that his mouth touches the upper curve of my ear, he whispers, "We can play I'm the virgin and you're the experienced upperclassman after I pop your cherry."

I hit him because he deserves it, but it only makes him laugh more. And even though he's laughing at my expense, I'm glad because I like happy Reed over quiet, angry Reed.

His good mood doesn't last, though. Callum greets us at the door with a stern look.

"Good to see you're enjoying yourself," he says flatly as we enter the kitchen.

When I notice Steve at the counter, I jump in surprise. I know it's crazy, but I keep forgetting about him. It's like my brain isn't capable of handling more than one crisis at a time, and Reed possibly going to jail is the only thing I can focus on.

Each time I see Steve, it's almost like I'm hit with the news that he's alive over and over again.

I don't miss the way his blue eyes narrow as they land on Reed's arm around my shoulders. Steve's expression looks vaguely like parental disapproval, something I haven't experienced before. Mom was as easygoing as they came.

I slide out from under Reed's arm under the pretense of going to the refrigerator. "Want something?" I offer.

Reed gives me an amused smile. "Sure, what're you offering?"

Jerk. He knows exactly why I left him at the kitchen doorway, and now he's making fun of me for it. Resisting the urge to give him the finger, I grab a container of yogurt.

Callum claps his hands together to get our attention. "Get a spoon and meet me in the study."

"Us," Steve corrects.

Callum waves a hand as he walks away.

"Stop it with the innuendo," I hiss to Reed as I grab a spoon out of the drawer.

"Why? Dad knows about us."

"But Steve doesn't," I point out. "It's weird, okay? Let's just pretend to be—"

Reed quirks an eyebrow.

"Friends," I finish, because all the alternatives are too weird.

"Pretend? I thought we *were* friends. I'm hurt." He slaps an exaggerated hand over his chest.

"You're not now, but I can change that." I wave my spoon at him threateningly. "I'm not afraid to get physical with you, pal."

"I can't wait." His hand falls to my hip and drags me closer. "Why don't you get physical with me right now?"

I lick my lips, and his gaze zeroes in on my mouth.

"Reed! Ella!" Callum yells. "Study. Now!"

I jerk away. "Let's go."

I swear I hear him say *cockblocker* under his breath.

In Callum's office, we find Steve leaning against the desk while Callum paces. All traces of humor evaporate when we spot Halston Grier sitting in one of the leather club chairs situated in front of the desk.

"Mr. Grier," Reed says stiffly.

Grier rises to his feet. "Reed. How are you doing, son?"

Reed reaches around me to shake the lawyer's hand.

"Should I leave?" I ask awkwardly.

"No, this involves you, Ella," Callum answers.

Reed comes to my side immediately and places a protective hand at my back. I notice for the first time that Callum's tie is askew and his hair is sticking up, as if he's dragged his hand through it a hundred times. My gaze skips over to Steve, who's wearing jeans and a loose-hanging white shirt. He doesn't appear to be concerned.

I don't know who to take my emotional cues from. My eyes bounce between the rattled Callum and the calm Steve. Does this have to do with me and not the murder case?

"You should sit down." This comes from Grier.

I shake my head. "No. I'll stand."

Sitting seems dangerous. It takes longer to get up from a seated position and run than it does if I'm already on both legs.

"Dad?" Reed prompts.

Callum sighs, this time scrubbing the heel of his hand down one side of his face. "Judge Delacorte came to me with an interesting offer." He pauses. "It's regarding the DNA they found under Brooke's fingernails."

Reed frowns. "What about it?"

"Delacorte's willing to lose this evidence."

My jaw hits the floor. Daniel's father is a *judge*. And he's willing to "lose" evidence? That's the most corrupt thing I've ever heard.

"What's the price?" I demand.

Callum turns toward me. "Daniel would be allowed to come back to Astor Park. You would recant all your accusations and admit you took the drugs willingly." He glances at his son. "When you and your brothers found her, she made up a story so you wouldn't dislike her more than you already did. That's the price."

Every atom inside of me revolts at Callum's scenario.

Reed erupts like a volcano. "That motherfucker! No way!"

"If I do it…" I take a breath. "Will Reed's charges be dropped? Will the case go away?" I direct my questions to the lawyer.

"You're not doing this," Reed insists, his hand clamping onto my arm.

I jerk out of his grasp and advance on the lawyer. "If I do this," I repeat through gritted teeth, "will Reed be saved?"

Behind me, Reed yells at his father for even entertaining the idea. Callum tries to soothe him, explaining that he's not recommending I take this path.

But obviously he wants me to or he wouldn't have brought it up in the first place. It hurts, a little, but I get it. Callum's trying to save his son from life in prison.

Steve, meanwhile, says nothing. He's just taking it all in. But I don't care about any of the other men in this office. Only the lawyer has the answer I need.

Grier folds his perfectly manicured hands in his lap, clear-eyed and unruffled by all the chaos in the room. I'm not sure what he sees when he looks at me. A frail girl? A stupid one? A silly one? How about one who loves her boyfriend so much she'd be willing to swallow swords for him?

This...this would be nothing. A few months of Daniel Delacorte in my life, a few more awful Astor Park kids whispering behind my back, a reputation as a drug addict? All of that in exchange for Reed's freedom?

It'd be worth it.

"It can't hurt," Grier finally admits.

And Reed loses it again.

CHAPTER 10

REED

"No way!" At the attorney's words, I immediately abandon Dad and storm over to Ella's side, stepping between her and the snake before any more damage can be done. "That's absolutely not happening. Ever."

Ella shakes me off. "What about the video evidence?"

"It can all disappear," Grier replies. "It seems that getting rid of evidence is something Delacorte has some experience with."

"I can't believe any of you would even consider this a good idea. Daniel shouldn't be within a hundred miles of Ella," I say hotly. "This is so fucked up."

"Language," my dad chides, as if he's ever cared before when I've dropped F-bombs.

"Is it?" Ella counters. "How about going to prison for twenty-five years? If swallowing my pride means keeping you free, it doesn't sound fucked up to me."

Nobody reprimands Ella for *her* language, which just pisses me off more.

I turn toward Dad because he's the one who needs convincing. Ella can't pull off this trade by herself. Only Dad and this gutter lawyer can.

"This is the lowest thing ever. That asshole is a psycho and you'd bring him back? Worse, you'd subject Ella to a lifetime of harassment?"

Dad glares at me. "I'm trying to keep you out of prison. It's not a great idea, but it's one you both deserve to hear. You want me to treat you two like adults? Then you get to make the adult decisions," he snaps.

"I'm making it then. Daniel stays where he is and we win this case on the merits, because I didn't. Fucking. Kill. Her." I enunciate each word so that there's no mistake.

Ella grabs my wrist. "Reed, please."

"Please what? Do you know what it'll be like at school if you say you lied about Daniel? You wouldn't be able to walk the halls alone. One of us would have to be with you at all times. Jordan would tear you up."

"Do you think I care about that? It'll only be for a few more months."

"And what about next year? I won't be around to protect you," I remind her.

At the desk, I see Steve narrow his eyes. "I appreciate the sentiment, Reed, but Ella doesn't need your protection. She has her father to protect her." He purses his lips. "In fact, I think it's time for me to take my daughter home."

My blood runs cold.

Ella's grip tightens on my fingers.

Steve straightens from the desk. "Callum, I appreciate you taking care of her when I was gone, but I'm Ella's father. You have your hands full with your own children right now—Ella and I don't need to be here."

Oh hell no. She's not leaving me or this house.

"Dad," I say in warning.

"Steve, your place hasn't been released yet," Callum reminds the other man. "And it doesn't sound like it will be for a while." He looks at the attorney for confirmation.

Grier nods. "The sheriff's office said they'll be collecting evidence for another two weeks, at least."

"That's fine. Dinah and I procured the penthouse suite at the Hallow Oaks." Steve reaches into his pocket and pulls out a plastic keycard. "I've added your name to the reservation, Ella. Here's your key."

She makes no move toward it. "No. I'm not sleeping in the same house as Dinah." Hastily, she adds, "No offense."

"Ella's a Royal," I say coldly.

Steve's gaze falls to where Ella's hand is white-knuckling my wrist. "You better hope not," he murmurs in amusement.

"Be reasonable, Steve," Dad says. "Let's get you settled first. We have a number of legal matters to work out. This is new for everyone."

"Ella's seventeen, which means she's still under her parent's authority, isn't that right, Halston?"

The lawyer tips his head. "That is correct." He rises and shakes out his pant legs. "It sounds like all of you have private matters to work through. I'll get out of your way now." He stops when he's halfway to the door and frowns at me. "I assume I don't need to tell you to stay away from the funeral on Saturday?"

I frown back. "What funeral?"

"Brooke's," Dad says tightly, before glancing at Grier. "And no, Reed won't be attending."

"Good."

I can't stop a bite of sarcasm. "What happened to your whole stand-united-as-a-family thing?"

Grier's response is just as biting. "You can stand united anywhere but that funeral home. And for the love of God, Reed, keep your nose clean. No more fights at school, no bullshit, all right?" His eyes fall to Ella with an unspoken warning.

My biggest weakness? No way. Ella's the steel in my spine, but Grier only sees her as evidence of my motive. I step closer to her.

He shakes his head and turns to Dad, adding, "Let me know if you want me to arrange another meeting with Delacorte."

"There's no meeting," I snap at them.

Dad pats the lawyer on the back. "I'll call you."

Frustration jams in my throat. It's like I'm not even here. And if no one's going to listen to me, then there's no point in *being* here.

"Let's go," I tell Ella.

I pull her out of the study without waiting for her agreement—or anyone else's.

A minute later, we're upstairs, and I throw open her bedroom door and hustle her inside.

"This is stupid!" she blurts out. "I'm not moving into some hotel with Steve and that horrible woman!"

"Nope," I agree, watching as she climbs onto her bed. Her uniform skirt rides up and I get a nice view of her ass before she sits down and draws her legs up under her chin.

"And you're being stupid, too," she grumbles. "I think we should take Delacorte's deal."

"Nope," I say again.

"Reed."

"Ella."

"It would keep you out of prison!"

"No, it would keep me in that bastard's pocket for the rest of my life. It's not happening, babe. Seriously. So get the idea out of your head."

"Fine, let's say you're not taking the deal—"

"I'm not."

"—then what do we do now?"

I take off my white dress shirt and kick off my shoes. Wearing my pants and a wife-beater, I join Ella on the bed and draw her into my arms. She snuggles up against me, but only for a brief moment. Then she's sitting up again, scowling at me.

"I asked you a question," she grumbles.

I exhale in frustration. "There's nothing for us to do, Ella. It's Grier's job to deal with everything."

"Well, he's not doing a very good job of it if he's recommending you make deals with shady judges!" Her cheeks redden with anger. "Let's make a list."

"A list of what?" I ask blankly.

"All the people who could have killed Brooke." She jumps off the bed and hurries to her desk, where she grabs her laptop. "Other than Dinah, who else was she close to?"

"Nobody, as far as I know," I admit.

Ella sits on the edge of the bed, opening the laptop. "That's not an acceptable answer."

Exasperation shoots through me. "It's the only answer I've got. Brooke didn't have any friends."

"But she had enemies—that's what you said, right?" She pulls up a search engine and types Brooke's name into it.

About a million results pop up for a million different Brooke Davidsons. "So it's just a matter of finding out who those enemies are."

I rise up on my elbows. "So you're, what, Lois Lane now? You're going to solve this case on your own?"

"Do you have a better idea?" she counters.

I sigh. "Dad's got investigators. They found you, remember?"

Ella's hand pauses over the mouse, but her hesitation lasts only for a second before she clicks on what appears to be Brooke's Facebook page. While the page loads, she throws me a thoughtful glance.

"The funeral," she announces.

"What about it?" I ask cautiously. I don't like where she's going with this.

"I think I should go."

I sit up in a rush. "No way. Grier said we couldn't go."

"No, he said *you* couldn't go." Her gaze returns to the screen. "Hey, did you know Brooke had a BA from North Carolina State?"

I ignore the useless tidbit. "You're not going to that funeral, Ella," I growl.

"Why not? It's the best way to get an idea of who was close to Brooke. I can see who shows up and—" She gasps. "What if the *killer* shows up?"

Closing my eyes, I try to will up some much-needed patience. "Babe." I open my eyes. "Do you really think whoever killed Brooke is going to waltz up and say, 'Hey guys! I'm a murderer!'"

Indignation flashes in her blue eyes. "Of course not. But haven't you ever watched those crime documentaries on TV?

Those FBI commentators always talk about how killers will return to the scene of the crime or attend the victim's funeral as a way to taunt the police."

I stare at her in disbelief, but she's already focused on the laptop again.

"I don't want you going to the funeral," I grind out.

Ella doesn't even look my way as she says, "Too fucking bad."

CHAPTER 11

ELLA

"WHAT NUN DID YOU KILL for that outfit?" Easton asks when I climb into his pickup early Saturday morning.

I slap the dashboard. "Shut up and drive."

He obediently puts the truck in gear and peels down the driveway toward the massive steel gates that block the mansion from the main road. "Why? Who's after us? Is it Steve?"

Even though Steve is now living with Dinah in their suite of hotel rooms at the Hallow Oaks, he's still lurking around the mansion all the time. He puts Callum in a good mood, but I feel awkward around him and try to avoid spending time with him. I guess that hasn't escaped anyone's notice.

"It's Reed," I reply. "He didn't want me to go today."

"Yeah, he wasn't thrilled about me going, either."

I glance out the back window to make sure Reed isn't running after the truck or anything. He was unhappy when I left, but like I told him the other night, too bad. I plan on scoping out every single person who attends Brooke's service today.

Besides, someone needs to be there with Callum today while his fiancée is being buried. I can't let him do that alone, and since Reed is out of the question and the twins refused, that leaves me and Easton. Callum went on ahead of us with his driver, Durand, because he has business in the city after the service.

"So what'd you do? Sex him into submission? Is he passed out in orgasmic bliss?"

"Shut up." I find my girl power mix on my phone and plug the music in.

But that doesn't silence Easton. Instead, he just shouts over the lyrics. "Are you still not putting out? Poor guy's balls are probably purple by now."

"I'm not talking about my sex life with you," I inform him, and turn the music up even higher.

Easton spends the next five miles laughing.

The sad truth is, Reed's the one who's torturing us. For the last three nights, he's slept in my bed again and we've fooled around a ton. He's fine with me touching him everywhere. He loves it when I go down on him and he's equally generous in return. Heck, he'd spend *hours* with his head between my legs if I let him. But the final deed? That's off the table until "this Brooke thing," as he calls it, isn't hanging over our heads.

I'm in a weird state of satisfaction and anticipation. Reed's giving me nearly everything, but it's not enough. Still, I know that if our situations were reserved, he'd totally respect my wishes. So I have to respect his. Which sucks.

When we arrive at the funeral home, Callum is waiting for us at the entrance. He's wearing a black suit that probably cost more than my car, and his hair is slicked back away from his face, which makes him look younger.

"You didn't have to wait for us," I say when we reach him.

He shakes his head. "You heard Halston—we need to show family unity. So if we're going to be here together, then everyone will leave believing we're a happy, non-guilty group."

I don't say it out loud, but I'm pretty sure no one in there is going to be impressed with a Royal show of strength, considering we're all members of the alleged murderer's family.

The three of us enter the somber-looking building, and Callum leads us to an arched doorway to our left. Inside is a small chapel with rows of polished wooden pews, a raised area with a podium, and…

A casket.

My pulse speeds up at the sight. Oh my God. I can't believe Brooke is actually in there.

As a morbid thought occurs to me, I stand on my tiptoes to whisper in Callum's ear. "Did they do an autopsy on her?"

He responds with a grim nod. "Results haven't come back yet." He pauses. "I assume they'll conduct DNA testing on the, ah, fetus, as well."

The thought makes me sick, because for the first time since this all started, it suddenly occurs to me that *two* people died in that penthouse. Brooke…and an innocent baby.

Swallowing a rush of bile, I force my gaze away from the sleek black box. Instead, I stare at the huge framed photograph that sits on an easel beside it.

Brooke might have been an awful person, but even I can't deny that she was beautiful. The picture they picked shows a smiling Brooke in a pretty patterned sundress. Her blonde hair is loose and her blue eyes are sparkling as she beams at the camera. She looks gorgeous.

"Shit. This is depressing," Easton mumbles.

It totally is.

I was so poor growing up that I couldn't afford a funeral for my mom. The memorial service was twice the cost of the cremation, so I decided not to have a service. No one would've attended it anyway. Mom would've liked it, though.

"Coming?" Easton prompts, nodding his head toward the front.

I follow his gaze to the casket. It's open, but I refuse to go up. So I shake my head and find a seat near the middle while Easton ambles up the center aisle, hands tucked into his pockets. His suit coat strains across his broad shoulders as he leans forward. I wonder what he sees.

Glancing around the room, I'm a bit surprised by the turnout. Or rather, the lack of turnout. There are fewer than ten people in attendance. I guess Brooke really didn't have any friends.

"*Get out!*"

I jerk at the sound of Dinah's high-pitched wail. Well, Brooke had one friend, at least.

It takes a second to register that Dinah is speaking to *us*. She's glaring daggers at me and Easton, who's just coming back from the casket.

"This is shameful!" she screams, and I don't think I've ever seen her look so unhinged before. Her face is one red splotch, her green eyes wild with outrage. "You Royals don't belong here! And *you*—"

She's talking to me now.

"—you're not even family! Get out! All of you!"

I don't know what not-guilty looks like, but I'm putting

Dinah at the top of my suspects list. A woman who'd blackmail some poor guy into her bed is a woman who'd do other terrible things.

Callum stalks over, a hard look in his eyes. Steve, who's in a similar black suit, tails him. Steve's gaze flicks at my black sack of a dress that I found on the first sale rack at the mall department store. It's two sizes too big, but the only other black dress I have is a body-con one from my mother. That was absolutely too morbid—and much too sexy—to wear to a funeral.

"We're not going anywhere," Callum says tightly. "In fact, we have more right to be here than you, Dinah. I was engaged to marry her, for Pete's sake."

"You didn't even love her," Dinah growls. She's trembling so violently that her entire body is swaying. "She was nothing but a sex toy for you!"

My gaze darts around the room to see if anyone heard that.

They all did. Every single pair of eyes is glued to this confrontation, including the minister's. He's frowning at us from the podium, and I'm not the only one who notices.

"Dinah." Steve's voice is low and more commanding than I've ever heard it. Usually he speaks in an easygoing manner, but not right now. "You're making a spectacle of yourself."

"I don't care!" she roars. "They don't belong here! She was *my* friend! She was like a sister to me!"

"She was Callum's fiancée," Steve snaps. "Whatever feelings he may or may not have had for her, we know what *her* feelings were. She loved Callum. She'd want him here."

That shuts Dinah up. For about half a second. Then she aims her furious gaze at me. "Well, *she* doesn't belong here, then!"

Steve's eyes narrow into dangerous slits. "Like hell she doesn't. Ella's my daughter."

"She's been your daughter for all of five minutes! I'm your goddamn *wife*!"

The minister clears his throat. Loudly. I guess he doesn't appreciate her taking the Lord's name in vain in the middle of a chapel.

"You're acting like a child," Steve says harshly. "And you're embarrassing yourself. So I suggest you sit down before you're the one who gets thrown out of here."

That shuts her up for good. With a thunderous glower in our direction, she stomps to the front of the room and slams her ass down on a pew.

"I'm sorry about that," Steve apologizes, but he's only looking at me. "She's a little…emotional."

Easton snorts softly, as if to say "A *little*?"

Callum gives a curt nod. "Let's just sit down. The service is about to begin."

I breathe in relief when Steve walks away to join his horrible wife. I'm glad he's not sitting with us. Every time someone reminds me that I'm his daughter, my discomfort skyrockets.

To my surprise, Callum abandons us, too, settling onto a front-row pew on the opposite aisle of the O'Hallorans.

"He's giving a speech," Easton tells me.

My eyebrows soar. "Seriously?"

"He was her fiancé," is the shrugged response.

Right. I keep forgetting it's not public knowledge that Callum hated Brooke by the end of their destructive relationship.

"It'd look suspicious if he—ah, fuck." Easton stops abruptly, his gaze swinging to the right.

Tension coils in my neck when I see what made him curse. The police detective who came to Astor Park earlier this week—Cousins?—has entered the chapel. A short, dark-haired woman is at his side. They both have shiny gold badges clipped to their belts.

As uneasy as their presence makes me, I can't help but feel a burst of triumph. I wish Reed were here so I could say, *See! The cops are here because they also think the killer might show up!*

"They better not try to interview us," I mumble to Easton as I scrutinize the guests.

One of them could be the killer. My gaze pauses on the back of Callum's head. He had motive, but there's no way he would let his son take the heat for a crime he committed. Plus, Callum was in D.C. with us.

My gaze moves to Steve. But what would be the motive? If it was Dinah in the casket, he'd be my prime suspect, but he's been gone for nine months, which means there's no way he could've been the father of Brooke's baby. I dismiss him.

The other handful of people, I don't know. It must be one of them. But who?

"Dad's lawyers are still stalling about that," Easton mumbles back. "If it happens, it'll be next week. They talked to Wade, though."

I suck in a breath. "They did?" I wonder why Val didn't say anything, but then I think, when would she have had the opportunity?

I've barely spent any time with my best friend since this whole mess began. I know she misses me, and I miss her, too, but it's hard to hang out and gossip and have a good time when life is so screwed up right now.

"They asked him all these questions about Reed's fighting," Easton confesses. "And about all the chicks Reed's been with."

"What the hell? Why is that important?" I'm oddly resentful about that. I don't like the idea of these cops dissecting Reed's previous relationships. Or his current one with me.

"I don't know. Just telling you what Wade said. That was pretty much it. They didn't even talk to him about Brooke or—" He halts again. "Okay, seriously? This is just weird."

When I turn again, this time it's to find Gideon walking in our direction.

Easton mutters to me out of the side of his mouth. "Why is Gid here? Who drives three hours to attend a funeral of some bitch he couldn't even stand?"

"I asked him to come," I admit.

He gapes at me. "Why?"

"Because I need to talk to him." I don't offer any other details, and Easton doesn't have time to cross-examine me, because Gideon reaches us.

"Hey," the eldest Royal brother murmurs. His eyes aren't on us, though. He's staring at Brooke's casket.

Is he imagining Dinah there? I wouldn't be surprised if he was. Steve's wife has been blackmailing Gideon for six months, maybe longer.

I move down to make some space, and he sits beside Easton. Gideon's a Royal anomaly. He's little thinner than his younger brothers, and his hair isn't as dark. He has those blue, blue eyes, though.

"How are classes?" I ask awkwardly.

"Fine."

I haven't spent much time with Gideon at all because he goes to college a few hours away. I only know a handful of things about him. He's a swimmer. He dated Savannah Montgomery. He's sleeping with or has slept with Dinah. He sends dirty pictures to his girlfriend.

If Gideon would kill anyone, it'd be Dinah.

But...Dinah and Brooke look similar. They both have blonde hair styled in that magazine cover blow-out fashion. They're both skinny as sticks with huge racks. From the back, they could easily be mistaken for sisters.

"Thanks for coming," I tell him. Covertly, I study his face, which is hard and tense. Is that what guilt looks like?

"Still not sure why you summoned me," is the terse reply.

I hesitate. "Can you stick around after the service? It feels weird discussing stuff while..." I nod toward the enormous picture of Brooke.

He nods back. "Yeah. We can talk after."

Easton sighs, also staring at the photo. "I hate funerals."

"I've never been to one before," I confess.

"What about your mom?" he asks with a frown.

"Didn't have the money for it. I was able to pay for a cremation and then I took her ashes and threw them in the ocean."

Gideon turns to me with surprised eyes at the same time that Easton says, "No way."

"Yes way," I say, unsure of why they're both staring at me.

"We spread our mom's ashes in the Atlantic," Gideon says quietly.

"Dad was going to bury her, but the twins were freaked out

about worms eating their way into the coffin. They watched some Discovery Channel special on it or some shit. So he caved and agreed to the cremation." A genuine smile spreads across Easton's face, not the cocky fake grin he constantly wears, but a soft, honest one. "We took the urn out and waited for the sun to rise because mornings were her favorite. At first, there was no wind and the water was like glass."

Gideon picks up the story. "But the minute the ashes hit the water, a huge gust came out of nowhere and the tide rolled out so far I swear I could've walked a mile without the sea hitting my knees."

Easton nods. "It was like the ocean wanted her."

We sit silently for a moment, thinking about our own losses. The grief over my mom's death doesn't feel so sharp today, not while I'm sandwiched between the broad shoulders of the two Royal brothers.

"That's a beautiful memory," I whisper. My suspicion that Gideon is the killer wanes. He loved his mother so much. Could he really murder a woman?

Easton grins impishly. "I like that our moms are watching over us from one coast to another."

I can't help but smile back. "Me, too."

My gaze strays to the front row where Steve and Dinah sit, and my smile fades when I notice that Steve has his arm stretched across the back of Dinah's chair. She's leaning against him, her shoulders shaking slightly. Her grief reminds me of why we're all here. This isn't some mixer in a church basement.

It's a funeral for a woman who was only ten years older than me. Brooke was young, and no matter her flaws, she didn't deserve to die, especially not a violent death.

Maybe Dinah isn't the killer at all. She's the only one here who's showing any true grief.

The minister walks up to the podium and asks for us to all take our seats.

"Friends and loved ones, we are gathered here today to mourn the passing of Brooke Anna Davidson. Let us stand together, join hands, and pray," the gray-haired man intones.

Music starts playing as we all rise. The boys brush their hands down the front of their ties. I shake out my dress and clasp their hands, wishing Reed were here. After a short moment of silence, the minister's low voice recites a scripture about how there's a time and season for everything. Apparently this was Brooke's time to die, at the age of twenty-seven. He doesn't mention Brooke's unborn child at all, which makes me wonder if maybe the police are keeping that detail from the public.

At the end of the prayer, he instructs us to sit, and then Callum strides to the podium.

"Awkward," Easton mutters under his breath.

If Callum thought so, you'd never guess it. He calmly speaks of Brooke's charitable work, her devotion to her friends, and her love of the ocean, ending with a declaration that she will be missed. It's short, but surprisingly heartfelt. When he's done speaking, he nods politely in Dinah's direction and retakes his seat. Dinah has the decency not to freak out on him again. She simply nods back.

At the podium once more, the minister asks if anyone else has any memory they would like to share. Everyone seems to pivot toward Dinah, whose only response is to sob loudly.

The minister closes with another prayer and then invites

everyone to remain for refreshments served in the next room. All in all, the service takes less than ten minutes, and something about the speed of it and the lack of people here for Brooke chokes me up.

"You crying?" Easton asks with a note of worry.

"This is just awful."

"What? The funeral in general or that Dad got up to speak?"

"The funeral. There's hardly anyone here."

He surveys the room. "Guess she wasn't a very nice person."

Did Brooke have any family? I strain to remember if she ever told me. I don't think I ever asked. Her mom died when she was young, I know that much.

"Maybe, but I don't think I'd have more people at mine," I admit. "I barely know anyone."

"Nah, every kiss-ass in the state would be here to extend their sympathies to Callum. It'd be big. Not as big as mine, but it'd be good-sized."

"Nothing's ever as big as yours, is it, East?" Gid says dryly.

My eyes widen in surprise. I don't think I've ever heard him make a joke.

Easton cackles. "You know it, bro."

His laugh is a little too loud for Callum, who turns around to glare at us. Easton shuts up immediately, looking slightly abashed. Gideon, on the other hand, glares right back. He folds his arms across his chest as if daring his father to come over and yell at us. Callum turns back to Steve with a sigh of resignation.

"Ready to talk?" Gideon asks.

Nodding, I follow the boys out of the aisle and the three of us walk into the hallway. Everyone else is moving into the next room to take the minister up on the refreshments offer, but we stay put.

"Reed and I were talking the other night," I start, though technically *I* was talking and Reed was telling me I was nuts. "We think maybe we should look into Brooke's past, figure out if there's anyone else who might have wanted her"—I lower my voice—"dead. I was hoping you could help with that."

He looks startled. "How exactly can *I* help? I barely knew Brooke."

Easton, however, instantly understands why I've come to Gideon with this. "Yeah, but you're boning Dinah, and she knew Brooke better than anyone."

Gideon clenches his jaw. "Are you serious right now? Are you suggesting I hop back into bed with that…that…bitch," he hisses, "just to try to squeeze some info out of her?"

The anger reddening his face makes me take a timid step back. This is the first time I've seen Gideon lose his temper. He's always been the most levelheaded of the Royals.

"I'm not asking you to sleep with her," I protest. "Just to grill her for some details."

He looks incredulous. "Are you really that naïve, Ella? You think I can spend a second with that woman without her trying to hump me?"

I cringe in embarrassment.

"So forget it," he snaps. "Ever since Brooke died, Dinah's been too upset to even pick up the phone and call me. As long as she doesn't remember I exist, I get to live my fucking life without having to deal with her. Hopefully with Steve back, she'll forget I ever existed."

"I'm sorry," I whisper. "It was a stupid idea."

Beside me, Easton shakes his head in disapproval. "Wow, Gid. That's harsh. You don't want to help Reed?"

His brother's jaw drops. "I can't believe you just said that to me. Of course I want to help Reed."

"Yeah? Well, we both know he'd bang every cougar in the state if it was *your* neck on the line. Reed would do whatever it took to save you."

I can't disagree with that. Reed is loyal to his core. He'd die for his family.

Hell, he might've even killed for it.

Stop it!

I banish the awful thought and focus on Gideon. "Look, you don't have to do it if you're not comfortable. All I'm asking is, if you're around Dinah for some reason, maybe you can ask her if there's anyone out there who may have hated Brooke? Like, what about any of these people inside?"

He goes quiet for a moment. "Fine. I'll see what I can do."

"Thank—"

"But only if you do something for me," he interjects.

I wrinkle my forehead. "What?"

"When are you moving in with Steve?"

"What?" I'm even more bewildered.

"When are you moving in with Steve?" he repeats.

"Why would she move in with Steve?" Easton demands.

"Because he's her father," Gideon says impatiently before focusing on me again. "Dinah must keep all her blackmail shit at her place. I need you to find it and get it back for me."

I frown. "Even if I was moving in with Steve," which I don't want to ever, "I wouldn't know the first place to look."

"There must be a safe or something," he insists.

Gideon shrugs. "I'm not opposed to sledgehammering that shit out of the wall. We'll tell Steve you and Reed got into a fight."

I gape at him. "That's a terrible idea and I'm not going to do it."

Gideon grabs my arm. "I'm not the only one who you could save." His voice is low, deadly. "Savannah's up to her eyeballs in this. Dinah's got a DA in her pocket. He visited me up at State and showed me two criminal complaints, one for Sav and one for me. They were going to charge us with things I didn't even know were illegal."

Sympathy tugs at me as I stare at his pale face. There's a bead of sweat along the top of his forehead. "I don't know," I say slowly.

"At least think about it," he begs. The fingers at my elbow are tight and desperate.

"I'll do what I can," I finally say. I might not be close with Gideon or Savannah, but what Dinah is doing to them isn't right.

"Thank you."

"But only if you return the favor," I counter, raising one eyebrow.

"I'll do what I can," he mimics.

"So Savannah can actually get in trouble for sending you those naked pics?" Easton asks his brother as we walk toward the exit.

"Dinah and the DA claim she can, but I don't know," Gideon admits. "I didn't want to take the risk, so I broke up with her. I was hoping it would remove her from the equation, but…" He curses softly. "Dinah never lets me forget that Sav is involved in all this. It's her go-to threat when I'm not feeling cooperative."

Wow. Every time I think Dinah O'Halloran can't get any worse, the woman proves me wrong.

Hands in his pockets, he lumbers past us toward the parking lot. He pauses with his hand on his car door and looks over his shoulder. "Want to know who's here?" He jerks his head toward the entrance. "Check the guestbook."

Easton and I exchange a wide-eyed why-didn't-I-think-of-that look.

"Anyway, I gotta go," Gideon mutters. "It's a long drive back to school."

"Later, bro," Easton calls out.

Gideon gives us a brisk wave before climbing into his car and driving off.

"I feel so sorry for him," I admit to Easton.

His blue eyes flicker with pain. "Yeah. So do I."

"Let's go look at that guestbook."

I turn to head back inside, only to run into Callum.

"You kids heading home?" he asks. Steve is right behind him. Dinah must still be inside where the guestbook is.

Easton waves his keys. "In a sec. I gotta use the little boys' room."

His father nods. "Good. And I'd prefer it if you stayed in tonight." He gives Easton a warning look. "No wild parties or dock fights. I mean it."

"We'll order some takeout and chill by the pool," Easton promises, surprisingly obliging. He tilts his phone toward me, indicating that he'll take a picture of the guestbook while I stall the dads. "I'll be right back."

The moment that Easton is out of earshot, Steve speaks up. "Actually, I'd like Ella to come back with me."

My eyes immediately seek out Callum's. He must see my panicked expression, because he's quick to shoot down Steve's request. "That's not a good idea. I don't think Ella should be around Dinah tonight."

I say a silent *thank you* to Callum, but Steve clearly isn't happy about this. "With all due respect, Callum, Ella is my daughter, not yours. I've been more than accommodating about letting her remain with you—temporarily. But I'll be honest, I'm not comfortable with her living in your house any longer."

Callum frowns. "And why's that?"

"How many times do we need to go through this?" Steve sounds impatient. "It's not an ideal environment for her, not when Reed is facing a life sentence. Not when the cops are sniffing around and talking to everyone at Ella's school. Not when—"

Callum angrily cuts him off. "Your wife verbally attacked Ella before the service. Do you truly believe that your home— *Dinah's* home—is a better environment for Ella right now? Because you're delusional if you think that."

Steve's blue eyes darken to a metallic cobalt. "Dinah might be unstable, but she's not charged with murder, now is she, Callum? And Ella is *my* daughter—"

"This isn't about you, Steve," Callum growls. "Contrary to what you believe, the world does not revolve around you. I've been Ella's guardian for months. I've clothed her and fed her and made sure her every need is met. At the moment, *I* am the closest thing this girl has to a father."

He's right. And for some reason, I get a little choked up at Callum's impassioned speech. Other than my mom, nobody has ever really fought for me. Nobody has cared about "meeting my every need."

Swallowing, I speak up in a small voice. "I want to go back with Easton."

Steve narrows his eyes at me. There's a glint of betrayal there, but it doesn't trigger any guilt on my part.

"Please," I add, locking my gaze with Steve's. "You said so yourself—Dinah's super emotional right now. It'll be better for both of us if I'm not around her, at least for a little while. Besides, the Royals' house is really close to the bakery."

"The bakery?" he says blankly.

"Her job," Callum clarifies in a brusque tone.

"I work mornings at a bakery right near the school," I explain. "If I stay in the city with you, it'll add another thirty minutes to my drive, and I already have to wake up at dawn. So, um, yeah. This makes more sense for me."

I hold my breath as I await his answer.

After a long pause, Steve's head jerks in a nod. "Fine. You can go back to Callum's. But it's not permanent, Ella." A warning note rings in his voice. "I need you to remember that."

CHAPTER 12

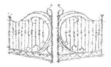

ELLA

"Anything special you want from the bakery this morning?"
I ask Reed as he pulls into the parking lot in front of the
French Twist.

From the driver's seat, he turns to glower at me. "Are you
trying to bribe me with food?"

I roll my eyes. "No, I'm just trying to be a nice girlfriend.
And would you quit sulking already? The funeral was two days
ago. You can't still be mad at me."

"I'm not mad at you. I'm disappointed," he says solemnly.

My jaw falls open. "Oh my God! Don't you dare give me
the 'I'm not mad, I'm disappointed' crap. I get it—you didn't
want me to go. But I did, and it's over, and you need to move
on. Plus, we got that list."

Although, the guestbook turned out to be worthless,
because Callum told us that his investigators had already
looked into the six people I didn't know at the funeral. They
were all accounted for the night of Brooke's death.

To say that Easton and I were bummed is an understatement.

"Which was a total dead end." Reed runs a hand through his dark hair. "I don't like how the detectives showed up," he mumbles. "That means they're watching all of us."

His distressed expression makes my heart ache. "We knew they'd be watching," I remind him, sliding closer so I can rest my chin on his shoulder. "Your lawyer warned us about that."

"I know. But that doesn't mean I have to like it." His voice is low and tortured. "Honestly? It's…"

"It's what?" I ask when he doesn't go on.

Reed's distress turns into pure torment. "It's getting harder to convince myself that this whole mess is gonna go away. First there was the DNA evidence, then Judge Delacorte's shady offer, and the cops interviewing everyone I know. It's all starting to feel too…real."

I bite hard on my lower lip. "It is real. That's what I've been trying to tell you since you got arrested."

"I know," he says again. "But I was hoping…"

This time he doesn't have to finish, because I know exactly what he was hoping for. That the charges would magically be dropped. That the person who killed Brooke would walk into the police station and confess. But none of that is happening, and maybe it's time Reed fully understood how much trouble he's actually in.

He might go to *prison*.

Still, I can't bring myself to toss another dose of reality his way, so I simply cup his chin and twist his head toward mine. Our lips meet in a soft, slow kiss, and then we pull apart, resting our foreheads against each other.

For once, he doesn't force a smile and try to tell me that everything will be okay, so I do it for him.

"We'll get through this," I proclaim with confidence I don't feel.

He just nods, before gesturing to the bakery's front window. "You should go. You'll be late for work."

"Don't overdo it with the weights this morning, okay?" Reed's doctor cleared him for practice this week, but with some restrictions. Even though his stab wound is healing nicely, the doctor said that he shouldn't push himself too hard.

"I won't," he promises.

I give him another quick kiss and hop out of the car, hurrying toward the French Twist.

My boss is kneading dough when I walk into the kitchen. The gray of the stainless steel countertop is barely visible under the coating of flour. Behind her is a stack of bowls that need to be washed.

I hang up my jacket and am rolling up my sleeves when she suddenly seems to notice me.

"Ella, you're here." She blows a strand of hair away from her forehead. The bouncy curl falls back immediately, forcing her to peer at me through the spirals.

"I'm here," I say cheerfully, even though I can tell by her tone that the *you're here* statement wasn't one of greeting but almost of warning. "I'll start washing the dishes and then you can tell me what you want me to do next."

I hustle over to the sink as if having my hands wet will prevent her from unloading the bad news.

She straightens and wipes her hands on her apron. "I think we'd better talk."

My shoulders go rigid. "Is it because of Reed?" Panic creeps into my voice. "He didn't do it, Luce. I swear."

Lucy sighs and rubs the back of her hand under her chin. The crowd of curls around her face gives her the look of a worried angel. "It's not about Reed, honey, although I can't say I'm pleased about that situation, either. Why don't you grab yourself a cup of coffee and a pastry and we'll sit down?"

"Nah, I'm good." Why delay the inevitable? Caffeine isn't going to make this conversation less awkward.

She presses her lips together in slight frustration, but I don't feel like making it easy for her. Yes, I totally left her in the lurch when I disappeared a few weeks ago, but I came back and haven't missed another day since. I've never been late, even though getting here at five in the morning requires me to wake up before the birds.

I fold my arms across my chest, lean my butt against the sink, and wait.

Lucy walks over to the coffeemaker and mutters something to herself about needing at least three cups before she feels human. Then she turns back to me. "I didn't realize your father was found alive. That must've been a huge shock."

"Wait, this is about Steve?" I say in surprise.

She nods, takes another sip of courage, and says, "He came to talk to me last night before closing."

"He did?" A nervous feeling flutters in my stomach. Why the hell would Steve come to the bakery?

"He told me he doesn't want you to work," Lucy continues. "He feels that you're missing out on activities and socialization by coming here so early in the morning."

What?

"He can't stop you from employing me," I protest.

This is beyond ridiculous. What does Steve care if I work?

He's back less than a week and thinks he can dictate what I do? Bull. Shit.

Lucy clicks her tongue. "I don't know if he has that right, but I'm not really in a position to fight it. Lawyers are expensive..." Her voice trails off even as her eyes plead for understanding.

I'm horrified. "He threatened to sue you?"

"Not in so many words," she admits.

"What exactly did he say?" I push, because I can't let it go. I honestly don't understand why Steve would object to me having a job. When I mentioned it to him after Brooke's funeral, he didn't say a word about not being on board with it.

"He simply said he didn't think it was appropriate for you to be working so many hours and taking a job away from someone who really needs the money. He wants you to focus on your studies. He was very nice." Lucy drains her coffee and sets the mug down. "I wish I could keep you on, Ella, but I can't."

"But I'm not taking a job away from anyone! You said yourself that you didn't have anyone who would work the morning shift."

"I'm sorry, honey." Her tone has a ring of finality.

No matter what I say, Lucy's mind is made up. It was made up before I even got here.

She bustles around the kitchen and grabs a white to-go box. "Why don't you pick a few things out for your classmates? Your, um, stepbrothers enjoy the éclairs, right?"

I almost say no because I'm mad, but then I decide I might as well accept everything Lucy is offering since she's taking my job away.

I stuff a dozen pastries into the box and get my coat. Just

as I reach the doorway, Lucy says, "You're a good worker, Ella. If things change, let me know."

I nod sullenly, too pissed off to mutter anything more than a *thanks* and *goodbye*. The walk to school doesn't take very long. When I arrive, the grounds of Astor Park are mostly empty, but the parking lot is surprisingly full.

It's too early for most of the students to be here. The only ones who come early are the football players. Sure enough, as I approach the front doors of the main building, I hear a few shouts and faint whistles coming from the practice field. I could go over and watch Reed and Easton practice, but that sounds about as exciting as watching paste dry.

Instead, I slip inside the school, shove the pastries inside my locker, and text Callum.

Why is Steve dictating where I work?

There's no immediate reply. It occurs to me that Callum wasn't a fan of me working at the bakery, either. Reed got mad, too, when he heard about it, saying that my job implied to everyone that the Royals were mistreating their ward. I explained to both of them that I got the job because I was used to working and wanted money of my own. I don't know if they understood it, but eventually they accepted it.

Maybe Steve will come around, too? For some reason, I'm not too hopeful about that.

Lacking anything better to do, I wander down the hall to find the owners of all the cars outside. In a computer lab, a bunch of students are clustered around one screen. Toward the end of the hall, I hear the clashing of metal against metal. A peek inside the window reveals two students waving swords at each other—advancing, retreating, and slashing at one another. I watch the sword play for a few minutes before moving on. On the other side of the hall, a huge number of students are silently engaged in a different kind of battle. This one is comprised of boards and chess pieces. In almost every hallway, I see huge posters for the Winter Formal, as well as signup sheets for what seems like a million different clubs and organizations.

Seeing all this makes me realize that I don't know much about Astor Park. I assumed that it was like any other school with its football in the fall and baseball in the spring, only stocked with wealthier kids. I hadn't paid much attention to extracurricular events or activities or groups because I didn't have time for that.

Now it looks like I have nothing but time.

My text alert goes off. Callum's response flashes on the screen.

He's your father. Sorry, Ella.

Seriously? Two days ago Callum was making a grand speech about how *he* feels like my father. Now he's backing down? What changed between then and now?

And what gives Steve the right to do this? Can parents really prevent their kids from working? My mom didn't care what I was doing so long as I could assure her I was safe.

Furiously, I key in a response. *He has no right!*

Callum replies with, *Fight the important battles.*

It's good advice, I guess, but it causes an ache to develop in my chest. If Mom were alive, I wouldn't have to deal with Steve on my own. But...if she were alive, would I even know Reed? Easton? The twins?

No, I probably wouldn't. Life is so unfair sometimes.

I pull up in front of the main gym. The double doors are propped open and hip-hop music blares in the background. I spot Jordan inside, wearing booty shorts and a bralette. Her back is to me as she curves one arm elegantly over her head, and then she spins around on one foot, using her other leg to whip herself into a pirouette.

I rub one foot against the other. Mom and I used to dance around the house. She told me she wished she could've been a professional dancer. In some ways, she was. Like a dancer, she moved her body and got paid for it. The only difference was no one in the audience wanted to see a pirouette or appreciated the graceful arch of a limb.

Plus, she had to take all her clothes off.

I don't have any real classical training—not the kind that I suspect Jordan has. The few classes Mom was able to pay for were more of a tap and jazz mix. Ballet was too expensive because you were required to buy specific shoes and leotards. After seeing my mom's despondent face when we checked out the prices of gear, I told her I thought ballet was stupid, even though I was dying to try it.

The other dance classes only required me to show up in socks or bare feet, and I was happy with that, but…I won't deny that I sometimes stood outside the door of the ballet room, watching the girls dance by in their pastel leotards and toe shoes.

I can't help superimposing those images over the one I'm watching now—until Jordan spins to a stop with her eyes shooting fire at me. Too bad I can't pin the murder on Jordan.

"What the hell do you want?" she snaps.

Her hands are on her hips and she looks ready to come

over and kick my ass. Fortunately, I already know I can hold my own with her. We threw down, literally, just a few weeks into classes.

"Just wondering who you ate for breakfast," I answer sweetly.

"Freshmen, of course." She smirks at me. "Don't you know? I like them young and tender and weak."

"Of course you do. Anyone strong would scare the shit out of you." Which is why Jordan doesn't like me.

"You know what would scare the shit out of me? Climbing into bed with a murderer." Tossing her long dark hair over one shoulder, she walks over to her gym bag and pulls out a water bottle. "Or are you so jaded from all the guys you've slept with that normal ones don't turn you on anymore?"

"You wanted him before," I remind her.

"He's rich and hot and supposedly has a good dick. Why wouldn't I want him?" Jordan shrugs. "But unlike you, I actually have standards. And unlike the Royals, my family is actually respected around these parts. My father has won awards for his philanthropy. My mother heads up half a dozen charity committees."

I roll my eyes. "What does that have to do with you wanting Reed?"

She scowls. "I just told you—I don't want him anymore. He's bad for my image."

A laugh pops out. "You're saying all this as if you and Reed hooking up is actually a possibility—which it isn't. He's not interested in you, Jordan. Never has been, never will be. Sorry to burst your delusional bubble."

Her cheeks flush. "You're the delusional one. You're screwing a killer, sweetie. Maybe you should be careful. If you make him angry, you might be the next person in the coffin."

"Is there a problem?"

Mr. Beringer, the headmaster of Astor Park, appears out of nowhere. Even though he's all bluster—I've seen Callum pay this guy off more than once—I still don't want to make any waves.

"Not at all," I lie. "I was just admiring Jordan's form."

He eyes me suspiciously. The last time he saw us together, I'd taped Jordan's mouth shut and paraded her, bloody nose and all, in front of the school.

"I see. Well, perhaps you can do that another time," he says in a clipped voice. "Your father is here. You're being excused for the day."

"What?" I blurt out. "But I have classes."

"Your father?" Jordan echoes in disbelief. "Isn't he supposed to be dead?"

Crap. I forgot she was here. "It's none of your business."

Jordan stares at Beringer, then at me, and then collapses on the gym floor, laughing so hard she needs to wrap her arms around her stomach.

"Oh God! This is amazing," she gasps between giggles. "I can't wait to see the next episode where you're pregnant but we don't know if it's Reed's or Easton's baby."

I scowl at her. "Every time I start thinking of you as a human being, you have to ruin it by opening your mouth."

The headmaster directs a glare at my nemesis. "Ms. Carrington, this behavior is completely uncalled for."

Beringer's reprimand only makes her laugh harder.

Visibly clenching his teeth, he takes my arm and guides me away from the doorway. "Come along, Ms. Royal."

I don't correct him about my last name, but I wrench my elbow out of his grip. "I'm serious. I have classes."

He bestows a smarmy smile on me, the kind he probably gives to old ladies when he asks them for a donation to the Astor Park endowment. It says that he's doing me a favor. "That's all been taken care of. I've informed your teachers that you've been excused. And you won't even need to make up your coursework."

Yup. He thinks he's doing me a favor. "What kind of bullshit school are you running if you can just excuse a junior from classes and not have her do the makeup work?"

His already thin lips flatten in a disapproving line. "Ms. Royal. Just because your father has returned from the dead doesn't mean you can mouth off to me like that."

"Give me a thousand demerits, then," I mock. Or maybe I'm pleading. "I'll serve them today."

He simply smirks. "I don't think I will. It sounds like you're already serving a punishment."

Seriously, I hate everyone in this school. They're the *worst*. I wonder what Beringer would do to me if I just refused to walk out the front doors. Would the police show up and drag me away?

The headmaster stops at his office and tips his head down the hall toward the lobby. "Your father is waiting." He gives a slight shake of his head. "I don't understand why you aren't excited to spend time with him. You're a strange girl, Ms. Royal."

With that, he disappears into his office, as if he doesn't want to spend one more moment with the weird kid who doesn't want to see her father.

I rest my head against one of the lockers and force myself

to face the truth I've been dodging ever since Steve showed up.

I don't want to spend time with him because I'm scared.

What if he doesn't like me? I mean, he left my mom. Whatever she had wasn't enough to keep him, and Maggie Harper was an angel—beautiful, sweet, and kind.

And then there's me... Prickly and difficult to get along with, not to mention foul-mouthed and set in my ways at the ripe old age of seventeen. I'm bound to say something that embarrasses me and offends him.

But no matter how badly I want to hide in these poison-infested halls, Steve is waiting and I've got two choices. Stay and meet him, or run and lose Reed.

And if those are my only choices, there's really no decision to make.

I point my feet toward the lobby and start walking.

CHAPTER 13

ELLA

When I walk up, Steve is waiting in the lobby with his hands in his pockets, reading the bulletin board notices.

"This place hasn't changed much," he tells me as I approach.

My forehead creases in confusion. "You went here?"

"You didn't know?"

"No. I didn't think Astor Park was that old."

A wry smile lifts the corners of his mouth. "Are you calling me old?"

My cheeks heat up. "No. I just meant—"

"I'm only teasing. I think the first class graduated in the thirties? So yeah, this place is old." He takes his hands out of his pockets before facing me full on. "You ready to go?"

My spine stiffens. "Why?"

"Why what?" Steve looks confused.

"Why are you taking me out of classes?"

"Because you can't hide behind Beringer like you do Callum and his boys."

I can't hide the surprise that leaps across my face. And Steve is perceptive enough to notice.

He smiles. "Thought I didn't notice you were avoiding me?"

"I don't know you." And I'm scared. Too many things are out of my control. I'm used to being in charge. For as long as I can remember, Mom relied on me to pay the bills, shop for groceries, get myself to school.

"That's why I'm taking you out for the day. Let's go." This time his smile is laced with steel.

That's me, I realize with a jolt. My mom was soft. My dad? Not so much, I guess.

I follow him outside because I sense there's no getting out of this. At the curb sits a low-slung sports car full of curves. I've never seen anything like it. Except for the color. It's the exact shade as my own car—a patented color called Royal Blue, according to Callum.

The wonder must show in my face because Steve says, "Bugatti Chiron."

"I have no idea what you just said," I say matter-of-factly. "It sounds like a brand of spaghetti."

With a chuckle, he holds the door open for me. "It's a German car." He runs his hand along the top of the roof. "Best in the world."

He could be making all this up, and I wouldn't know. I'm not a car person. I like the independence of having wheels, but even I can tell that this car is something special. The leather is softer than a baby's bottom and the dials are shiny chrome.

"Is this a spaceship or a car?" I ask when Steve settles into the driver's seat.

"Maybe both. It goes from zero to sixty in two-point-five seconds and has a max speed of two hundred and sixty-one miles per hour." He flashes a boyish smile in my direction.

"Are you the rare female who's also a car enthusiast?"

"I'm offended for my gender. I bet there are lots of female car fans out there." I buckle my seatbelt and offer a reluctant grin in return. "I'm not one of them, though."

"Too bad. I could let you drive it."

"No thanks. I actually don't like to drive all that much."

Steve mock-glares at me. "Are you sure you're my daughter?"

Not really.

Out loud, I say, "DNA says I am."

"That it does," he murmurs.

An awkward silence hangs between us. I hate this. I just want to go back inside and attend my classes and make out with Reed during lunch period. Hell, I'd rather exchange insults with Jordan right now than sit here with Steve.

My father.

"So what should we do today?" he finally asks.

I toy with the strap of my seatbelt. "You don't have something planned?" *Then why did you pull me out of school?* I want to shout.

"I thought I would leave it up to you. Ladies' choice."

This lady chooses to go back to class.

But I have to remind myself that continuing to avoid Steve isn't going to make this awkwardness go away. Might as well face it head on.

"How about the pier?" I suggest, naming the first place that pops into my head. It's November, so it'll be too cold to sit outside, but maybe we could go for a quick walk or something. I'm pretty sure I brought some gloves.

"That's a very good idea." He starts the engine, and the entire car vibrates from the power of it.

As Steve drives through the massive front gates of the school, my gaze strays to the right, in the direction of the French Twist. Just like that, my body tenses again, the memory of what he'd done returning in full, angry force.

"Why did you get me fired from my job?" I blurt out.

He glances over in surprise. "You're upset about that?"

"Yeah. I am." I cross my arms. "I loved that job."

Steve blinks a couple of times, as if he can't understand what I'm saying. I'm wondering if I should try saying it in a different language, when he finally snaps out of his trance.

"Shi—I mean, shoot. I thought Callum was forcing you to work." Steve shakes his head in dismay. "Sometimes he does strange things to enforce responsibility in his kids."

"I haven't seen any of that," I answer tightly, feeling oddly defensive of Callum.

"Oh, he used to threaten the boys with military school all the time."

My annoyance rises up again. "Working at a bakery is nothing like military school."

"Your shifts start at five in the morning, Ella. You're what? Sixteen? Surely you'd rather be sleeping in."

"I'm seventeen and used to working," I retort, then force myself to soften my tone. My mother always said you caught more bees with honey than vinegar. "But you didn't know that, so I get why you made assumptions." My voice goes even softer. "But now that you know I love my job, can you go back and tell Lucy that it's okay for me to work?"

"I don't think so." His hand waves dismissively. "My daughter doesn't need to work. I'll take care of you."

Steve hits the accelerator and the car zooms forward.

I resist the urge to cling to the dashboard, fear for my life overshadowing the irritation that his comment evokes.

"Now, tell me about yourself," he says as he drives down the road like a maniac.

I bite my lip in frustration. I don't like the way he just ended the bakery conversation. *You're not working. The End.* His parenting skills need work. Even Callum, who's not winning any father awards, was willing to have a lengthy discussion about me working.

"You're a junior, right? What did you do before coming here?"

Steve is completely oblivious to my unhappiness. His blue eyes are fixed on the windshield, his hand skillfully shifting gears as he weaves through traffic.

Feeling unusually petty, I respond in a saccharine tone. "Didn't Callum tell you? I was stripping."

He nearly drives off the road.

Crap. Maybe I should have kept my mouth shut. I proceed to hang on for dear life as he swerves back into the correct lane.

"No," Steve sputters. "He forgot to mention that."

"Well, I was." I stare at him in challenge, waiting for him to lecture me.

He doesn't. "I can't say I'm thrilled to hear it, but sometimes you've got to do whatever it takes to survive." Steve pauses. "You were on your own before Callum found you?"

I nod.

"And now you live in the shrine of Maria. I'm surprised Brooke didn't have that portrait taken down."

There's a giant painting of Maria that hangs over the fireplace, and when Callum and Brooke announced their engagement, Brooke sat under it with a smug smile. The boys were so mad about the engagement, the way it was announced, even about Brooke's ring—which was a match for the one Maria wore in the portrait. The whole setup was like a human-sized middle finger.

"She didn't have the time," I mutter.

"I suppose not. I imagine the first thing she'd do is redecorate the place from top to bottom. Everything in that house has Maria's fingerprints all over it." He shakes his head. "Those boys all idolize her. Callum, too, but no living person is a saint." He tilts his head slightly, sliding a glance in my direction. "It's not good to place a woman on a pedestal. No offense, sweetheart."

Is that…resentment in Steve's voice? I really can't tell. "None taken," I mumble.

If Steve had intended to make the conversation between us even more awkward, he picked the perfect topic.

"So this car is really fast," I say in a desperate attempt to distract him from the Maria train of thought.

A faint smile touches the corners of his mouth. "I hear you. No more questions about Maria. What about your mother? What was she like?"

"Kind, loving." *What do you remember about her?* I want to ask, but before I can, he's already moving on.

"How are you enjoying school? Grades okay?"

This man has a serious case of ADHD. He can't stay on one topic for more than two seconds.

"School's fine, I guess. My grades are fine."

"Good. That's good to hear." He throws me another curveball. "You're dating Reed?"

My mouth snaps open in shock. "I…ah…yeah," I finally admit.

"Is he treating you well?"

"Yes."

"Do you like seafood?"

I fight the urge to rub my confused eyes. I don't understand this man. All I know is that he drives too fast and has spitfire conversations that make my head spin.

I can't make sense of him. At all.

"THAT. WAS. THE. WORST."

Hours later, I stomp into Reed's bedroom and throw myself onto his bed.

Reed sits up and leans against the headboard. "Aw, come on. It couldn't have been that bad."

"Didn't you hear me?" I grumble. "It was the worst."

"What was the worst?" Easton asks from the doorway, then barrels into the room.

"Dude, you need to learn how to knock," Reed tells his brother in exasperation. "What if we were naked?"

"Naked implies you're having sex. And we all know you're not."

I stifle a sigh. I should probably be used to the frank way Easton discusses Reed's and my sex life, but I'm not.

"You weren't in Chem," Easton informs me, as if I wasn't aware of my own absence. "You and Val skip?"

"No." I grit my teeth. "Steve pulled me out of school for some father/daughter bonding."

"Ah. Gotcha." Easton flops down on the bed next to me. "Didn't go well, huh?"

"Nope," I say glumly. "I don't get him."

Easton shrugs. "What's there to get?"

"*Him.*" I run a hand through my hair in frustration. "He's like a man-child. We had breakfast at the pier, then took a drive up the coast and had lunch at this restaurant on top of a *cliff*. I swear, all he did was talk about cars and how much he loves flying planes. Then he told me about all the times he almost died on his crazy adventure trips and how he wishes he was still a Navy SEAL because he loved blowing shit up."

Reed and Easton snicker. They'd stop laughing pretty darn fast if they heard the comments Steve had made about Maria, but I don't want to poison that well, so I concentrate on the other weird stuff. And there was plenty.

"He changes subjects so fast it's impossible to keep up," I say helplessly. "And I can never tell what he's thinking." My teeth sink into the inside of my cheek as I look at Reed. "He knows we're together."

My boyfriend nods. "Yeah, I figured. We weren't exactly trying to hide it."

"I know, but…" I swallow. "I got the feeling he doesn't like it. And that's not even the worst part."

"Am I the only one who thinks this sounds like a badass day?" Easton pipes up. "I want to eat on a cliff."

"He wants me to move in with him and Dinah."

That shuts Easton up. Both he and Reed go stiffer than the bedposts.

"Not happening," Easton says.

"According to Steve, it is." I moan unhappily and climb into Reed's lap. His strong arms instantly wrap around my waist, anchoring me. "He didn't push the issue about me staying at the hotel with them, but he said that the second the police release the penthouse, he expects me to move in. He asked me if I had any design ideas for his interior decorator. He's hiring someone to decorate my room!"

Reed tucks a strand of hair behind my ear. "Dad won't let that happen, baby."

"Your dad doesn't have a say in it." My throat tightens to the point of pain. "Steve is the one who gets to decide, and he wants me to live with him."

Easton makes a growly sound. "It doesn't matter what Steve wants. You belong with us."

He's right. I do. Unfortunately, Steve doesn't agree. At lunch, he even asked me to consider legally changing my last name from Harper to O'Halloran. If I was going to change it to anything, it would be Royal, but I didn't say that to him. I simply nodded and smiled and let him babble and babble for hours. I honestly think he just likes hearing the sound of his own voice.

"Stop stressing," Reed advises, running one hand over my lower back.

"I can't. I don't want to live with him and that bitch. I won't."

"It won't even come down to that," he promises. "The thing about Steve—he's all talk and no action."

Easton nods fervently. "It's true. You totally nailed it when you called him a man-child. Uncle Steve is a big kid."

"Easton's right. Steve has all these big ideas but he never follows through on any of them," Reed admits. "He gets distracted."

"Yeah, by his dick," Easton says, and I cringe at that. "He could be in the middle of a board meeting and you put a hot chick in front of him and he's outta there."

Yeah. My father sounds awesome. Not. "Please don't talk about my dad's penis in front of me. That's disgusting."

"He's just caught up in this whole I'm-a-father thing," Easton says with another shrug. "Once that wears off, he'll probably forget you exist."

I know he's trying to reassure me, but he only succeeds in bumming me out even more. Every new thing I learn about Steve brings a new knot of anxiety to my stomach.

And now I'm scared again, but not at the idea that Steve might not like me.

I'm afraid I won't like *him*.

CHAPTER 14

ELLA

Since Val doesn't have a car, and I don't have a job anymore, there's nothing stopping me from driving her home after school on Friday. I was hoping we would catch up during the drive, but she's surprisingly quiet, so at the next red light I glance over and come right out with it.

"You're mad at me, aren't you?"

Her gaze flies to mine. "What? No! Of course not."

"Are you sure?" I say anxiously. "Because I've been a really crappy friend this week. I know I have."

"No, you've been a busy friend." She smiles sadly. "I totally get it, Ella. I'd be distracted too if my boyfriend was being accused of murder."

"I really am sorry I haven't been around. Life…sucks."

"Tell me about it."

We trade grim smiles.

"What's going on with you and Wade?" I ask as I drive through the intersection.

"Nothing." Her tone is vague.

"Nothing? Seriously?" They've both been super cranky every day this week, barely even looking at each other at lunch. That's not *nothing*.

I turn onto Val's street and slow down in front of the Carrington mansion. Before she can escape, I click the locks so she can't open her door.

Val snickers. "You realize this is a convertible, right? I can just climb out."

"Well, you're not going to." I give her a stern look. "Not until you tell me what's up."

"Nothing's up." She sounds exasperated. "Wade is…Wade. We're not together."

"But do you *want* to be?" I press.

She heaves a huge, exaggerated sigh. "No, I don't."

I narrow my eyes. "Really?"

"Yes… No… Maybe. I don't know, okay?"

I sigh, too. "Are you pissed at him because he hooked up with someone else?"

"Yes!" she bursts out. "Which is so stupid. It's not like we were even going out in the first place. We just fooled around a couple of times in the bathroom. But…I was having fun again, you know? I wasn't obsessing over Tam anymore."

Sympathy tugs at me. Val took her breakup with Tam, her old boyfriend, pretty hard. I was so happy to see her finally getting over it.

"And then Wade asks me to hang out one weekend," Val goes on, "and I was busy, so he was like, okay, rain check. So I get to school on Monday and find out he made out with Samantha Kent on Sunday at the golf club! That is *so* not cool." Her expression clouds over. "It reminded me of Tam screwing around on me and…" She trails off.

I reach out and gently squeeze her arm. "I get it. You got burned and you're not looking to get burned again. You were too good for Tam. And you're too good for Wade." I hesitate. "But for what it's worth, Wade seems to feel really bad about everything."

"I don't care. I told him before we hooked up that I wanted it to be exclusive. If he's with me—even if it's just casual—then he's *just* with me." She stubbornly sticks out her chin. "He broke the rules."

"So I take it you're not coming to the game tonight?"

"Nope. I'm staying home and waxing my legs."

I laugh.

"Want to come over?" she asks. "We can make it a spa night."

"I can't," I say glumly. "Unlike you, I don't have a choice about going to the game. Callum told us last night that the whole family is going—no exceptions. It's a show of force."

Val's lips twitch. "I didn't realize we were at war."

"We might as well be." I shove a strand of hair out of my eyes. "You've heard all the whispers at school. People are saying the most terrible stuff about Reed, and apparently some of the Atlantic Aviation board members are giving Callum grief about it, too."

"Are there reporters camped out in front of the mansion?"

"Shockingly, no. Callum must have thrown his weight around or something, because any other case like this would cause a huge media storm." I slump down into the seat. "Reed's lawyer wants us to act like Reed did nothing wrong. We're supposed to stand together as a family and all that." Only I'm not supposed to stand too close. Reed didn't tell me that, but

Callum took me aside the other day and suggested that we cool it on any PDA.

She rolls her eyes. "And going to a football game will convince people that Reed is innocent?"

"Who knows." I shrug. "Plus, Callum thinks it's a good time for Steve to 'come out' to the other families. He's hoping maybe it will cause enough of a stir and take the heat off Reed."

Val's dark eyes probe my face. "How's that going, anyway? You and Steve."

A groan slips out. "Not great. He keeps trying to spend time with me."

She mock gasps. "How dare he!"

I can't stop a giggle. "Okay, I know that sounds crazy. But it's weird, okay? He's a total stranger."

"Yeah, and he's gonna stay that way as long as you keep avoiding him." She wrinkles her nose. "Don't you *want* to get to know him? I mean, he's your dad."

"I know." I chew on my bottom lip. "I tried to be open-minded when he showed up at school on Monday and insisted we spend the day together, but all he did was talk about himself. For hours. It was like he didn't even notice I was there."

"He was probably nervous," she suggests. "I bet this is hard for him, too. He comes back from the dead and finds out he has a kid? Anyone would have a hard time with that."

"I guess." I unlock the doors. "Anyway, you may leave now, milady. I need to head home and get ready for the game," I say in a tired voice.

Val snickers. "Careful, girl. Your enthusiasm is *so* contagious I might do cartwheels all the way to my front door." She pulls on the door handle and hops out of the car, then taps the doorframe and grins at me. "Good luck tonight."

"Thanks," I answer.

I have a feeling I'm going to need it.

THERE IS AN OCEAN OF space around us. An *ocean.*

All week, I've seen kids at school whispering about Reed, but I didn't think those whispers would extend to Callum. Callum Royal has always seemed untouchable to me—confident and in control, a captain of industry who everyone sucks up to. The last time he came to a game, there was a *ton* of sucking up. Every other second, a parent stopped him to chat about something.

Tonight, Callum is getting the silent treatment. We all are—me, Steve, and the twins. We're sitting in the stands in the row right above the home team bench, and everyone around us is sneaking peeks in our direction. I can feel their accusatory gazes boring into the back of my head.

And as uncomfortable as it is for me, it's a million times worse for Reed. He can't play tonight because he still has stitches in his side from the stabbing orchestrated by Daniel Delacorte. He's benched for another week, but he's still expected to stand on the sidelines.

I wish he could sit up in the stands with us. I hate how alone he looks right now. And I *hate* that people keep whispering and pointing at him.

"That's the Royal boy," some woman hisses loud enough for all of us to hear. "I can't believe they let him come here tonight."

"It's shameful," another parent agrees. "I don't want him around my Bradley!"

"Someone needs to talk to Beringer about this," a male voice ominously chimes in.

I wince. So does Callum. Beside me, Steve seems totally unconcerned by all the negative attention. As usual, he's talking my ear off, this time about some European trip he's planning for us. I don't know if *us* means me and him, or if that includes Dinah, too. Either way, I'm not interested in going on a trip with him, even if he is my father. He still makes me so nervous.

The funny thing is, I can totally see why my mom was drawn to him. In the week he's been back, he's been filling out. His face is no longer gaunt, and his clothes are actually starting to fit his lean, muscular frame. Steve O'Halloran is decent looking—for a dad—and his blue eyes always hold this boyish twinkle. Mom had a thing for the playful types, and Steve definitely fits that bill.

But as his daughter, and not someone who's romantically interested in him, I think the boyish act is kind of annoying. He's a grown-up. Why doesn't he act like one?

"You're sulking," Sawyer murmurs in my ear.

I snap out of my thoughts and turn to the younger Royal. "No, I'm not," I lie, before looking past his shoulder. "Where's Lauren?" Technically, Lauren is Sawyer's girlfriend, so she's usually his date for these types of things.

"Grounded," he answers with a sigh.

"Aw. Why?"

"She got caught sneaking out to meet me and—" He stops when he notices Steve listening in. "Me," he finishes. "Just me."

I hide a grin. I don't get Lauren Donovan at all, but I think it's kind of ballsy that she's so open to dating two boys. I can barely handle one.

Speaking of my *one*, Reed looks miserable on the sidelines. His gaze is glued to the touchdown zone. Or the end zone? I can't remember what it's called. No matter how many times Reed and Easton try to teach me how the game works, I still don't like or care about football.

I can tell Reed is upset that he's not out there with his teammates. The defense is on the field—I know this only because one of the blue-and-gold jerseys down there reads "ROYAL." Easton is lined up in front of an opponent. I see his mouth moving behind his facemask, which tells me he's making some smartass comment.

Yup, he totally is. When the play starts, the opposing player lunges at Easton like he wants to murder him. But East is dangerous out there—he sweeps by his opponent, who falls to his knees, while two other Astor Park players tackle Marin High's quarterback before he can throw the ball.

"That was a sack," Sebastian says helpfully, leaning over his brother to explain the play to me.

"I don't care," I reply.

On my other side, Steve chuckles. "Not a fan of football, I gather?"

"Nope."

"We've been working on her," Callum says from the end of the row. "But no luck yet."

"It's all right, Ella," Steve tells me. "The O'Hallorans are a basketball family, anyway."

Just like that, I tense up again. Why does he keep saying stuff like that? I'm not an O'Halloran! And I hate basketball more than I hate football.

I muster up a smile and say, "Harpers are anti-sports. All sports."

Steve's mouth curves in a tiny smirk. "I don't know about that... If I recall correctly, your mother was very...ah...sporty."

My mouth slams shut. Was that some sort of disgusting innuendo? I'm not sure, but I think it was, and I really don't like it. He's not allowed to talk about my mom that way. He didn't even know her. Not outside of the biblical sense, anyway.

On the field, the Astor Park offense is lining up. Wade is our quarterback, and he's shouting unintelligible words to his teammates. I think I hear him yell "STUDMUFFIN!" at one point, which prompts me to poke Sawyer in the side.

"Did he just say 'studmuffin'?"

Sawyer snickers. "Yeah. Peyton Manning has 'Omaha'—Wade has 'Studmuffin.'"

He might as well be speaking gibberish. I don't know what a Peyton Manning is, and I don't bother to ask. Instead, I watch as Wade throws a perfect spiral on the first play, which lands right in the capable hands of some Astor kid running fast down the sidelines.

My phone buzzes in my purse. I pull it out and find a text from Val.

Ugh! He's not allowed to play this good!

Instantly, my head swivels to search the crowd, but my best friend is nowhere to be seen.

Where r u?? I text back.

Concessions. No food at home so I drove here to buy a hot dog.

I snort out loud. The twins glance over, but I wave off their curious stares and send another message to Val.

U r SO busted. U came 2 C Wade!

NO. I was hungry.

For Wade.

I hate u.

Just admit u like him.

Never.

Fine. Then at least come up and sit w/ us. I miss ur face.

A loud cheer rocks the stands. I look down to catch the tail end of the play—another perfect pass from Wade. I'm not surprised when Val texts back immediately.

Nah. Going home. Stupid idea 2 come here 2nite.

Sympathy floods my system. Poor Val. I know this thing with Wade started off as a rebound for her, or maybe as a way to pass the time before she was ready to seriously date again after her breakup, but I'm positive she's developed real feelings for the guy. And I think Wade likes her, too. They're just too stubborn to admit it.

Like you and Reed? an inner voice taunts.

Okay, fine. Reed and I were the same way in the beginning. He was such a jerk to me, and I spent weeks fighting my feelings for him. But we're together now and it's awesome, and I want Val to experience that same awesomeness.

"Who are you texting?"

I instinctively slap my hand over the screen when I realize that Steve is peering at my phone. Why the hell is he trying to read my texts?

"A friend," I answer tersely.

His narrowed gaze focuses on the home bench, as if he's expecting to see Reed typing into his cell phone. But Reed has his hands on his knees and is intensely watching the game.

I don't like the suspicion in Steve's eyes. He already knows I'm with Reed. And even if he doesn't like it, he has absolutely no say in who I date.

"Well, why don't you put the phone away?" he suggests, and there's a bite to his tone. "You're out with your family. Whoever you're talking to can wait."

I shove the phone back in my purse. Not because he ordered me to, but because I might've hurled it in his face otherwise. Callum never cared if I texted my friends during a football game. If anything, he was happy that I had friends in the first place.

Beside me, Steve nods in approval and refocuses his attention on the game.

I try to do the same, but I'm all riled up again. I want to catch Reed's eye and mouth to him how much I dislike Steve, but I know Reed will just tell me to ignore him, that Steve will get "bored" of this father stuff eventually.

Except I'm starting to think that's not going to happen.

CHAPTER 15

REED

AFTER THE GAME, DAD AND Steve insist on taking us out for a late dinner at some French place in the city. I don't want to go, but I'm not exactly given a choice. Dad wants us to be seen in public. He says we can't hide, that we need to act like nothing's wrong.

But *everything* is wrong. All those stares at the game tonight… Shit, my back and my ears are still burning from all the condemning eyes and scornful whispers that pierced me.

At dinner, I sit in stony silence and wish I were at home, preferably with my lips on Ella's and my hands all over her body.

Beside me, East stuffs his face like he hasn't eaten in weeks, but I guess he's earned the right to pig out. Astor Park kicked Marin High's ass tonight. We finished the fourth quarter four TDs ahead, and everyone was in high spirits afterward.

Well, except for me. And maybe Wade, who—for the first time since I've known him—didn't announce that he would be celebrating the win with a BJ followed by lots and lots of sex. He was in a crappy mood as he stripped out of his gear and stomped out of the locker room. I think he said he was going home, which, again, isn't very Wade-like.

On my other side, Ella is also stone-faced. I think Steve said something to rub her the wrong way at the game, but I'm not going to ask her about it until we're alone. Steve's been on some weird power trip ever since he came back from the dead. He keeps talking about how he has a daughter now, so he has to set a better example. Dad, of course, nods in approval every time Steve says shit like that. In Callum Royal's eyes, Steve O'Halloran can do no wrong. It's been that way for as long as I can remember.

When we get back from dinner, Dad and Steve hurry off to the study, where they're probably going to chain-drink Scotch and drone on about their SEAL days. East and the twins disappear into the game room, which leaves just Ella and me.

Finally.

"Upstairs?" I growl, and I know she doesn't miss the predatory gleam in my eyes.

Riding the bench tonight sucked ass. Forget the fact that everyone in the stands was talking about me, and that some asshole coughed the word "killer" into his palm when he passed me. Not playing was a thousand times worse. I felt like a useless sack of potatoes, not to mention more than a little jealous as I watched my friends pummel the other team.

All the aggression I didn't get to expend tonight is rearing up now. Luckily, Ella doesn't seem to mind. She flashes me that beautiful smile and tugs me toward the staircase.

We practically sprint to her bedroom. I lock the door, then lift her up in my arms and march over to the bed. She squeaks in delight as I fling her onto the mattress.

"Clothes," I order, licking my lips.

"What about them?" She toys with the bottom of her loose green sweater, all innocence.

"Off," I growl.

She smiles again, and I swear my heart soars to the sky. I don't think I could have survived this week if I didn't have Ella by my side. The murmurs at school, the phone calls from my lawyer, the police investigation that's still going strong. As much as I hated Brooke, it's not like I'm jumping for joy that she's dead. I'm not going to miss her, that's for sure, but nobody deserves to die like that.

"Reed?" Ella's humor fades when she sees my face. "What's wrong?"

I swallow. "Nothing. I was just thinking about stuff I shouldn't be thinking about."

"Like what?"

"Nothing," I say again, and try to distract her by peeling my long-sleeve shirt over my head.

It works. The moment she lays eyes on my bare chest, she makes a breathy little sound that goes right to my dick. I love that she loves my body. I don't care if that makes me some cocky, superficial jerk. The way her eyes darken with pleasure and her tongue comes out to lick her bottom lip is the biggest ego boost a guy could ever get.

"Your stitches," she says, as she's done all week when we've fooled around.

"Healing nicely," I answer, as I've done all week when we've fooled around. "Now take off your clothes before I do it for you."

She looks intrigued, as if she's wondering whether to be difficult just so I'll follow through on the threat, but I guess she's as horny as I am, because her clothes start coming off in the next moment.

My entire mouth turns to dust when her pink bra and matching underwear are revealed. Ella has no idea how gorgeous she is. Every girl at Astor Park would die to have those curves, that golden hair, the flawless features. She's pure and total perfection. And she's all fucking mine.

Keeping my pants on, I climb onto the bed and press my body against her, my mouth finding hers again. We make out forever. Kissing and groping and rolling around on the bed until finally I can't take it anymore. Her underwear comes off. My pants are undone. Her hand is on me and my hand is between her legs and it's so good I can't think straight.

"Lie back," she murmurs.

Holy hell, she's bent over me now, and her mouth is doing things that drive me absolutely crazy.

Her hair falls over my thighs. I thread my fingers through the soft strands, guiding her over me. "Faster," I whisper.

"Like this?"

"Yeah. Like that."

Her lips and tongue shove me right over the edge, and even though it's probably the biggest cliché in the book, once my body settles I pull her up and tell her I love her.

"How much?" She gives me a teasing smile.

"So much," I say hoarsely. "Like, an insane amount."

"Good." She plants a kiss on my lips. "I love you an insane amount, too."

She lies down beside me, stroking my abs while her lower

body slowly rolls against my hip. Damned if that doesn't get me going again. I might've gotten off, but she hasn't yet. I love being the one to get her there. She makes the hottest noises when she comes apart.

"My turn," I rasp as I move down her body.

She's so ready for me it's not even funny. I get hard again, because the thought of being the first one to slide into her welcoming body is hot enough to melt the entire continent of Antarctica. But I can't. Not tonight. Not until I know for sure that I'm not going to be locked up for a crime I didn't commit.

But I can do *this* instead. Torture her with my mouth and my fingers and make her moan and plead—

"Ella," a sharp voice commands from behind the door. "Open up."

She shoves my head away and bolts up as if the bed is on fire. "Oh my God, it's Steve," she hisses out.

I sit up, shooting a wary look at the closed door. I locked it, right? Please fucking say I locked—

The doorknob jiggles, but the door doesn't budge. I breathe a sigh of relief.

"Ella," Steve barks again. "Open the door. Now."

"One second," she calls, her tone hasty and her eyes wild with panic.

We hurriedly throw our clothes on, but I don't think we do a good job of looking put-together, because when she lets Steve in, his gaze turns into a thundercloud.

"What the *hell* are you two doing in here?"

I arch a brow at the rage in his voice and the redness of his cheeks. I get that he's Ella's father, but it's not like the two of us were filming a porno in here or something. We were just messing around.

"We were...watching TV," Ella mumbles.

Both Steve and I turn toward the black screen across the room. Steve clenches his fists to his sides before turning back to Ella.

"Your door was locked," he practically growls.

"I'm seventeen," she says stiffly. "I'm not allowed to have any privacy?"

"Not this much privacy!" Steve shakes his head. "Is Callum out of his mind?"

"Why don't you ask him yourself?" comes my father's dry voice.

Steve spins around to the doorway, where Dad stands with his arms crossed.

"What's going on here?" Dad asks calmly.

"Your son just had his hands all over my daughter!" Steve snaps back.

My mouth actually. But I keep quiet. The vein in Steve's forehead already looks like it's about to burst. No sense in speeding the process along.

"This is unacceptable to me," he continues, his tone colder than ice. "I don't care what kind of parenting role you've decided to take. Your boys can screw to their hearts' content, but my daughter is *not* one of Reed's sex toys."

My shoulders snap straight. Who the hell is he to say that?

"Ella is my girlfriend," I say coolly. "Not a sex toy."

He jabs a finger at the messed up bedspread. "So it's perfectly okay for you to take advantage of her like this?" His icy glare shifts to Dad. "And you! What kind of father allows two teenagers this much freedom? Next thing you're going to tell me they sleep in the same room!"

Ella's guilty expression doesn't go unnoticed by anyone. When Steve sees it, his face turns redder.

He takes a deep breath, slowly relaxes his fists, and then says, "Pack your bags, Ella."

There's a beat of silence, followed by three incredulous exclamations.

"What?" Ella.

"No way." Me.

"Steve, that isn't necessary." Dad.

Ella's father only addresses the last remark. "Actually, I think it's very necessary. Ella is my daughter. I don't want her living in this kind of environment."

"You're saying my home isn't a good environment for a child?" Dad's tone sharpens. "I've raised five sons here, and they're all doing fine."

A loud laugh booms out of Steve's throat. "They're doing *fine*? One of your boys is charged with murder, Callum! Sorry to be the one to break it to you, but Reed's not a good kid."

Outrage slams into me. "The hell I'm not."

"He's a bad influence," Steve goes on as if I hadn't spoken. "They all are." He looks at Ella again. "Pack your bags. I mean it."

She juts her chin. "No."

"She's only just settled into a routine here," Dad says in another attempt to calm Steve down. "Don't rip her away from the place she considers home."

"Her home is with me," Steve retorts. "You're not her father—I am. And I don't want my daughter shacking up with your son. I don't give a shit if that makes me old-fashioned or unreasonable or whatever the hell you want to call it. She's coming with me. You want to fight me on this? Fine. I'll see you in family court. But right now, you can't stop me from taking her out of this house."

Ella's panicked gaze darts over to Dad, but the look in his eyes says it all—defeat.

She turns her imploring gaze to Steve. "I want to stay here."

He's unmoved by her plea. "Sorry, but that's not an option. So, I repeat. Pack. Your. Bags." When she doesn't budge from my side, he claps his hands together as if she's a trained seal. "*Now*."

Ella fists her hands at her side, waiting for my dad to jump in. When he remains silent, she stomps out angrily.

I'm about to go after her when Steve stops me. "Reed. A minute of your time," he says tersely.

It's not a question. It's a command.

The two men exchange glances. Dad's face tightens and then he backs out of the room, leaving me alone with Steve.

"What?" I say bitterly. "You gonna tell me again what a bad influence I am?"

He walks over to the bed and stares at the rumpled covers before shifting his gaze to me. I fight the urge to fidget. Nothing Ella and I were doing in here was wrong.

"I was once your age."

"Uh-huh." Damn. I think I know where this is going.

"I know how I treated girls, and in retrospect, I regret that a bit." Steve runs his hand along the edge of the bed frame. "Ella's right—I haven't been involved in much of her life. But I'm here now. She's had a troubled childhood, and those types of girls often look for affection in the wrong places."

"And I'm one of those wrong places?" I tuck my hands into my pockets and lean against the dresser. It's sort of ironic that one of the most straight-laced girls I know with the shittiest upbringing has an absentee father giving me a lecture on doing right by his daughter. During the entire nine months or so that I dated Abby, her dad's entire conversations with me were about the Astor Park football team.

"Reed." Steve softens his tone. "I love you like you're my own son, but you have to admit that you're in a challenging situation here. Ella's obviously very attached to this family, but I hope you won't take advantage of her loneliness."

"I'm not taking advantage of Ella in any way, sir."

"But you are sleeping with her," Steve accuses.

If he expected me to be embarrassed or ashamed, he's pegged me all wrong. Loving Ella is one of the best things I've done in my short life. "I'm making her happy," I answer simply. I have no intention of talking about our sex life. Ella would be mortified.

Steve's lips press together in a tight line. He's not pleased with that response. "You're a physical guy, Reed. You like to fight because you enjoy the impact of your fist against someone else's flesh. You enjoy the clash of strength against strength. By the same token, you probably can't go without sleeping around. I'm not judging you, because, hell, I'm the same way. I'm not a big believer in fidelity. If a girl's available, who am I to say no, am I right?" He grins, inviting me to be part of that trashy lifestyle.

"I've said no plenty of times," I tell him.

Steve snorts in disbelief. "All right, let's just go with that. When it comes to Ella, though, if you really love her, then you're not trying to paw her clothes off every second. I see how you look at her, kid, and it's with a belly full of lust and not much more." He closes the distance between us and places a heavy hand on my shoulder. "It's not wrong. I'm not expecting you to change. I'm just saying that Ella's not the girl to screw around with. Treat her like you'd want your own sister to be treated."

"She's not my sister," I bite out. "And I do treat her with respect."

"You have a murder charge hanging over your head. You might go to prison for a very long time. How's Ella going to cope when you're there? Do you expect her to wait around for you?"

I speak through clenched teeth. "I didn't do it."

Steve doesn't answer.

Does this man, who's been part of my life for as long as I have memories, actually believe I'm capable of killing someone?

Embittered, I study Steve's expression. "Do you really believe I did?"

After a beat, he squeezes my shoulder—hard. "No, of course not. But I'm thinking about Ella. I'm trying to put her first." Those vivid blue eyes, the ones that Ella has, stare at me in challenge. "Can you honestly say you're doing the same?"

CHAPTER 16

ELLA

"You know, the reason why there's no floor thirteen is because a large number of patrons are secretly superstitious. Hallow Oaks is rumored to be built over an old Confederate cemetery. There might be ghosts here."

Like the ghost of your dead body, I think sourly.

Steve waves the keycard in front of a sensor and punches the "P" button. He's all smiles now, as if he didn't just drag me out of my home and to this stupid hotel.

"So you're not going to talk to me?" Steve asks.

I stare straight ahead. I'm not making chitchat with this guy. He thinks he can waltz into my life after seventeen years and order me around? *Welcome to parenthood, Steve. You're in for a bumpy ride.*

"Ella, you can't honestly believe I'd allow you to continue living with the Royals with your boyfriend down the hall."

It's probably childish, but I continue to give Steve the silent treatment. Besides, if I open my mouth, something bad's going to come out. Such as, *Where the hell were you when my mom was dying of cancer? Oh, that's right, you were hang-gliding with your evil wife.*

He sighs, and we finish the ride up to the penthouse in silence. The doors open into a wide hallway. Steve leads me down the hall, rolling my suitcase behind him. He presses the keycard against the door at the end of the hall.

Inside, I find a living room, a dining room, and a set of stairs. I've spent my share of time in crappy, low-budget hotel rooms, and the stairs have never been *inside* a room before. I try not to gawk, but it's hard.

Steve picks up a leather pad from the table. "Before I show you your room, why don't you have a look? We'll order room service while you get settled."

"We just ate an hour ago," I remind him in disbelief.

He shrugs. "I'm hungry again. Should I order a salad for you, Dinah?" he yells.

Dinah appears at the top of the stairs. "That'd be fine."

"Why don't you call this in while I show Ella around?" He waves the menu and then sets it back on the table. Without waiting for an answer, he places a hand on my back and pushes me forward. "I'll take the T-bone. Rare, please."

Past the dining room is another door. Steve opens it and gestures for me to come inside. "This is your room. It has an exterior door that leads to the hall. You'll need your key to get up to this floor." He holds out a plastic card, which I reluctantly pocket. "There's daily maid service and twenty-four-hour room service. Feel free to order whatever you like. I can afford it." He winks. I'm too busy looking around to respond. "Do you want someone up here to unpack for you?" he continues. "Dinah can help you if you'd like."

Dinah would probably rather drink a bottle of bleach than help me.

I muster up a, "No, thank you," which generates another big smile from Steve. He apparently thinks we're getting along swimmingly. I'm wondering if I can get the front desk to create a new keycard for Reed. Exterior door? Maybe I won't hate it here.

"All right. If you need anything, just holler. We're in tight quarters here, I know, but it'll only be a couple of weeks." He taps the top of the suitcase before leaving.

Tight quarters? Granted, the room is smaller than my bedroom at the Royals', but it's still larger than any place I've ever lived before. Definitely larger than any hotel room I've ever stayed in. I didn't even realize they made hotel rooms this large.

Ignoring my suitcase, I throw myself on the bed and text Reed.

I have an exterior door.

He texts back immediately. *I'm on my way.*

I wish.

I can b...

Steve wld lose it.

Don't kno whts up his ass. He's had more women than a rock star.

That's a lovely thought. Pls stop with the ur dad is a dog comments. It really grosses me out.

Kk. Virgin. How is everything else?

I'm a virgin bc u won't give it up.

I will, baby. U kno I'm dying 2. Wait till this is all cleared up. I'm not visiting u in prison. BTW.

Not going to prison.

Whatevr. What ru doing?

In response, I get a picture of him and his brothers sitting in my bedroom.

Why?

Why what? Why r we in ur room? Game's on.

U have a media room.

We like it here. Besides, E says ur room is full of good luck.

I groan. Easton has gambling issues. A bookie once attacked us outside a club and I had to pay him off.

E betting on anything?

If he is, he's winning bc he's not shitting a brick over the score. I'll watch ovr ur little East, don't u worry.

Ha. Thanks. I miss every1.

A knock sounds at the door.

"Yeah?" I'm not happy at the interruption and make no effort to keep the irritation out of my voice.

"It's Dinah," comes the equally irritated response. "We're ready to eat."

"I'm not eating," I call back.

She laughs cruelly from behind the door. "As you shouldn't. You could stand to lose a few pounds. But your *father* has requested your presence, Princess."

I clench my teeth. "Fine. I'll be right out."

Gotta go. Eating with Dinah & S. 8-)

I push the suitcase out of the way and walk into the living room. A uniformed man is rolling a cart inside. While he carefully places everything on the large dining room table, Steve takes a seat at the head.

"Sit. Sit." He waves a hand, completely ignoring the nice

man who is removing the silver domes from the plates. "I ordered you a burger, Ella." He sighs when I don't answer. "Fine, don't eat it, then. But I ordered it in case you'd changed your mind."

The server lifts a silver dome off my plate to reveal a huge burger on a bed of lettuce. I give him an awkward smile and say, "Thanks," because he doesn't deserve my rudeness. It's useless, though, because he doesn't look at me at all.

With a sigh of my own, I sit down. Dinah takes a chair on the opposite side of the table.

"This is nice," Steve announces. He snaps a napkin and drapes it across his lap. "Oh hell. I forgot my drink over on the coffee table. Will you get that for me, Dinah?"

She rises immediately, grabs the glass, and brings it over to Steve.

He kisses her cheek. "Thank you, darling."

"Of course." She resettles herself in her chair.

I force my gaze to my plate so no one can see the astonishment. This is a completely different Dinah than the one I met before. Heck, it's a different Dinah than the one who just summoned me to dinner.

I've only had two other encounters with her, and both of them were not good. She was confrontational at the will reading. And then, at Callum's house, I caught her having sex with Gideon in the bathroom.

Tonight, Dinah is quiet, almost shy, and it's like watching a coiled snake hiding under a big banana leaf.

Oblivious, Steve takes a sip. "It's warm."

There's a long moment of silence. When I drag my eyes away from the table, I see Steve staring pointedly at Dinah.

She smiles thinly. "Let me get you some ice."

"Thanks, dear." He turns to me. "Would you like some water?"

The interplay between these two is so weird that I forget I'm supposed to be giving him the silent treatment. "Sure."

Rather than pour it himself, he calls out toward the kitchen area. "Dinah, bring Ella a glass of water." Then he begins cutting into his steak. "I spoke with the DA's office this morning. We should be able to take possession of the apartment soon. That'll be nice for all of us."

I'm pretty sure it will be nice for *none* of us.

Dinah returns with two glasses—one full of ice, one full of water. She sets the water glass in front of me with enough force that some of the liquid splashes over the rim and soaks my sleeve.

"Oh, I'm sorry about that, Princess," she says sweetly.

Steve frowns.

"No prob," I mutter.

Steve drops a couple of ice cubes into his drink, swirls it around, and then takes a sip. Dinah has just picked up her fork when Steve makes a face. "Too watery," he states.

She hesitates, her fingers growing white around the fork handle. I wonder if she's going to stab Steve with it, but instead she sets it down in a slow, deliberate fashion. Pasting a smile on her face, she rises from the table for the third time and makes her way to the bar, where big bottles are lined up like little soldiers in a row.

At this rate, I might start drinking from them.

"Ella, I spoke with your headmaster today," Steve tells me.

I tear my eyes away from Dinah's stiff back. "Why would you do that?"

"I just wanted to check on your progress at Astor Park. Beringer informed me that you have no extracurricular activities." He slants his head. "You mentioned you like dancing. Why not the school dance team?"

"I, ah, I was working at the time." I don't feel like getting into my feud with Jordan. It sounds stupid saying it out loud.

"Then perhaps the school newspaper?"

I try not to grimace. Writing articles sounds more painful than sitting here at dinner. Actually, I take that back. This dinner is so uncomfortable that I'd rather be sparring with Jordan Carrington, so the school newspaper would be a welcome distraction.

"What did you do as electives?" I counter. Maybe if I can get him to admit he was a slacker in high school, he'll ease up a little.

"I played football, basketball, and baseball."

Great. One of those.

But hadn't Callum implied that Steve wasn't interested in running a business and preferred just having fun? Why can't he let me enjoy myself?

"Maybe I'll try out for the, um…" I think frantically of some girl sport—"soccer team."

Steve smiles encouragingly. "That would be good. We can talk to Beringer about it."

Ugh. I guess I can try out for it, and when they see how terrible I am, they'll kick me off the grounds and ask me to never return. It's not a bad plan, actually.

I pick up my burger and take a bite, even though I'm not at all hungry. But it gives me something to do with my hands, and it keeps my mouth full so I don't have to make any more conversation.

As I chew, I think strategy for the best way to get around Steve. I need to pretend like I'm meeting his demands while actually doing whatever the hell I want—hanging out with Val, fooling around with Reed, and having fun with East and the twins. Besides, watching out for Reed and Easton is a full-time job. In the meantime, I can hunt down possible suspects. I think I might be the only one interested in finding the real criminal.

By the time I've arranged this perfectly in my head, Dinah returns with Steve's latest drink.

"What did *you* do in high school?" I ask her, trying to be polite.

"I worked two jobs to support my family." She smiles. "Neither of which required me to take off my clothes."

I cough mid-sip.

Steve frowns again.

"Did you know that Ella was stripping when Callum found her?" Dinah asks her husband. Her tone is sweeter than sugar. "How unfortunate."

"As I recall, you've never had any problems taking your clothes off in public," he answers cheerfully. "And nobody had to pay you to do it."

That shuts her up.

The hotel phone rings. Steve ignores it, and it rings and rings until finally Dinah gets up to answer. His gaze follows her all the way into the living room. When she turns her back on us, Steve shifts his attention to me.

"You think I'm being mean to her, don't you?" he murmurs.

Faced with a choice between lying or finding out what the hell is going on, I opt for truth. "Yeah, kinda."

"Well, try not to feel bad for her." He shrugs. "I think she intentionally messed with my equipment and tried to kill me."

My mouth drops open. Speechless, I watch as he slices into his steak and takes a huge bite.

After swallowing, he wipes his mouth and continues. "I can't prove it with the guide missing, but I can torment her. Don't worry. You're safe, Ella. It's me she can't stand."

Wrong. I still remember the threats she hurled at me when she found out I was heir to Steve's fortune. Besides, I've seen Discovery Channel specials on snakes. They're the most dangerous when they feel threatened, but I doubt Steve's going to listen to any of my warnings. He's going to do whatever it is he wants.

But now I have Dinah soaring to the top of my suspect list. Maybe moving in with them is a good idea. I can find not only Gideon's stuff, but evidence that she killed Brooke.

Then common sense takes over. If the police, not to mention Callum's investigators, couldn't find anything that pointed to someone other than Reed, how am I supposed to?

Despondently, I shove the lettuce around my plate. "I don't think you should poke a bear. Why don't you just divorce her and move on?"

"Because Dinah always has a plan up her sleeve, and I want to see what it is. Besides, I don't have proof." He reaches out a hand to touch mine. "And maybe it's foolish of me to bring you into this mess, but you're my daughter and I don't want to miss another day of your life. I've missed too many before. I know you don't like the decisions I'm making. And hell, maybe they're all wrong. In my defense, I've never had a daughter before. Will you at least give me a chance?"

I sigh. It's pretty hard to be a bitch in the face of that.

"I'll try," I tell him.

"Thank you. That's all I ask." He squeezes my hand before drawing back and resuming eating. A moment later, Dinah joins us at the table again.

"It was the furniture store. The police aren't allowing them to deliver the new bed you ordered." Dinah's face is red and she sounds like she's choking on something.

Steve leans toward me with a feral smile. "Dinah was using our current bed to screw someone who isn't her husband, so I'm having it replaced."

Wow.

Just...*wow*.

He turns toward his wife. "Have the building store it, then, until we all move in."

With that statement, the rest of dinner is a stilted, awkward affair. Dinah goes off to relay Steve's instructions, and when she returns, she's ordered around shamelessly. She meekly obeys every command, but still manages to throw a cutting remark my way here and there. And every time Steve turns his head, she flashes me an evil smile, which goes a long way to proving my theory about not trusting snakes.

"Mind if I go?" I ask once Steve puts away the last of his meal. There's only so much of this I can take, and after thirty minutes of it, I need a break. "I've got homework."

"Of course." As I walk past his chair, he grabs my wrist and tugs me down to plant a kiss on my cheek. "I feel like we're really a family tonight, don't you?"

Um. No.

But I can't diagnose what's going on inside me. The kiss

on the cheek from my dad feels odd. He's a stranger to me in all the ways that count, and the urge to escape rides me hard.

When I hurry into my room, the expensive leather suitcase tempts me. I could take it and leave. Be done with this weird family and not have to face the emotions that Steve's existence brings out in me.

But I just shove the suitcase into the closet, pull out my homework, and try to concentrate. Outside, I hear the television flick on and then off. The phone rings. There are other signs of life, but I'm not leaving this room.

Finally, around nine, I yell that I'm going to bed. Steve wishes me a good night. Dinah doesn't.

After brushing my teeth and slipping into one of Reed's old T-shirts, I climb into bed and call him.

He answers after the second ring. "Hey, how's it going over there?"

"Bizarre."

"How so?"

"Steve is awful to Dinah. He said he thinks she might have tampered with his equipment, so his revenge is to make her life hell. He's doing a good job of it."

Reed snorts, clearly not feeling any sympathy for Dinah. "Ella, she's an original See You Next Tuesday."

"Ugh, don't use that word."

"I didn't. I used several words. Four of them. How you choose to interpret them is your business."

"Dinner was so awkward. Worse than the night Brooke announced her pregnancy."

Reed whistles. "That bad, huh? Do you want me to come over? You said you have your own room."

"I do, but we better not. Steve's so...I can't read him. I'm afraid of what he'd do if he caught you in here tonight."

"All right. Say the word, though, and I'll be there."

I snuggle deeper under the covers. "Do you think Dinah did it?"

"I'd like to pin it on her, but Dad's investigators say she was on an international flight from Paris when Brooke died."

"Shoot." No motive then. "What about hiring someone? Like Daniel hired someone to knife you."

"I know." He blows out a heavy breath. "But there are three sets of surveillance cameras at the building. The lobby and elevator cameras show only me."

"And the others?"

"The stairwell cameras show nothing. The third set are in the service elevators. Staff, movers, delivery people use those. They were down for maintenance that night, so there's nothing there."

My heart beats a little faster. "So someone could've gone up the service elevator."

"Yeah. But the DNA all points in my direction." He sounds miserable. "And Dinah and Brooke were friends, so what's the motive? Brooke had a rough childhood, made friends with Dinah when they were teens. She and Dinah worked their way into a circle of rich men, hoping to land one of them. Dinah got lucky with Steve a couple years back, and Brooke set her sights on Dad. But he wasn't willing to put a ring on her finger."

"Do you think your dad..." I'm reluctant to say it, but... Callum could have hired someone, too.

"No," Reed says sharply. "No one in my family offed her. Can we talk about something else? Where are you?"

I don't want to talk about anything else, but I give in because I've had too much conflict tonight. I'll never get to sleep at this rate. "In my room. You?"

"I'm in yours." I hear him inhale. "Smells like you. You wearing my T-shirt?"

"Yeah."

"And?"

"I'm not having phone sex with you before actual sex," I reply tartly.

"Aww, poor Ella. I'll make you feel good at school on Monday."

His low-voiced promise makes me tingle, but since Monday is a whole forty-eight hours away, there's no point to this conversation. I change the subject to the game, and we talk for a long time about nothing and everything and just hearing his voice makes me feel better.

"Goodnight, Reed."

"Night, baby. Don't forget about Monday." He laughs quietly as he hangs up.

Cursing him, I shove the phone on the nightstand and am about to turn off the light when my door swings open with no warning.

"What the hell!" I shoot up and glare at Dinah, who's walking in as if she belongs here. "I locked that!"

She waves her keycard in the air. "These babies open any door in the suite."

Oh my God. Really? I'd noticed the keycard slot under the handle, but I thought only *my* card could open it.

"Don't open this door again," I say coldly. "If I want you to come in, I'll invite you in." Which will never happen, because

I'm never going to want her to come in. Ever.

She ignores that, tossing her long blonde hair over one shoulder. "Let's get one thing straight, sweetie. It doesn't matter if we're in a hotel or in the penthouse—it's still *my* house. You're nothing but a guest here."

I raise a brow. "Isn't it Steve's house?"

Dinah scowls at me. "I'm his wife. What's his is mine."

"And he's my father. Who, by the way, left *me* everything after he died. Not you." I smile sweetly. "Remember?"

Her green eyes flash, making me regret taunting her. I'd warned Steve not to poke a bear, and here I am, doing the same thing. I guess I'm my father's daughter.

"Well, he's not dead anymore, is he?" Her lips twist in a smug smile. "So I guess you're back to having what you're used to—nothing."

I falter, because she's right. I didn't particularly care about all the money Steve left me in his will, but now that it's gone, I really do have nothing. No, that's not true. I have the ten thousand dollars Callum gave me when I got back to Bayview after running away.

I make a mental note to hide that cash the first chance I get.

"You have nothing, too," I point out. "Steve controls everything around this place, and it didn't look like he was too happy with you at dinner. What'd you do to piss him off so hard?" I pretend to think it over. "I know. Maybe you killed Brooke."

Her jaw drops in outrage. "Watch your mouth, little girl."

"What? Did I hit a nerve?" I narrow my eyes at her. "Am I getting too close to the truth?"

"You want the truth? Brooke was my best friend—*that's* the truth. I'd kill you before I'd ever kill her. Besides, I've learned that accidents aren't the best way to get rid of people." She smiles savagely. "I have a gun and I'm not afraid to use it."

I gape at her. "Did you just confess to trying to kill Steve?" Oh man. Where's a recorder when you need it?

She lifts her chin as if she's proud of her actions. "Watch yourself, Princess. When it comes to children, I'm a big believer in the saying *seen but not heard*. As long as you stay out of my way, I'll stay out of yours."

I don't believe her, not for a hot second. She's going to get some serious pleasure out of tormenting me now that I live under her roof. And was that comment about the gun a threat? Holy *hell*.

"Watch yourself," Dinah says again, then flounces out of my room and closes the door behind her.

I stay in bed. There's no point in getting up and locking the door when I know that any keycard can open the darn thing.

Taking a breath, I shut off the light and close my eyes. Visions of Dinah flashing a gun in my face pop up, along with ones of Reed behind bars.

Sleep is elusive.

Don't lose ur temper with S. Not worth it. He'll come around.

That's the text Reed sends me before he leaves for practice on Monday morning, and it's pretty much the same thing he's been saying to me this whole weekend.

This whole long, terrible, long, frustrating, *long* weekend.

Come around, my ass.

Steve has already gotten me fired from my job and decided

I'm trying out for a school team—you'd think that would be enough. But nope, it's not.

Last night, he informed me he was imposing a curfew. I have to be home by ten each evening, and I have to turn on the location finder on my phone so he can keep tabs on me. I've already decided that in the future I'll be leaving my phone at home. There's no way I'm making it easier for him to find me.

The problem is, this Friday is the Riders' first playoffs game. Reed was cleared to play, and I desperately want to go because I've decided I'm done with Reed's reluctance. Every day that he's the prime suspect in Brooke's case is a day that rattles my sense of security. If we're supposed to act normally, if we're supposed to at least pretend that all is well in our lives, then this distance between us should not exist.

It's time for us to have sex. I don't care if I have to play dirty to make that happen. So I'm going to seduce him. The away game is the perfect place to do it, and there's an amusement park thirty minutes away that a bunch of kids were talking about going to. The plan is—or was—to use that as an excuse to stay overnight.

Except now, with Steve's stupid curfew, I don't know how I'll be able to swing it. Hopefully Val can help me figure it out today. But I'm going on that away trip, one way or another.

I finish brushing my hair, tuck my shirt into my skirt, and grab my backpack.

Out in the living room, Steve is lounging on the couch, paging through a newspaper. Doesn't he ever work?

Dinah is at the dining table, sipping a flute of orange juice. Or maybe it's a mimosa because I don't think people use fancy glasses for their OJ.

She eyes me over the rim, a smirk forming on her pouty lips. "That skirt is rather short for school, don't you think?"

The paper rustles as Steve lowers it. He frowns as he examines my uniform.

I look down at my white shirt, open blue blazer and ugly pleated skirt. "This is my uniform."

Dinah glances at her husband. "I didn't realize the headmaster at Astor Park Prep encouraged his female students to dress like whores."

My jaw drops. First of all, the skirt goes all the way down to my *knees*. Second of all, who says things like that?

Steve continues to study my skirt. Then he slaps the paper down by his side and glares at me. "Go back to your room and change."

I glare right back. "This is my uniform," I repeat. "If you don't like it, take it up with Beringer."

He points a finger at my legs. "You can wear pants. I'm certain that in this day and age, that's an option for a school uniform."

This is a stupid conversation, so I walk toward the door. "I don't have pants." Well, actually, I do. But those khaki monstrosities are ugly as hell, no matter that they have a three-hundred-dollar price tag. I'm not putting those things on my body.

"Of course she has pants," Dinah says, laughing gleefully. "But we all know why she chooses not to wear them. Easier access with a skirt."

Another frown slashes Steve's face. "She's right," he tells me. "I had my share of fun times with girls in skirts. They're easy lays. Is that what you want to be? Easy Ella?"

Dinah titters.

I clutch the strap of my backpack and turn the doorknob. If I had a gun, maybe I'd shoot Dinah with it.

"I'm going to school," I say stiffly. "I've already missed one entire day of classes so you could drive around Bayview. I'm not going to be late because you have a problem with my school uniform."

Steve stomps over and lays his palm on the door. "I'm trying to help you. Girls who put out are disposable. I don't want that for you."

I pull the door open with a sharp jerk. "Girls who put out are girls who want to have sex. There's nothing immoral about that. Or gross. Or deviant. If I choose to have sex, then that's what's going to happen. It's my body."

"Not while you live in my house," he thunders, hurrying after me down the hall. Dinah's laughter follows us all the way to the elevator.

I jab the *down* button. "Then I'll move."

"And I'll have you hauled back here. Is that what you want?" At my silence, he sighs with frustration. In a softer tone, he says, "I'm not trying to be a bad guy, Ella, but you're my daughter. What kind of dad would I be if I just let you run around and sleep with your boyfriend?"

"My boyfriend is your best friend's son," I remind him. I will the elevator to arrive faster, but it seems to be climbing the forty-four floors one excruciating second at a time.

"I know. Why do you think I'm so anxious about you dating him? Callum's kids are wild. They're *experienced*. That's not what I want for you."

"Being a little hypocritical here, aren't you?"

"Yes." He throws up his arms. "I don't deny it. The last thing in the world I want for you is to date the guy I was in high school. I had no respect for girls. All I wanted was to get in their pants, or under their skirts." He throws a pointed gaze at my hemline. "And once I had them, I moved on."

"Reed's not like that."

Steve gives me a look of pity. "Honey, I told all the girls I wanted to have sex with that they were special and the only ones for me, too. I've used all those lines before. I would've said anything to get a girl to say yes." I open my mouth to protest, but Steve keeps talking. "And before you say that Reed is different, let me point out that I've known that boy for eighteen years and you've known him for a few months. Who has the more informed perspective?"

"He's not like that," I insist. "He's the one who's holding out on me. Not the other way around."

Steve laughs abruptly. Shaking his head, he says, "Damn, that boy's got moves I hadn't even thought of. I'll give him that."

I blink in confusion.

"Pretending to be reluctant and forcing you to make all the moves? He must be loving that." He sobers up. "No, Ella, you're just going to have to take my word on this. Reed's been around the block so many times, there's probably a trench built from all his activity. There've got to be other nice boys at Astor for you to date. Why don't you find one and we'll revisit this conversation?"

I can't mask my astonishment. "I don't work that way. I don't discard people like that. Reed is not disposable in my life." *I'm not like you.*

"Let's see how long his affections last when he doesn't have access to you. Don't be so easy, Ella. It's not attractive."

If I'd been the child Steve pretends that I am, I would've shouted an insult back. One burns at the back of my throat. One that says he needs to stop measuring me by his own miserable stick. But I'm not going to get anywhere by confronting Steve. Thankfully, the elevator finally fucking arrives.

"I need to get to school," I inform him as I step inside the car.

"Classes are over at three forty. I expect you here by four."

The elevator doors slide shut.

A tension headache pounds at my temples as I speed out of the basement parking garage three minutes later. The relentless throb of frustration doesn't let up until I reach Astor Park.

How ironic that the place I once hated now feels like a refuge.

CHAPTER 17

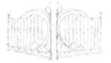

REED

Worst weekend of my life. No lie.

I spent all of Saturday with Halston Grier going over the details of my case. My lawyer maintains that the DNA—my DNA—they found under Brooke's fingernails is the most damning piece of evidence the cops have. He admitted that my explanation about Brooke scratching me out of anger might not sway a jury if this goes to court, especially combined with the video surveillance.

I can't even remember her scratching me. My memory of the event is her demanding money, me laughing at her, her swinging a hand toward my face and not connecting. She wobbled on her feet. I caught her and pushed her away. She must've grazed me then.

Which makes all of this so much bullshit. I didn't kill that woman. Just because her fingernails didn't break any of my skin doesn't mean she didn't scratch me. I've offered to take a lie detector test, but Grier says that even if I pass with flying colors, polygraph results aren't admissible in court. And if I fail the thing, he warned that the police might find a way to leak those results to the press, who would crucify me.

Sunday, I wallowed around the house missing Ella, and not because I want to bone her, like Steve thinks. I miss her company, her laughter, and her smart-ass taunts. Steve kept her busy all weekend, so we were only able to text and talk on the phone a couple of times. I hate that she's not living with us anymore. She belongs here. Even Dad agrees, but when I pushed him to talk to Steve about it, he shrugged and said, "He's her father, Reed. Let's just see how it goes."

When Monday finally comes, I'm practically dying of anticipation. Even though I'm released to practice, Coach has me running no-contact drills only, and he says there's no guarantee I'm going to see playing time on Friday. He's still pissed at me about the fight with Ronnie last week.

Speaking of Ronnie, the asshat wanders over to the bench a few times to harass me, calling me "killer" under his breath so Coach can't hear.

I don't give a crap what he thinks of me, though. The only opinions that matter belong to my family and Ella, and none of them believes I'm a killer.

"You're going the wrong way," East says with a grin as we walk across the south lawn after practice. "Don't you have Bio?"

I do, but I'm not going there. Ella just texted to meet her at her locker. It's in the junior wing of the school, the opposite direction of the senior buildings.

"I've got somewhere to be," is all I say, and my brother waggles his eyebrows mischievously.

"Gotcha. Tell little sis I said hi."

We part ways at the front doors, East darting off to his first class while I march down the hall toward the junior locker banks. Several girls smile at me, but just as many frown. Furtive whispers tickle my back as I walk. I hear the word "police" and someone else says, "father's girlfriend."

Other guys might flush with embarrassment or cower in shame, but I don't care about any of these kids. My shoulders are straight and my head is held high as I brush past them.

Ella's entire face lights up when she spots me. She launches herself at me, and I catch her easily, burying my face in her neck and breathing in her sweet scent.

"Hey."

"Hey," she says with a smile. "I missed you."

"Missed you, too." A groan slips out. "You have no idea how much."

Sympathy fills her eyes. "Are you still upset about the meeting with the lawyer?"

"A little. But I don't want to talk about that right now. I want to do *this*."

I kiss her, and she makes the hottest sound against my lips. Kind of a whimper crossed with a happy moan. I slip her some tongue just so I can hear her make that noise again. She does, and my body tightens.

"Ahem."

A loud throat-clearing has us breaking apart.

I turn, nodding politely at the teacher standing behind us. "Ms. Wallace. Morning."

"Good morning, Mr. Royal." Her lips flatten in a severe line. "Ms. Harper. I think it's time for you two to go to class."

I nod again and take Ella's hand. "On our way," I assure the frowning teacher. "I'm walking Ella there now."

Ella and I hurry away from the locker, but I don't walk

her to class like I said. Instead, I turn left at the end of the hall. Once we're out of Ms. Wallace's line of sight, I tug Ella into the first empty classroom I find. It's one of the junior music rooms, completely dark because the heavy gold drapes are drawn shut.

"What are we doing?" Ella hisses, but she's laughing.

"Finishing what we started back there," I reply, my hands already landing on her slim hips. "One kiss wasn't enough."

One *anything* is never enough with this girl. I don't know how I ever lived without her. I mean, I went out with other girls. Slept with a few of them. But I've always been picky as hell. Nobody ever really held my interest for more than a week or two, sometimes not more than a day, an hour.

Not Ella, though. She got under my skin the moment I met her, and she's still there, in my blood, in my heart.

Our lips meet again, and this kiss is hotter than the first. Her tongue is in my mouth and my hands are on her ass, and when she starts wiggling her lower body against my crotch, I lose all awareness of our surroundings.

"C'mere," I mutter, dragging her to the teacher's desk.

She hops up, and I instantly move between the cradle of her thighs. Her legs wrap around my waist and then we're rocking against each other. It's hot as hell. Even hotter because we're at school and I can hear footsteps thumping up and down the hall outside the door.

"We shouldn't be doing this here," she says breathlessly.

"Probably not. But tell me to stop. I dare you." I'm not going to have sex with her, but I can't keep my hands off of her, and I know I can make her feel good. I'm totally putting her first—just not in the way her dad wants. Screw Steve, though.

She laughs again.

I slip my hand under her skirt and wink at her. "Gotta love the easy access."

That gets me a startled snicker.

"What?" I ask with a frown.

"Don't worry about it." She grins widely, then squeaks in pleasure when my fingers find her.

Rather than push me away, she arches into my greedy hand. Her hands are equally greedy, undoing the buttons of my dress shirt.

"Need to touch you," she mumbles.

I'm not complaining. The feel of her small, warm palms on my bare chest sends a jolt of heat up my spine. We've never fooled around at school before, but Steve is making it really fucking hard to see each other outside of it. He hasn't let me come over to the hotel even once since he moved Ella out of the mansion.

Our kisses get sloppier, more frantic. I slide a finger inside her and groan against her mouth. I want to get her off before class so she'll be thinking about me all day. Maybe I'll do it again at lunch, take her to the bathroom that Wade dubbed the Hook-Up Zone and—

The door flies open and light suddenly floods the room.

Ella and I break apart, but not fast enough. The tall, gray-haired music teacher in the doorway gets an eyeful of my hand flying out from under Ella's skirt. Of my half-open shirt and our swollen lips.

He sighs in disapproval, then snaps, "Fix yourselves up. You're going to see Beringer."

Shit.

THE HEADMASTER CALLS OUR PARENTS. I'm fuming when Dad and Steve stalk into the waiting room outside Beringer's office, because, come on. Since when does Beringer call in the big guns over a couple kids making out in school? It happens every other minute. Wade has *sex* here, for fuck's sake.

It doesn't take long for understanding to dawn on me, though. Because the first thing Steve does after he storms in is shake Beringer's hand and say, "Thank you for calling me. I feared something like this might happen."

In the chair beside mine, Ella is beet red. She's clearly embarrassed, but there's fire in her eyes, too. Anger. Like me, she knows that Steve is responsible for this. He must've warned the faculty to keep an eye out for us.

"Get up," Steve tells Ella. "You're coming home with me."

She bursts out with an objection. "No! You can't take me out of school again. I'm not missing any more classes, Steve."

His tone is like ice. "You had no problem missing class before. Francois says you were ten minutes late for first period."

Ella falls silent.

Dad is unusually quiet, too. He's watching me with an indescribable expression. It doesn't look like disapproval or disappointment. I can't figure it out at all.

"This kind of behavior is unacceptable," Steve fumes. "This is a place of learning."

"Yes, it is," Beringer agrees coldly. "And I assure you, Mr. O'Halloran, these kinds of shenanigans won't be tolerated."

My jaw drops. "Really? But letting Jordan Carrington duct-tape a freshman to the front entrance is A-OK?"

"Reed," my father warns.

I spin toward him. "What? You know I'm right. Jordan

freaking *assaulted* another student, and he"—I rudely gesture at the headmaster—"totally let it slide. Ella and I are caught making out like two normal teenagers and—"

"Normal teenagers?" Steve echoes with a harsh laugh. "You've got a plea hearing this week, Reed! You're facing a murder charge."

Frustration shoots through me. Christ. I don't need the reminder. I'm well aware of how screwed I am right now.

Then I register what he'd said. "What plea hearing?" I ask my dad.

His features go strained. "We'll discuss it when you get home from school."

"You can discuss it on your way home," Beringer interjects, "because I'm suspending Reed for two days."

"What the fuck?" I demand angrily.

"Language," the headmaster snaps. "And you heard me. Two-day suspension." He glances at Steve. "Ella can remain at school, if that's acceptable to you."

After a long, tense moment, Steve nods. "It's acceptable. As long as he's not here, I'm all right with letting her stay."

Steve says *he* like I'm a carrier for Ebola or some shit. I don't get it. I really don't. Steve and I never had any problems in the past. We weren't close, but there was no hostility between us. Now, the air is so hostile I can hardly breathe.

"Then it's settled." Beringer walks around his desk. "Mr. Royal, I'm releasing Reed into your custody. Ella, you may return to class."

She hesitates, but when Steve offers a hard glare, she quickly moves to the door. Right before she walks out, she gives me the most miserable, frustrated look on the planet. I'm pretty sure I'm wearing the same expression.

Once she's gone, Steve shifts his scowl to me. "Stay away from my daughter, Reed."

"She's my girlfriend," I reply through clenched teeth.

"Not anymore. I asked you to respect her, and when I thought you were going to do so, I was open to the idea of the two of you dating. After what happened this morning, I'm no longer on board with it." He addresses my father. "Our kids just broke up, Callum. If I see or hear of them together again, you and I are going to have words."

Then he marches out of the office and slams the door behind him.

CHAPTER 18

ELLA

For the second day in a row, I go to school angry. Yesterday, Steve and Dinah ganged up on me about my skirt. Today, Reed is suspended because Steve has some kind of parental stick up his ass. The single good thing about my anger at Steve is that I don't have the emotional energy to worry about Dinah any longer.

I can't believe he ordered Beringer to tell all the teachers to narc on us. That is *so* not cool. I'm still fuming about it as I pull into the parking lot. Luckily, I spot Val on the front lawn, which distracts me from my rage.

"Hey, sexy," I shout out my window.

Her dark bob spins around, her middle finger ready. When she realizes it's me, she jogs over. "Hey! I was worried about you. Did you have to deal with the never-ending lecture when you got home from school yesterday?"

I maneuver into an empty parking space, then turn off the car. "You have no idea."

She already knows all about yesterday's stupidity because

I spent the entire lunch period bitching about it. Then I wrapped it up by griping and moaning for a good ten minutes about how I won't be able to go to the away game and seduce Reed. And have sex for the first time!

"What happened?" Val asks as I grab my backpack and hop out of the driver's seat.

"There was a lot of arguing, shouting, insults thrown. It ended with Steve telling me that I needed to stop being so easy. That guys didn't find it attractive."

Val grimaces. "Wow, that's harsh."

"It's getting so bad, I'm actually thinking I need to spend more time at school."

"It can't be that bad," she says, knowing my great aversion to joining anything here at Astor. "It just seems bad because you're not used to having a parent who imposes rules and stuff. From what you've told me, your mom was the kid in your household, and Callum kind of lets his boys do anything they want as long as they don't make too big of a mess."

"So you're saying that Steve's behavior is normal?" I challenge.

Val shrugs. "It's not that abnormal. I think your mom and Callum are more lenient than other parents."

"You have parties at your house. And you don't have a curfew."

She laughs. "Well, sure I do. I have to be home by ten on school nights and midnight on the weekends unless I tell Uncle Mark or Aunt Kathy first. And I wouldn't be allowed to have a boy spend the night. It was easy to fool around with Tam because he lived in the same house." Tam is the Carringtons' housekeeper's son. "I think most parents don't allow boys to sleep over. I mean, why do you think Wade has so much sex at school? His mom is kind of strict at home." She pats me on the shoulder. "Steve might be going overboard, but it just means that he cares. Don't take it personally."

Is she right? I mean, I have almost no experience with normal parents, but here's Valerie, who I presume does, telling me that Steve's reaction is...well, ordinary. Am I overreacting?

Maybe. But still, I don't see myself ever being okay with all these rules and shit.

"Even if that's normal, I don't want to live like that," I admit as we walk into the building.

"Ride it out," she recommends. "You're both so new at this. You're a kid and Steve's trying to be the adult. You're bound to have clashes. I bet you'll figure something out."

"I'm not a kid. I'm seventeen."

"Ha. That's where you're wrong. My mom always says that no matter how old I get, I'll always be her baby. That's just how parents are." She nudges my shoulder with hers. "Honestly, I think it's pretty cool that he came back from the dead. You're not alone anymore."

The thing is, I didn't *feel* alone before Steve came along. And that's the piece that's missing for me. He's not filling something inside of me that was empty. The Royals were already there, and Steve's trying to push someone out to make room for himself.

Val must read the skepticism on my face. "Don't break your head obsessing about this. You should go to him with a counteroffer."

"What do you mean?"

"Steve doesn't want you hanging around with Reed because why?"

"He says Reed's a dog."

Val tips her head back and stares at the sky as if praying for patience. "Honey, Steve is totally being a dad."

I feel the need to defend Reed, again. It seems like I'm always defending him. "Maybe Reed was a dog before, but he's not with me. Besides, he's not like Easton. He doesn't sleep around. He's picky."

Val opens her mouth to respond, but before she gets anything out, the bell rings. "Hold that thought. Meet me in the south bathroom at lunch? We'll talk more."

"The south bathroom?" I have no idea what she's talking about.

"It's the one by the boys' locker room. Wade always does his business there."

With that, she's gone, leaving me to wonder if I'm the unreasonable one.

THE MOMENT THE LUNCH BELL rings, I make a stop at my locker to shove my books inside, then hurry toward the south bathroom. It takes me about ten minutes to find it, because this school is so ridiculously big.

Pushing open the door, I stop abruptly at the sight of the full bathroom—there are about six girls in here. Val's putting on lipstick in front of the far sink, and I quickly make my way to her.

"Why is it so crowded?" I hiss under my breath. "I thought Wade has sex in here."

"In the boys' room." She smacks her cherry-red lips together. "This is the girls' bathroom."

"Right." Duh. For some reason I thought we were having a private powwow.

"Dance team is having extra rehearsals for the away game performance. Apparently Gibson High is their main rival in state dance competitions," Val explains, tucking the lipstick into her purse. "Anyway, I've been giving this some thought, and I think what you need to do is go to Callum. Have Callum work it on your behalf."

"I don't think that's going to make a difference. Callum already told Steve that I should live with the Royals, and Steve gave him the look of death and dragged me out by my hair."

Val's mouth twitches. "By your hair?"

"Okay, maybe not by my hair, but it felt like it."

"I was just kidding. I like seeing you get all angsty over hooking up with Reed. Sometimes you come off so together, it's intimidating." She pauses. "What's Steve's weakness?"

I meet her reflection in the mirror. "What do you mean?"

"When I want something from my aunt, she likes to see a sacrifice. So let's say I want to go to a concert. I'll tell her I'm studying super hard, doing extra work around the house, essentially laying the groundwork for what a fucking awesome kid I am. And *then* I'll ask for the concert tickets."

"Does she know you're manipulating her?" I ask.

"Of course. It's our game. She gets to see me being responsible and that gives her warm fuzzies, and then I'm rewarded for my sacrifice."

"My dad likes it when I write him a paper justifying all the reasons I want something," some girl next to me chimes in.

I glare at her in the mirror, but she's unfazed. Or maybe she can't tell I'm glaring because she's busy putting on mascara.

"My mom needs to hear it's okay from ten other moms before she says yes," another girl near the door says.

I flick an irritated gaze toward Val at how all these girls are up in my business. She merely smiles, mischief glinting in her eyes.

"What do you want?" the girl by the door asks. I think her name is Hailey.

The blonde next to me grins. "She wants Reed, right?"

My first reaction is pure discomfort. I don't like discussing my personal issues with strangers. But the two girls actually look...friendly.

So I sigh and lean against the sink. "I want to go to the away game, but my..." It's hard saying the word, but I spit it out. "My father won't let me."

"He's being overprotective?" the blonde guesses.

"Making up for lost time, probably," Hailey suggests.

"Oh right!" the blonde exclaims. "Your dad's Steve O'Halloran. I forgot about his grand resurrection."

Val snickers.

"Yeah, he's definitely making up for lost time," Blondie agrees.

Val leans around me. "See?" She pokes me lightly. "This is all normal."

"It totally is," Hailey agrees. "My dad freaked out when he found a condom in my car. My mom took me to the clinic the next day and put me on birth control. She told me to hide that shit and be more careful next time."

"But it's your body," I point out.

She sidles over. "Your dad is going to want to control you until you're fifty. My oldest sister is twenty six, has a law degree, and when she came home for Christmas with her boyfriend, my parents made him sleep in the basement. Dads are the worst when it comes to sex."

"Ella doesn't have a mom to run interference," Blondie reminds everyone.

I shift awkwardly again. It's so messed up that everyone at this school knows my business.

Hailey taps her chin. "Doesn't Katie Pruett live with only her dad?"

"Yeah, she does," a curly-haired brunette says as she leans against the door of the fourth stall. "And she's totally having sex with Colin Trenthorn. They've been doing it since she was a soph."

"Does her dad know?"

"I think he pretends he doesn't know, but she's on birth control so he has to have some idea."

"My mom told my dad that my birth control was for my period," Hailey says, "so maybe Katie used that excuse, too."

"I don't need an excuse to go on birth control," I tell them. "I've been on it since I was fifteen." Because I actually did have terrible cramps, not just because my mother was worried about the pregnancy thing. "I need an excuse to get out of town overnight."

"Say you're staying with a friend."

"And hide in the car while the game's going on? That's not going to work," Val says impatiently. "Everyone knows the Royals, and someone is bound to mention that they saw Ella at the game."

A sympathetic murmur spreads through the bathroom.

"Not to mention that Callum will definitely be there and

probably rat me out to Steve," I remind them. I'm not sure why I'm suddenly okay with all of these girls offering me advice, but I am. It feels weirdly welcoming in some way.

Before anyone can come up with a workable solution, the bell rings. Everyone's heads pop up and there's a flurry of activity as the girls jostle each other to get their makeup reapplied and their stuff packed away.

"We'll think of something," Hailey says on her way out. About six girls stream out after her, all of them waving goodbye to me.

"That was..." I trail off, my confused eyes focusing on Val.

"Fun? Helpful? Entertaining?" She grins. "Not everyone here is awful. Besides, now you know Steve's behavior is completely normal. You just need to figure out how to work him."

A little dazed, all I can do is nod. Okay then. I guess he *is* being normal.

"I tell my parents what they want to hear and then do my own thing," a familiar voice offers coolly.

I spin around to see Jordan stepping out of a stall.

"Did you crawl out of the sewer or have you been there the whole time?" I accuse.

"Eavesdropping the whole time," she says blithely. "So you want to have a little sexcation with Reed Royal, hmmm?"

I don't answer her right away. This girl has disliked me from the moment I stepped foot onto Astor Park's hallowed prep school grounds. When I was ordered to try out for the dance team, she left me a stripper's uniform. I'm sure she meant for me to be too embarrassed to come out of the locker room, but I put on the gear, marched into the gym, and punched her in the face.

"Maybe," I finally say.

"So you need my help." She nudges Val out of the way and passes her hands under the automatic soap dispenser.

"No. I came to *Val* for help."

Jordan scrubs her hands clean, shakes the excess water off, and then grabs a paper towel from the stack in the basket next to the sink.

"And Val's here and so were six of my teammates, but you haven't come up with a solution," she says smugly. "Meanwhile, I have the perfect one."

I doubt it, but her confident tone keeps my feet glued to the floor.

"Why would you help me?" I watch her with narrowed eyes, but I can't read anything on her face. Damn, she'd be an impressive poker opponent.

She tosses the towel in the trash. "Because you'd owe me."

Owe her? That sounds miserable. But…what if she really does have a solution to my problem?

"What would you want in return?" I ask suspiciously.

"A favor to be paid later." She pulls out a little pot from her purse and dabs her perfect lips with shiny gloss.

I watch her, waiting for the rattler's tail to sting me. "What favor?"

"I don't know yet. Depends on what I'll need from you."

"Tell me your solution first." I expect her to say no, but she surprises me.

"Sure." She puts the lip gloss away. "You're a good dancer. Layla Hansell sprained her ankle the other day jumping with her little sister on a trampoline. You can fill Layla's spot on the team."

"Shit." That comes from Val.

Shit, indeed. It *is* the perfect solution. Steve wants me to do extracurricular stuff. Dancing is the only thing I'm capable of and somewhat interested in doing. The dance team's going to travel to this playoff game, which means I can be on the field and sell Steve on the idea of spending time with Astor Park kids.

It's diabolical how perfect this plan is.

Jordan smirks. "Let me know your answer by the end of the day. You can text Val. Bye now."

She saunters out of the bathroom, her hair a dark ribbon streaming behind her.

"I hate her even more," I say to Val.

"I don't blame you." My friend drapes an arm around my shoulders. "But damn, that's a good excuse."

"The best," I say despondently. "The very best."

CHAPTER 19

ELLA

"W‌HAT ARE YOU DOING HERE?" I exclaim when I find Reed leaning against my car after school. "You're suspended!"

He rolls his eyes. "School's over. What are they going to do, suspend me again for standing in the parking lot?"

Good point.

I walk over and give him a hug, which he turns into a kiss that lasts long enough to leave me breathless. I'm smiling like a fool by the time he lets me go.

"You look happy." His eyes narrow suspiciously. "What's wrong?"

I sputter in laughter. "I'm not allowed to be happy?"

He flashes a grin. "Of course you are. It's just that the last time we talked, you were threatening to punch Steve in the face for all his crazy rules."

"I think I found a way to get around the rules."

"Yeah? How?"

"That's for me to know and for you to find out," I say mysteriously, because I want everything to be worked out before I tell him the news. I'm not entirely sure Steve is going to buy into this, so I don't want to get Reed's hopes up if I fail. "Val and I are working on a secret project."

"What kind?"

"I just told you—a secret one."

Reed rests an elbow against the car hood. "Should I be worried?"

I run a hand down his chest to rest on the top of his belt. Somehow Reed manages to make a pair of black cargo pants and a blue sweater look as hot as if he was shirtless.

"You should always be worried," I tease, giving his belt a tug. I'm tired of being stressed, scared, and unhappy all the time. I'm going to enjoy Reed and all my moments with him. Screw the rest of the world.

He allows his body to press into mine until we're pancaked against the side of the car. His hand skims down my side until he reaches the top of my ass. My lips part, waiting for another kiss, the mingling of our breaths, the moment we shut out the entire world—

"Look at them," someone says as they pass. "Perfect trashy couple."

Reed's head flies up. "Got a problem with me, Fleming? Come say it to my face."

I see a short, dark-haired boy stiffen and then quickly walk away.

"Yeah, I thought so," Reed mutters.

"Jerk," I say angrily.

Reed takes my chin between his fingers. "Don't worry about it, baby. Let them run their mouths. It can't hurt us."

He pinches me lightly before dropping a kiss on my lips.

I'm tempted to linger, but if I do, I'll be late. I push him away regretfully. "I've got to get back to the hotel. If I'm not there at four o'clock sharp, Steve might lock me in a dungeon."

Reed snickers.

"Call me tonight?"

"'Course." He leans down to give me one final kiss, and by the way his hand digs into my butt, I know it's going to be one of those long, drugging ones. Oh gosh. I have to get out of his embrace before I turn into a puddle of mush.

"Okay. I'll text you later."

He wanders off to where his Rover is parked, and I wait until he's driving away before calling Val. I put the phone on speaker as I pull out of the parking lot.

"Tell me the downside of this deal," I say the moment she picks up. "What kinds of favors would Jordan ask of me? Like, I don't want to tape any girl up to the side of the school because she talked to Jordan's boyfriend."

"I've been thinking about this since lunch," Val answers.

"And?"

"And I think just because she asks you to do something doesn't mean you have to do it. You owe her *a* favor, not a specific one."

"Good point." I press down on the gas, even though I hate driving fast. Well, I hate driving, period. But I especially hate driving fast. If I don't hurry, though, I'm going to be late. "I like the way you're thinking."

"Let's say she asks you to do something you're not comfortable with. You just tell her to come back with something else."

"Right. So I'm going to keep my word, if I give it, but

it's within the spirit of the agreement to exercise a veto over shitty acts."

"Right," she confirms. "So you gonna do it?"

"I think so."

Jordan's proposal does solve all my problems. Steve wants me to be involved in activities so I'll be less interested in spending time with the Royals. I like dancing. The only downside is that I have to spend time with Jordan.

"This thing is only temporary until that other girl gets back," I say. "So really, I'll just be an alternate."

"Do you want me to tell her yes?" Val asks.

"Is she there with you right now? Blink twice if you're in danger," I tease, pulling into the hotel's parking garage.

Val laughs. "Nope, she's at practice. Actually, you'll appreciate this. Jordan scheduled all the dance team practices at the same time as the football team workouts."

"Even better." I grin to myself. "Okay, tell her I'm in, with payment to be made later."

Val chuckles again. "Gotcha. I'll relay the message when she gets home."

THE ELEVATORS DON'T APPRECIATE THAT I'm five minutes late and take forever to arrive and carry me up the forty-plus floors. However, when I walk in the door ten minutes after four, Steve isn't even home. It's just Dinah.

"Well, look at you," she sneers from her perch on the leather sofa. "You're surprisingly obedient. Like a little dog that comes when you're called, sits when you're told, and stays when you're ordered to stay."

In her hand is another stemmed glass, or maybe it's the same glass from this morning and she's just been refilling it all day.

I'm tempted to snark at her to get a job, but then I remind myself that she's just lost her best friend and that Steve's brutal to her. Then again, he thinks she tried to kill him, which doesn't seem all that far-fetched considering what a witch she is.

"I'm going to my room," I mutter as I walk past her. "I have homework."

Her taunting voice tickles my back. "Your father brought you a gift, Princess. It's lying on your bed."

By the way she says that, I know I'm not going to like whatever Steve got me.

Sure enough, when I dump out the contents of the shopping bag on the bed, I find three pairs of cotton khakis.

Too bad there isn't a fireplace in this hotel suite.

"I hear there's an away game this weekend," Dinah drawls from the door.

I look up to find her leaning against the frame. Her long legs are encased in a pair of loose-fitting pants and she has a sheer floral top on. It's kind of a dressy look for hanging around the suite, and I wonder who she's been visiting.

"How do you know that? Are you blackmailing some poor high school student, too?"

She smirks. "Is that why you think Gideon's in my bed? Darling, you are delightfully naïve. Have you ever heard of a Royal doing anything he doesn't want to do?" She drags her hand down her body to settle at her waist, emphasizing the tininess of it. "Gideon can't get enough of me."

I hold back a barf. "I know you're blackmailing him," I reply coldly.

"Is that the excuse he uses?" She juts her delicate chin forward. "He sleeps with me because he wants to. Because he can't stay away."

Ugh. I don't need to hear another word of this.

"Why are you still married to Steve, then? It's obvious you guys don't love each other." I sweep the pants back into the bag and set it onto the floor.

"Oh my goodness. Is that why you think people get married? Because they love each other?" She starts to laugh. "I'm here for Steve's money and he knows it. Which is why he treats me like shit, but don't worry, he pays for each word he says to me." She waves a hand over her outfit. "Like this? It cost him three thousand dollars. And every day that he's an asshole to me, I'll spend a little more. And while I'm with him, I'm fantasizing about Gideon."

"That's beyond gross." I walk to the door, pushing her out. Dinah's my favorite for the killer, mostly because I can't stand her. Finding evidence against her is the problem. "I'm going to study now."

I slam the door in her face and pull out a sheet of paper that I title *Dinah*. Underneath, I write *means, motive,* and *opportunity*.

Then I stare at it for an hour without writing another frickin' letter.

I'm still hiding in my room, doodling all over the Dinah page while *Orange is the New Black* plays on my laptop, when

Steve knocks on my door.

"You decent?" he says.

I shove the paper under my laptop and hop to my feet. "Yeah."

"How was school?" he asks, poking his head inside.

"Good. How was work?" I grab a sweatshirt from the chair near the window and slip it on.

Steve eyes the top with a smidge of unhappiness, guessing from the size that it's not mine but Reed's. "It was good. The R&D team is getting close to having a prototype finished of a hypersonic delivery vehicle."

I raise one eyebrow. "That sounds dangerous."

He shrugs. "It's primarily a research vehicle and would be flown remotely as a UAV." At my blank look, he expands. "Unmanned aerial vehicle."

"A drone?"

He bobs his head in a considering motion. "I suppose, but not exactly. Similar concept, although ours is much more sophisticated. Essentially the UAV is launched like a rocket into the upper atmosphere. It's definitely not as fun as flying an aircraft, but unfortunately most military aircraft is heavily focused in the unmanned area."

He sounds disappointed, which reminds me of how Callum told me that Steve enjoyed testing the machines out, rather than designing, building, and selling them.

"Seems safer that way," I say lightly.

"Probably is." A rueful smile tilts up one side of his mouth. "I get bored easily. Callum kicked me out of the meeting because I kept launching paper airplanes around the room."

He's bored, huh? Is that why he's so intense on this

parenting thing? It's new and he's trying to find something that interests him?

I think that's what the girls were trying to tell me earlier, so maybe they're right about everything else. I just need to learn to manage him. Once I'm eighteen, I'll be back in control for good.

"I thought about what you said this morning," I inform him.

"Oh?" He leans against the desk, his fingers brushing the side of my laptop. I can see the *D* of *Dinah* poking out. Nervously, I slide toward the desk.

"Yes. I'm going to join the dance team. It's supposed to be really good." I'm not even lying. According to the banners outside the gym, Astor Park has won the state dance competition for the last eight years, except for one time. I wonder what the story is behind that.

Steve straightens, a pleased look on his face. "That's excellent." He crosses the distance between us and pulls my stiff body against his in a hug. "High school and college are all about experiences, and I don't want you to miss out on any of them."

I let him hug me for another second even though this type of contact makes me uncomfortable. The only attention I've ever gotten from men Steve's age hasn't been good.

Stepping back, I walk into the living room and away from the blank list of investigative notes. From the table, I pick up the room service menu. In the short time I've been here, I'm getting tired of room service.

"When do you think we'll be back in the penthouse?" I ask Steve. If there's any evidence that could clear Reed, it's going to be there.

"Why? Are you getting stir crazy?" At the wet bar, he mixes himself a drink. "I spoke with the detective today. We should be allowed back by the end of the week."

I pretend to study the menu more carefully. "How's the investigation going?" Reed and Callum are so tight-lipped about everything, so I'm dying for more details. Really, I just want someone to tell me the cops have nothing and that the case will be dropped any day now.

"Nothing for you to be concerned about."

"Did Brooke's, um, autopsy results come back?"

"Not yet." Steve's back is to me, but I don't need to see his face to know he's not interested in talking about this subject. "Tell me about this dance team."

"Well, it costs some money, because I'll need to buy a uniform." I actually have no idea what the details are. I'm winging it here. "And we travel."

"That's no problem."

"It means staying at hotels with only the dance coach as a chaperone," I point out.

He waves his hand. "I trust you."

Now's the perfect time to tell him the rest. If I wait, that trust will erode. If there's actually any trust there—he could be lying. Then again, what I'm planning to do is definitely against his rules, so he'd be right not to trust me.

But it's Reed, and I want to be with him. I'm afraid he's going to prison, and I need to get all the time I can in with him right now.

I shove those despairing thoughts into the back of my head, muster up a bright smile, and dive in. "In the interest of full disclosure and all, the dance team travels with the football team."

The drink in his hand halts halfway to his mouth. "Is that right?" he drawls, and I feel like he can see through my entire charade.

"Yeah. I know that puts me near Reed, which you don't want." I feel myself blushing, because this is totally TMI for a dad. "But that thing you're worried about? I haven't done anything. With anybody."

Steve sets down his glass. "Are you serious?"

I nod, wishing this awkward discussion was over already. "I might wear a skirt to school—" I offer a wry smile. "But I'm not easy. I guess because of my mom, I haven't had any desire to go down that route."

"Well." He seems at a loss for words. "Well," he repeats and then half-chuckles to himself. "I really stuck my foot in my mouth the other morning, didn't I? I think I let Dinah rile me up with all those comments about your skirt."

I force myself not to shift uncomfortably, because while I haven't lost my virginity yet, I've still done a lot, and I have big plans for this weekend.

"I really misjudged you," Steve says ruefully "I'm sorry about that. I'm messing up all over the place. I read this book on parenting and it said that I should listen more. I'm going to do that," he declares, lobbing another promise out there like his paper airplanes.

"So it's okay that we travel with the team? I mean, it's not like we spend a lot of time with the players, and we drive up in different buses."

"It should be fine."

I give an internal fist pump. Now it's time to go in for the kill. "Also, I was talking to some of the girls and they said that everyone's staying overnight at a hotel so we can go to this amusement park the next day." I fake a grimace. "It sounds totally juvenile, but apparently it's supposed to be some kind of team-building thing. I convinced Val to come up and keep me company."

His eyes narrow. "Will the football players be going, too?"

"No, they're all riding back on the bus to Bayview on Friday night." Except half the starters, including Reed and Easton, but I don't mention that. I've told most of the truth. That counts, right?

"All right." Steve nods. "I'm okay with that." He holds up a finger. "Hold on. I'll be right back. I got you a few things."

Apprehension builds inside me as I watch Steve jog up the stairs. Oh God. What did he get me now? I hear a drawer opening and closing, and then he reappears a minute later with a small leather case in his hand.

"A couple things," he tells me. "First, Callum said he hadn't gotten you a credit card yet, so I took care of it."

He holds out a black card.

I warily accept it. The card is shiny and heavy. For a second, I'm excited to have it—until I see the name embossed on it with gold lettering.

ELLA O'HALLORAN.

Steve notices my frown but answers it with a broad smile. "I've already secured the paperwork to legally change your surname. I figured you wouldn't mind."

My jaw drops. Is he serious? I flat-out told him I wanted to keep my mom's last name. I'm Ella Harper, not O'Halloran.

Before I can object, he turns toward the stairs. "Dinah, get down here," he orders. "I have something for you."

Dinah appears, her shrewd eyes focused on Steve. "What is it?"

He beckons her. "Come down."

The snake inside her looks ready to pounce, but she obviously manages to restrain it, because she descends the stairs and walks stiffly to Steve.

He holds out another credit card. This one is silver rather than black.

"What's this?" She stares at it as if it might explode in her hand if she tries to touch it.

Steve smiles, but it's cold and mean. "I was going over your recent credit card statements and they seemed exorbitantly high. So I canceled those cards. This is the one you'll use from now."

Fire flashes in her eyes. "But this is a basic card!"

"Yes," he agrees. "The limit is five thousand. That should be more than enough for you."

Her mouth opens. And closes. And opens. And closes. This goes on for a while. I hold my breath as I examine her face, waiting for her to lose it. Five thousand dollars might be a fortune for me, but I know it's peanuts for Dinah. There's no way she's going to take this well.

Except…she does.

"You're right. That seems like more than enough," she answers in a sweet voice.

But when Steve bends his head to take something else out of his leather case, Dinah gives me a look so icy and scathing that I find myself shivering. When her gaze lowers to the black card I'm holding, I'm afraid she might actually hit me.

"The last item of business," Steve announces, handing me a sheet of paper.

I glance at it and see a printout of airline tickets. "What's this?"

"Tickets to London," he says happily. "We're going there over the holidays."

I wrinkle my brow. "We are?"

He picks up his drink. "Yes. We'll stay at the Waldorf, visit a few castles. You should make a list of the things you want to see," he encourages.

"All of us are going?" Reed never said a word to me about the Royals going to London for Christmas. Maybe he doesn't know?

"No, just us. If you're calling in our dinner, I'd like the salmon." He tips his head toward the menu I'd left on one of the end tables.

"London is so lovely in the winter," Dinah remarks, her demeanor brightening. She mockingly waves her silver card in the air. "I guess I'll have an opportunity to put this to use."

"Actually, you're staying behind." Steve is darn near smirking. He's clearly enjoying tormenting her. "It'll just be Ella and me. A father/daughter bonding trip, if you will."

I frown deeply. "What about the Royals?"

"What about them?"

"Are they going, too?" I give him back the printout.

He tucks the paper in the leather case and tosses it onto the sideboard. "I have no idea what they're doing for the holidays. But Reed can't leave the country, remember? He had to surrender his passport to the DA's office."

I can't keep the dismay off my face. It's true—Reed can't leave town.

But I can't believe Steve's planning on taking me out of town for the holidays. I'm going to miss my first Christmas with Reed? That's so unfair.

Steve reaches out and dabs his knuckle under my chin. "It'll only be for a week." He arches a brow. "Besides, after seeing Reed at all those games, you'll probably need a break, don't you think? I can even arrange it that we go for longer..."

The message is clear. If I don't go to London with him, I don't get to travel with the dance team. Like the deal I struck with Jordan, it's imperfect, but I force myself to smile and nod, because in the end I'm still getting what I want.

"No, a week is great," I say with forced cheeriness. "I'm excited. I've never been out of the country before."

Steve breaks out into a giant smile. "You'll love it."

Dinah, meanwhile, is glaring at me with the heat of a million suns.

"Darling, go upstairs and change for dinner," Steve tells his fuming wife. "I'll order you a salad."

As she storms off, I call in the order and then listen to Steve babble while we wait for dinner. After it's over, I escape to my room and text Reed immediately.

I'm allowed 2 go 2 the game! Be prepared. Bring a big box of condoms and eat a few energy bars. Ur going 2 need it.

For the game?

The game is easy-peasy compared to the workout I'm putting u through after.

Do u want me to walk arnd w/ a permanent HO?

Yup.

We're supposed to be waiting.

I'm done waiting. Get ready.

I punctuate that with a smiley face and then put the phone away and do some homework.

CHAPTER 20

ELLA

Say what you will about Jordan, but the girl has a serious work ethic. For the rest of the week, I'm forced to endure twice-a-day dance practices—one in the morning and one after school. And although we're practicing on the same field and in the same gym as the football team, I don't have time to even look at Reed, let alone talk to him.

To make matters worse, I only have three days to learn the routines that these girls have been performing for months. Jordan pushes me so hard that my limbs feel like jelly by the time I get home every night. Reed makes fun of me because every time we talk on the phone, I'm icing a different part of my body. Steve thinks it's great, though. He keeps telling me how proud he is to see me throwing myself into this extracurricular stuff.

If he knew the real reason I was working so hard, he'd probably have a heart attack.

On Friday morning, we have our last official practice before tonight's game. One of the girls—Hailey—pulls me aside when we're done and whispers, "You're *such* an amazing dancer. I hope you stay on the team after Layla gets better."

The compliment makes me blush with pride—on the inside. On the surface, I answer with a careless shrug. "I doubt it. I don't think Jordan can stand to be around me any more than absolutely necessary."

"Well, Jordan's an idiot," Hailey murmurs with a grin.

I try to stifle a snort, but it ends up popping out anyway. The sound draws frowns from Rachel Cohen and Shea Montgomery, Savannah's older sister.

"What are you two whispering about?" Shea asks suspiciously.

Hailey just smiles and says, "Nothing."

Okay, I like this girl. She's not Val, but she's cooler than I thought. So are most of the other girls. These past three days I've learned that Jordan's mean-girl control only really applies to Shea, Rachel, and Abby, Reed's ex-girlfriend. Abby's not on the team, thankfully, but she comes by to watch the practices sometimes, which is super uncomfortable.

I don't like Abby, and not just because she's Reed's ex. The girl is too passive. She walks around like the eternal victim, wearing this sad doe-eyed look and talking in a soft whisper. Sometimes I think it's all an act and that deep down she's got claws to rival Jordan's.

In the center of the blue mats strewn on the floor, Jordan claps her hands, the loud sound bouncing off the gym walls. "The bus leaves at five," she announces. "If you're late, we leave without you." She gives me a pointed look.

Ha. Like I'm going to be late. I plan on being there early just to make sure the bus doesn't zoom away without me on it. I'm kind of worried that this sudden show of niceness on Jordan's part isn't real, that she doesn't want a favor from me at all and is planning some horrible humiliation for tonight.

I'm going to take my chances, though. With the way Steve is constantly keeping tabs on me, this is my only opportunity to be alone with Reed.

"I'll see you later," Hailey tells me as we walk out of the girls' locker room ten minutes later.

I wave goodbye and head outside to the parking lot, where Reed is waiting beside my car. His SUV is parked in the next space. I wish I was still living with the Royals and we were driving home together, but I'll take whatever stolen moments with him that I can get.

He pulls me into his arms the moment I approach. "You looked so hot out there," he rasps in my ear. "I love those little dance shorts."

A shiver shimmies up my spine. "You looked hot, too."

"Liar. You didn't even look my way once. Jordan was standing over you like a drill sergeant."

"I was looking at you in spirit," I answer solemnly.

He snickers, then bends down to kiss me. "I still can't believe Steve is letting you stay overnight."

"Me neither," I admit. A pang of worry hits me. "What did you tell Callum about where you're staying tonight? He doesn't suspect you'll be at the hotel, right?"

"If he does, he hasn't said anything." Reed shrugs. "I told him East and I are crashing at Wade's. That we don't want to drive home drunk because we'll probably be pounding booze at the after party."

I frown. "He's actually cool with you going out drinking?

After that whole speech about keeping your nose clean?"

Another shrug. "As long as I'm not fighting, I don't think he cares what I do. Look, about the sex thing—"

I give him an irritated look. "You said you were waiting until I was ready. Well, I'm ready. The only way we're not having sex is if you don't want it."

He returns my irritated stare with a frustrated one. "You know I'm dying for it."

"Great. We're on the same page." I push up on my tiptoes and give him a cheery kiss.

Reed's arm tightens around me and then I feel the tension leave him in a rush. He's on board. Oh, thank God. I was expecting him to put up more of a fight, try to be all honorable again.

My fake cheeriness morphs into real delight. "I've gotta go. Steve wants us to have an early dinner before the bus leaves."

Reed smacks my butt as I walk around the side of the car. "I'll see you later," he calls out.

I turn to smile at him. "You know it."

THE FOOTBALL GAME IS IN a town called Gibson, a two-hour drive from Bayview. I was really hoping I'd get to drive up with Val, but as Jordan not-so-nicely told me, "The dance team travels together—no exceptions." So Val's driving my car while I bus it with the team.

But even though I was dreading being stuck on a bus for two hours with Jordan and her cronies, the ride ends up being surprisingly fun.

"I still can't believe you were actually a stripper," Hailey says from the window seat. She insisted that we sit together, and I didn't put up much of a fight. "I can't imagine taking off all my clothes in front of strangers. I'm too shy."

My cheeks grow hot. "I didn't take it *all* off. The club where I worked wasn't a full-nudity place. Just a G-string and pasties."

"Still. I'd be way too self-conscious. Was it fun?"

Not at all. "It wasn't terrible. The money was decent and the tips were great."

Jordan makes a derisive sound from across the aisle. "Yeah, I'm sure all those dollar bills stuffed down your panties added up to, what, twenty whole dollars?"

I bristle. "Twenty bucks is a lot of money when you're working to support yourself," I shoot back.

She bats her eyelashes. "Well, at least these days you're rolling in the dough. I bet Reed pays as high as a hundred for your services."

I flip up my middle finger but don't bother with a retort. I'm not going to let this catty girl ruin my good mood. I'm finally out from under Steve's watchful eye and about to spend the night with my boyfriend. Jordan can suck it.

To my disbelief, some other girl sticks up for me. "Ha! Reed doesn't pay her a dime," the brunette—I think her name is Madeline—says from the seat behind me. "That boy is freaking in love with a capital L-O-V-E. You should see the way he stares at Ella during lunch."

I blush again. I thought I was the only one who noticed that Reed's intense gaze is *always* on me.

"How sweet," Jordan says dryly. "The killer and the stripper love each other. It's like a Lifetime movie."

"Reed didn't kill anyone," another girl pipes up, her tone as dry as Jordan's. "We all know that."

My head swivels toward her in shock. Does she seriously believe that, or is she being sarcastic?

"Yeah," someone else agrees. "He probably didn't."

"And even if he did," the first one says, waggling her eyebrows, "who the fuck cares? Bad boys are *hot.*"

"Killers are killers," Jordan sneers, but I notice that some of the venom has left her voice. Her expression is almost... thoughtful.

Fortunately, the conversation ends because we arrive at our destination. The bus pulls into the parking lot behind Gibson High School, and we all climb off with our gym bags. I'm the only one who's also carrying an overnight bag.

I squeal when I notice a familiar car parked across the lot. "You beat us!" I yell to Val, who hops off the hood and meets me halfway.

She throws her arms around me in a hug. "Your car is built for speed, babe. I had so much fun letting it loose on the highway. Do you have time to pop over to the hotel before warm-ups? I want to give you something."

"Hold on. Let me ask Satan."

Val snickers as I hurry over to the crowd of girls and tap Jordan on the shoulder. Technically Coach Kelly is the one in charge of the team, but I learned pretty quickly that it's on paper only. Jordan calls all the shots here.

She turns around with an annoyed look. "What?" she snaps.

"When do we warm up?" I ask. "Val and I are staying in town overnight and we just wanted to drop off our stuff at the hotel."

Jordan makes a big show of checking the time on her phone, but then she heaves a sigh. "Fine. But be back by seven-thirty. The game starts at eight."

"Yes, sir." I give her a mock salute and dart back to Val.

It only takes three minutes to drive from the high school to the hotel. It's a sprawling, three-story building with tiny patios on the ground-floor rooms and balconies on the upper floors. It looks clean, and Val and I researched it online and determined that the area is completely safe.

We check in at the front desk and then climb the stairs to our third-floor room and deposit our bags on the beige carpet. I take out my phone and find a text from Reed saying the football team arrived an hour ago and is warming up soon.

"I should head back," I say regretfully, watching as Val plops down on one of the double beds.

"Not yet. First you have to open this!"

She unzips her backpack and removes a striped pink bag with the words *Victoria's Secret* emblazoned on the front.

A groan slips out. "What did you do?" I accuse.

She smiles broadly. "What any good wingman does. I'm making sure my friend gets laid tonight."

Curiosity has me reaching for the gift bag. I sift through the pink tissue paper and find a matching bra and panty set in my size, though I have no clue how Val knows my exact cup size. The demi bra is ivory-colored, with thin straps, pretty scalloped lace, and hardly any padding. The underwear matches it, a teeny scrap of ivory lace that makes me blush.

"Oh my God. When did you get this?"

"After school today. I got my aunt to drop me off at the mall."

The thought of Mrs. Carrington accompanying Val to

purchase lingerie for me makes my face go pale.

Val is quick to assure me. "Don't worry, she dropped me off and left. I took an Uber home." She beams at me. "Do you like?"

"I love," I confess, running my fingers over the lacy edge of the bra. My throat tightens suddenly. I've never had a real friend before and now it seems like I won the friend lottery. "Thank you."

"Thank me later," she says with a grin. "Reed is going to lose his mind when he sees you in that."

My cheeks heat up again.

"By the way, I expect details. It's in the best friend code."

"I'll think about it." I roll my eyes and tuck the naughty items back in the bag. "But it works both ways, you know. I expect details, too."

"Details about what?"

"You and Wade."

Her smile fades. "There is no me and Wade."

"Yeah?" I raise one eyebrow. "Then why did you drive three hours to watch him play football?"

She huffs in outrage. "I didn't come here for *him*. I came for you!"

"Uh-huh, even though I'm not even going to see you tonight because I'll be with Reed?"

Val scowls. "Someone needs to have your back at the game. What if Jordan tries something?"

My lips twitch. "We both know I can handle Jordan. So why don't you just admit it? You came for Wade."

"It's the first matchup of the playoffs, and it's an away game," she grumbles. "Astor Park needs all the support it can get."

I burst out laughing. "Oh, now you have school spirit? God,

Val, you're such a terrible liar."

She flips me the bird. "You know what? I don't like you right now." But she's laughing as she says it.

"That's okay," I answer sweetly. "You can fill your liking quota with Wade, because, um, we both know you do."

That gets me a pillow to the head. I catch it easily, then toss it back to Val. "I'm just teasing you," I assure her. "If you like Wade, great. If you don't, also great. I support you in everything you do."

Her tone softens, and there's a crack in her voice as she says, "Thank you."

CHAPTER 21

ELLA

EVEN AS I WARM UP with the other girls, I'm still expecting some sort of ambush. My wary gaze darts toward Jordan after each stretch and exercise I complete, but she seems focused on her own stretches. Maybe this is legit? I mean, I practiced with these girls all week, and I didn't get so much as a hint that they might be up to something. I'm praying that nobody is going to throw a bucket of pig's blood on me when I'm in the middle of a tumbling routine.

As Hailey and I head for the bench to rehydrate, she leans in closer and whispers, "There are, like, a hundred girls staring at you right now."

I frown and follow her gaze. Sure enough, there are *a lot* of female eyes on me. Male ones, too, because of the booty shorts and crop top I'm wearing. But the girls aren't checking me out—they're all looking at me in…envy?

It doesn't make sense to me at first, but when I pass a group of jersey-wearing girls in the front row, the pieces suddenly slide together.

"That's his girlfriend!" one hisses loud enough for me to overhear.

"She's *so* pretty," her friend whispers back, sounding sincere rather than catty.

"She's lucky, more like it," the first one responds. "I'd die to go out with Reed Royal."

This is about Reed? Wow. I guess that girl on the bus was right—bad boys *do* have major appeal. I glance at the away bench, where Reed is sitting with Easton, then at the stands, and realize that a ton of girls are looking covetously at Reed.

Jordan sidles up to me. "Quit eye-fucking your boyfriend," she mutters. "We're going on soon."

I glance over at her. "I'm pretty sure every chick in this stadium is doing the same thing. I guess it's every girl's fantasy to hook up with a murder suspect?"

My nemesis snorts in amusement, then slaps a hand over her mouth as if she realizes what she'd done. I'm kind of surprised, too, since Jordan and I aren't exactly joking-around friends. Or friends, period.

The non-toxic exchange must have freaked Jordan out, because she suddenly snarls at me. "Your shorts are riding up. I can see half your ass. Fix yourself up, will you?"

I fight a grin as she stalks off, because we both know the industrial double-stick tape on my ass means my shorts haven't moved an inch. Maybe I've been going about this the wrong way—instead of shooting insults and antagonizing Jordan, maybe I should be extra sweet and friendly. That would drive her insane.

I turn toward the bleachers again in search of Val. When I spot her a few rows behind the away bench, I give her a happy wave. She waves back and then shouts, "Break a leg!"

Grinning, I rejoin the team and bounce up and down on my heels a little, mentally preparing myself for the routine. I think I have it down pat, but hopefully I don't forget all the moves once the spotlight is on me.

Since it's the first playoffs game, the pre-show is ridiculously extravagant. There's a drum line routine punctuated by fire shooting out of big pillars on either side of the field and a short display of fireworks. The Gibson High cheerleaders put on a routine that involves a lot of butt-shaking and hip-swaying, causing all the guys in the stands to jump to their feet and whistle and catcall. Then it's our turn. The girls and I run onto the field. I catch Reed's eye as I get in position next to Hailey.

He gives me a thumbs up, which I return with a huge grin.

The music starts, and we're off.

All my nerves disappear the moment the beat injects into my bloodstream. I nail every spin and turn. I kill it on the short tumbling routine that I do side by side with Hailey. Adrenaline sizzles inside me, my heart racing in excitement as the fast-paced dance routine draws deafening cheers from the crowd. The team moves in perfect precision, and when we finally wrap up, we get a standing ovation.

Now I get why Astor Park has won all those national championships. These girls are *talented*. And although this started off as just a way for me to attend this game, I can't lie—I'm kind of proud to have been a part of this performance.

Even Jordan is in an ecstatic mood. Her cheeks glow as she hugs and high-fives her teammates—including me. Yep, she actually gives me a high-five, and it's *genuine*. I guess hell must have frozen over.

Any thoughts of murder and verdicts and prison are relegated to the very back of my head. No one else seems to be bothered by it, either.

After we clear the field, there's some discussion with the refs and the coaches, a coin toss, and then the game gets underway. The Riders' offense is up first, and my eyes follow Wade as he jogs onto the field. He's a tall guy, but for some reason he looks even bigger in his uniform and with his helmet on.

On the first play, Wade throws a short pass to a receiver with the name Blackwood on his jersey. Blackwood catches the ball, but then there's a long, boring halt as the refs try to decide if he gained enough yards for a new set of downs—Hailey helped me with some of the lingo on the bus ride up here when she found out how little I knew about the game. A little man darts out and measures the distance from the ball to the line, then holds up his hands and makes a signal I don't understand. Hailey and I didn't cover hand signals.

The Astor Park fans cheer in approval. Me, I'm just bored from how long it took to decide if our guys got a few measly yards. I search the sidelines until I spot Reed. At least I think it's Reed. There are two players with ROYAL stitched on their jerseys and they're standing side by side, so for all I know, I'm ogling Easton's butt and not Reed's. He shifts his head and I see his profile. Yup, it's Reed.

He's chewing on his mouth guard, and then, as if he senses me watching him, he sharply turns his head. The mouth guard pops out and he grins at me. It's a wicked, private smile reserved just for me.

The excitement vibrating in the stadium only gets more intense when Gibson ends up tying the score right before halftime. In retaliation, Reed and Easton tackle the Gibson quarterback the next time he's on the field, and the guy fumbles the football. Someone else on the Astor defense scoops it up and runs it in for a touchdown.

The Astor Park fans are freaking out. The home fans are booing loud enough to rock the bleachers. Some of the Gibson kids start chanting, "Killer, killer," but are quickly shut down by some administrators. The verbal attacks only seem to fire up the Astor Park team even more.

In the end, the Riders win the game, which means they're moving on to the next round of the playoffs. I grin as I watch Coach Lewis slap his players on their asses after the win. Football is so freaking weird.

The teams form two lines and exchange handshakes. A few of the opposing players don't shake Reed's hand. For a moment I wonder if there's going to be a fight, but Reed doesn't seem to care. The moment they're done, Easton races toward me. He plucks me right off my feet, then carries me down to the field and whirls me around.

"Did you see that sack in the second?" he exclaims.

I strain my head toward Val, who's hurrying down the steps toward us.

"Wait for Val!" I grumble at him, but he carts me down the sidelines and doesn't release me until we reach the entrance of the tunnel that leads to the locker rooms.

Reed is there, helmet in hand, sweaty hair matted to his head. "Enjoy the game?" he asks before bending his head and kissing me.

A laughing Val finally catches up to us, and she and Easton start making gagging noises as Reed's kiss drags on and on.

"Come on, guys, we're standing right *here*," Val announces. "Royal, stop mouth-mauling my best friend so we can walk back to the hotel already."

I break away from the kiss. "You didn't drive?" I ask her.

She shakes her head. "It was a ten-minute walk. I figured there wouldn't be any closer parking spots, anyway."

Reed gives me a stern look. "I don't want you two walking back to the hotel alone. Wait for us outside the stadium and we'll all walk back together."

I respond with a brisk salute. "Yes, sir."

His mouth finds mine again. This time there's something different about his kiss. It's rippling with promise. When he pulls back, I see a familiar gleam in his blue eyes. We're away from the Royal mansion. There's no risk of Callum or Steve or anyone else interrupting us. Whatever reservations Reed had about saving himself until after the investigation is over were left behind in Bayview. There's only one reason I'd join Jordan's dance squad and it's not to cuddle.

We both know what's going to happen tonight.

REED AND I WALK BACK to the hotel with Easton, Valerie... and Wade. Needless to say, Val is *not* happy about this latest development.

The moment we reach the parking lot, she plants her feet and crosses her arms. "Why is *he* here?" Her accusatory gaze is laser-pointed at me. "You said it was just Reed and Easton."

I hold up my hands in defense. "I didn't know."

Wade looks uncharacteristically wounded. I always

thought nothing fazed this guy, but Val's obvious unhappiness about his presence brings a sad look to his face.

"Come on, Val," he says hoarsely. "Don't be like that."

She bites her lip.

"Please," he adds. "Can't we just go somewhere and talk?"

"You're staying with us anyway," Easton pipes up, "so you guys might as well call a truce before the slumber party begins."

I turn to Val in surprise. "You're not rooming with me?"

A flicker of humor shines through her cloudy expression. "Didn't I tell you? Reed and I reached an agreement. I agreed to bunk with Easton."

I glance from Reed to Val in suspicion. When did they decide *that*?

Val's humor fades and the clouds take over again. "But I didn't agree to bunk with *him*."

Wade looks hurt again. "Val…"

"Wade," she mimics.

Easton heaves a huge sigh. "Okay, I'm tired of this lovers' quarrel. I'm going to hit the hotel bar while you two figure this shit out." He grins at Val. "And if you figure out that you guys want to be alone tonight, text me and I'll get my own room."

With that, he saunters inside, leaving the four of us in the parking lot.

"Val?" I prompt.

She hesitates for a long, long time. Then she groans. "Oh fine. I'll talk to him." She says it to me rather than Wade, whose whole face lights up at her words. "I need to come up and grab my bag, though."

We climb up to the third floor, where I swipe the keycard to open the door. As Val ducks inside to get her backpack,

Reed and I linger in the doorway with Wade, who decides to offer me his unsolicited advice.

"Make sure my man doesn't skimp on the foreplay. That's important. Warms that virginal body of yours right up."

I whirl toward Reed. "You told him I was a virgin?!"

Wade answers for him. "Nah, East did."

Frickin' Easton. That boy can never keep his mouth shut.

"Also," Wade adds solemnly, "don't freak if you don't have an orgasm the first time. You're gonna be all tense and nervous. Besides, Reed won't last more than twenty seconds—"

"Wade," Reed says in exasperation.

"Leave them alone," Val snaps, slinging her backpack over her shoulder. "You should be worrying about your own technique. From what I saw in that supply closet at school, you need a lot of work."

He slaps a hand to his heart as if she shot an arrow into it. "How dare you, Carrington. I'm a modern-day Romeo."

"Romeo dies," she says tersely.

I fight a smile as the two of them disappear back toward the stairwell. Wade has his work cut out for him, that's for sure. Val is clearly not going to make this easy for him.

Reed and I exchange a grin and enter the hotel room, where he sits on the bed and gestures for me to join him.

Nerves flutter in my tummy. "Um…" I swallow hard and then clear my throat. "Give me a second?"

I dash into the bathroom before he can answer. The moment I'm alone, I stare at my reflection in the mirror, noting the deep blush on my cheeks. I feel stupid. I mean, Reed and I have fooled around before. I shouldn't be nervous, but I am.

Breathing deeply, I reach for the gift bag I stashed under

the sink and spend an excessive amount of time getting ready. Smoothing out my hair. Fixing the bra straps so they're not crooked but perfectly parallel. I glance in the mirror again and can't deny I look hot.

Reed agrees, because the second I step out of the bathroom, he groans, "Holy fuck, baby."

"Thought I'd change into something a little less comfortable," I say in a wry voice.

He wheezes out a laugh. He took off his shirt when I was in the bathroom, and now he rises to his feet, bare-chested and utterly gorgeous.

"You like?" I ask shyly.

"I more than like."

He advances on me like a hungry animal, blue eyes raking over my body until every inch of me feels hot and achy. He comes closer, and he's so much taller than me, so much bigger. Strong arms pull me in. His lips find my neck and he kisses me there.

"FYI?" he murmurs against my heated flesh. "You don't need to dress up for me. You're beautiful no matter what you wear." He lifts his head and gives me a wicked smile. "You're even more beautiful when you're wearing nothing at all."

"Don't ruin this," I scold. "I'm too nervous. I need to feel pretty."

"You *are* pretty. And there's no reason to be nervous. We don't have to do anything you don't want to."

"Are you backing out?"

"No way." He drags his hand down my side to settle at my waist. "Nothing or no one could drag me away at this point."

I want this so badly I can hardly breathe. I never gave much thought to my first time. I never fantasized about rose petals and candles. I never even thought it would be with someone I loved, if I'm being honest.

"Good, because I don't want to wait another minute," I tell him.

"Lie down." His voice is husky as he nudges me toward the bed.

Without a word, I stretch out on my back with my head on the pillows.

He stands at the edge of the mattress. Then he takes off his pants.

My lungs stop working as Reed crawls up beside me. He brings his mouth to mine, kissing me softly at first, then with more urgency as I part my lips for him.

The hard length of him presses against my thigh, and the drumbeat of desire that played in the background all week as I thought about this night thuds loudly in my head. His tongue traces my lips, his mouth whispers a path across my cheek. His hands roam my body, mapping the valleys and the rises with equal interest.

A thumb across my nipple sends shudders from the tip to my core. A kiss behind my ear makes my whole body quiver in delight.

We make out for what seems like hours, until we're both breathless and painfully turned on.

Reed's lips release mine abruptly. "I love you," he mumbles.

"I love you, too." I press my mouth to his again and we stop talking. My heart is pounding. So is his. And his hands tremble as they begin a slow descent.

To my frustration, he won't let me touch him. Every time

I reach for him, he swats my hands away. "It's all about you," he whispers after my third grabbing attempt. "Close your eyes and enjoy it, dammit."

And gosh, I do. I enjoy every torturous second of it. It's not long before my brand-new underwear is cast aside. I can't focus on anything but the incredible sensations he's eliciting. He's touched me before here, in the same intimate ways, but it's different tonight. It's the start of something, rather than the end. Every caress of his hand, every press of his lips against my skin, is a promise of more to come. And I can't wait.

Two calloused fingers slide down my stomach until he's there, inside me, and I moan as the pleasure explodes in a blinding rush. The sensations shake me from the inside out. His mouth meets mine, swallowing my whimpers, stroking me to completion. My hips arch to meet his fingers, and he rides the wave with me as I shudder against the mattress.

He doesn't even give me time to recover. I'm still shaking wildly when he starts all over again, this time sliding between my legs and using his mouth to send me soaring. He licks and kisses and teases until I can't take it. It's too much, too good. But not enough.

A frustrated groan flies out. "*Reed*," I beg, clutching his broad shoulders to yank him up.

The heavy weight of his body presses me to the bed. "You ready?" he rasps. "Really ready?"

I nod wordlessly.

He leaves me, just for a moment, so he can dig around in his jeans pocket. He comes back with a condom.

My heart stops.

"You okay?"

His deep voice is like a warm blanket of reassurance. "I'm good." I reach for him again. "I love you."

He whispers, "Love you, too," and then kisses me at the same time he enters me.

We both make a strangled noise, because it feels impossibly tight. The pressure triggers an achy feeling, a strange sensation of emptiness.

"Ella," he breathes as if he's the one in pain.

When he hesitates, I dig my nails into his shoulders and urge him on. "I'm okay. Everything's good."

"Might hurt for a second."

He drives his hips forward.

The pain startles me even though I expected it. Reed stops abruptly, his eyes inspecting me carefully. Sweat beads on his forehead, and his arms shake as he holds himself still until my body accepts his sweet invasion.

We wait until the pain has abated, the empty feeling is gone, and all that's left is a feeling of wondrous fullness. I lift my hips experimentally, and he groans.

"Feels so good," he chokes out.

It does. It really does. Then he starts to move and it only gets better. There's only slight pain when he withdraws, and I instinctively wrap my legs around him. We moan in unison. He moves even faster. The muscles of his back flex under my grip as he pushes into me, over and over again.

Reed whispers how much he loves me. I clutch him tight with both hands and gasp at each thrust and retreat.

He knows exactly what I need. Easing off me slightly, he brings his hand between my legs and presses down on the spot that aches for him. The second he does, I go up in flames.

Everything ceases to exist. Everything but Reed and the way he's making me feel.

"God, Ella." His rough voice barely penetrates the blissful glow that surrounds me.

One last thrust and he's trembling on top of me, his lips pressed to mine, our bodies glued together.

It takes forever for my heart to beat at a regular pace again. By then, Reed has withdrawn and taken care of the condom, only to return and drag me against his chest. He's breathing just as hard. When my limbs are finally strong enough to support my weight, I rise up on one elbow and smile at the look of utter satisfaction on his face.

"Was it okay?" I tease.

He snorts. "You need to erase the word *okay* from your vocab, baby. That was…"

"Perfect," I fill in, my voice a happy whisper.

He holds me even tighter. "Perfect," he agrees.

"Can we do it again?" I ask hopefully.

His laughter tickles my face. "Did I just create a monster?"

"I think so?"

We're both laughing as he rolls over to kiss me again, but we don't start anything, at least not yet. We just kiss for a bit and then snuggle together, while he plays with my hair and I stroke his chest.

"You were incredible," he tells me.

"For a virgin, you mean?"

Reed snorts. "No. *This* was beyond incredible. I was talking about the routine. I couldn't take my eyes off you."

"It was fun," I confess. "More fun than I thought it would be."

"Do you think you'll stay on the team? I mean, if you can

stomach being around Jordan, then maybe you should. You looked so happy when you were out there."

"I *was* happy." I chew on my bottom lip. "Dancing is…it's a thrill. It's my favorite thing in the whole world. I always—" I stop, a bit embarrassed to reveal my silly hopes.

"You always what?" he pushes.

A breath slides out. "I always dreamed that maybe one day I could take actual classes. Get some real training."

"There are arts colleges. You should apply," Reed says immediately.

I rise up on an elbow again. "You really think so?"

"Hell yeah. You're so freaking talented, Ella. You have a gift, and it would be a waste of that gift not to do anything with it."

Warmth unfurls like ribbons in my chest. Other than my mom, nobody has ever told me I was talented.

"Maybe I will," I say through the lump of emotion in my throat. Then I kiss him and ask, "What about you?"

"What about me?"

"What's your dream?"

His features crease unhappily. "Right now? My dream is not going to jail."

Just like that, the relaxed mood in the hotel room dissolves into tension. Crap. I shouldn't have said anything. For this one perfect moment, though, I completely forgot about Brooke's death and the police investigation and that Reed's entire future is nothing but uncertain right now.

"Sorry," I whisper. "I forgot about all that."

"Yeah, me, too." He runs his big hand over my bare hip. "I guess…if I didn't have these charges hanging over my head… I'd want to work for Atlantic Aviation."

My jaw drops. "Seriously?"

A sheepish gleam fills in his eyes. "Don't you dare tell my father," he orders. "He'd probably throw a parade."

I giggle. "It's okay to please Callum, you know. As long as you're pleasing yourself, too, then who cares?" I study his face. "You would really want to be involved in the family business, though?"

Reed nods. "I think it's kind of fascinating. I wouldn't want to design anything, but the business side of it would be pretty cool to get involved in. I'd probably get a business degree in college." His features become pained again. "But none of that is even an option. Not if…"

Not if he's found guilty of killing Brooke.

Not if he goes to jail.

I force myself to banish those thoughts. I want to focus on good things right now. Like how happy I am to be lying here with Reed and how amazing it felt when he was inside me. So I climb on top of him and end the conversation by planting my lips on his.

"Round two?" he teases against my mouth.

"Round two," I confirm.

And off we go.

CHAPTER 22

REED

"You look like you're in a good mood," Easton notes on Sunday morning.

I join him out on the terrace. "Smoothie?" I ask, tipping the extra bottle in his direction. At his nod, I toss it to him. "Can't complain."

I try but fail to keep from smiling, and the way my brother's eyes roll to the back of his head tells me he can read the satisfaction all over my face. But I don't give a rat's ass, because between the murder charge and Steve's striving for a Father of the Year award, things have been tense between Ella and me. After this weekend, we're back on track. Nothing's going to ruin my good mood today.

If Steve asks, I respected the hell out of his daughter. Three times.

"Nice sweatshirt, though," I tell East. "What trash bin did you fish that out of?"

He pulls the ratty thing away from his chest. "I wore this crabbing three summers ago."

"Is that the trip where Gideon got his balls bitten?" The summer before Mom died, we went to the Outer Banks as a family and fished for crabs.

Easton lets out a roar of laughter. "Oh shit, I forgot that happened. He walked around with a hand in front of his crotch for a month."

"How'd that happen anyway?" I still can't figure out how the crab jumped from the bucket to land in Gid's lap, but his scream of pain made every seagull within a hundred yards fly off in terror.

"Dunno. Maybe Sav knows some magic voodoo and stuck him." East holds his stomach with one hand and wipes tears away from his face with the other.

"They were just starting to go out then."

"He was always an ass to her."

"True." Gid and Sav never made much sense, and it flamed out in a spectacular way. Can't blame the girl for being bitchy toward us.

"So Wade and Val getting it on again?" East asks curiously.

"Well, you ended up having to get your own room on Friday night, so you tell me."

"I think they are."

"Why do you care? Did you want a shot at her?"

He shakes his head. "Naah. I got my eye on some other chick."

"Yeah?" This surprises me, since Easton's never settled down. He seems like he wants to tap every ass in Astor. "Who is it?"

He shrugs, pretending to be absorbed with his smoothie.

"Not even gonna give me a clue?"

"I'm still debating what my options are."

His uncharacteristic reserve piques my interest. "You're

Easton Royal. You have all the options."

"Shockingly enough, there are some people who don't subscribe to that theory. They're wrong, of course, but what can you do?" He grins and then chugs the rest of his drink.

"I'll sic Ella on you. You can't hold out against her."

He snorts. "Neither can you."

"Who'd want to?"

Whatever comeback he was going to make is halted by Dad's appearance at the door.

"Hey, Dad." I raise my drink. "We're having breakfast…" My happy greeting trails off as I take in his somber expression. "What's up?"

"Halston is here and he needs to see you. Now."

Shit. On Sunday morning?

I don't spare a look at East, who's likely frowning. I slide my stone face into place and walk through the space my dad makes for me.

"What's this is all about?"

I'd rather know what I'm going to be confronting, but Dad just shakes his head. "I don't know. Whatever it is, we'll deal with it."

Meaning Grier wouldn't tell him. Awesome.

Inside the study, Grier's already seated on the couch. A stack of papers about two inches high sits in front of him.

"Hello, son," he says.

It's Sunday and he's not at church. That's my first warning. Everyone but the worst kind of people go to church down here. When Mom was alive, we went like clockwork. After we buried her, Dad never made us go again. What was the point? God hadn't saved the only worthy Royal, so there wasn't much hope the rest of us were getting past the pearly gates.

"Good morning, sir. I didn't realize lawyers work on Sunday."

"I went into the office last night to catch up on some things and there was mail from the prosecutor's office. I spent all night reading it and decided I should come here this morning. You'd better have a seat."

He gives me a thin smile and waves to a wing chair opposite him. I notice that he's not even wearing a suit, but khakis and a button-down shirt. That's my second warning. Shit's going to go down.

Stiffly, I sit down. "I'm guessing I'm not going to like what you have to say."

"No, I don't think you will, but you're going to listen to every word." He points to the stack of paper. "For the past couple of weeks, the prosecutor's office and the Bayview police have taken statements from your classmates, friends, acquaintances, and enemies."

My fingers itch to grab the papers and toss them all in the fireplace. "You have a copy of those? That's normal?" I reach for the pile, but he shakes his head until I settle back in my chair.

"Yes, as part of your constitutional rights, you get access to all the information they acquire, except for some documents the courts deem attorney work product. Witness statements are produced so that we can prepare a defense. The last thing the prosecution wants is for us to get a conviction overturned because they didn't give us the appropriate evidence prior to trial."

Over the pounding of my heart, I say, "That's good, right?"

As if I hadn't spoken, Grier continues. "It's also a way for them to show us if they have a strong case or a weak case."

My fingers curl over my knees. "And by the look on your

face, I guess the case against me is strong?"

"Why don't I read you the statements and then you can make your own judgment? This one is from Rodney Harland the Third."

"I have no idea who that is." Feeling faintly better, I rub my palms against my sweatpants.

"Nickname Harvey."

"Still doesn't ring a bell. Maybe they're interviewing people that don't even know me." It sounds ridiculous as I say it out loud.

Grier doesn't even look up from the page. "Harvey the Third is five-eleven but likes to brag that he's six-two. He's wider than he is tall, but because of his massive size, no one disputes his obviously false claim. His nose is broken and he has a tendency to lisp."

"Wait, does he have curly brown hair?" I remember a guy like that at the dock fights. He doesn't get in the ring much, because despite his size he hates taking hits. He ducks and runs away.

Grier looks up from the sheet of paper. "You do know him then."

I nod. "Harvey and I fought a couple times a while back."

What could Harvey say? He was involved in this up to his tiny ears.

"Harvey says that you fight on a fairly regular basis down in the warehouse district, usually between Docks Eight and Nine. That's your preferred space because one of the fighters' fathers is the dock manager."

"Will Kendall's dad is the dock foreman," I confirm, feeling a bit more confident. Every guy down there is fighting because he wants to. Mutually agreed upon beatings are not illegal.

"He doesn't care that we use it."

Grier plucks his shiny pen off the table. "When did you start fighting?"

"Two years ago." Before my mom died, when her depression was spiraling out of control and I needed an outlet that didn't include being pissed off at her.

He jots something down. "How did you hear about it?"

"I don't know. In the locker room?"

"And how often do you go there now?"

I sigh and pinch the bridge of my nose. "I thought we went over this before." The fight thing came up the first time Grier and I met over this murder mess—the one I'd wrongly thought would go away because I didn't do it.

"Then you won't mind going over it again," Grier says implacably. His pen is poised, waiting for me.

Dully, I recite the answers. "We usually go after football games. We fight and then go to a party."

"Harvey says you were one of the more regular participants. You would fight two or three males a night. These fights never lasted more than approximately ten minutes each. Usually you came with your brother Easton. 'Easton is a real dick,' according to Harvey. And you are 'a smug asshole.'" Grier pulls down his eyeglasses and peers over the top of the lenses. "His words, not mine."

"Harvey's a narc, and he cries if you so much as glare in his general direction," I say tersely.

Grier arches his eyebrows for a second and then resettles his glasses. "Question: 'How did Mr. Royal appear during fights?' Answer: 'Usually he pretended to be calm.'"

"Pretended? I *was* calm. It was a dock fight. Nothing was

on the line. There wasn't anything to be excited about."

Grier keeps reading. "'Usually he pretended to be calm, but if you said anything bad about his mom, he'd go ballistic. About a year ago, some guy called his mom a whore. He beat that kid so hard the poor shit had to go to the hospital. Royal was banned after that. He broke this kid's jaw and his eye socket.' Question: 'So he never fought again?' Answer. 'No. He came back about six weeks later. Will Kendall controlled dock access and said Royal could come back. The rest of us went along with it. I think he paid Kendall off.'"

I stare at my feet so Greer doesn't see the guilt in my eyes. I did pay off Kendall. The kid wanted a new engine for his GTO, which would've set him back two grand. I gave him the money, and I was back in the fights.

"Nothing to say?" Grier prompts.

Swallowing the lump in my throat, I try to shrug carelessly. "Yeah, that's all true."

Grier makes another note. "Speaking of fights over your mother..." He pauses and picks up another stapled document. "Jaw breaking appears to be a particularly favorite pastime of yours."

I clench my own jaw and stare stonily back at the lawyer. I know what's coming next.

"Austin McCord, age nineteen, still reports problems with his jaw. He was forced to eat soft foods for six months while his jaw was wired shut. He required two teeth implants and to this day has difficulty eating solid foods. When asked about the cause of his injury, Mr. McCord was"—Grier shakes the document a little—"pardon the pun, closemouthed, but at least one friend of McCord's explained that McCord had been in an altercation with Reed Royal, which resulted in serious injuries to his face."

"Why are you reading that? You made that deal with the McCords and you said it was confidential." As per the deal, Dad set up a trust to fund McCord's four-year tuition costs at Duke. A gaze in my father's direction reveals his own distress. His mouth is a thin line and his eyes are red-rimmed, as if he hasn't slept for days.

"Confidentiality of those deals are meaningless in a criminal case. Eventually McCord's testimony can be subpoenaed and used against you."

Grier's words pull my attention back to him. "He had it coming."

"Again, because he called your mother a bad name."

This is bullshit. As if Grier would ever stand for his momma being badmouthed.

"You're telling me that a man isn't going to stand up for the women of his household? Every juror would excuse that." No southern male would ever allow that kind of insult to pass unchecked.

It's one reason the McCords took the deal. They knew prosecuting that kind of case would go nowhere, especially against my family. You can't call someone's mother a drug-addled slut and get away with it.

Grier's face tightens. "If I had known that you were engaged in disreputable activity to this extent, I wouldn't have suggested to your father that we settle this matter in a monetary fashion. I would've suggested military school."

"Oh, was that your idea? Because Dad always throws that threat around whenever he doesn't like what we're doing. I guess I can thank you for that," I say sarcastically.

"Reed," my father chides from his place near the bookshelves. It's the first thing he's said since we walked in here, but I've been watching his expression and it just keeps getting bleaker.

Grier glares at me. "We're on the same team here. Don't fight me, boy."

"Don't call me *boy*." I glare back, dropping my arms to my knees.

"Why? Are you going to break my jaw, too?"

His eyes fall to the hands I've got curled into fists in my lap.

"What's your point here?" I mutter.

"My point is—"

A soft ringing cuts him off.

"Hold that thought." Grier reaches for the sleek cell phone on the desk and checks the screen. Then he frowns. "I need to take this. Excuse me."

Dad and I exchange a wary look as the lawyer steps out into the hall. Since he closes the door behind him, neither of us is able to hear what he's saying.

"These statements are bad," I say flatly.

Dad gives a bleak nod. "Yes. They are."

"They make me look like a psycho." A powerless sensation squeezes my throat. "This is freaking bullshit. So what if I like to fight? There're guys out there who fight for a living. Boxing, MMA, wrestling—you don't see anybody accusing *them* of being bloodthirsty maniacs."

"I know." Dad's voice is oddly gentle. "But it's not just the fighting, Reed. You've got a temper. You—" He stops when the door swings open and Grier appears.

"I just got off the phone with the ADA," Grier says in a

tone I can't decipher. Confused, maybe? "The lab results from Brooke's autopsy came back this morning."

Dad and I both straighten our shoulders. "The DNA test on the baby?" I ask slowly.

Grier nods.

I take a breath. "Who's the father?"

And suddenly I'm…afraid. I know there's zero chance of me being that kid's father, but what if some corrupt lab tech rigged the results? What if Grier opens his mouth and announces—

"You are."

It takes me a second to realize he's not talking to me.

He's talking to my dad.

CHAPTER 23

REED

Silence crashes over the study. My father is gaping at the lawyer. I'm gaping at my father.

"What do you mean, it's *mine*?" Dad's tortured eyes are fixed on Grier. "That's not possible. I had a…"

Vasectomy, I finish silently. When Brooke announced her pregnancy, Dad was certain the baby couldn't be his, because he'd gotten snipped after Mom had the twins. And I was certain it couldn't be mine, because I hadn't slept with Brooke in more than half a year.

Looks like only one of us was right.

"The test confirmed it," Grier answers. "You were the father, Callum."

Dad swallows hard. His eyes glaze over a bit.

"Dad?" I say tentatively.

He stares at the ceiling as if it's too painful for him to look at me. A muscle in the back of his jaw flexes, and then he shudders out an unsteady breath. "I thought she was lying to me. She didn't know I'd had the vasectomy, and I thought…"

Another breath. "I thought, it had to be someone else's."

Yeah. He decided it was *mine*. But I can't blame him for reaching that conclusion. He'd known about me and Brooke, so of course the thought had entered his mind. I guess the other thought—that it could actually be *his*—never did.

Sympathy ripples through me. Dad might've hated Brooke, but he would've been a good father to her kid. The loss has to be killing him.

He inhales heavily before finally looking my way. "I…ah, do you need me here or can you handle the rest of the meeting on your own?"

"I can handle it," I answer gruffly, because it's obvious he can't handle a damn thing at the moment.

Dad nods. "All right. Shout if you need me."

His legs don't appear to be steady as he leaves the room. There's a beat of silence, and then Grier speaks up.

"Are you ready to continue?"

I nod weakly.

"All right. Let's talk about Ella O'Halloran." He shuffles through the endless fucking pile of papers and pulls out another set. "Ella O'Halloran, formerly known as Ella Harper, is a seventeen-year-old runaway who was found masquerading as a thirty-five-year-old and stripping in Tennessee just three months ago."

Has it only been three months? I feel like Ella's been a part of my life forever. Anger begins to pound at my temples. "Don't talk about her."

"I'm going to have to talk about her. She's part of this case whether you like it or not. In fact, Harvey said you brought her along to some of the fights. She was unfazed by the blood."

"What's your point?" I repeat through gritted teeth.

"Let's go through a few more statements, shall we?" He holds up a document and jabs it. "Here's one from Jordan Carrington."

"Jordan Carrington hates Ella's guts."

Grier once again ignores my comments. "'We invited Ella to come try out for the dance team. She showed up wearing a thong and a bra, prancing through the gym. She has no shame and even fewer morals. It's an embarrassment. But for some reason Reed likes this. He was never like this until she came along. He used to be decent, but she brings out the worst in him. Whenever she's around, he's extra mean.'"

"That is the biggest bunch of bullshit I've ever heard. Jordan taped some freshman girl up to the side of Astor Park's walls, and *I'm* extra mean? Ella didn't change me one bit."

"So you're saying you were prone to violence even before Ella came along."

"You're twisting my words," I spit out.

He laughs harshly. "This is a cakewalk compared to what a trial will be like." He throws down Jordan's statement and picks up another. "This is from Abigail Wentworth. Apparently you two were dating until you hurt her. Question: 'How do you feel about Reed?' Answer: 'He hurt me. He hurt me really bad.'"

"I never touched her," I say hotly.

"Question: 'How did he hurt you?' Answer: 'I can't talk about it. It's too painful.'"

I explode from the chair, but Grier's relentless.

"'Interview was cut short because subject was distraught and could not be consoled. We will need to follow up.'"

I grab the back of the chair and squeeze it hard. "I broke

up with her. We dated until I wasn't feeling it anymore and then I broke it off. I didn't hurt her physically. If I hurt her feelings, I'm sorry about that, but she must not be too sad because she fucked my brother last month."

Grier's left eyebrow pops up again. I feel the urge to pin him down and shave that fucker off.

"Great. The jury will love to hear about your deviant brothers."

"What about them?"

He rattles more pages at me. "I have about ten statements here that say two of them date one girl."

"What does that have to do with anything?"

"It shows the kind of household you're living in. It shows that you're a kid of privilege who is in constant trouble. Your father cleans up your messes by paying people off."

"I break jaws, not women."

"You're the only person on the video surveillance entering the building the night Brooke Davidson died. That's opportunity. She was pregnant—"

"And the baby wasn't mine," I protest. "It was Dad's."

"Yes, but you were still having sex with her, as Dinah O'Halloran will testify to. That's motive. Your DNA is under her fingernails, suggesting that she fought you off. The bandage on your side was newly applied that night. You have a history of physical violence, particularly when a woman in your life is verbally maligned. Your family is, if I can quote Ms. Carrington, without shame or morals. It's not a stretch that you would kill someone if you felt threatened. That's means. Finally, you have no alibi."

When I was four or five, Gideon pushed me into the pool.

At the time, I hadn't really learned how to swim, which is dangerous when you live on the shore. I was fighting Mom about getting into the water, so Gideon up and threw me into the pool. The water rushed over my head and into my ears. I thrashed around like a helpless, dumb fish on dry land, thinking I would never get to the top. I probably would've grown up afraid of the water had Gideon not hauled me out and pushed me back in again and again and again until I learned that the water wasn't going to kill me. But I still remember the fear and can taste the desperation.

That's how I'm feeling now. Afraid and desperate. A cold sweat breaks out at the back of my neck as Greer picks up the last page.

"This is a plea deal," he says quietly, as if he senses just how much he's rattled me. "I worked it out with the prosecutor this morning. You plead to involuntary manslaughter. The sentence is for twenty years."

This time when I clutch the chair, it's not out of rage but helplessness.

"The prosecutor will recommend ten years. And if you're good, no fights, no altercations of any kind, you could be out in five."

My throat is dry and my tongue feels three sizes too big. I have to force the words out. "And if I don't plead?"

"There are about fifteen states in the union that have abolished the death penalty." He pauses. "North Carolina isn't one of them."

CHAPTER 24

ELLA

Steve and I have just finished eating dinner when my phone buzzes with a text from Reed. It takes all my willpower not to snatch up the phone and read what it says, but I know I can't do that in front of Steve. He has no idea that I spent Friday night (and most of Saturday afternoon) in bed with Reed, and I'm not about to tip him off.

"Are you going to check that?" Steve asks as he sets down his napkin. There isn't a trace of food left on his plate. In the week I've lived with him, I've discovered that Steve is a voracious eater.

"Later," I answer absently. "It's probably just Val."

He nods. "She's a nice girl."

I don't think he and Val have ever exchanged more than ten words, but if he approves of her, I'll take it. God knows he doesn't approve of Reed.

My gaze darts to my phone again. Willpower. I need willpower.

But I'm *dying* to know what the message says. I didn't see Reed at school today, not even at lunch. I know he was there, because his suspension is over and I caught a glimpse of him on the practice field this morning. I think he might be avoiding me, but I have no idea why. When I asked Easton about it, he just shrugged and said, "Playoffs."

As if that explains why Reed hasn't called or texted me since Saturday night. I get that the team is focused on winning the championship, but Reed's never let football distract him from our relationship before.

Some tiny, insecure part of me wonders if maybe he didn't enjoy the sex as much as I did. But that *can't* be true. I know when a guy is into me—and Reed was very, very, very into me this weekend.

So it must be something else. It has to be.

"Mind if I go to my room?" I blurt out, then curse myself for sounding so eager to get away.

Lately, things with Steve have been…okay. He still doesn't want me seeing Reed, but I think he's happy I'm part of the dance team now, and he's been really nice to me since I got back from Gibson. I don't want to threaten this fragile trust we're building by revealing that I'm lying to him about Reed.

"Homework?" he asks with a chuckle.

"Tons," I lie. "And it's all due tomorrow."

"All right, have at it. I'll be upstairs if you need me."

I try to look as casual as possible as I walk away. It isn't until I reach the hallway that I start sprinting. In my room, I devour the sight of my phone screen.

Can I see u 2nite?

My pulse instantly races. God. Yes. I totally want to see him tonight. Not just because I miss him, but because I want to know why he's been avoiding me.

However, Steve's rules are clear when it comes to Reed. Meaning, I can't see Reed outside of school. Ever.

Yes! But how? S won't let me come ovr. And my curfew is 10.

Reed's response makes my eyebrows soar.

I've already worked it out. Tell him u have a date 2nite.

Confused, I hurry into the bathroom and blast all the faucets before pulling up Reed's number. Hopefully the running water will muffle my voice if Steve happens to walk past my room.

"Who do I have a date with?" I hiss after Reed picks up.

"Wade," he answers. "But don't worry, it's not a real date."

My forehead crinkles. "So you want me to tell Steve I'm going out with Wade tonight?"

"Yeah. It can't be an issue, right? I mean, he said you're not allowed to date *me*. Not that you're not allowed to date *anybody*."

True. "Okay," I say slowly, wondering how I can swing this. "Maybe I'll play up the reverse psychology thing?"

Reed snickers.

"No, seriously, it's genius. I'll tell him that somebody else asked me out, and how I really, really don't want to go because I'm not over you, yada yada." I grin to my reflection in the bathroom mirror. "I bet he'll beg *me* to go out with Wade."

"That's evil. I love it." Reed chuckles again. "Text me if it's a go. Wade can pick you up at seven. He'll sneak you in here and then drop you back at the hotel before curfew."

"What's in it for Wade?" I ask suspiciously. When Reed hesitates, I know I'm right to be distrustful. "Oh no—what did you promise him?"

"Val," Reed admits. "I told him you'd talk to her about forgiving him."

I stifle a sigh. "I don't know if that's possible."

"They hooked up this weekend," he points out.

"Yeah, and she was kicking herself for it afterward." Her exact words had been *I'm such a stupid stupid-face!* "She doesn't want to be one of Wade's girl toys."

"She's not," he assures me. "Seriously, I've *never* seen Wade Carlisle go to this much trouble for a chick. He really likes her."

"Are you just saying that so we can see each other tonight?"

"No way. Honest, babe. You know I'd never put your best friend in a situation where she's going to get hurt. Wade wants to make it right. He feels like shit for the way he treated her."

I lean against the vanity and tuck a strand of hair behind my ear. "Let me call her and see if she's willing to talk to him. If she says no, then we have to respect her wishes." Even if it means that Wade backs out tonight. But I'm hoping he'll still help us even if Val isn't part of the equation.

Reed's tone turns serious. "Try to make it happen, babe. I…" There's a pause. "I really need to see you."

An alarm bell goes off in my head as we hang up. Is he breaking up with me?

No, of course not. That's crazy.

But then why did he sound so upset just now? And why didn't he try to track me down at school today?

Pushing aside my fears, I call Val.

VAL AGREES. I'M A BIT shocked by how willing she is to talk to Wade, but I guess maybe she doesn't regret this weekend's hook-up as much as she let on at school earlier.

Now it's just a matter of working on Steve, which I waste no time doing. I wander past the bedroom he's using as his office, purposely walking very, very slowly as I pretend to talk into the phone.

"I'm not ready for that!" I say loudly. "Ugh. I'm hanging up now. Later, Val."

Then I heave the biggest, most exaggerated sigh.

Sure enough, the aggravated sound lures Steve out of his office. "Everything okay?" he asks in concern.

"It's fine," I mutter. "Val is just being crazy."

A smile plays on his lips. "And why's that?"

"She wants me to—" I deliberately cut myself off. Then I grumble. "It's nothing. Forget it. I'm going to the kitchen. I'm thirsty."

Steve chuckles and follows me downstairs, which was what I was hoping for. "You can talk to me, you know. I'm your father—I've got wisdom to dispense. Lots of it."

I roll my eyes. "Now you sound like Val. She was trying to offer me her 'wisdom,' too." I air-quote that.

"I see. What about?"

"It's guy stuff, okay?" I wander toward the fridge to grab a bottle of water. "You don't want to hear it."

His eyes instantly narrow. "You're not seeing Reed anymore?" It's voiced as a question, but we both know he means it as a statement.

"No. That's over." I tighten my jaw. "Thanks to you."

"Ella—"

"Whatever, Steve. I get it. You don't want me seeing Reed. And I'm not. You won, all right?"

He lets out a frustrated breath. "It's not a matter of winning or losing. It's about me wanting to protect you." He braces both hands on the granite countertop. "That boy might go to prison, Ella. That's not something either of us can ignore."

"Whatever," I mumble again. Then I straighten my shoulders and paste on a defiant look. "But me dating the school quarterback? I bet you'd be all over that, right?" I make a noise of disgust. "Of course you would, because it's not Reed."

He blinks. "I don't understand."

"Wade Carlisle asked me to go to a movie tonight," I say darkly. "That's what Val and I were arguing about. She thinks I should go, but I said no."

Steve's forehead gets a deep groove in it. His gaze becomes thoughtful, then shrewd. "You said no," he echoes.

"Yes, I said no!" I slam my water bottle on the counter. "I'm still into Reed, in case you haven't figured it out."

That calculated gleam in his eyes deepens. "Sometimes the best way to get over someone is to go out with someone else."

"Great advice." I shrug. "Too bad I'm not doing that. I'm not interested in Wade Carlisle."

"Why not? He comes from a good family. He's part of a school team." Steve lifts a brow. "He's not being investigated for murder."

He's a man-ho. He's interested in my best friend. He's Reed's best friend.

There are a million reasons why I *shouldn't* go out with Wade, but for Steve's sake, I pretend to consider it. "I guess. But I hardly know him."

"Isn't that the point of a date?" he counters. "To get to know someone?" Steve clasps both hands and laces his fingers together. "I think you should go."

"Since when?" I challenge. "You don't want me dating, remember?"

"No, I don't want you dating Reed," he corrects. "Look, Ella. I love the Royal boys to death—I'm their godfather, for God's sake—but they've been screwed up ever since their mother died. They don't have good heads on their shoulders, and I don't think they're the best influence for you, all right?"

I stare back defiantly.

"And while I don't think you need to be in a serious relationship at your age, I'd rather that you experienced what else was out there before you declared your undying love to Reed Royal," Steve says dryly.

I still don't answer.

"Wade Carlisle… He wants to take you to a movie, you said?"

Reluctantly, I nod.

"Tonight?"

Another nod.

Steve nods back. "As long as you're back by eleven, I'm fine with you going."

Oh, so it's eleven now? Funny how the curfew was *ten* when I was with Reed. *Am* with Reed. We're still together, for Pete's sake. Steve just doesn't know that.

"I don't know…" I feign reluctance again.

"Think about it," he encourages as he edges to the doorway. "If you decide to go, let me know."

I wait until he's out of the room before letting my smile surface. It takes a huge effort not to break out in a happy dance. Instead, I slip my phone out of my pocket and text Reed.

It's a go. Tell W to be here at 7.

CHAPTER 25

ELLA

At seven o'clock sharp, the concierge rings our suite to tell us that Wade Carlisle is here.

"Let him up," Steve says into the phone, then disconnects and appraises the outfit I've chosen for my "date."

I decided to go with a wholesome look, so I'm wearing skinny jeans, a flowy gray sweater, and black boots with no heel. My hair is down and pulled away from my face with two green barrettes. I look nauseatingly cute.

Clearly, Steve approves. "You look great."

"Thanks." I pretend to toy nervously with the hem of my sweater. "I don't know about this date."

"You'll have fun," he says firmly. "It'll be good for you."

A knock on the door has both of us walking toward it. Steve reaches it first and opens it, and we find Wade standing in the doorway with a polite smile on his handsome face.

"Hi," he tells my father. "I'm Wade. I'm here to pick up Ella."

"Steve O'Halloran."

As the two of them shake hands, I can tell Steve is impressed by Wade's clean-cut appearance and classic good looks. They chat about the playoffs for a couple of minutes, and then Wade and I leave the suite while Steve gives me a not-so-discreet thumbs up.

The moment we get into the elevator, I roll my eyes. "He's trying to be such a dad," I say with a sigh.

Wade snickers. "He *is* a dad."

As we ride down to the lobby, I make sure to put at least three feet between me and Wade. For some stupid reason I'm paranoid that Steve might have access to the elevator cameras, so I don't want to do or say anything that might be construed as strange.

But once we're in the safety of Wade's Mercedes, the first thing I do is throw my arms around him. "Thank you *so* much for doing this."

"No prob," he answers. His grin falters slightly. "Did you talk to Val?"

I nod. "She said to call her after you drop me off later."

His expression fills with hope. "Yeah?"

"Yep." I reach over and pat his arm. "Don't blow this, Carlisle. Val is good people."

"I know." He groans in frustration. "I mean, before you started hanging out with her, I always saw her as Jordan's poor cousin, you know?"

My jaw falls open. "Oh my God. That's a terrible thing to say!"

"But it's true." He puts the car into gear and drives away from the curb. "She wasn't on my radar until you moved to town and hooked up with Reed. And then suddenly she's having lunch with us, and…" He shrugs. "She's really cool. And hot."

"Do you seriously like her or is this just a game for you?"

"I like her," he assures me. "For reals."

"Good. Then I repeat, don't blow this."

The rest of the drive passes by quickly. I'm a bundle of excited nerves by the time Wade pulls into the Royals' driveway. I fly out of the Mercedes before it even comes to a stop, which causes Wade to burst out laughing.

"Man, I don't think I've ever seen a chick look this eager to get laid," he says as he joins me on the steps of the Royal castle.

"I'm eager to see my boyfriend," I answer primly. "It has nothing to do with getting laid."

"Uh-huh. Keep telling yourself that."

The front door swings open the moment we reach it, and suddenly I'm in Reed's arms and his face is buried in my neck.

I jerk away, nervously glancing around the empty parlor. "Is Callum home?"

"He called to say he's working late tonight," Reed answers, tugging me back toward him.

Our mouths collide and the kiss we share is hot enough to spike the temperature in the parlor. Behind us, Wade moans unhappily.

"Guys! Stop it! I can't believe I'm the one saying this, but get a room."

I release a burst of laughter against Reed's lips and then turn toward Wade. "I thought you were all about PDA," I tease.

He pouts. "Since neither of you let me play, it's no fun."

With his arm still around my waist, Reed reaches his free hand out to slap Wade's palm. "Thanks for making this happen."

"No problem. I'll be back in a couple hours. That enough time?"

No, but it'll have to do. "It's perfect," I tell him. "Now go call Val."

With a cheery salute, Wade speeds out the door. Reed locks it before swinging me up in his arms.

"Where're we going?" I ask, looping my own arms around his neck.

He climbs the stairs two at a time. "Figured we'd watch a movie with Easton."

"Seriously?" My heart falls. I thought for sure we were getting together for happy times.

"Um, no," he replies with a laugh. "I was kidding."

When we reach the landing, he doesn't stop at my bedroom but hauls ass all the way to his. Inside, he drops me to the floor. I wait for him to reach for me, to pull off my shirt, to take his shirt off, but nothing happens.

I look around awkwardly. "Is something wrong?"

"I wanted to talk to you about the case. And, ah, other things," he admits. He clasps his hand around the back of his neck and gives me an unhappy look.

"No fun times?" I say in a small, disappointed voice. It's not that I need to have sex with him, but when I'm in his arms, none of the bad things in our lives exist. It's only us.

"Not yet." He tries to summon up a smile, but it fades fast. I guess he knows that fake grins aren't going to cut it with me. "Sit down?"

There aren't too many options in Reed's room. It's sparse—a boat-sized bed, a dresser, and a small loveseat positioned in front of his big screen. I plant my butt on the bed, wishing I could burrow under the covers until all this blows over.

"The paternity test on Brooke's baby came back," he begins.

My heart stops. Oh no. The bleak look in his eyes tells me this isn't going to be good news, and suddenly I feel sick. There's no way the baby could have been Reed's—

"It was Dad's kid," he finishes.

Both relief and shock slam into me. "What? Seriously?"

Reed nods. "I guess the vasectomy failed."

"Is that even possible?"

"In a few cases, yeah." He shoves his hands in his pockets. "Anyway, Dad took it pretty hard. I mean, he didn't want to be with Brooke, but he would've been there for their kid. I think he's grieving for the baby now that he knows it was his."

My hand flies to cover my heart. That poor man. "I feel so bad for him."

"Me, too. The sad thing is, it doesn't matter who the dad is, because Brooke was still threatening *me* about it, and I'm still the only person with motive. And the only one they have on camera entering the penthouse that night."

I bite my lip. "When did the paternity test results come back?"

"Yesterday."

I scowl at him. "And you didn't tell me until now?"

"I was waiting on Dad. He hasn't even told East and the twins yet. I told you, he's kind of down about it. But I had to tell you. I promised I wouldn't keep secrets anymore, remember?"

A lump forms in my throat. "You were avoiding me all day at school today," I accuse.

Reed lets out a breath. "Yeah. I know. I'm sorry. I was just trying to figure out how to tell you about, uh, the other thing."

Suspicion climbs up my spine. "What other thing?"

"The trial date for my case is set for May," he confesses.

I shoot to my feet. "That's six months away!"

He smiles grimly. "Grier says it's my constitutional right to have a speedy trial."

My stomach heaves. "Tell me Callum's guys have found something. They found *me*, for crying out loud."

"Nothing." Reed's expression holds no hope. "They've come up empty." He pauses. "Grier says I might not win."

I'm beginning to hate every sentence beginning with *Grier says*.

"What now, then?" As hot tears flood my eyes, I keep my gaze pinned to the carpet. I don't want my own torment to be heaped on top of the anguish I hear in his voice.

"He wants me to plead guilty."

I can't stop a moan of pain from escaping. "No."

"It's a twenty-year sentence, but the DA's office will recommend ten. Because of the overcrowding, Grier says I should be out in five. I think I should—"

I fly toward him, covering his mouth with my hand. I don't want him to say it. If he says he's going to take the deal, that he's going to leave me, I won't be able to change his mind. So I jerk his head down and plant my mouth over his, shutting him up in the only way I know how.

His lips part, and I attack him—with my tongue, my hands, everything.

"Ella, stop," he groans against my mouth. But Reed's one weakness, if he has one, is me, and I exploit that vulnerability mercilessly.

My hands are down his pants. Then I'm on my knees, taking his full length into my mouth. Staring up at him, I dare him to stop me now.

He doesn't. He just thrusts deep, groans, then picks me up

and throws me on the bed.

His hand finds me needy and wanting. "Is this what you want?" he growls.

"Yes," I say fiercely, wrapping my legs around his waist. "Show me how much you love me."

Lust sparks in his eyes. He may have wanted to talk, but all of that is shoved onto the backburner now.

When he enters me a moment later, I wait for the pleasure to drive away the sadness, but the pain doesn't recede. It's filling my heart, and even the strength of his body, the comforting weight of his frame against mine, can't completely drive the ache out.

He makes love to me fiercely, almost frantically, as if he thinks it will be the last time we're together. His body hammers into mine. He fills me hard and deep and leaves me breathless. But I'm equally savage. My nails dig into his shoulders. My legs lock around his hips. In some small corner of my brain that is now in control, I feel like if I love him hard enough, long enough, I can keep him with me forever.

And when lightning flashes through my body, when the bliss finally, finally overtakes the pain, I forget why I was angry and let the pleasure rocket through me.

When I fall down from that high, sweaty but not sated, I reach for him again, wanting to stay on this emotional high where only Reed and I exist. But unlike the night of the game, he draws away.

"Ella," he says softly, running a hand over my shirt, which we never bothered to take off. "We can't solve anything by having sex."

Stung by his words, I retort, "Excuse me for wanting to be

close to you."

"Ella—"

I sit up, acutely aware of how naked I am from the waist down. Reaching down beside the bed, I snag my jeans and put them on. "I mean, if you're so eager to get locked up for twenty years, shouldn't I be getting all my sex in now? After that, all I'll have is memories to keep me warm."

Reed bites his lip. "You're going to wait for me?"

I stare at him dumbly. "Of course. What else would I do?" Then it dawns on me. He hasn't thought this through. He hasn't weighed all the repercussions of the plea. Encouraged, I press him. "That's right. We're going to be apart for twenty years."

"Five," he corrects absently.

"Five if we're lucky. Five if the prison system or whoever is in charge thinks you deserve to get out. The sentence is for twenty years, you said. I'll be nearly forty when you get out."

Reed is the first person I've ever really loved besides my mother. Before I met him, a man didn't figure into my future. My experience with Mom's boyfriends led me to believe that I'd be better off. Now I can't envision a future without Reed, but the road ahead of us is depressing, and the crushing loneliness that I lived with for the months following my mom's death hovers over my head.

If I lose Reed, too, I don't know how I'll take it.

Fighting a burst of panic, I kneel beside him on the bed. "Let's go. Right now. We'll get my backpack and we'll get out of here."

His eyes fill with disappointment. "I can't. I love you, Ella, but I already told you—running isn't gonna make this go away for us. It'll be worse if I run. We'll never see my family again.

We'll always be worried that we're going to be caught. I love you," he repeats, "but we can't run."

CHAPTER 26

REED

HALSTON GRIER IS SITTING IN the front room when I get home from school the next day. Last night's date with Ella was so strained, even after the sex, and now I know why.

No matter what we do, the shadow of the case is going to keep hanging over our heads until all this shit is resolved.

"More witness statements?" My question comes out snider than I intend.

Grier and Dad exchange a weighted look before Dad gets to his feet. He grabs my shoulder and pulls me toward him, almost as if he feels the need to give me a hug, but he stops before he can complete the act.

"Whatever you decide, I support," he says gruffly before walking out.

Grier wordlessly points to the couch. He waits until I'm seated before pulling one of those typewritten statements out of the briefcase at his feet.

If I never see another piece of copy paper in my life, I'll die a happy man.

The lawyer reaches forward and hands me the statement.

"Not going to read this one to me?" I say. My eyes skim over the header that declares it's the statement of a Ruby Myers. "Never heard of her before. Is it someone's mom?" I rack my brain for the last name. "There's a Myers who's a junior. I think he plays lacrosse…"

"Just read it."

I settle in, scanning the neatly typed words on the page.

I, Ruby Myers, declare under penalty of perjury, the following is a true and accurate account, to the best of my knowledge:

1. I am over the age of eighteen and competent to testify of my own volition.
2. I reside at 1501 8th Street, Apt. 5B, Bayview, North Carolina.
3. I was called in to serve food at a private catering event at 12 Lakefront Road in Bayview, North Carolina. I got a ride with a friend because my car wasn't working. They told me it was the alternator.

That's my address. I think back to the last time we had servers here. It would've been when Brooke and Dinah came over for dinner. But I can't think of anything that was worth reporting that night. East and Ella found Gideon and Dinah screwing in the bathroom. Is that what this is about? And if so, what does it have to do with my case?

I open my mouth to ask, but the next line catches my eye.

4. After dinner, at approximately 9:05 PM, I was using the bathroom upstairs. I was curious about the house because it was really pretty and I wondered what the rest of it looked like. Dinner was over so I snuck up there, even though I wasn't supposed to. I heard two people talking in one of the bedrooms and peeked inside. It was the second oldest boy, Reed, and the blonde lady who is now dead.

I don't read another word. I set down the two-page affidavit and speak in a calm voice. "This is a lie. I was never upstairs with Brooke that night. The only time she was in my room in the last six months was the night Ella ran."

The lawyer merely moves his shoulders in that maddening, useless way of his. "Ruby Myers is a nice lady who works two jobs to support her children. Her husband left her about five years ago. All of her neighbors say that there's no better single mom in the world than Ruby Myers."

"A woman with values and morals?" I mock, repeating the accusations Jordan Carrington made in her statement. I start to hand the papers back, but Grier won't take them.

"Keep reading."

Unhappily, I scan the rest of the paragraphs.

5. The blonde lady, Brooke, said she missed the boy. I took that to mean that they had been together at one point. He asked her what the hell she was doing in his room and to get out. She pouted a bit and said he never complained about it before.

"She pouted a bit? Who's writing this shit?"

"We encourage affidavits to be written by the witnesses themselves. Makes it sound more authentic if it's in the witness's own voice."

If Grier wasn't supposed to save me, I think I would break his jaw.

> 6. *Brooke claimed she was pregnant, and that Reed was the daddy. He said it wasn't his and good luck with her life. She said she didn't need luck because she had him. He kept telling the lady to get out because his girl was coming home.*

"What's the penalty for perjury?" I demand. "Because none of this happened. We had dinner with Brooke and Dinah around this date, but I never talked to any server."

Grier shrugs again.

I keep reading.

> 7. *The lady wanted his help to arrange a marriage with his daddy. Reed refused and said that she'd be part of this family over his dead body.*
> 8. *I heard a noise and thought I might get caught so I ran downstairs and helped put all the catering dishes and supplies away. Then I got into the van. My friend dropped me off at my house.*

"This is bullshit." I toss the lies onto the coffee table and scrub a hand down my face. "I don't even know this Myers chick. And this conversation she's describing happened between Brooke and me the night Ella left. Everyone else was gone. I don't know how she knows this happened."

"So it happened?"

"I never said that she'd be part of this family over"—I grab the paper and read the exact, lying words—"'over his dead body.'"

"How'd she know what happened, then?"

I try to swallow, but my throat's so dry, it hurts. "I don't know. She must've known Brooke somehow. Can't you track people's cell phones and find out if she and Brooke ever had contact?" I know I'm reaching, but I can feel the walls closing in on me.

"In light of this…" Grier pushes the statement toward me until it's almost falling off the table. "Take the plea deal, Reed. You'll be out by your twenty-third birthday." He tries to smile. "Think of it as a different type of postsecondary education. You can take college courses while you're inside, even get your degree. We'll do everything to make your life comfortable."

"You can't even get me off on a charge I'm innocent of," I snap. "How can I trust you to do anything?"

He reaches down and grabs his briefcase, an expression of disappointment on his face. "I'm giving you the best legal advice there is. A less scrupulous lawyer would take this to trial and bill your father for a hell of a lot more money. I'm advising you to take this plea deal because your defense is not good."

"I'm telling you the truth. I've never lied to you." I clench my jaw since I can't clench my fists.

Grier gazes at me mournfully over the top of his stupid glasses. "Sometimes innocent people go away for a long time. I do believe you, and I think the DA's office might, too, which is why I was able to get the plea deal. Involuntary manslaughter can carry with it a twenty-year sentence. Ten years is very generous. This is the very best deal."

"Does my father know about this?" I nod toward the Ruby Myers statement.

Grier readjusts the briefcase in his hand. "Yes. I gave it to him to read before you arrived."

"I have to think about it," I choke out.

"Delacorte's deal is off the table. There's too much evidence here," Grier adds, as if I would even entertain the Delacorte option. He already knows I won't let Daniel come back to hurt Ella.

The ground is shifting beneath my feet. I'm eighteen and my once limitless world is narrowed down to the choice of five years in prison or rolling the dice and growing old in a tiny cement cell.

"If I—" My throat is raw and I can feel embarrassing hot tears prick at the back of my eyes. I force the words out. "If I take this deal, when do I start my sentence?"

Grier's shoulders sag in relief. "I recommended, and the DA's office seems amenable to this, that you would start your sentence after the first of January. You'd be able to finish out your semester and spend the holidays with your family." He shifts forward, his voice taking on a slight animation. "I think I can get you into a minimum security facility. Those house mostly drug offenders, some white-collar crime, a few sex offenders. It's a very mild crowd." He smiles, as if I should be rewarding him for this great gift.

"I can't wait," I mutter. I stick out my hand, remembering a few manners Mom drilled in me. "Thank you."

"You're welcome." We shake, and he turns to leave, but he pauses at the door. "I know your first instinct is to fight. It's an admirable trait. But this is the one time you need to surrender."

TEN MINUTES LATER, DAD FINDS me in the same spot, rooted to the floor. The enormity of everything is sinking in.

"Reed?" Dad says quietly.

I raise my stricken eyes to him. Dad and I are about the same size. I'm a little heavier than he is because I lift a lot of weights. But I remember when I was a kid, I rode on his shoulders and thought he'd always keep me safe. "What do you think I should do?"

"I don't want you to go to prison, but this isn't like going to Vegas and putting down even a few million at the craps table. Going to trial means we're gambling with your life." He looks as old and as tired and as defeated as I feel.

"I didn't do it." And for the first time, it's important for me to tell him that, for him to believe me.

"I know. I know you never would've hurt her." The side of his mouth quirks up. "No matter how much she might've deserved it."

"Yeah." I tuck my hands in my pockets. "I want to talk to Ella. Do you think Steve's gonna have a problem with that?" If I only have a little time left, I want to spend it with the people I care the most about.

"I'll make it happen." He reaches inside his suit coat to grab his phone. "You want to talk to your brothers? You don't have to. At least, not until you make your decision."

"They deserve to know. But I only want to go through it once, so I'll wait until Ella comes over."

We walk out into the hall, and I have a foot on the first step when a thought occurs to me.

"Are you telling Steve about this mess?" I wave a hand toward the living room, where Grier just dropped a bomb on my life.

Dad shakes his head. "This is Royal information only." He gives me another half-smile. "That's why Ella needs to be here."

"Truth." I take the stairs two at a time, texting Ella when I reach the top.

Dad's gonna make it so u can come over.

Really? :) I feel like I'm under house arrest here. Not to complain or anything but Steve said this hotel suite was 2 small. I thought he was nuts, but after living here for 3 weeks, it feels like a cracker box.

I wonder how big a prison cell is.

I text back, *I hear u.*

My mind starts to race as I think about the plea deal. If I take it, I'll be shoved in a concrete room and kept there for five years. Nearly two thousand days. Can I do it? Would I survive it?

My heart starts pounding so fast I wonder if I'm going to have a heart attack.

I force my fingers back to the phone.

When are u going to be let back in2 the penthouse?

Soon, I hope. G wants me 2 look 4 blackmail stuff. Do u think I shld?

Yeah. If it's not obv.

Damn it, I want to break Dinah and Brooke's hold over my family. Getting rid of this murder charge is a step toward that. I could fight, but what's the point? Grier says my case is hopeless.

I don't want to drag my family through a trial. I don't want a parade of witnesses up there talking about Easton's struggles with gambling, drinking, and drugs, the twins' private life, distorted stories about Gideon and Dinah, me and Brooke and Dad. And then there's Ella's past. She doesn't need to be dragged through the mud again.

Our family has already gone through so much. The prosecutors will rake up the details of Mom's death if I go to trial. Everything we fought so hard to keep behind these closed doors would come spilling out.

I have the ability to stop that from happening. The price of tucking those secrets away is a slice of my freedom. And it isn't long. Five years. *Five if you're lucky.* I can live through that. It's just a fraction of my entire life. What's that worth against the trauma that the trial would inflict on my family?

Nothing.

Yeah, I've made up my mind. This is the right decision. I know it is.

Now I just have to sell it to Ella and my brothers.

ELLA SHOWS UP AN HOUR later. When she breezes through the front door, my heart feels immediately lighter. I barely have time to brace myself before she throws herself at me. After planting a long, dick-raising kiss on my lips, she wriggles out of my arms.

"Gosh, you feel like a block of ice." She pinches my bare arm. "Put some clothes on."

"Thought you liked it when I was naked," I counter, forcing a light note into my voice. "I think you once said it was a crime for me to wear shirts."

She wrinkles her nose but doesn't deny it. "What do you think Callum said to Steve? Steve told me I could come right over and he didn't even make a fuss. Maybe he's coming around?"

She's smiling so brightly, thinking I have good news for her. I don't want to tell her, but I have no choice. This is her future, too.

"Come on." I grab her hand and tug her up the stairs. "Let's go to your room."

I march down to my brothers' rooms. Knocking on their doors, I yell, "Ella's here."

My brothers pop out of their rooms immediately.

"Little sis!"

Pangs of jealousy curl in my stomach as I watch Easton wrap Ella up in a big hug before passing her off to Sawyer and Seb. But the closeness they all share with her is a good thing. Especially for East.

I turn my back and walk into Ella's room, forcing myself to quash my negative feelings. They'll need each other after I'm gone. I can't be angry about this.

I'm the one who put myself in this situation when I decided to sleep with Brooke. And then I made stupid decision after stupid decision. The *what if* game will probably drive me insane in prison. *What if* I'd flown to D.C. for dinner with my family? *What if* I hadn't answered Brooke's call? *What if* I hadn't gone over there, thinking I could reason with Brooke?

It was my own damn pride that got me into this.

I wait for everyone to walk in before I start. "I wanted to give you guys an update on the case."

My brothers perk up. I know they're starving for details. But Ella... She's frowning deeply at me.

"Is this about...?" She trails off, glancing at my brothers

and back at me. She's obviously not sure if I've told them about the plea offer yet.

I nod. "Yeah. And there's another new development."

Slowly, I go through the statements that I've read so many times I can recite them by heart. I offer only the highlights and leave out the stuff about Easton and the twins' relationship with Lauren and focus on the crap the police have compiled against me, finishing with the statement from Ruby Myers.

Ella grows paler and paler with each passing minute.

"That's an incredible amount of bullshit," East declares once I'm done.

"If Brooke was still alive, I'd kill her myself," Ella mutters darkly.

"Don't say that," I chide.

"We should fill out our own statements," she suggests.

"Yeah." East nods. "Because that shit with that waitress never happened."

Seb and Sawyer join the chorus, swearing that they'll testify, too. I realize I have to put a stop to this before their bedroom lawyering gets out of hand.

"I'm going to take a plea deal," I announce.

Easton's jaw drops. "What the fuck!"

He and the twins stare at me as if I've gone crazy, but I can't take my eyes off Ella, whose face is full of fear.

"You can't," she protests. "What about the Delacorte deal?"

East perks up. "What's that?"

Ella starts talking before I can shut the idea down. "Judge Delacorte offered to lose evidence if Daniel gets to come back from juvie military jail and if I agree to say I lied about the drugging." She crosses her arms. "I say we do that."

"Yeah," Seb agrees. Sawyer nods excitedly.

"Not happening. Ever." I glare at my brothers until they turn their hopeful expressions to the floor.

Ella holds up her hands, mimicking the scales of justice. "You going to prison for twenty-five years, or me living with Daniel." Her left hand drops down and her eyes burn angrily at me. "Take the Delacorte deal."

"Even if I was remotely okay with that, which I'm not, there's too much evidence to get rid of. There is no Delacorte deal anymore," I say through clenched teeth. "They have no one else to pin this on. Grier says they have me on means, motive, and opportunity, which is all they need to convict me of a crime."

"You're not pleading guilty, Reed." Her tone is harder than steel.

I swallow hard. Then I lock my gaze to hers and say, "Yes. I am."

CHAPTER 27

ELLA

My emotions are all mixed up right now. I hate Reed for thinking I'd ever be okay with his stupid plea deal, but I love him for wanting to make this whole mess go away. I know that's why he's not fighting this. He's decided that he needs to save his family from a stain on their reputation.

I get it, but I hate it.

"For the record, I'm not on board with this plan," Easton tells the room.

"Same," the twins say in unison.

Reed nods at them. "Noted. But it's happening whether you like it or not."

Bitterness jams in my throat. Well, I guess that's the Royal decree. And to hell with what anyone else thinks about it, right?

A soft tap on the doorframe has our heads turning. "Everything okay in here?" Callum asks, his tone oddly gentle.

Nobody says a word.

He sighs. "I assume Reed's told you about the deal?"

Easton frowns at his father. "And you're cool with it?"

"No, but it's your brother's decision. I'm going to support him no matter what." Callum's stern eyes imply that we should all be doing the same thing, supporting Reed.

"Can I have a moment alone with Reed?" I ask tightly.

At first, nobody moves, but then they notice the look on my face, and whatever they see spurs them into action.

"Come on, boys, let's go down to the kitchen and rummage up some dinner," Callum tells his sons. Before he leaves the room, he glances my way. "Oh, and Ella, I've already arranged it with Steve that you can spend the night here. I'm sending Durand over to your hotel to pick up your uniform."

"Steve was okay with that?" I say in surprise.

"I didn't give him much of a choice." With a wry smile, Callum ducks out of the room and closes the door behind him.

Once I'm alone with Reed, it's impossible to contain my anger anymore.

"This is crazy! You didn't kill her! Why would you ever, ever, *ever* say you did!"

He slowly sits down beside me. "This is the best option, baby. Five years in prison isn't the end of the world. But the alternative? Going to prison for the rest of my *life*? That *is* the end of the world. I can't take that chance."

"But you're innocent. You can go to trial and—"

"Lose," he finishes flatly. "I'll lose."

"You don't know that."

"The statement from Ruby Myers is too damaging. She's going to tell a jury that I threatened to kill Brooke." He sounds frustrated. "I don't know why that woman is lying about me, but her testimony will put me away."

"Then let's prove she's lying," I say desperately.

"How?" His voice is low, defeated. "She signed an affidavit." Reed takes my hand and squeezes it tight. "This is happening, Ella. I'm taking the deal. I know you don't like it, but I really need you to support me on this."

Never.

Out loud, I only manage a weak croak. "I don't want to lose you."

"You won't. It's only five years. It'll fly by, just watch." He hesitates suddenly, raking one hand through his dark hair. "Unless…"

I narrow my eyes. "Unless what?"

"Unless you've changed your mind about waiting for me," he says sadly.

I gape at him now. "Are you kidding me?"

"I wouldn't blame you." His fingers tighten through mine. "And I don't expect you to, either. If you want to break up, I'd totally underst—"

I cut him off with a kiss. A furious, incredulous kiss. "I'm not breaking up with you," I hiss angrily. "So erase that thought from your stupid head, Reed Royal."

Rather than answer, he yanks me toward him again, his mouth locking with mine. His broad body pushes me onto the bed as he kisses me so deeply that it sucks all the breath from my lungs.

His hands are down my pants. Mine are busy tugging at his shirt. His lips break away from mine for the second that it takes to pull his T-shirt over his head. Then that mouth is back on mine. His hand reaches between my legs. I rock my lower body against the hard, hot length of him.

We sink into the mattress, his body pressing against me.

My shirt comes off. A thigh nudges its way between my legs as his mouth finds my breasts, lavishing attention on the aching tips. A light tug of his teeth has me arching off the bed and crying his name.

"Reed, please."

He licks lower, taking away that exquisite pressure to give a different kind of kiss—one that drives me mad with need until I'm splintering into a thousand different pieces. Then he surges to his knees and grabs a condom from the nightstand. In my dazed state, I hadn't even been thinking about that, but he is. Reed's not the destroyer. He's never destroyed anything in his life; he's always been the protector, even at this moment when he battles his own lust for control.

I reach between us and guide him between my legs. The broad head pierces my body, but there's no pain this time. Sweat dots his brow as his body shakes with the effort to let me set the pace. Slowly, tenderly, desperately, he pushes into me over and over until the friction builds into a bomb of pleasure that explodes once again.

Afterward, he buries his head in my neck. "I love you, baby. I love you so damn much."

"I love you, too." I'm glad he's not looking at me, because I can't stop the tears from filling my eyes. I clutch him to me, wrapping myself around him as if I can keep him there, safe with me forever.

He wakes me up twice more during the night to tell me with his mouth and hands and body how much he loves me, how desperately he needs me, how he can't live without me. I say the same things right back, until we're both too exhausted to keep our eyes open.

But I don't know if either of us believes anything we're saying at this point. We're just a tangle of wild, hopeless emotions trying to find peace with our bodies. No matter how hard we try to forget, we can't.

Because Reed's going to prison and it feels like death.

In the morning, Reed and Easton take me to school. I run through dance practice listlessly, because most of my attention is pinned on the other side of the gym, where the football players are lifting weights. I stare at Reed's back until Jordan finally snaps at me.

"I know your felon boyfriend is over there, but can you try to keep your attention on the team for one measly second?"

"Why am I even here?" I snap back. "Layla isn't injured anymore." I point to the senior, who's taping her ankle.

Jordan purses her lips and places her hands on her tiny waist. "Because you agreed to join the team, not hang out for a weekend on an away game."

"I don't give two shits about your team!"

A group of girls behind me gasp, and I instantly regret losing my temper. Truth is, I *do* care about the team. It might have started off as a deal with Satan, but I loved every second of performing at the away game. I'm even willing to put up with Jordan if it means getting to do what I love the most.

But it's too late. My outburst causes Jordan's eyes to blaze.

"Then get out," she orders, jerking her arm in the direction of the locker rooms. "You're officially off the team."

"Fine by me." The lie burns my throat on the way out, but

there's no way I'm letting Jordan see how devastated I am. So I just pick up my water bottle and march across the gym.

Only when I enter the locker room do I allow my emotions to surface. Tears sting my eyes. I want to punch myself for lashing out at Jordan. She deserves a good lashing, usually, but not when it comes to the dance team. She's actually not a bad captain, and from what I've seen, she only ever does what's best for the team. Yelling at her was such a mistake. Now there's no way she'll let me come back.

Reed catches me at my locker before class, his heated gaze searching my face. "What was that all about at practice? Jordan say something to you?" He's all worked up, ready to defend me.

I give his biceps a weak pat of assurance. "No, it was all me," I admit. "I snapped at her, and she kicked me off the team."

Reed sighs. "Aw, baby. I'm sorry."

"Whatever," I lie again. "It's no biggie. It was just supposed to be a one-time thing anyway."

I grab my books and slam the locker shut.

"All right then." He slides a hand under my hair until his fingers curl around my neck. "See you at lunch?"

"Yup. I'll save you a seat. Or we can share one—I'll just sit on your lap."

Reed's response is to bend down and kiss me so thoroughly that I forget my spat with Jordan, that we're not supposed to have any physical contact at school, and my worries about the future. I might even forget my name for a few seconds.

When he finally lifts his mouth from mine, I'm glassy-eyed and shaken. Then I realize that the bells ringing in my head are the school alerts. Classes are about to start.

"You look gorgeous right now." He leans forward and

whispers in my ear. "I hear conjugal visits are real hot."

Immediately, my gooey mood hardens to displeasure. "Don't say stuff like that."

His expression goes serious. "I'm sorry, but—"

"You should be."

"—if I can't joke about it, then I'm probably gonna cry about it, and that's not an option."

He looks so miserable that I feel bad for snapping at him. God, I'm just losing my cool all over the place this morning.

But I just...I refuse to accept that Reed is going to prison. I can't let that happen.

I *can't*.

SINCE I NO LONGER HAVE dance practice after school, I'm free to pursue what I call Operation Justice. I bring Val along, not just because I need the backup, but because I'm hoping if we're trapped in a car together, she'll finally tell me what's going on with her and Wade. I know they met up to talk, but she hasn't given me any details about it.

"So how was the talk with Wade?" I demand as I drive out of the school lot.

"Fascinating."

Her tone is off. I tilt my head and study her. "I can't tell if you're being sarcastic."

"I am. And I'm not." She sighs. "He said all the right things, but I don't know if..."

"If you believe him?" I finish.

"Yeah. Or if I'm willing to even go there with him. Like, to the relationship zone."

"Is it because you're not over Tam yet?"

"No, I think I'm over Tam. I'm just not sure I'm ready to be…*under* Wade."

We both snort.

"Do you want me to stop asking about it? Because I'll shut up. But if you want to talk, I'm here." Thinking about Val's problems is kind of a relief from my own.

"No, I don't want you to stop asking about it. I just don't think Wade and I are in the right headspace for each other. He's fun and all, but he's *all* about fun. I can't get anywhere with him." She gives me a slight smile, this time actually looking at me so I can see her bemused expression.

"I think Wade has hidden depths but maybe is afraid to show them?" I suggest.

"Maybe." She sounds dubious.

"Are you going to Winter Formal with him? Reed said he asked you."

She grimaces. "No. I'm staying home. I hate Winter Formal."

"Is it that bad? Everyone at Astor acts like it's the best thing ever."

"This is the South. Any time you can get dressed up and parade around, it's going to be celebrated."

"But not by you?"

"Nope. I hate that stuff. Is Steve letting you go with Reed?"

"Um, I doubt it. I haven't talked to him about it, but I don't think he'll be on board with it at all. Besides, I don't even have a dress. You never told me I'd need one for this."

We share a grin. When we first met, Val told me I needed dresses for every event from weddings to funerals, but not a dress for a school dance. "You'll need to get on that," she says.

"Mmm," is all the enthusiasm I can muster up. Dancing, dresses, and parties hold no interest for me right now, not until I find evidence to get Reed out of this mess. I am *not* going to let an innocent guy go to prison. The rest of the Royals might be down for that, but not me.

Ten minutes later, I pull up at the curb in front of a low-rise building in the city. I kill the engine and glance at Val. "Ready?"

"Remind me why we're here again?"

"I need to talk to someone."

"And you can't call them?"

"I don't think she'll answer my calls," I admit, shifting my attention out the window.

All of the statements Reed told us about are essentially true—or some variation of the truth. But Reed insists that this one isn't. Plus, none of us ever remember seeing this server upstairs. So I decided to seek her out. I want her to tell this lie to my face.

"This place looks sketchy," Val observes, leaning across the console to look out my window at the sprawling apartment complex.

She's right. All the buildings look tired and worn. The cement sidewalk is cracked and buckling. Weeds creep up the chain link fencing that encloses the parking lot in the center of the buildings. But I've lived in far worse conditions than this.

"Do you think I should knock on the door or wait for her to come out?" I ask.

"Do you know what she looks like?"

"Yeah, she was part of the catering staff that came to the

house once. I'd recognize her if I saw her."

"Then let's wait. If she's not going to answer the phone, I can't see her opening the door to you."

"Good point." I tap my fingers against the wheel impatiently.

"You ever think Reed did it?" Val says quietly after a few minutes.

"Yeah, I think about that." All the time.

"And?"

"I don't care." And then, because I want Val to be clear on this, I abandon my stakeout for a second. "I don't think he did it, but if it was an accident and they got in a fight where she fell and hit her head, then I don't see why Reed should be punished for that. Maybe that makes me a terrible person, but I'm Team Reed."

Val smiles and reaches out to cover my hand with hers. "For the record, I'm Team Reed, too."

"Thank you." I squeeze her hand and turn back to the window in time to see the door to apartment 5B swing open. "There she is!"

I scramble out of the car, nearly taking a header on the pavement in my haste.

"Ms. Myers," I call out.

The petite, dark-haired woman stops, just inside the fence. "Yeah?"

"I'm Ella Harper."

To my relief, her face registers no recognition. I straighten my blazer—one that I ruined by ripping the Astor Park badge off in hopes that it makes me look like a journalist. "I'm a reporter for *The Bayview News*. Do you have a minute?"

Immediately, a shield falls over her face. "No. I'm busy."

She turns away, but I yell her name sharply. "Ruby Myers, I'd like to ask you a few questions about the statement you gave in the Davidson murder."

I can only see the side of her face, but it's pale and stricken. Suspicion spikes through me.

"I-I got nothing to say," she stutters, then puts her head down and rushes to a vehicle parked three spaces away.

I can only watch as she climbs in and speeds out of the parking lot.

"Did you see that?" Val demands.

I turn to find her at my elbow. "What? That I suck as an investigator?" I want to stomp my foot on the ground like a spoiled kid. "I couldn't even get one answer out of her."

"No. Did you see what she was driving?"

"God, not you, too. Reed was hassling me about not knowing the difference between a truck and a car. It was an SUV?"

"That's a Lincoln Navigator and it runs about sixty grand. This one still has the showroom shine, it's so new. You said she was a catering waitress, right? You're telling me she just found a bunch of money?"

"You think someone paid her to lie about Reed?"

"Maybe?"

I think it over for a beat, then hiss out a breath. "There's only one person who really has anything to gain by pinning this on Reed."

"Who?"

I lock eyes with Val. "My stepmother."

CHAPTER 28

ELLA

AFTER I DROP VAL OFF at home, I immediately speed back to the hotel. It takes me all of two seconds to find Dinah. She's lounging on the sofa when I storm in, her eyes glazed and her hair slightly mussed up.

"Where's Steve?" I demand, glancing around. If I'm going to confront Dinah about possibly paying off Ruby Myers, then I don't want an audience. Steve will just antagonize her, and then she'll clam up.

Dinah lifts one shoulder, her barely-there nightgown sliding halfway down her slender arm. "Who knows? Probably buying a sixteen-year-old hooker down at the wharf. He likes them young, you know. I'm surprised he hasn't crawled into your bed yet."

Disgust fills my throat. "Do you do anything but sit on your ass all day?"

"Why, yes. I shop. I go to the gym. Sometimes I fuck your stepbrother, Gideon." She laughs drunkenly.

I loom over the couch, my arms crossed, but a part of me

is hesitating. My plan was to come out and confront her about Myers, but I don't know how to start. How would she have paid Myers off? Cash, right? I wonder if Steve would let me look at their bank withdrawals. Or does she carry around a bunch of cash?

Instead of accusing her right off the bat, I decide to use a different approach. Drunk people have lower inhibitions. Maybe I can squeeze some information out of her without her knowing I'm even doing it.

So I sit on the opposite end of the couch and wait for her to keep talking.

"How was dance practice? You don't look very sweaty."

I shrug. "That's because I quit."

"Ha!" she exclaims way too loudly. She points a shaky finger in my direction. "I told Steve that you joined just so you could sleep with your boyfriend."

I give another shrug. "What do you care what I do with Reed?"

"I don't. I just enjoy making the Royals miserable. Your unhappiness is a little extra something special."

"Nice," I say sarcastically.

"Nice gets you nowhere," she snarls. But then her whole face crumples, and for the first time since I walked in, I notice that besides smelling like a brewery, her eyes are rimmed with red.

"Are you okay?" I ask uneasily.

"No, I'm not okay," Dinah snaps, except this time her voice shakes a little. "I miss Brooke. I really miss her. Why did she have to be so greedy and stupid?"

I swallow my shock. I can't believe she's the one who's bringing it up! Okay, this is perfect. I sneak a hand into my pocket and fiddle with my phone. Do I have a recording app? Can I get Dinah to say something incriminating?

"What do you mean?"

Dinah's eyes take on a faraway glimmer. "She said you were like us. Are you?"

"No," I blurt out, and immediately regret it. Damn it. I should've said yes.

But Dinah seems too lost in her own world to notice my disagreement. "You need to be careful of those Royals. They'll take you in and then stab you in the back."

I watch my words this time. "How so?"

"It happened to me."

Was this before or after you slept with Gideon? Before or after you decided to take down the Royals?

"How?" I ask instead.

She fiddles with one of the heavy rocks on her fingers. "I knew Maria Royal. She was the queen in Bayview. Everyone loved her, but no one saw how sad she was. I did, though."

I frown. Where is she going with this?

"I told her I knew where she'd come from and how lonely it could be when you weren't born into these circles. I was being friendly," Dinah mutters. "But did she appreciate that?"

"No?"

"No, she certainly did not." Dinah slams a hand on the coffee table, and I flinch in surprise. "The Royals are like the apple in the fairy tale. Golden on the outside, but rotten to the core. Maria didn't come from money. She was poor trash from the wharf who opened her legs at the right time to the right man—Callum Royal. Once she was pregnant, he had to marry her. But Maria wasn't satisfied with Callum's devotion.

She always wanted more, and woe to any woman who stood in her way of total domination over the males in her circle. She was a manipulative bitch who enjoyed playing both sides of the table. To the women, she was spiteful and cruel, running others down constantly. To the men, she was nothing but sweet words and compliments."

Wow. This is a side of Maria Royal I'd never heard about. Reed and his brothers remember her as a saint. But then the comments Steve made when he dragged me out of school pop up in my head.

No living person is a saint.

On the other hand, Dinah isn't exactly the most trustworthy person. And she probably paid someone off to send Reed to jail. I'd be stupid to believe anything she says.

Besides, even if Maria *was* a bitch, Dinah's obsession with the Royals still doesn't make sense. "You and Brooke had it in for the Royals and Steve because Maria Royal was rude to you at one time?" I ask in disbelief.

She sighs heavily. "No, honey. Maria Royal represents every other rich bitch around here. You've encountered these types at school. They're the kind who believe their own shit doesn't stink."

Like Jordan Carrington. I guess in some ways, Dinah's lecture isn't completely crazy. Except the difference between us is that I don't give a crap about Jordan while Dinah obviously cared a lot about Maria's opinion.

"And the one time I tried to reach out to her, she slapped me down. Called me a whore and said I was nothing like her."

"I'm sorry."

It doesn't come out sincere enough, because Dinah starts

to cry. Big, fat tears roll down her face as she sobs. "No, you're not. You don't get it. You still think the Royals are wonderful. The only person who understood was Brooke, and she's gone. She's gone."

It's the perfect opening, so I take it. "Did you kill Brooke because she was trying to horn in on your piece of the pie?"

"No, damn you, I didn't kill her." Anger drips from Dinah's tone. "Your precious Reed did."

"He did not," I answer between clenched teeth.

"Keep telling yourself that, sweetie."

I face her mocking gaze head on. "Did you pay Ruby Myers to say that Reed threatened to kill Brooke? Did you?"

Dinah smiles. A cold, humorless smile. "And what if I did? How will you prove it?"

"Her financial records. Callum's investigators will find out the truth."

"Will they?" She releases a short, angry laugh, her hand snaking out to grab my chin. "The Royal resources won't buy Reed's freedom. I'm going to do whatever it takes to see that piece of murderous shit in prison, even if it's the last thing I do."

I slap her hand away and jump off the couch. "You're not going to pin this on Reed!" I spit out. "I'm going to prove that you paid off Ruby Myers. And maybe I'll even prove that you killed Brooke."

"Go ahead, Princess. You're not going to find anything on me." She tosses back her booze and then refills her glass.

Sick of her smug, awful face, I hurry off to my room and slam the door. The moment I'm calm enough to hold my phone without dropping it, I call Reed.

"What's up?" he asks.

"I went to Ruby Myers' house and—"

"*What?*"

He yells so loud that I have to pull the phone away from my ear.

"Are you kidding me? What are you trying to do? Get yourself killed?"

"You and I both know her statement is a lie," I shoot back. Then, lowering my voice to a whisper, I say, "Dinah is up to her ears in this. She virtually admitted to buying Myers off."

"Ella, dammit, stay out of this. Dad has investigators crawling all over this case and we haven't been able to turn up new information. If Dinah's involved, then you poking a hornet's nest is only gonna get you hurt. I can't have you hurt."

"I can't just sit around." I stomp over to the window and yank the curtains open. Housekeeping always shuts them for some stupid reason.

Reed sighs. "Look, I know. I know it's tough for you. But you just gotta accept that this is the right thing for all of us. If I accept the plea deal, it goes away. Instead of a year of uncertainty and then a few more years of appeals with all our dirty laundry parading across the front page, we get it over and done with." More quietly, he adds, "It's not gonna last that long."

Tears well up in my eyes. "It's not right. And I don't want you gone for even a day."

"I know, baby."

But does he? There's aloofness in his voice, as if he's already putting distance between us. A little desperately, I say, "I love you."

"I love you, too." His voice is rough and low and gravelly. "Let's not fight. Let's try to put this aside and enjoy the time that I'm still here. Before you know it, I'll be back." He pauses. "It's going to be okay."

But I just don't believe him.

THE NEXT DAY, I TRY to act as if nothing awful is happening in our lives. As if Reed didn't just announce he's going to prison for a minimum of five years. As if my heart isn't breaking every time I look at him.

He's right in one sense. If we spend the next five weeks or so dwelling on the horrible future, he might as well start his sentence today.

So I go through the motions at school, acting like nothing's wrong, but by the time the final bell rings, I'm exhausted from all that pretending and more than ready to go home.

I'm halfway across the parking lot when a sharp voice calls my name.

Instantly, I go stiffer than a board. Great. Jordan.

"We need to talk," she says from about ten yards away.

I try to get the car door open, but Jordan's at my side before I can escape. I turn around with a sigh. "What do you want?"

An evil gleam lights her gaze. "I'm calling in the favor."

Every muscle in my body coils tight. Crap. I was really, really hoping she'd forget all about that. But I should've known better than to think that Jordan Carrington forgets anything, especially when it's to her advantage.

"All right." I fake a smile. "So who am I duct-taping to the school doors?"

She rolls her eyes. "Like I'd get an amateur to do my dirty

work." With a wave of her manicured hand, she says, "I think you're going to like this favor, actually. It requires almost little effort on your part."

Suspicion trickles down my spine. "What do you want?" I repeat.

Jordan gives me a big, broad smile. "Reed Royal."

CHAPTER 29

ELLA

It takes a few seconds for Jordan's words to sink in. Once they do, I can't stop a loud burst of laughter. She wants Reed? Um, yeah. Not happening, bitch.

"I'm not sure what that even means, but either way, Reed's not on the table," I say cheerfully. "So you should probably come up with something else."

She cocks a brow. "It's this or nothing."

I grin. "Then I pick nothing."

Jordan laughs at that. Or maybe she's just laughing at me. "Sorry, did I say *nothing*? I meant, if you don't uphold your end of the bargain, then 'nothing' is what your social life will be. As in, I'll tell your father all about how you lied to him about the dance team so you could bang your boyfriend at a hotel. I'm pretty sure you'll be grounded for life after he finds out." She bats her eyelashes. "Or maybe he'll pick up and move you to another state. Actually, maybe I'll recommend that to him. I'll even give him some brochures for really good prep schools upstate."

Damn her. That's totally something Steve would do, force me to transfer schools. If he finds out I lied about the away game and spent the night with Reed, he'll lose his shit.

"So," she says, her smile returning. "Should I tell you the details?"

"What do you want with Reed?" I ask through clenched teeth.

"I want him to take me to Winter Formal."

My jaw falls open. Is she freaking serious?

Jordan rolls her eyes at my shock. "What? It's not like *you* can go with him, unless your dad is suddenly on board with you dating a killer?"

I stare at her. "What happened to your whole speech about *you* not wanting to be with a killer?"

She shrugs. "I changed my mind."

"Yeah? And why's that?" I mutter.

"Because Reed's star has never shone brighter." She flips her dark, glossy hair over one shoulder. "When he was first arrested, his social status plummeted, but now he's all these pathetic chicks can talk about. Unlike your trashy ass, the social hierarchy matters to me." She shrugs again. "I want to go to the formal with Reed. That's the favor."

A disbelieving laugh pops out. "I'm not lending you my boyfriend for a night!"

Frustration darkens her eyes. "He's a trophy, dumbass. Don't you get that?"

Reed's not a trophy! I want to shout. He's a human being. He's smart and gorgeous and sweet when he allows himself to drop his tough-guy act. And he's *mine*. This girl is insane if she thinks I'm going to say yes to this.

Jordan sighs when she sees my immovable expression. "I'll tell you what—how about I throw in a spot on the dance team?"

"What the hell does that mean?"

"It means I'm letting you rejoin the team," she answers in exasperation. "God, are you fucking dense? We both know you didn't want to quit—you were just being a bitch for no reason. So you can come back if you want."

I falter. I did really enjoy my time on that stupid team.

"And I won't even ask for another favor," she says with an overly bright smile. "All I want is Reed on my arm at Winter Formal."

That's *all* she wants? Gee, she's asking for *so* little. Not.

I plant my hands on my hips. "And then what?"

"What do you mean?"

"What happens after the dance? Do you think he's going to be your boyfriend or something? Because he won't."

Jordan snorts. "Who wants a boyfriend who's going to be in jail for the rest of his life? I want Snowflake Queen. That's it."

"Snowflake Queen?" I echo blankly.

"Everyone at Winter Formal votes for a king and queen. Like homecoming." She flips her hair over her shoulder. "I want to be queen."

Of course she does.

"I mean, I'm already a lock for it, but going with Reed will seal the deal. A bunch of people are talking about voting for him because they feel sorry for him."

Astor Prep kids are weird as hell. I study her face. "If I agree to this, we'll be even?"

"Even Steven," she chirps.

Swallowing my irritation, I fling open the car door and

flop onto the driver's seat.

"Well?" Jordan hovers at the side of the convertible, her expression expectant.

"I'll think about it," I spit out. Then I start the engine so I can drown out the sound of her laughter.

REED

WHEN I GET HOME FROM practice, I find Ella curled up on her bed, wearing what looks like a pair of my old sweatpants and a tiny, tiny tank top. I'm surprised to see her.

"Steve know you're here?" I ask warily.

She nods. "I told him I needed to study for a chem test with Easton." Her chemistry book is beside her, but Easton is nowhere to be found.

I grin. "Do you actually need to study or was that an excuse?"

"No, I really do have to study," she answers glumly. "But we both know your dumb brother isn't going to help me. I figured if I studied here, at least I could see you. Steve's downstairs, though, so we need to be quiet."

I walk over to the bed to give her a quick kiss. "Let me change into sweats and then I'll help you. I took Chem last year, so I remember all the work."

Before I can duck into the bathroom, she sits up and says, "Wait. I need to tell you something."

My gaze sweeps over her barely there tank top. Knowing I'm only going to have a few more weeks with Ella makes the fire burn hotter every time I lay eyes on her. "Can you tell me while your shirt is off?"

She grins. "No."

"Fine. Be that way." I hop up on the bed and roll onto my back, folding my fingers across my abdomen. "What is it?"

She clears her throat. "You need to take Jordan to Winter Formal."

I bolt upright. "Are you nuts?" I stare at her in astonishment. "I didn't know we were even going. I thought we'd do something else. Just the two of us." I freaking hate Winter Formal.

"I thought everyone went." Ella tosses her phone toward me. "See?"

I pick it up and see Astor Park's Instagram feed, which is full of pictures of the Winter Formal preparations. The school's obsessed with this dance, and I've been grateful for that, because it's taken some of the heat off of Ella and my brothers over my case.

"The girls go because it's the social event of the semester. The guys go so that they can get laid afterward," I say bluntly.

"Nice. Well, you don't have to sleep with Jordan after the dance. The bargain was for you to take her to the party and nothing else."

"Bargain?" I'm losing my train of thought because Ella's shirt is riding up and I can see a sliver of skin above her waist.

"For me being on the dance team and going to the away game."

I swallow a groan. "So this is what you promised her? That I'd take her to Winter Formal?"

"No, it was just a debt to be called in later."

"Why does she want to go with me? I thought she hated me."

"I don't think she hates you. I think it's some kind of weird notoriety thing. You go with her and she gets to parade you around like a dog on her leash. The beauty and the beast sort of thing."

"She's the beast, right?"

Ella responds by tweaking one of my nipples. Which hurts, dammit.

"Oh, and she wants to be crowned Snowflake Queen or some shit," Ella adds. "She thinks going with you will up her chances."

I grab her fingers and drag them to my mouth. "I don't want to go to a dance with Jordan. If I go, you're holding the leash."

"I'm not a leash holder."

I place her hand at the base of my neck. "I belong to you. Everyone at Astor knows that."

She turns an adorable shade of pink. "I belong to you, too. But I made a deal."

"Why are you even paying off this debt? No one's holding you to it."

Her fingers trace my collarbone, sending a buzzing sensation down my spine. "Because a deal's a deal. I always keep my word."

"Deals with the devil don't count."

"If you don't do it, then she's going to tell Steve I lied about the away game," Ella admits, pulling her hand away. "And she said she'll try to convince him to send me to another school. Maybe even out of state."

The school thing, I could handle, especially since I won't even be around after January. But another state? No way. That means Ella wouldn't be able to visit me. Plus, my brothers need her and she needs them. This is her family. She doesn't deserve to be separated from them.

Still, I can totally see Steve doing something drastic like that. Ever since my dad told him about the plea deal, Steve's been better about letting Ella spend time here, but he doesn't want us dating. He's made that more than clear. If he finds out I took her virginity at the away game? He'll freaking kill me.

Ella sits up and swings a leg over my waist. "You have to do it, Reed. Please?"

One thing I've learned about Ella is that if she sets her mind to something, there's no moving her. She's that stubborn. She's going to fulfill her end of the deal with Jordan no matter what the cost, and this cost isn't that terrible, I guess.

I grab her hips and hold her still. "Are there any details to this deal? What does she expect from me?"

Ella picks up her phone and checks her text messages. "She said you have to wear something. Can't remember what it is."

"Did you already agree to this before you even asked me?" I demand.

"No, I swear. I just told her I'm okay with it if you are." Ella's hands drop to my chest. Her hips start moving.

My eyes flutter shut, but I hear myself respond, "We always wear tuxes. What the hell else would she want me to wear?" Another thought pops into my head. I snap my eyes open. "Are you planning to go, too, or are you leaving me at Jordan's mercy?"

"Aw, I'd never abandon you like that. I thought I'd go with Wade. Val's not going, so I can keep an eye on him."

Oh hell, no. I don't like this plan at all. "Wade can't keep his dick in his pants," I growl.

"I know. Why do you think Val's not going?"

"So I'm supposed to go with the she-demon, and you're going to hang out with a guy whose mission is to bang every available chick along the Atlantic coast?"

"Give your friend more credit," Ella chides. "Wade knows better than to hit on me."

"He better," I say sullenly.

She leans down to kiss me, but pulls back before I can slip her some tongue. "So you'll do it?"

"Yeah, I'll do it," I grumble. "Even though I still can't believe you'd be okay with me going to a dance with *Jordan*."

"Hey, at least it's not with Abby," she grumbles back. "I can handle you going with Jordan because I know you hate her, but Abby would bother me a lot."

"Because she's my ex?"

"Because she's your ex."

"But she's my *ex*. Meaning, I no longer want to go out with her, haven't wanted to go out with her for a long time, and do not intend to go out with her in the future. That kind of ex."

Ella makes a growly sound. "She better stay that way."

A chuckle escapes. "I like jealous Ella." Something else occurs to me. Winter Formal is in two days and this is the first time Ella's even brought it up. "Do you have a dress?"

"Can't I buy one at the mall?"

"Oh, babe. You still haven't learned, huh?" I lift her off my aching dick and set her on the side of the bed. I stalk over to the dresser and fish out a sweatshirt for her. "Put this on. We'll talk to my dad."

"Right now? The stores are all closed."

She stands there without moving, so I shove the sweatshirt over her head. "Winter Formal is like a prom on steroids.

These chicks spend more money on their dresses than some folks spend on a car." I shove her arms into the sleeves and roll them up. "I don't want you to have a hard time that night."

"Jeez, Val was right. You guys really do have a special dress for everything. Where should I get the dress, then, if not the mall? You know, where many, many dresses are on sale?"

"I don't know where you buy it, but Dad probably will."

Downstairs, we find Dad and Steve in the study. The two men are bent over some papers that look like a flight plan.

"Got a minute?" I ask, knocking on the door.

Steve glowers at the sight of Ella in my clothes.

"Nothing happened," I feel compelled to mutter. "We were talking about Winter Formal and Ella said she doesn't have a dress."

"So the two of you are attending Winter Formal together?" Dad asks, peering over the papers at the two of us.

"Like hell they are," Steve says stiffly.

Ella glowers at her father. "We're not going together. Reed's taking Jordan Carrington, and I'm going with Wade."

Steve instantly relaxes. "All right."

I hide my displeasure at his obvious relief. "Anyway, Ella needs a dress," I mutter.

"Is this really a big deal?" she says in irritation. "I've got dresses."

"I don't know," Dad says slowly, "but I chaperoned the formal a few years back and I remember seeing a lot of designer dresses. If Reed is telling me you need a dress, then I suppose you do." He rubs his chin and then turns to Steve. "You dated that one woman…Patty, Peggy—"

"Perri Mendez?" Steve supplies. "Yes, she owned the

Bayview Boutique."

"She still does. I saw her at the Chamber of Commerce dinner a few weeks ago. Let's see if she can make something happen." Dad gestures for Ella to come to the desk. "Sit down and look at Perri's website. Find a dress you like, and we'll get it for you."

Ella takes a seat. "What am I looking for?"

"As fancy as you can find," I recommend. "This is pageant country."

She clicks through a series of photos, then stops on a page. "I like this one."

I can't see which one she's talking about, because her hand is blocking the screen.

"Save the picture and I'll send it to Perri," Dad tells her.

"Thanks."

"Told you Dad would handle it," I say with a grin.

She rises from the chair, and the two of us edge back toward the door, only to halt when Steve's sharp voice pierces the air.

"Where are you two going?"

"Just up to my room. Don't worry, Easton is already there," Ella says, her feet already across the threshold.

Steve frowns. "Keep the door open. Your new boyfriend wouldn't like it if he knew you were hanging around Reed so much."

Dad gets a frustrated look on his face while I glance at Ella in confusion. *New boyfriend?* What in the world is she telling Steve?

Ella drags me upstairs, explaining as we go. "Steve thinks Wade is my new boyfriend because he took me out on the fake date. And I guess now that we're going to the dance together, we're an official couple."

"You're not a couple," I remind her.

"Duh."

Once we're alone, I waste no time ridding her of her sweatshirt and kissing her, reminding her with my mouth exactly who she's going out with.

"We didn't leave the door open," she murmurs.

"I know," I say into her breasts. "Want me to stop?"

"Hell, no."

We get about five minutes of fooling around before Easton bursts in.

"I didn't interrupt anything, did I?" he asks, completely unrepentant. "I heard I'm watching television with you."

Ella throws a pillow at his face, but moves over to make room for him. I flick the TV remote. As the screen flickers on, my girl tucks herself under my arm.

I don't have much time before I go to prison. Spending even one night with Jordan isn't how I want to use that precious time, but I'll just have to suck it up. For Ella's sake.

Because my goal for the weeks we have left is to make Ella Harper happy every second of every day.

CHAPTER 30

ELLA

On Friday night, Steve drives me over to the Royals', grumbling the entire time. "In my day, the boy drove to the girl's house. He didn't drive to his best friend's house to pick up the girl."

"It was easier than Wade driving all the way to the city to get me," I answer with a shrug. That, and I really wanted to get a sneak peek of Reed in his tux. But I keep that to myself.

As we roll through the Royal gates, I can't help but think about what my life is like now versus when I first arrived. A few months ago, I was stripping at a seedy club called Daddy G's. Today, I'm sitting in some ridiculously expensive car, wearing a dress that Val told me must have cost more than one year of tuition at Astor Park and shoes that have brand name crystals glued all over them. Val pronounced the name of the crystal maker three times and I still can't get the hang of it. I look like a real-life Cinderella complete with the ball gown and glass slippers. I'm not sure if the fairy godmother in this situation is Callum or Steve, though.

Steve maneuvers the sports car around the fountain in the courtyard. I throw open the door as soon as we pull up to the front steps, but the car is so darn low that it's hard for me to get out, what with the hundred layers of chiffon.

Steve chuckles. "Hold on. I'll come pull you out."

He lifts me up and sets me on my four-inch stilettos.

"What do you think?" I ask, holding out my arms.

"You look beautiful."

I find myself blushing at the compliment. It's so surreal to think that this is actually my father staring at me with this awed kind of pride.

He takes my arm and helps me up the wide steps. The moment we walk inside, I see Reed descending the staircase. He looks so good in his black tuxedo that I have to stop myself from drooling.

"Hey, Reed. You look nice," I say blandly, because Steve is standing right beside me.

"You look nice, too," he answers in an equally indifferent voice. But his heated gaze says otherwise.

"I'll be in Callum's study," Steve tells us. "Ella, come get me when your date arrives."

He disappears down the hall, which surprises me since I know he doesn't like it when I'm alone with Reed. And he has a reason not to like it. The moment he's gone, Reed bends down and presses his mouth on my neck. He lays a searing kiss at my pulse point that has my knees buckling.

Then he backs me up against the wall and continues his exploration of all the skin conveniently exposed by the strapless sweetheart neckline. My hands fall onto the crisp cotton of his dress shirt. The idea of stripping him out of his clothes grows more appealing by the second. Unfortunately, the sound of an engine roaring outside pops that balloon.

At the honk of the horn, Reed lifts his head from my upper chest reluctantly. "Your date's here."

"No kiss on the lips?" I smile, trying to catch my breath.

His thumb presses at the corner of my mouth. "Didn't want to mess up your lipstick."

"Mess away," I invite.

His lips curve up. "There's so much more of your body I'd like to have my mouth on right now." His hand falls to the top of my breast, still damp from his kisses. I gasp as one long finger slides under the tightly corseted bodice to swipe across my nipple.

"Hey man, are you mauling my date?" Wade demands as he bursts through the front doors without knocking.

Reed sighs, removes his hand and rocks back on his heels. "I'm expressing my appreciation for my girlfriend's rocking bod."

I take a deep, calming breath before turning to face Wade. Thankfully, the bodice of my dress is thick enough that my excited state doesn't show through the silk. "If you're my date, you better have brought me an awesome floral arrangement. Someone told me you can tell the size of a guy's dick based on the amount of flowers he buys."

Wade stops short, his eyes falling to the long white box in his hands. "Really? They say that?"

Reed and Wade exchange alarmed glances, and I nearly die laughing at them.

"You're an evil woman." Wade marches past me without even handing me the box.

We all turn at the sound of footsteps on the stairs. Easton and the twins appear, each clad in his own tux.

Sawyer nods when he sees me and Wade. "Finally. Let's get this show on the road. We need to pick up Lauren."

Everyone marches out the door, with Easton and me taking up the rear. Smiling, he reaches out and flicks my skirt. "I thought you'd go for something slinky and sexy."

"I've worn slutty clothes for a long time. I've never done princess." I shake out the dress, which I fell in love with the moment I removed it from the box. The bare shoulders give me all the sexy I need, but even if it were high-necked and long-sleeved, I'd still be obsessed with the full skirt and the thousands of layers of chiffon that swish around my legs as I walk.

Easton grins. "You're always doing the opposite of what anyone expects. The girls will be killing themselves."

"I'm just doing what I want. They should, too." I didn't choose the dress because I wanted to tweak anyone's noses at Astor. I picked this one because it looked like a dream—and if this is the only Winter Formal I'll ever be attending with Reed, even though he isn't technically my date, I wanted to wear the most beautiful gown on the earth.

"Doesn't matter. If you wore a tight dress, they'd call you a slut, and now they're going to call you something else, but I'm going to take care of you while Reed's away."

Easton's declaration makes me feel warm inside. Not because I need watching over, but because I sense he's growing up a little. In a burst of insight, I realize that Easton needs someone to watch over and take care of. I'm not going to be that person, but until he finds her, we can watch out for each other.

"And I'll take care of you, too," I promise.

"Deal."

We shake on it.

Steve and Callum wander outside just as we reach the courtyard. "You kids taking off now?" Callum calls.

"Yup," Easton answers.

Wade stops by Steve's Bugatti. He smooths a hand above the hood, not daring to lay his palm on the steel. "I think you should let me drive this, Mr. O'Halloran. For your daughter's sake."

"I think you should stop breathing on my two-million-dollar vehicle, Mr. Carlisle, and take my daughter to the dance."

Holy mother of Mary. I gape at my father. "Two million?" I echo.

All of the men look at me like I'm ridiculous for asking, but they're the ridiculous ones. Two million bucks for a car? These people have way too much money.

"It was worth a shot." Grinning, Wade jogs to his own sports car and holds open the door for me. "Your chariot awaits."

"Hey listen," Wade says fifteen minutes later, as we idle behind a long line of cars waiting to turn into the country club. "I want you to know that you can come to me if you have any problems."

I frown. "What do you mean?"

"Next semester," he clarifies. "After, ah, Reed's gone."

"What problems do you anticipate me having? Like if I forget a tampon, will you have extras in your locker?"

His head jerks around. "Reed keeps tampons in his locker for you?"

"No, you dumbass, but that's about how stupid your statement is. I can take care of myself." His words remind me eerily of Easton's, though, and a note of suspicion strikes me. "Did Reed put you up to this?"

Wade looks out the window. "Did Reed put me up to what?"

"Don't play dumb."

His shoulders sag. "Okay, maybe."

"Is he going to dictate instructions from his prison cell like some mafia don?"

Reed's over-protectiveness will probably only get worse when he can't see me every day. I guess it should make me feel suffocated, and for some girls, maybe it would—but for me, it's comforting. I'm not going to let him control my life, but I don't mind the gesture.

"I dunno. Maybe?" Wade seems unbothered by this. He shifts and slides a sly glance in my direction. "So…conjugal visits?"

I roll my eyes. "What is it with you guys and conjugal visits?"

"Dunno," he says again. "Seems kinky." His eyes become unfocused as he engages in some fantasy regarding jail cells and sex games.

And because I don't want to sit next to Wade while he's playing some porno in his head, I ask, "Speaking of kinky, what's up with you and Val?"

His lips tighten into a rigid line.

"Cat got your tongue?" I taunt, but his mouth stays glued shut.

He'll talk about anything but Val, huh? Very, very interesting.

"Fine, don't talk, but just know that Val's an awesome girl. Don't play with her." It's not an overt threat, but Wade should know me by now. I'll hurt him if he hurts her.

"Is that what you think?" he bursts out. "That *I'm* the problem? Women," he mutters and then adds something under his breath that I can't make out.

I raise my eyebrows, but he turns up the music, and I drop the subject because his outburst is answer enough.

By the time we make the turn into the Bayview Country Club property, Wade's natural good humor has resurfaced. He loses his stiffness, and his characteristic easy smile is back on his face. "Sorry I snapped at you. Val and I are…complicated."

"I'm sorry I pried. I just love Val and want her to be happy."

"How about me?" he says in mock offense. "Do you want me to be happy?"

"Of course." I reach out and squeeze his hand. "I want everyone to be happy."

"Even Jordan?"

"Especially her," I tell him as he pulls up in front of the club's entrance. "If she's happy, I think she'd be less of a terror."

He snorts in disagreement. "Doubtful. She feeds off the fear and unhappiness of others."

The valet opens my door before I can respond, but Wade's assessment is depressingly correct. Jordan does seem to be happiest when everyone around her is miserable.

"Be careful. It's my baby," Wade tells the valet as he tosses his keys over. Then he pats the hood and winks at me. "Cars are less complicated than women."

"Can't have a conjugal visit with a car," I remind him.

He snickers. "Good point."

I haven't been to the country club before, so I don't know what it looks like when it's not decked out in the Astor Prep blue and gold, but it's pretty tonight. Wide swaths of white fabric hang from the center and outward, making the room look like a huge, luxurious tent. Along the white fabric hang tiny Christmas lights. Decorating the room are round tables covered with pristine white tablecloths and chairs wearing giant, shiny blue-and-gold ribbons. But despite the long line of cars outside, the room is surprisingly empty.

"Where is everyone?" I ask my date.

"You'll see," Wade says cryptically, leading me to a table at the entry.

Behind the table, a man and a woman dressed in black suits rise as we approach. "Welcome to the Astor Park Prep Winter Formal," chirps the lady. "Name, please?"

"Wade Carlisle and Ella—" He stops and looks at me questioningly. "Royal? Harper? O'Halloran?"

"I have an Ella Harper." The woman holds out a silk bag and a mini bottle of sparkling cider with my name on it.

"What's this?" I ask slowly.

Wade grabs everything and moves me away from the table so the couple behind us can get their goodies. He tucks the bottles in one pocket and the silk bags in the other. "You're given five hundred dollars' worth of chips to play in here."

"Here" ends up being a room filled with felt-covered gaming tables and so many people that I feel a bit suffocated. The girls are beautifully dressed, most of them wearing slinky gowns with slits up the side. The guys are wearing black tuxes.

It looks like a movie set.

"I wish Val was here," I whisper.

I think Wade says, "Me, too," but I'm not completely sure.

"So I use the chips to play these games?" I wave a hand toward the casino tables, trying to take both our minds off our missing friend.

"Yep, and then you bid on stuff."

We wander in. There are two tables—one where kids are playing poker and another where they're playing blackjack. "What kind of stuff?"

"Trips, jewelry, experiences."

"Who pays for it?"

"It's all donated. But your chips are paid for by a parent or guardian, I guess."

"Is this why there's no dancing?" Deeper in the room, I see a table full of purses, envelopes, and baskets. It looks like a raffle table at a bingo hall, only much nicer.

"There's dancing in the dinner area."

I vaguely recall a small open square in the middle of the tables. "But that space is so small."

"No one dances."

Well, duh. Who wants to dance when you could gamble? "When did this start?"

"Maybe ten years ago?" Wade slaps the hands of one of the football players as we pass by. "None of the guys danced, and a huge number of them just stopped coming altogether, so some smarty set this casino thing up. Boom, boys were back in town."

We stop in front of a table. The items range from purses to jewelry to placards with the words *Aspen* and *Las Vegas* and *Puerto Vallarta* written on them. Those must be the experiences Wade referenced. "None of these is five hundred," I tell him, pointing to the bolded numbers on the bottom of each explanation sheet.

"Right, well, you're supposed to win the chips and then your date's supposed to give you his."

"That's not sexist," I mutter under my breath.

Wade snorts. "Astor Prep's not real enlightened. You're just figuring that out?"

I wonder if this is why Val didn't come. On top of the dress, there's the added cost of buying five hundred dollars' worth of chips to buy what I presume to be worthless stuff. "Sucks if you're a scholarship student."

Wade frowns. "You don't have to play."

I turn to inspect the room. "I don't see Liam Hunter here, either. Isn't he a scholarship student like Val?"

"Huh." Wade's eyes widen as the realization sinks in of who exactly attends these charity dances.

The whole setup reeks of rich kids keeping the poor kids out, and some of the magical gauze that covers the place is torn away.

Impatiently, I check the door. "Where's Reed?" Everything's more tolerable when he's around. Only if he has his way, he won't be around much longer.

I shove that depressing thought aside.

Wade shrugs. "He'll be late. Jordan likes to make an entrance."

CHAPTER 31

REED

"You're late," Jordan snaps as she throws open the mansion's door.

I check my watch. "A whole minute late," I answer, rolling my eyes. And even though her sharp tone scrapes across my nerves, this devil's bargain Ella made was so fucking worth it. It's not going to kill me to be civil. "Are you ready to go?" I ask politely.

Jordan's gaze rakes over me. "Where's your gold tie?"

That's not the question I expected. I peer down at the black one hanging down my front. "I don't think I own a gold tie."

Her eyes narrow into thin strips. "Part of the deal is that you wear a gold tie to match my dress."

I follow her hand as she Vanna Whites it down her body, which is wrapped in what looks like gold tissue. Really thin gold tissue. Holy hell, are her nipples visible? I try not to stare, but it's not easy.

I catch a glimpse of Jordan's smug face as I avert my eyes. "Like what you see?"

"Your tits? Every girl's got a pair, Jordan."

Her smirk turns to a sneer. "Tell Ella the deal's off and she still owes me."

The door starts to close on my face. I slap my hand on the wood frame and push my way in. *Be nice, Reed. It's not going to kill you to be nice to this chick.*

"You look nice," I manage to grind out.

"Ahh, there you go." The demon pats my arm, and it takes a lot of effort on my part not to flinch. "Was that so hard?"

Yes. Really hard. And I don't want to be touched by her or any other girl whose name isn't Ella Harper. But I don't say that to Jordan. Instead I repeat my question. "Are you ready?"

Considering she was mad that I was late, I expect her to say yes, but she doesn't. "We're not going until you put on a gold tie."

For fuck's sake. What the hell is wrong with this girl? "I don't have one, and even if I did, I'm not driving twenty minutes to get it. Get your purse or whatever else you need and let's go."

She lifts her chin. "No, we're taking pictures first. Mom," she yells. "Reed Royal is here. We're ready for pictures."

Pinching the bridge of my nose, I pray for patience. I'm not standing around like a mannequin so that Jordan can memorialize this farce of a date. "I didn't sign up for pictures. I'm here to take you to the dance. That's the deal."

"The deal is what I say it is," Jordan hisses.

"We both know Ella's the only person who would actually honor this deal. The rest of Astor would tell you to go fuck yourself." Including me, but I'm trying to keep my nose clean, so I try to keep the insults to a minimum. "I'm here. I'm willing to take you to the dance. I'll sit with you during dinner and give you my bag of chips to buy whatever the hell you want. But that's it. We can either keep arguing for the next two hours or we can haul ass to the party. We might even make it in time for dinner if we move."

"I deserve a picture," she insists.

As if on cue, Mrs. Carrington pops around the corner with Mr. Carrington, who's carrying a camera.

I sigh. If I don't give in, my guess is we're going to be here all night. "Fine. Take your picture and let's go."

"Five pictures."

"One."

Her mother's face is a picture of confusion. "Well, perhaps we could take a few by the mantle," she suggests quietly.

"We'll start there," Jordan agrees.

"Just a couple ground rules," I murmur so I don't embarrass her in front of her parents. They're already wondering what in the hell is going on. "We're not kissing, hugging, or doing couple shit in this photo."

"You'll put your arms around me and you're going to like it," she snipes and then grabs my sleeve to haul me snug up to her side.

Calmly, I pull the fine wool out of her grasp. "Be careful. Tom Ford isn't cheap." The tux is custom fit. Every year, we get a new one. Dad's a big believer in dressing for the occasion.

"Are you ready?" Mrs. Carrington asks, gesturing for her husband to come forward with the camera.

After a little maneuvering where Jordan tries to grind her ass against my dick and I try to avoid even our clothes coming into contact, the pictures are taken and we're at the door.

Mark Carrington clears his throat loudly as we're about

to leave. "Mr. Royal, I don't approve of my daughter's choice of dates given your current situation, but I also want her to be happy."

"Dad," Jordan protests.

Her father ignores her and looks me square in the eye. I respect that.

"Don't worry," I assure him. "She'll be home by ten."

I duck out the door and jog down the steps, with Jordan huffing her displeasure behind me.

"The party doesn't end until midnight, asshole."

I hold the car door open for her. "Too bad I told your dad you'd be home earlier, then."

"And then there's the after party," she says between clenched teeth.

I wait for her to get her legs inside the truck and stare off into the distance. The skirt on her dress is so short that her panties would show, and it's not something I care to see.

"I signed up for one Winter Formal," I retort as I slam the door.

"Are you going to be like this the whole night?" Jordan demands as I settle into the driver's seat.

"Yup."

"That's not within the spirit of the deal."

"Your deal is with Ella, not me. I'm doing the bare minimum here."

"You're the worst. You and that trash deserve each other."

I slam on the brakes halfway down the driveway. My efforts at being nice have their limit and they stop at any insults toward Ella. "Call her trash and the date is off. I'll haul you out of the Rover and leave you on the side of the road."

"You would not," she says indignantly.

"I so would." In fact, I'd love to do it.

"You should be grateful I'm even being seen with you."

"Really? If it wasn't for you, I'd be with Ella right now."

"Just..." She sputters. "Just drive."

Some small part of her must realize I'm nearing the end of my rope. I release the brake and ease into traffic. It's ten to seven. I wonder if dinner's been served yet. Has Wade won any chips for Ella? He's kind of a shit poker player. Ella's probably not very good, either. Her face is too expressive. And Easton's too undisciplined.

I press harder on the gas.

The country club gates never looked so welcoming. When I pull up, the valet's so bored by the lack of traffic, he's almost sleeping. At the slamming of my car door, he jerks to his feet and runs over to help Jordan out. She must be giving him a good view of her crotch given the way his eyes bulge out of his face.

When we walk inside, the front table is abandoned.

"I can't believe no one's here to give me my chips," Jordan exclaims.

Before she can make a scene, I reach over the table, find a box and pull two sacks of chips out. Shoving them into her hands, I say, "Here."

Then I push her, none too gently, toward the casino doors. Heads turn as she enters, which is probably just what she intended, because her shoulders straighten and her face gets this weird satisfied expression.

My eyes scan the room looking for Ella. I spot her laughing in the far corner as Wade whispers something in her ear. Two other football players, McDonald Samson and Greg Angelis, hover to her left. Despite my designated role as Jordan's date, the gravitational pull to be next to Ella is irresistible.

I leave Jordan standing at the entrance, basking in the attention of her classmates, to join the most beautiful girl in the room. The moment Ella sees me, she breaks away from the group, a smile filling her entire face.

I feel better already.

"Am I imagining things or can I see Jordan's tits in that dress?" Greg squints toward my date.

"Why don't you go check it out up close?" I suggest, sliding an arm around Ella's waist. It'd be nice if everyone would go the hell away so I could be alone with my girl. I only have so much freedom left and I don't want to spend it with anyone but Ella and my brothers.

I drop a light kiss on her lips. Anything more heated and I'm bound to drag her off to the nearest dark corner, lift that pretty skirt of hers, and do at least six of the million dirty things that run through my mind every time I touch her.

"Aren't you supposed to be Jordan's date?" Ella says.

"Don't remind me. I brought her, didn't I?" But as I look into my girlfriend's stubborn face, I realize I'm not going to weasel out of this at all.

Wade gives me a sympathetic look. "How about we go play poker?"

With relief, I take him up on the offer. "That I can do."

Before we can find an empty table, Rachel Cohen—Wade's mid-day fuck buddy—comes by, decked out in a slinky red dress with cutouts at the side. "Wade, sweetie! I've missed you!" The pretty brunette flips his tie with her finger and smiles devilishly. "You want to find a quiet place to, um, catch up?"

And we all watch with astonishment as the guy who never says no stares down at his feet. Awkwardly, he shifts from one foot to the other as he struggles to find some way to let this poor girl down easy. "I can't right now, honey. I'm about to play some poker."

"Aw, okay. We can meet up later, then?" Rachel is apparently a dim bulb and doesn't catch the signal.

Wade casts a silent plea for help in our direction.

Only Ella responds. "Oh, Rachel, I think I see Easton struggling with his cards."

The brunette perks up. "Really? I was with him earlier and he said he didn't need any help."

"He's embarrassed. Tell him that I sent you." Ella pats Rachel on the back.

"Okay," the girl says happily. She takes a couple of steps and then turns back. "If you want to join us later, I'm cool with that. See ya, Wade."

We wait for a few seconds before turning on my buddy.

"Seriously?" McDonald exclaims. "That chick just threw herself at you and you said no? You lose your balls or something?"

Wade scowls. "No. I just wasn't in the mood."

"Dude, you're always in the mood," McDonald says.

Greg and I nod in agreement, but Ella is smiling broadly at Wade, as if she knows something we don't. I guess it's about Val? I kind of figured Wade was over that already, though.

"Fuck. Whatever." Wade grabs Ella's arm. "Baby, I'm your date tonight and I'm not abandoning you." He drags Ella toward a nearby table, calling over his shoulder, "You losers coming or what?"

"I'M OUT," I TELL WADE a bit later as I lose the last of my chips at one of the poker tables.

He frowns. "You only played a hundred bucks."

"I gave the rest to Jordan."

He grunts. "Is it worth it? Being shackled to her all night?"

"Who's shackled? I haven't seen her in an hour."

It turns out my date might have a gambling addiction, because she hasn't moved from the craps table since we got here. Not that I'm complaining. The less time I spend with her, the better.

"And even if she was glued to my side, yeah, it's worth it," I admit. Making love to Ella for the first time was the best night of my life. It's an event I'll replay every night for the five or so years I'm in my lonely cell. "If you wouldn't do that for Val, then maybe she's not the one for you."

"I'm eighteen, dude. Since when do I have to find the one?" Wade frowns at his cards, and I don't think it's because he has a bad hand. He's falling for Val and struggling with it.

I leave him alone because this is something he needs to deal with on his own. I guess eighteen is kind of young to be tying yourself to someone permanently, but I can't imagine my future without Ella in it.

I just hope she feels the same way, especially since we'll be separated for the next five years. Is she going to wait for me? I know it's selfish to ask, but is it too selfish?

"You okay?" the object of my thoughts, the subject of all my desires, whispers in my ear.

I guess I'm frowning as hard as Wade. "Yeah, I'm fine. I spaced out for a moment there."

Ella squeezes my shoulder. "Okay, well, I'm going to hang

with Lauren for a bit. You know, since technically I'm not your date and your actual date is glaring big holes in my back."

Ella's only gone five seconds when someone softly taps my shoulder. I turn around to find Abby Wentworth standing there.

My chest instinctively softens at the sight of her pale pink dress and flowing white-blonde hair. What had drawn me to Abby was how gentle and delicate she is. She reminded me so much of my mom, and being around her was...comforting.

But now that I'm with a girl who's so full of fire, I don't think I could ever go back to one with the strength of a puff of steam.

And especially not a girl who would say all that shit about me to the cops.

The reminder has me stiffening. "What's up?" I mutter to my ex.

"Can we talk?" Even her voice is delicate. Everything about Abby is so damn fragile.

"Got nothing to say to you," I grunt, drawing startled glances from my friends. They're all aware that I've always had a soft spot for this girl. But not anymore. The only thing I feel for Abby now is pity.

"Please?" she begs.

I get up only because I don't want to embarrass her in front of everyone, but the moment we're out of earshot, I pin her with an angry scowl.

"You told the cops I *hurt* you," I hiss out.

Abby's pale blue eyes widen. "Oh. I-I..." She visibly swallows and then her expression collapses. "You did hurt me!" she moans. "You broke my heart!"

Frustration bubbles up inside me. "For fuck's sake, Abby,

this is my *life* we're talking about. I read your statement. You implied that I physically abused you and we both know that's a goddamn lie."

Another anguished moan rips out of her throat. "I'm s-sorry. I know it looks bad, but I swear to you I'll go back and give another statement and make it clear that you never—"

"Don't bother," I snap. "I don't want you to say another word, you hear me? You've already done enough."

She flinches as if I've hit her. "Reed," she whispers. "I…I really miss you, okay? I miss us."

Oh shit. Discomfort wedges into every crevice in my chest. What the hell do I even say to that? We broke up more than a year ago.

"Everything okay here?"

Saved by Satan.

I've never been more relieved to see Jordan Carrington in my life, and maybe that's why I lay a hand on my date's arm as if she's *actually* my date.

"Everything's fine," I say tersely.

But Abby viciously shakes her head. For the first time since I've known her, pure anger blazes in her eyes. "Everything is *not* fine!" she snaps at Jordan, and it's also the first time I've ever heard her raise her voice. "I can't believe you came with him tonight! How could you, Jordan?"

Her friend doesn't even blink. "I already explained why I—"

"Because of your stupid *image?*" Abby is seething, her cheeks redder than apples. "Because you want to be crowned the queen of some stupid dance? I told you I didn't want you to go with him, and you totally ignored my feelings! What kind of friend does that? And who cares about your stupid social status!" She's shrieking now, and nearly the whole room is staring at us. "I was with Reed because I love him, not because it helped my reputation!"

Again, Jordan is unfazed. "You're making a scene, Abigail."

"*I don't care!*"

We all cringe at the deafening pitch of her voice.

"You don't deserve him!" Abby yells between panted breaths. "And neither do *you!*"

It takes me a second to realize that Ella is at my other side.

"Why did you have to move here?" Abby growls at Ella. "Reed and I were doing fine before you got here! And then *you* showed up in your cheap clothes and your trashy makeup and your...your...*whore* ways—"

Jordan snickers.

"—and you ruined everything! I *hate* you." Her desperate, furious gaze swings back to me. "And I hate you, too, Reed Royal. I hope you rot in jail for the rest of your stupid life!"

Abby finishes in a breathless rush.

Silence has fallen over the room. Every pair of eyes is glued to my unhinged ex-girlfriend. When she realizes it, she releases a horrified gasp and slaps a hand over her mouth.

Then she runs right out the door, her pink fairy princess dress flapping behind her.

"Well." Jordan sounds amused. "I always knew she wasn't the meek little thing she pretended to be."

Ella and I don't respond. I stare at the doorway Abby just barreled through, a weird lump of pity forming in my throat.

"Should we go after her?" Ella finally asks, but she doesn't sound like she wants to.

"No," Jordan answers for me, her tone haughty and her

head held high. She possessively clutches my arm and yanks me away from Ella. "Come on, Reed. I want to dance. It'll be good practice for when we're crowned king and queen."

I'm still too stunned by Abby's outburst to protest, so I just led Jordan lead me away.

CHAPTER 32

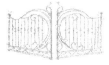

REED

"So. That was...intense," Ella murmurs when we walk into my bedroom a couple of hours later.

I stare at her. Intense? Talk about an understatement.

This entire night was a disaster, starting with the photos Jordan and her parents made me pose for and ending with Abby falling apart in front of a room full of people. I almost fell over in relief when Jordan didn't press me about taking her to the after party. I guess the stupid Snowflake Queen tiara was enough to satisfy her, and luckily I didn't even have to participate in the nausea-inducing king and queen waltz, because Wade beat me out for the king title. The only highlight of the night was watching Wade grope Jordan's ass during their big dance, while she kept hissing for him to stop.

Ella and I were able to escape by ten o'clock, and since Steve's not picking her up until eleven, we have an entire hour of alone time. But we're both a little shell-shocked as we sit side by side on the edge of my bed.

"I feel really fucking bad for her," I admit.

"Abby?"

I nod.

"Well, you shouldn't," Ella says bluntly. "I hate to say this, but I think Abby might be a tad delusional."

I sigh. "A tad?"

"Okay, a lot delusional." Ella squeezes my hand. "But it's not your fault. You broke up with her. You haven't led her on since. She's the one who isn't able to move on."

"I know." But I still can't erase the image of Abby's grief-stricken eyes from my mind.

I've run through these last few years with little regard for anyone but myself. I was proud of being an unfeeling asshole. Is this karma? Is me going to prison for five years punishment for the guys I've beaten, the girls I've hurt?

I've tried to act like nothing's wrong. I've gone to classes, played football, went to Winter Formal. I've acted as if every day is an ordinary day in the life of a high school senior. But I can't pretend anymore that everything is okay. Abby's not okay. Brooke's murder is not okay. My life isn't okay.

Every night, I lie awake staring at the ceiling, wondering how I'll survive inside a prison cell. It's the wait that's the hardest.

"Reed? What's wrong?"

I take a breath as I meet Ella's worried eyes. No amount of sweet words is going to take the sting away, so I speak abruptly, like pulling off a Band-Aid. "I'm going to sign the plea deal early."

She whips around so fast, she loses her balance. I reach out and steady her, but she jerks out of my grip and shoots to her feet.

"What'd you say?"

"I'm going to sign it early. Agree to start serving the sentence starting next week instead of the first of January." I swallow. "It's the right thing to do."

"What the hell, Reed?"

I rake a hand through my hair. "The sooner I go in, the sooner I'm out."

"This is bullshit. We can solve this. Dinah paid off Ruby Myers, so that means there's new evidence—"

"There's no new evidence," I interrupt.

It kills me that she's holding on to this dream that something's going to magically appear to get me off. Her inability to accept me going to prison or to understand why I want this sentence over with tells me all I need to know.

I can't keep asking her to wait for me for five years. I'm a selfish jerk for even entertaining that idea. She'll miss out on everything. What kind of senior year will she have with everyone believing her boyfriend is a murderer? What about college? I may be an asshole, but I'm not this big of one. Not to her, at least.

I brick up my heart, the useless, shitty thing, and stare down at my feet because I can't look into her pale, beautiful face while I say the rest of the words that are galloping around my head.

"We should take a break. I'll be inside and you'll be out here."

The bedroom grows so quiet, I can't help glancing in her direction. She's frozen in place, a hand to her mouth, her eyes as wide as platters.

"I want you to enjoy your time at college. It's supposed to be the best time of your life." The words taste bitter, but I push them out. "If you meet someone, you shouldn't be thinking of me."

I stop then, because I can't get the rest of the lies out. The ones where I'm supposed to say that I won't be thinking of her. That she was just a convenience. That I don't love her.

If I say those things, it'll truly be over. There'd be no coming back from it. No way she'd forgive me.

Be a man, I tell myself. *Let her go.*

I take another deep breath and gather up some more courage. But before I can open my mouth, Ella flies into my lap and mashes her lips against mine. It's not so much a kiss as it is a slap across my face. A scolding for everything I just said and every awful thing that sits in my throat.

And while I know I shouldn't, my arms close around her waist and I hold her, letting her kiss me.

The tears fall, sliding between our lips. I swallow her tears, my words, our despair, and kiss her back until she's crying too hard to keep kissing me. I press her face against my chest and feel the tears soak my shirt.

"I don't want to hear that crap from you," she whispers.

"All I'm saying is that you shouldn't feel guilty about moving forward with your life," I say gruffly.

She stabs her finger into my chest. "You don't get to tell me how I feel. No one does. Not you. Not Steve. Not Callum."

"I know. I'm just saying..." Hell, I don't know what I'm saying. I don't want her to date anyone else. I don't want her to move on. I want her thinking about me the entire time I'm thinking about her.

But I also hate the idea of her being alone, wanting me and not being able to have me, all because I did something stupid.

"I'm trying to be a better person," I finally say. "I'm trying to do right by you."

"You decided what was right for yourself without asking me," she says flatly.

I struggle to find the words to explain my position, but then her hands tangle with my belt buckle and all my good intentions fly out of my head.

"E-Ella…" I stammer. "Don't."

"Don't what?" she taunts. Her hands deftly unzip my tuxedo trousers, sliding inside to hold me in her palm. "Don't touch you?"

"No." This time I'm the one backing away. My body throbs with need, but I'm not going to put my own selfish desires ahead of hers.

"Too bad. I'm touching you." She grabs my wrist and holds it against her stomach. "And you're touching me. Do you really want someone else to touch me like this? Are you really going to be okay with that?"

The images her words conjure in my head are terrible. The hand I have planted on her ass curls into a fist. "Don't," I choke out. "Don't say that to me."

"Why? You said it to me. I would never, ever be okay with you 'moving on' to another girl. That kind of betrayal would ruin us. Not you going away for five years. Not a raft full of Daniels or Jordans or Abbys or Brookes. You moving on, even for a day, for an hour, is what I'd hate."

"I'm trying to do right by you," I repeat. Dammit, every waking thought I have is about her these days.

"Right by me is not rejecting me. Right by me is not dictating how I'm supposed to feel. I love you, Reed. I don't need to be told that I'm too young to know my own feelings. Maybe there is someone else out there that I might love, but I don't care about that person. I love you. I want to be with *you*.

I want to wait for *you*. What do you want?"

Her fierce declaration makes it impossible for me to stick to my guns. My own declaration bursts out of my mouth before I can stop it.

"You. Us. Forever."

"Then don't push me away. Don't tell me how to feel, what to think, who to love. If you're really taking this plea deal, then you can't be too embarrassed to see me. You can't stop writing me. You can't turn away from my visits. This is our countdown. This is our wait. Every day brings us closer together. We either do this together or not at all." Her blue eyes flash like molten sapphires. "So what'll it be?"

Man up, is what she's really telling me. Man up and act like a member of our team. The Ella and Reed team.

I grab her chin with my free hand and kiss her hard. "I'm all in, baby."

Then I rip her expensive dress off her body and show her exactly how *in* I'm going to be. For the rest of our freaking lives.

CHAPTER 33

ELLA

ON SATURDAY MORNING, STEVE ANNOUNCES that we're moving back to the penthouse. Today.

"Today?" I echo dumbly, setting down my glass of orange juice.

He leans his elbows on the kitchen counter and beams at me. "Well, tonight, actually. Isn't this great news? Now we won't be stuck in these five rooms anymore."

Truthfully, the idea of leaving does sound enticing. Living in this hotel has grown old, which is something I would've never said a year ago, but Steve's right—we do need more space from each other. Steve and Dinah have started to fight constantly. While I might've had a trace of sympathy for her at the beginning, I'm sick at the sight of her. Not only did she pay off Ruby Myers, but I know she's involved in Brooke's death somehow. I just can't prove it, damn it.

Reed told Callum about my suspicions, but so far Callum's army of investigators have come up with nothing. They need to find it *soon*, because if Reed has his way, he'll be signing that plea deal on Monday morning and going to prison the moment the ink is dry.

Maybe the penthouse holds some clue.

Steve tilts his head. "What do you say? Are you ready to move out?"

He gives me a hopeful, puppy smile that reminds me so much of Easton. Steve's not all bad. He tries hard, I guess. I can't help but smile back. "Yeah. That works."

"Good. Why don't you go pack a suitcase with your necessities? The hotel will send the rest of the stuff over. Dinah's called to get the place cleaned before we arrive."

I'm about to answer when my phone buzzes. Reed's calling, and I discreetly cover the screen with my hand so Steve can't see the display. "It's Val," I lie. "I bet she wants to know how Winter Formal went."

"Oh, that's nice," Steve says absently.

"I'll talk to her upstairs so I don't bother you," I say before darting out of the suite's kitchen.

He nods, off in his own head to another topic. Steve's biggest flaw is that if the conversation doesn't involve him, he quickly loses interest.

Once I'm alone in my room, I answer Reed's call before it goes to voicemail. "Hey," I say softly.

"Hey." He pauses. "I spoke to Dad about the waitress. Figured I should let you know."

"The waitress—oh," I say, realizing he means Ruby Myers. My pulse instantly speeds up. "What did he say? Do we have proof that someone paid her off?"

"She took out a loan," he says flatly. "Her mom died unexpectedly and had a small life insurance policy. Myers used that to put a down payment on the car. No signs of any wrongdoing there."

I swallow a frustrated scream. "That can't be true. Dinah all but admitted she paid Myers off."

"Then she did it in a sneaky way, because I've got a copy of the loan papers."

"God, I know Dinah's involved in this." Panic ripples through me. Why aren't these investigators making any progress? There *has* to be something that doesn't point in Reed's direction.

"Even if she did, Dinah's plane didn't land until hours after Brooke's time of death."

Tears fill my eyes and tighten my throat. I slap a hand over my mouth, but a muffled sob filters through.

"I have to go," I manage to say, my voice only wobbling a little. "Steve wants me to pack so we can be back in the penthouse tonight."

"All right. I love you, baby. Call me when you get settled."

"I will. I love you, too."

I hang up quickly and then bury my face into my pillow. I close my eyes and let the tears flow, just for a minute, maybe two. Then I tell myself to stop feeling sorry for myself and get up to start packing.

Brooke died in that penthouse. There *has* to be some kind of clue there.

And I intend to find it.

HOURS LATER, STEVE HUSTLES ME into the lobby of the swanky high rise. Dinah's already inside waiting for the elevator. She barely said a word on the ride over. Is she nervous about revisiting the scene of her crime? From the corner of my eye, I watch her avidly for any signs of guilt.

"I'm going to put you in the guest room," Steve babbles as the three of us step into the elevator. "We'll have it redecorated, of course."

I frown. "Isn't that where…" I lower my voice, even though we're in a cramped space and Dinah can hear every word, "Brooke was staying before she, ah, died?"

Steve frowns back. "Was she?" He turns to Dinah.

She nods stiffly and answers in an even stiffer voice. "She sold her apartment after Callum proposed, so she was staying at the penthouse until after their wedding."

"Oh. I see. I didn't realize that." Steve looks back at me. "Are you all right staying in that room, Ella? Like I said, we'll have it redecorated."

"Yeah. It's fine." Morbid as hell, but it's not like Brooke died in that room.

Nope, she died right *there*, I think as we enter the posh living room. My gaze instantly lands on the fireplace mantle, and a shiver runs up my spine. Steve and Dinah are both looking in that direction, too.

Steve is the first one to turn away. He wrinkles his nose and says, "It stinks in here."

I inhale deeply and realize he's right. The air *is* kind of stale. The apartment smells like a weird mix of ammonia and old socks.

"Why don't you open the windows?" Steve suggests to

Dinah. "I'll crank up the heat and light a fire."

Dinah is still staring at the fireplace. Then she makes a distressed sound and runs down the hall. A door opens and then slams shut. I stare after her. Is that guilt? Crap, how do I know what guilt looks like? If I killed someone, I'd run to my bedroom, too, right?

Steve sighs. "Ella, can you get the windows?"

Glad for something to do that takes my attention away from the crime scene, I nod and quickly move to the windows. Another shiver overtakes me when I pass the fireplace. God, it's creepy here. I have a feeling I won't be getting a wink of sleep tonight.

Steve calls in a delivery order, and it arrives about fifteen minutes later, filling the apartment with a spicy aroma that might have smelled good if my stomach wasn't churning from anxiety. Dinah doesn't come out of the bedroom, refusing to answer Steve's summons for dinner.

"We need to talk about Dinah," Steve says over a plate of steaming noodles. "You're probably wondering why I haven't divorced her yet."

"It's none of my business." I push a green pepper around my plate, watching it make tracks through the soy sauce. I haven't given the marriage much thought. I'm too obsessed with Reed's impending imprisonment.

"I'm arranging things," he admits. "And everything needs to be in order before I start the paperwork."

"It's really none of my business," I repeat more forcefully. I don't care what Steve does with Dinah.

"Are you going to be okay living here? You look…"

"Creeped out?" I supply.

He smiles slightly. "Yes, that's as good of a word as any."

"I'm sure I'll get over it," I lie.

"Maybe we'll find something else. You and me."

I'll be gone to college in a year, but I reply with, "Sure," because I don't want to see Steve's disappointment. Right now, I can't handle anyone's emotions but my own.

"I was thinking that you could take a bridge year and not go to college after you're done with school. Or maybe we could hire a tutor and go abroad."

"What?" I say in shock.

"Yes," he says, sounding increasingly enthusiastic. "I enjoy traveling, and since Dinah and I will be divorced, it'd be great if you and I went on a few trips together."

I stare at him in disbelief.

He flushes slightly. "Well, think about it, at least."

I clamp my lips tight around my fork so I don't say something hurtful. Or worse, stab him with my fork for such a ridiculous idea. I'm not leaving the state of North Carolina until Reed can.

After dinner, I excuse myself. Steve shows me to the guest room down the hall from the dining area. It's nice enough—all cream and golds. The design and setup isn't much different than the hotel room we left. I have my own bathroom, which is nice.

The only downside is that a dead woman once slept in this bed.

Pushing aside the thought, I unpack my school uniforms, a few T-shirts, and jeans. My shoes and jacket go in the closet. Next to the bed, behind the nightstand, I find an outlet for my phone charger. I plug in my phone and then lie down on the bed and stare at the ceiling.

Tomorrow I'll look for Gideon's stuff. I doubt it's in this room, though. Dinah wouldn't let the blackmail evidence far from her sight.

But…maybe if Brooke was sleeping on it, it would be just as safe?

I hop off the bed and look under the frame. The hardwood floor is clean, and none of the boards seem to be loose, which would be a telltale sign that something might be hidden underneath them.

How about between the mattress? It takes a few pushes to get the mattress on its side, but there's nothing underneath it but the box spring. I let it drop down with a thump.

I do a quick search of the nightstand, where I find a remote, four cough lozenges, a bottle of lotion, and a spare set of batteries. The dresser has extra blankets in the bottom, extra pillows in the middle drawer, and nothing in the top one.

The closet is empty. Dinah or the cops must've had Brooke's clothes taken away.

I run a hand along the wall and stop to inspect the bland abstract painting hanging over a thin console table across from the bed. There's no secret safe behind the painting. Frustrated, I collapse on the bed. There's nothing in this room but normal items. If no one had told me that Brooke slept in here, I would've never known about it.

With nothing to search for, my thoughts drift back to Reed. The large room suddenly feels oppressive, as if a heavy fog settled into the space.

Things are going to be okay, I tell myself. Five years is nothing. I'd wait twice that to have Reed back. We'll be able to write letters to each other, maybe even talk on the phone. I'll visit him as much as he lets me. And I do believe he can control his temper, if he wants. He has a huge incentive—good behavior equals less jail time.

There's a silver lining in every cloud, Mom always said. Granted, she said that mostly when we were leaving to go to some new place, but I believed it then. Even when she died, I felt like I'd survive. And I did.

Reed's not dying, even though it feels like I'm losing someone yet again. He's just…going on an extended vacation. It'd be like if he went to college in California and I was here. We'd have a long-distance relationship. Phone calls, texts, emails, letters. It's pretty much the same thing, right?

Feeling marginally better, I get up and reach for the phone. Except I forget I didn't put my suitcase away, and end up tripping over it. With a squeaky cry, I fall into the console table. The lamp on top of it teeters. I grab for it, but I'm too far away and the damn thing crashes to the ground.

"Everything okay in there?" Steve asks from the hall, sounding concerned.

"Yeah." I look at the shattered remains of the lamp. "Well, no." Sighing, I walk over to open the door. "I tripped over my suitcase and broke your lamp," I confess.

"Don't worry about it. We're redecorating, remember?" He holds up a finger. "Don't move. I'll get a broom."

"'Kay."

I bend down and start chucking the big pieces in a nearby trashcan. Something white pokes out from underneath one shard. Confusion wrinkling my forehead, I ease the paper out. From the way it's hastily folded and tucked against that one piece, I realize someone deliberately slid it inside the white porcelain base. Maybe it's the instructions for the lamp? Yeah, probably.

My hand is halfway to the trash bin when the word *Maria* catches my eye.

Curious, I unfold the paper and start to read.

Then I gasp.

"What've you got there?"

My head swivels to the door, where Steve is standing with a broom in his hand. I want to lie and say "Nothing," but I can't get my vocal cords to cooperate. I can't hide the paper, either, because every muscle in my body is frozen.

Looking concerned again, Steve leans the broom against the doorframe and marches over.

"Ella," he orders. "Talk to me."

I look at him with wide, frightened eyes. Then I hold up the paper and whisper, "What the hell is this?"

CHAPTER 34

ELLA

The paper crackles as I hold it between my trembling fingers. My mind is spinning with the few paragraphs I read—and I'm not even finished reading.

Before I can blink, Steve snatches the letter from my hand. As he scans the first few lines, his face drains of all color. "Where did you get this?" he chokes out.

My mouth is so dry with shock and horror that it hurts to talk. "It was hidden in the lamp." I continue to stare at him. "Why did you hide it? Why didn't you destroy it?"

His skin is as pale as mine probably is. "I…I didn't hide it. It was in the safe. It…" He curses suddenly. "That goddamned sneaky bitch."

My hands won't stop shaking. "Who?"

"My wife." He swears again, bitterness darkening his eyes. "My lawyers would have given Dinah the codes to the safe after my death." His fingers tighten, crumpling up the paper. "She must have seen this and—no, it would've had to be Brooke." He looks around the room, visibly shaken up. "She stayed here.

She was the one who hid it. She must've stolen it from Dinah."

"I don't care who hid the letter!" I shout. "All I care about is whether or not it's true!" My breathing goes unsteady. "Is it true?"

"No." He pauses. "Yes."

Hysterical laughter spills out of my mouth. "Well, which is it? Yes or no?"

"Yes." His Adam's apple bobs as he gulps. "It's true."

Disgust and anger shoot through me. Oh my God. I can't even believe what I'm hearing. This letter changes *everything* I knew about Steve, Callum, the Royals. If it really is true, Dinah had every right to be furious with Maria. To hate her, even.

"Let me read the rest of it," I order.

Steve takes a step back, but I grab the paper from his hand before he can move it out of my reach. The corner tears off and remains between Steve's limp fingers.

"Ella," he starts weakly.

But I'm too busy reading.

> *Dear Steve,*
>
> *I can't live with these lies any longer. They're tearing me apart. Each look from Callum weighs on my heart. This isn't the life I imagined for myself and not one that I can continue to pursue.*
>
> *My sons are the light of my life, but even they don't shine bright enough to erase the darkness in my soul. The stains of our actions will always be there. I don't know what to do.*
>
> *If I confess, our families will be torn apart. Callum will leave me; your friendship will be*

severed.

If I keep quiet, I will not live. I swear to you. I can't go on.

Why did you take advantage of me? You knew my weakness! You knew and exploited it.

I no longer believe that Callum has been unfaithful, or even if he has, I must learn to live with it. We can't continue like this, Steve, hiding the truth from Callum.

I need to tell him. I have to. Otherwise I won't be able to live with myself.

But while I can't live without Callum, I don't know that I can bear to be without you, either. You do things to me, bring me alive in ways I didn't think were possible. Every night when I close my eyes, I see your face, feel your touch.

When that other woman is near, I burn with anger. Why would you marry her? She's beneath you. Knowing that you go from me to her disgusts me. You ask me to leave Callum, but I don't trust you, either, Steve. I don't believe you. I don't believe in anyone any longer.

There's no choice for me. All of them have been taken from me. Don't try to stop me.

Maria

Once I'm finished, I let the letter drop to the carpet at my feet. This is so...*crazy.* How could Steve do that to Callum? How could Maria?

"I need to tell Reed," I blurt out.

Steve lunges forward before I can get my phone off the nightstand. "No," he begs. "You can't tell him. You'll tear them up. Those boys worship their mother."

"So did you, apparently," I say bitterly. "How could you *do* that? How could you!"

"Ella—"

Fear and hope and despair swirl around me, sucking all the air out of the room and making it hard to breathe or think. "You slept with Callum's wife," I accuse.

Steve's jaw clenches for a moment, his face haggard, and then he nods abruptly. He can't even bring himself to say it out loud.

"Why?"

"I always loved her," he admits in a hoarse voice. "And, in her way, she loved me."

"That's not what this letter says."

"She did," he insists. "We saw her at the same time, but Callum got to her first."

I just gape at him. Oh my God. He sounds like a little boy whose toy was taken away.

"So when Callum was busy saving your company, you told Maria he was cheating on her?" My thoughts are jumbled and crazy, one leaping after the other, but I think I'm starting to piece it all together. "That's how you got her into bed?"

His eyes shift away to stare somewhere over my shoulder.

"Was Callum actually cheating?" I demand. "Was that true?"

When he can't look me in the eye, I know it's not. The fragile relationship we were building crashes to the ground. I can't respect him. I barely like him right now. He slept with his best friend's wife. Worse, he told Maria that her husband betrayed her. And she'd killed herself! Steve O'Halloran pretty much drove that poor, messed-up woman to suicide.

I suddenly feel like throwing up.

Bending down, I pick up the letter and clutch it tight. "We're taking this to Callum. He thinks his wife killed herself because of him. The boys believe the same thing. You need to tell them all the truth."

Anger flickers in Steve's eyes. "No," he snaps. "This stays between us. I told you before, it would ruin those boys' lives."

"You think they aren't already dead inside because their mother killed herself? The only person this letter will ruin is *you*. And frankly, Steve, I don't care if it does. The Royals need to know the truth!"

With that, I grab my phone and barrel past him, practically hurling myself out the door.

"Don't you fucking walk away from me!"

His enraged voice brings a jolt of fear. I start to run, making it all the way to the living room before I'm suddenly yanked backwards. The momentum sends me flying butt-first onto the carpet, inches away from the fireplace where Brooke died—

And suddenly I'm struck with the most horrible thought.

"Was it you?" I blurt out.

Steve doesn't answer me. He just looms over me, breathing hard, his features creased with frustration.

"Did you kill Brooke?" My voice is weak now, shaky from horror.

"No," he growls. "I didn't."

But I see it—the flicker of guilt in his eyes.

"Oh my God," I whisper. "You did. You killed her and then tried to pin it on Reed. You *murdered* her—"

"It was an accident!" he roars.

The deafening volume has me flinching. I stumble to my feet, trying to put as much distance between us as I can, but Steve steps forward, and all I can do is back up, until my spine is flat against the fireplace.

"It was a goddamn accident, okay!" My father's eyes are wild now, red and narrowed and terrifying.

"H-how?" I stammer. "Why?"

"I just got off a damned plane after months of being trapped on some godforsaken island!" He's screaming now. "And I get home to see goddamn Reed leaving the penthouse! What the hell else was I supposed to think? I already knew that my wife was screwing Callum's eldest." His breathing is shallow. "And then Reed? You think I was going to take that lying down? After everything I'd just gone through?"

"Reed never touched Dinah," I croak.

"I didn't know that!" Each breath that leaves his mouth is sharp and laced with panic. "I took the service elevator up to the penthouse. I was going to confront my cheating bitch of a wife. The wife who fucking tried to *kill* me."

His fury is polluting the air, intensifying the fear pounding through my blood. I try to creep to the side, but he moves forward again. I'm trapped between his angry, shaking body and the hard stone of the fireplace.

"I walked in and she was *here*—looking at this damned picture of us!"

He snatches a framed photograph off the mantle and whips it into the wall over my head. Shards of glass rain down on us, a few pieces catching in my hair.

My heart pounds so fast I'm scared it will give out on me. I have to get out of here. I *need* to. Steve is confessing to *murder*. He's unraveling right in front of me.

I can't be here when he loses it completely.

"And I got angry, like any normal red-blooded man. Like your precious Reed. I grabbed her by the hair and slammed her forehead against the mantle. I'd never hit a woman before in my life, but goddamn, Ella, that woman needed hitting. She needed to pay for what she'd done to me."

"But it wasn't Dinah," I whisper.

Shame swamps his face, cutting through some of the anger. "I didn't know that. I thought it was. They look the same from behind, damn it. They…" He seems to be struggling for air. "I saw her face as she fell forward, but it was too late. I couldn't catch her. She hit her head on the mantle." He pants in dismay. "Severed her damned spinal cord!"

"I…" I gulp hard. "O-okay. Then it was an accident and you need to tell the police exactly what hap—"

"We're not involving the police!" he booms, then raises one hand as if he's going to hit me.

I brace myself, but the blow never comes. Instead, Steve's big palm falls to his side.

"Don't look at me like that," he orders. "I'm not going to hurt you! You're my daughter."

And Dinah is his wife, but he was still going to hurt *her*. My pulse careens again. I can't be here. I *can't*.

"You have to tell the truth," I plead with my father. "If you don't, Reed will go to jail."

"You think I don't know that? I've been racking my brain for weeks trying to figure out how to get him out of this. I might not want him screwing my kid, but I don't want to see that boy go to prison."

Then why haven't you saved him? I want to scream. But I already know the answer to that. No matter what he tries to say now, Steve was absolutely going to let Reed take the fall for Brooke's death. Because Steve O'Halloran only cares about himself. That's all he's ever cared about.

"You and me," he suddenly says, his eyes taking on an animated light. "We'll figure this out together. Please, Ella, let's just sit down and talk it through and see how we can save Reed. Maybe we can pin it on Dinah—"

"Like hell you will."

Steve spins around at the sound of Dinah's voice. Me, I've never been happier to see Dinah in my entire life. Steve's distraction is just the opportunity I need to dart away from the fireplace. I race toward the blonde as if my life depends on it. Because maybe it does.

"You killed Brooke?" Dinah spits out, her horrified gaze glued to her husband.

Her hand shakes. I see a glint of black, and that's when I realize what she's holding.

A small, black revolver.

"Put the gun down," Steve tells her, sounding annoyed.

"You killed Brooke," she repeats, and this time it's not a question.

I plaster myself to Dinah's side, but she surprises me by addressing me in a gentle voice. "Stand behind me, Ella."

"Put the gun down!" Steve orders again.

He lunges forward, but Dinah swings the gun up. "Don't take another step."

He stops in his tracks. "Put the gun down," he says for the

third time. His voice is soft now, measured.

"Ella, call nine-one-one," Dinah tells me without taking her eyes off Steve.

I'm too scared to move. I'm terrified that the gun might go off by accident, and I'll get caught in the crossfire.

"For God's sake, Dinah! You two are being ridiculous! Brooke's death was an accident! And even if it wasn't, who the hell cares! She was poison! She was a piece of garbage!"

He lunges toward us again.

And Dinah pulls the trigger.

It all happens so fast I can't even make sense of it. One second Steve is on his feet, the next he's on the carpet, groaning in agony as he clutches his left arm.

My ears are ringing like an entire row of carnival games. I've never heard a gunshot in real life before, and it's so deafening I'm worried it might've shattered my eardrums. I feel sick. Really sick, like I'm going to vomit all over my feet. And my heart is racing faster than it ever has before.

"You shot me, you bitch," Steve mumbles, staring up at Dinah.

Rather than acknowledge him, Dinah calmly turns to me and repeats her earlier request. "Ella. Call nine-one-one."

CHAPTER 35

REED

"What's wrong?" are the first words out of my mouth when I answer the phone.

"You need to come to the penthouse!" Ella gasps between deep, heaving breaths. "Come now. Bring Callum. Bring everyone. But especially Callum."

"Ella—"

The line goes dead.

Dammit. She hung up on me. I don't waste another second, though. She called and needs me. She needs all of us.

I'm off the bed and out the door in the next second. With my fist pounding on Easton's door and then Sebastian's, I scream downstairs for Dad.

"Dad! Something's wrong with Ella." I press redial, but she doesn't pick up.

"What's going on?" Easton bursts out of his room as I'm racing by.

"It's Ella. Something's wrong." Leaping five steps at a time, I fly down the stairs. Above and behind me, I hear the slamming of doors followed by running footsteps.

Dad meets me at the bottom of the stairs. "What is it?" he asks in concern.

"Ella's in trouble. She needs us."

"Us?" Confusion flickers across his face.

I shake my phone at him. "She just called. Told me she needs all of us to come over now."

His eyes widen, but he, too, jumps into motion. "We'll take my car. Let's go."

We run outside and pile into Dad's Mercedes. I take shotgun while the twins and East settle into the back. Dad presses the gas pedal to the floor and tears down the driveway, barely waiting for the gates to open wide enough for the car to speed through. Meanwhile, I'm redialing and redialing Ella's phone.

After my fifth attempt, she finally answers. "I can't talk, Reed. The police are here. Where are you?"

I tense. "The police?"

"Who's that?" Dad demands from the driver's seat.

"It's Ella," I tell him. To Ella, I ask, "Why are the police there?"

Her voice is strained. "I'll explain it all when you get here."

She disconnects again.

"Goddammit!" I slap my phone against my leg. I'm getting real tired of her hanging up on me.

East leans forward, sticking his head between the two front seats. "What did she say?"

Dad runs a red light, takes a hard right at about fifty miles an hour, and then careens wildly down another street. I brace myself against the door as I check the time. We're about ten minutes from the city. I quickly text Ella.

Be there in 10.

"What did she say?" East repeats in my ear.

I toss my phone into the center console and turn to look at my brothers. The twins are pale and quiet, but East is frantic. "She said that we needed to get to the penthouse—all of us…" I pause and turn to my father. "She said specifically to bring Dad."

"Why in the hell did she ask for me?" he wonders, not taking his eyes off the road.

Another hard turn has all of us sliding to the left before righting ourselves in our seats. "I have no idea."

"Steve," East pipes up. "Has to be about him."

Dad's jaw hardens. "Call Grier. Have him meet us at the penthouse."

Not a bad idea. I dial our lawyer, who, unlike Ella, actually answers his phone. "Reed, what can I do for you?"

"You need to meet us at Steve's place," I instruct.

There's a half beat of silence and then, "What in the world have you done?"

I pull the phone away from my ear to stare at the mouthpiece in disbelief. "This fucking guy thinks I did something."

Dad makes a frustrated noise in the back of his throat. "You've pled guilty to involuntary manslaughter. Of course he thinks you did something."

I frown, but place the phone against my ear again. "It's Ella. Something's happened and Dad thinks you should get over there." Then I hang up on him, because we've arrived at the condo complex and there are police cars everywhere.

Dad gapes at all the cruisers. "What in the hell?"

Heart in my throat, I jump out before the car stops.

"Reed, get back here!" my father yells. "Wait a damn second."

But more car doors slamming indicate my brothers are hot on my heels. The people in the lobby are a blur as I race toward the elevator bank. Miraculously, the brass doors are sliding open as I skid to a stop.

Impatiently, I wait for the two uniforms to step out and then I dive inside. My brothers jump into the car as the doors are closing.

"She's okay, man," East reassures me, slightly out of breath.

"Really?" I stare at him. "It's ten thirty. There are a dozen police cars out front. Ella called in a panic, saying she needed all of us here."

"She called, though," he points out.

The world's fucked up when East is the calm one, while my heart is beating so hard it feels like it'll leap out of my chest. I shove a hand through my hair and glare at the lights, willing the elevator to move faster.

"What do you think is going on?" Sawyer asks in a subdued voice.

"Probably Dinah," his twin guesses.

I slam my fist against the doors. That's my fear, too.

"You do that again and we might be stuck in here," East warns.

"Right. Then I guess I'll have to punch you in the face."

"Then Ella'll get mad at you. She loves my pretty face." He pats the side of his cheek.

The twins muffle nervous laughs. I ball my hands into fists and think about punching all three of them. Fortunately for them, the elevator grinds to a halt, and I bolt out.

There are two police officers in the short hallway leading to the double-door entrance of the penthouse. The tall, thin one places a hand on the door, while the female's hand moves to the top of her gun.

"Where are you going?" one of them demands.

"We live here," I lie.

The two officers look at each other. Behind me, I can feel all three of my brothers tense up. I don't care if I punch these two cops out. I'm already going to prison. I charge forward, but just as I close the distance, a familiar face appears in the door.

Detective Schmidt takes in the scene with one sweeping glance. Then she pushes the door open. "It's fine. They can come in."

I'm not about to question my sudden good fortune. I hurry inside, past the huge portraits of Dinah and into the living room, calling my girl's name. "Ella!"

I finally spot her, huddled next to Dinah of all people, on a sofa facing the terrace doors.

I rush over and drag her away from the couch. "Are you okay?"

"I'm fine," she assures me. "Where's Callum?"

Why is she so hung up on my dad? I run my hands up and down her arms while I look her over. There doesn't appear to be anything wrong with her. She's pale and cold. Her hair is tangled and crazy, but she doesn't seem to be hurt.

I clutch her to my chest, pushing her face flat against my hammering heart. "You sure you're okay, baby?"

"I'm okay." She hugs me back. Over her head, I stare at Dinah, whose normally immaculate face is tear-stained. Her eyes are red and her hair is messy, too.

"What the hell," Easton says, sounding as confused as I feel. "Did you—did one of you shoot Steve?"

I swing around and realize I'd run past Steve. He's slumped against the base of the fireplace, his back pressed against the stones.

He's in handcuffs.

Ella shudders.

"What the hell is going on?" Dad booms.

The grief lines on Dinah's face smooth out, a calculated gleam entering her eyes. She leans against the low-backed sofa and slides an arm across the top. "Steve attempted to silence Ella when she discovered that he was the one who killed Brooke. I saved her. You can thank me later."

I hear a couple of curses as I stare at Ella. "Is this true?"

She gulps and then nods slowly. "All of it."

There are other important things that Dinah just said, but the only one that sticks out is that Steve tried to kill Ella. That's almost too much for my tired brain to take in.

"Are you hurt?" I repeat, scanning her body again for signs of injury.

"I'm fine. I swear." She squeezes my arm. "Are you? Are you going to be okay?"

Because my mind is spinning, I just nod like an idiot, but the urgency in her voice suddenly registers. The new pieces of information tumble around and over and on top of each other until one by one, they fall into place.

Dinah's tears.

Ella's frantic request that I come—that we all come.

Steve trying to kill Ella.

It finally hits me. "Steve tried to pin Brooke's murder on me?"

At Ella's tiny grimace, I become so angry, I'm nearly blinded. I find myself halfway toward the fireplace before I realize I've even moved.

Dimly, I hear my name being called, but all my attention is focused on the man who helped me learn to ride my first bike, who threw footballs with me and my brothers. Hell, he gave me my first condom.

A medic kneels next to him, checking Steve's blood pressure while Detective Cousins stands to one side.

Ella appears beside me, placing a warning hand on my arm. "Don't," she whispers.

Somehow I find the strength not to lunge at Steve. All I want to do is beat the ever-loving piss out of my godfather, but I close my eyes and find an ounce of self-restraint in the bottom of my churning gut.

"Why?" I spit out in Steve's direction. "Why did you do it?"

My brothers form a wall behind me. Dad comes to stand on my other side. Steve's eyes skip from Seb to Sawyer, linger on Easton, land on me, and then fix on my father.

"It was an accident," Steve croaks.

"What was an accident?" Dad asks, his voice hollowed by pain. "You trying to kill your own daughter? Or trying to pin a murder charge on my son? How long have you been back? Were you screwing Brooke, too?"

Steve shakes his head. "It's not like that, man. She was a disease, though, turning you and Reed against each other."

Dad's arm lashes out, and a lamp crashes into the stone not far from Steve's head. We all flinch. "We were never against each other. A woman would've never come between us."

"Brooke would've. Dinah, too." He sneers at the blonde sitting ten feet away. "All these women we've been with, Callum—they're out to destroy us. Hell, including your wife."

Ella makes a small, distressed sound. Dad and I both look at her, but she quickly averts her eyes.

"What's wrong?" I ask roughly.

She sucks in a breath.

"Ella," Steve pleads from the fireplace. "They don't need to know."

She takes another breath.

"Damn it," Steve curses, then glances wildly at Detective Cousins. "Get me out of here, will you? It was a flesh wound—I don't need any medical attention. Just haul me off to jail. You've already read me my rights, goddammit."

And I know then what Steve is afraid to admit. What Ella must've discovered.

"This is about Mom, isn't it?" I say in a hoarse voice. I don't know if I'm asking Ella or Steve or Dad or the cosmic universe. All I know is that the second I mention my mother, Steve's entire face goes ashen.

Ella clutches my hand, but she's still not looking me in the eye. "Steve and your mom had an affair," she whispers.

Silence crashes over the room. Even Detective Cousins looks startled, and he didn't even fucking know my mother.

"Ella," Steve begs. "Please…"

She ignores him, turning her distraught gaze to my father. "Maria wrote him a letter saying that she couldn't live with the guilt anymore. I found it in the room where Brooke was staying. She tried to hide it." Her sad eyes shift back to me, then toward my brothers. "It wasn't your fault." Her voice catches on the last word.

Dad stumbles backward, catching himself against the edge of a table.

The words Ella just said aren't registering in my brain. They're just hard consonants, soft vowels. They aren't understandable. Sawyer and Seb are rooted to the tiled floor. I'm frozen, too, caught up in the horror of what I'm learning.

Only Easton can move. "You asshole! You asshole!" he screams and rushes at Steve.

Detective Cousins throws himself between the two of them. The twins rush over and drag East backward. Dad rights himself and stalks forward.

Every part of me wants to hurl myself at Steve again. Beat the shit out of him for what he did to me, to my mom, to my family. But Ella's slim hand rests lightly my shoulder, keeping me in check.

I once joked that she held my leash—and it's true. I'm a better person when she's around. More controlled. More worthy. And after all she's gone through tonight, I don't want to add to her pain by pummeling her father.

"How long did this go on?" Dad demands, his angry gaze fixed on his best friend.

Steve swipes a shaky hand across his mouth. "She came on to me."

"How long?" Dad roars.

Cousins radios for help. "I need some backup in here, stat. I've got five Royals and they're out for blood."

Steve's eyes never leave my father. "It was only once. She took advantage of me."

With a choked noise, Dad turns to Ella. "How long?"

"I don't know. There was just this letter." She holds out a crumpled piece of stationary with the lower left corner torn off.

I immediately recognize it. Mom had a set of personalized

paper and envelopes. She said every true lady sent a handwritten thank-you note rather than make a telephone call. And never a text or an email.

Dad snatches the paper from Ella's hand and scans the contents. Then, with what looks like enormous effort, he carefully folds it in half and gives it back to Ella. I nudge her arm and she drops the letter in my hand.

"You deserve to rot in hell," Dad hisses at Steve, his whole body vibrating with suppressed rage. "I stood by you for so long. Stuck up for you whenever anyone questioned your honor, your loyalty." He takes a deep, heaving breath. "I can't stand to look at you."

I only allow myself a quick glance at the letter, and just the sight of my mom's handwriting makes my heart ache. All this time, I thought I'd driven Mom to her death. Easton blamed himself, too. The twins were torn up for months. We fell apart as a family. We hated Dad, hated ourselves. When Ella arrived unannounced, we hated her, too. We treated her like dirt.

East and I left her on the side of the road one night and forced her to walk home. We followed her at a distance, because we're not *total* assholes, but we'd made her believe she was alone.

I don't know, or understand, how she forgave me, how she came to love me.

As I'm lost in my head, Dad shoves past East, sidesteps Cousins, and punches Steve in the jaw so hard that the sound of the impact echoes from one side of the large living room to the other. This time when Steve wipes a hand across his mouth, blood smears across his face.

"Enough. He's in police custody," Detective Cousins snaps.

Dad doesn't look away from Steve. "You bastard. You sleep with my wife, kill a woman, and try to pin it on my son?"

"Dad," I say hoarsely. "He's not worth it."

And he's not. Steve doesn't matter anymore. All that matters is I'm alive. Everyone I care about is alive and unhurt. I'm not going to prison. Ella's coming home with us, where she belongs. We're going to survive this, just like we survived our mother's suicide, our broken family, and our own demons.

I tuck Ella's hand securely in mine and say, "Let's go."

"Where are we going?" she asks.

"Home."

She's silent for a moment. "That's good."

"Yeah," Easton says, coming up on Ella's other side. "Your room's a mess."

"Because you keep watching football in there," she mutters as we lead her away. "I expect you to clean it the moment we get back."

Easton stops at the penthouse door and looks at her incredulously. "I'm Easton Royal. I don't clean shit."

Dad sighs. The twins snicker. Even the cops look like they're trying not to laugh.

I clasp Ella's hand more firmly in mine and walk out with each of my brothers falling in line. Behind us is the tormented and terrible past. In front of us is our unblemished future.

I'm not looking back again.

CHAPTER 36

REED

IT TAKES ALL OF FORTY-EIGHT hours for Halston Grier to get another hearing for me. This time, I'm not even annoyed that Judge Delacorte is assigned to the case. There's something awesomely ironic about the fact that he's going to have to rule on the motion to dismiss all the charges against me after he tried to bribe my father.

"Given your past with this judge, my advice is to look suitably penitent throughout the proceeding," Grier advises as we wait for Delacorte to appear from his chambers. The hearing was supposed to start fifteen minutes ago, but the judge is sulking in the back, trying to delay the inevitable.

Grier's warning is unnecessary. I haven't smiled much since I got the call from Ella on Saturday night.

"All rise, the Honorable Judge Delacorte is presiding."

"Honorable, my ass," East mutters loudly behind me.

Grier is facing forward, but his co-counsel, Sonya Clark, turns to glare at my brother.

Out of the corner of my eye, I see Easton making a zipping

motion across his lips. Ella is beside him, and she's sitting strangely close to Dinah. I guess the two of them formed a weird bond the night that Steve confessed to killing Brooke because he'd mistakenly thought she was Dinah.

I still think Dinah is a snake, but holy shit am I grateful to her. Yes, she blackmailed my brother, but she also saved Ella's life. If she hadn't grabbed that gun out of the safe and come to Ella's aid, things could have ended a lot differently. Thanks to Dinah, Ella is safe and Steve O'Halloran will be behind bars, charged with the crime that everyone thought *I* committed.

Every time I think about it, I want to punch something. That bastard was actually going to let me rot in jail for something I didn't do. I know he's Ella's father, but I'll never be able to forgive him for what he did. I don't think Ella can, either.

Grier tugs on my jacket as a reminder to get to my feet. I stand, as ordered, and then wait for the bailiff to give us the okay to sit down.

With his black robe and gray hair, Judge Delacorte looks the part of an honorable man, but we all know he's nothing but scum of the earth, burying the crimes of his punk-ass, rapist son.

Delacorte takes a seat and begins to leaf through the motion papers from the attorneys. All the while, the entire courtroom is on their feet. What a jackass.

After ten long minutes tick off the clock, the bailiff finally clears his throat. His red face displays his embarrassment. Not his fault his boss is a total dickweed. We all feel bad for him.

The cough gets Judge Delacorte's attention. He raises his head, looks us over, then nods. "You may be seated. Does the State have a motion to make?"

There's a lot of shuffling as people take their seats. The DA remains standing. It's got to be tough to do this—admit that they were wrong about all the evidence and nearly steamrolled an innocent kid into prison. "Yes, we do."

"And what is it?" Delacorte's impatience isn't even thinly disguised. He's irritated he has to be here, even though this is his job.

Stoically, the DA announces, "The DA would move to dismiss the charges."

"Under what grounds?"

It's all laid out in the paperwork in front of Delacorte, but because he hates his life, he's going to try to make everyone else equally unhappy.

"The grounds that new evidence suggests that the wrong individual has been charged. We now have another suspect in custody."

"And this new evidence is the testimony of the girlfriend of the formerly accused and the estranged wife of the newly accused?"

"Yes."

Delacorte huffs on the bench. "And the DA's office deems this credible?" He clearly doesn't want to let me off the hook.

I shoot a semi-worried glance toward Grier, who gives a nearly imperceptible shake of his head. Okay then. If Grier is unflustered, then I'm not getting my boxers in a bunch.

"We do. We have a recording of Mr. O'Halloran confessing to the crime. The statements of the victims are corroborated by the initial physical evidence at the scene, as well as post-incident statements heard by Detective Cousins, Detective Schmidt, and Officer Tomas wherein Mr. O'Halloran admitted that he'd mistaken the identity of the deceased for his wife."

"Are you absolutely certain you have the right person this time? The last time I was here, you swore that Mr. Royal was the perpetrator of this violent crime. In fact, we had a sentencing hearing scheduled due to the fact that *he* was going to plead guilty. Were you wrong then or now?" Delacorte says sarcastically.

The lawyer's cheeks grow red. "We were wrong then," he says, and despite his embarrassment, his voice is firm.

It's so obvious that Judge Delacorte doesn't want to rule in my favor. He wants me to rot. Unfortunately for him, he's going to bed tonight with bitter failure in his mouth.

He picks up his gavel. "Motion sustained," he snaps. "Anything else, counsel?"

"Yes, one more thing." The prosecutor turns and whispers something to his co-counsel.

Grier begins to pack up his things.

"Are we done here?" I ask.

Grier nods. "Yes. Congratulations. You're officially free of all of this."

I take my first full breath since walking into the courthouse. "Thanks." I shake his hand, even though the real person I should be thanking is behind me. Grier, on the other hand, believed I should plead guilty in spite of my innocence.

East reaches over the small railing, but his high-five halts in mid-air at the next words out of the prosecutor's mouth.

"We'd like to bring charges against Steven George O'Halloran."

I suck in a breath as Steve exits a side room, accompanied by a uniformed guard. Steve enters the courtroom and walks to the defense table, but his expressionless gaze doesn't once stray in my direction. Or his daughter's.

"Read them off, counselor," Judge Delacorte says in a bored tone, as if this is an everyday occurrence. I guess it is for him, but it's not for us.

Not for Ella.

I glance over my shoulder to find that her face is a mixture of horror and awful sadness. So I murmur to East, "Get her out of here."

My brother nods, obviously agreeing that Ella doesn't need to hear all these charges read out against her father. "Come on, Ella, let's go. We're done here," he says in a low voice.

But Ella refuses to leave. She grabs Dinah's hand, of all people. And Dinah, the gold-digger, the blackmailer, grips my girl's hand in return. The two of them lean against each other as the prosecutor reads from the indictment.

"Steven George O'Halloran, hereinafter known as defendant, in the county of Bayview and the state of North Carolina, did knowingly commit murder in the second degree which resulted in the death of Brooke Anna Davidson."

"Will the defendant step forward?"

I move out of the way and watch in stupefied amazement as Grier pulls out another file. Holy hell. He wasn't packing up. He was putting my case away and preparing to defend Steve.

Steve buttons his jacket as he approaches the bench. He looks confident and composed, but he still refuses to meet my eyes.

"How do you plead?" Delacorte asks.

"Not guilty," Steve says in a loud, clear voice.

My hand curls into a fist. Not guilty, my ass. I want to end him. I want to drive his face into the wood table until it's a bloody, unrecognizable mess. I want—

A hand clasps my wrist. I look up and stare at Ella's lovely, unhappy face and realize what I was on the verge of doing. Closing my eyes, I lean my forehead against hers. "You ready to go home?"

"I am."

I take her hand and then we leave the courtroom—and Steve—behind us, my family filing out after us. Outside, a few reporters rush at us, but the Royal boys are big and intimidating. We form a protective circle around Ella and keep the vultures away as we exit the courthouse.

Dad meets us by his Mercedes. "You're going to come home with us, Ella."

"For good?" she asks warily.

He smiles. "For good. Grier is filing guardianship papers as we speak." The smile fades quickly, though. "We're using Steve's current legal troubles as grounds for an emergency ruling."

I don't miss the sorrow swimming in my father's eyes. Steve's betrayal hurt all of us, but it hurt Dad the most. Steve is—was—his best friend, but the asshole was willing to let me go to prison for a crime that Steve committed.

And he…

My throat tightens as I remember the other betrayal.

Steve had an affair with my mom.

I want to throw up just thinking about it, and I almost wish none of us had read the letter. But a part of me is glad we did. For so long, I blamed myself for Mom's death, wondering if my fighting and my recklessness was what drove her to suicide. East thought it was his pill addiction that sent her over the edge.

At least now we know the truth. Mom killed herself because of guilt over her affair with Dad's best friend. And she thought Dad was cheating on her, too. Steve had led her to believe that.

Fucking Steve. I hope I never again have to lay eyes on that man in my life.

"Ella!"

The bastard's ears must've been burning because he suddenly appears on the courthouse steps.

"Oh shit," East mutters.

The twins echo his curse with more colorful ones of their own. I entertain the idea of throwing Ella over my shoulder, diving into the car, and speeding away. But I hesitate too long because Steve's already making his way across the parking lot.

Dad takes a menacing step forward, placing himself between Ella and Steve. "You should go," he commands.

"No. I want to talk to my daughter." Steve leans around Dad, pleading with Ella. "Ella, listen to me. I was drugged up the other night. I think Dinah must've put something in my drink. You know I'd never hurt you. And I didn't hurt Brooke, either. You misunderstood everything I said that night."

Pain flickers across her face. "Really? That's the story we're going with?"

"You have to trust me."

"Trust you? Are you kidding me? You killed Brooke and tried to pin it on Reed! I don't know who you are, and I don't want to know."

She wrenches the car door open and climbs inside. The slamming door puts all of us in motion. The twins and Easton get into Sawyer's Rover, while I join Ella in Dad's car.

Dad remains with Steve, but their angry voices are muffled behind the closed windows of the Mercedes. I don't even give a shit what they're saying. I trust Dad to tell Steve to go to hell, where he deserves to burn for eternity.

Ella peers at me with sad eyes as I gently put an arm around her. "You guys were rough on me when I first arrived," she starts.

I wince at this. "I know."

"But you all came around, and I…I had a family for the first time." Tears drip down her face. Her hands are clenched in her lap, white around the knuckles.

I cover them with my palm and feel the warm tears fall on the back of my hand.

"When Steve arrived, I gave him a hard time, but secretly I thought it was kind of cool that he was so excited to be a dad. His rules were ridiculous, but the girls at school said it was normal, and sometimes it made me feel like he really cared."

I swallow around the knot in my throat. Her words are so full of pain, and I don't know how to take it away.

"I thought," she continues between gulps of air, "sometimes I thought that my mom was wrong to haul me around the country, running from one bad relationship to another. I thought maybe it would've been better if I'd grown up with Steve. An O'Halloran, not a Harper."

Oh hell. I haul her into my lap, placing her wet face in my neck.

"I know, baby. I love my mom, but I think bad thoughts about her, too, sometimes. I get that she couldn't live with herself, but she should've *tried*. Because we needed her." I stroke Ella's hair and press a kiss on her temple. "I don't think being angry or resentful that our mothers let us down is disloyal."

Her small body heaves. "I wanted him to love me."

"Oh, baby, something's wrong with Steve. He's not capable of loving anyone but himself. That's his flaw, not yours."

"I know. It just hurts."

The driver's door opens, and Dad climbs in. "Everything okay back there?" he asks quietly.

His eyes meet mine in the rearview mirror. I remain silent, because I know it's a question for Ella.

She shudders and sighs and then lifts her head. "Yeah, I'm a mess, but I'm going to be okay."

She slides off my lap but keeps her head on my shoulder. Dad backs out of the parking lot and starts the drive home.

"I told Val once that you and I are mirrors," Ella whispers to me. "That we fit in some weird way."

I know exactly what she means. The complicated feelings we have for our mothers, for their weakness and frailty, for their hidden strengths and the love they showed us, for the selfishness that affected us...all these things are part of what twisted us up inside, but somehow those tangled strands fused until we were whole again.

Ella makes me whole. I make *her* whole.

I used to be scared of the future. I didn't know where I'd end up, didn't know if the anger and bitterness inside me would ever truly go away, if I could ever feel worthy or find someone who'd be able to see through the asshole I pretend to be to the rest of the world.

But I'm not scared anymore, and I did find someone who sees me. Who really, truly sees me. And I see her, too. Ella Harper is all I'm ever going to see, because she's my future.

She's my steel and my fire and my salvation.
    She's everything.

CHAPTER 37

ELLA

One Week Later

"What's this?" I ask when I get out of the bathroom dressed in my favorite hanging-out clothes—a T-shirt of Reed's and a pair of shorts.

Today's dance team practice ran long, so I told Reed to go on home without me. Once I got back, I made him wait until I showered, even though he claims he doesn't care if I'm sweaty.

Now, I walk into my room and find an assortment of colorful brochures on my bed. Most of them show pictures of teens clutching schoolbooks against their chests.

"Pick one," Reed says. His eyes are fixed on the TV.

As I get closer, I realize they're college brochures—about ten of them. "One what?"

"Pick where we're going to college."

"We?" Curious, I flip one open. *UNC*, the brochure declares, *has been granting degrees since the eighteenth century.*

"Duh." He rolls over on his side, crumpling half the glossy pamphlets under his fit body.

"We're choosing together?" I say in surprise.

"Yup. You said you wanted to dance, so there's a couple here that offer a good arts degree." He rummages through the pile and pulls out a red-and-white brochure. "So UNC-Greensboro offers a dance degree and so does UNC in Charlotte. They're both accredited by the National Association of Schools of Dance."

A familiar heat starts to course through my body. "Did you research all this stuff?"

"Sure did."

I suck in my lower lip so I don't break out in tears. This has to be one of the nicest, most thoughtful things anyone's ever done for me. I don't do a good enough job of hiding my emotions, because Reed vaults over the bed and drags me against him.

His eyes search mine. "Are you upset about this?"

"No. This is so sweet," I blubber.

Smiling, he sits on the edge of the bed and positions me between his legs. He looks half embarrassed, half proud. "I figured it was the least I could do. What were you planning to do before Dad kidnapped you?"

"Ha, so you admit he kidnapped me!"

He grins. "I just said that."

"Fine. I was going to go to community college and get an associates in business. And then take accounting classes for two years and hopefully find a steady job counting numbers all day. I planned to wear a lot of khaki, eat in the cafeteria, and maybe have a dog to come home to."

His smile grows broader. "Well, now you can go to an arts college and live off your trust fund."

"What about your business degree?"

He shrugs. "I can get that anywhere. It's not like Dad's not gonna hire me. He's dying for us to get into the family business. Gid has zero interest. East likes fast cars. The twins are more like—" He breaks off before he says Steve's name. "The twins like the planes and aren't interested in running the business."

I pull out of his embrace and go to the dresser, where I pull out the flier I found on the Astor Park bulletin board tonight—Hailey had pointed it out. I return to Reed and trade his UNC-Greensboro brochure for the flier.

"What's this?" He turns it over.

"It's an amateur boxing circuit. I know you like to hit things, but you probably shouldn't go to the docks anymore. This will let you hit and get hit and it's perfectly legal. I'm not saying you should do it for the rest of your life, but—"

"I like it," Reed declares.

"Yeah?"

"I can do this, go to classes, and come home to you, right?"

I melt against him. "Right." A grin lifts my lips. "Oh, and Val said to tell you to take Wade along. She thinks it'll be good for him to get punched in his pretty face every now and then."

Reed snickers. "I thought they were together now!"

"They are." I laugh as I think about our best friends. They've been an official couple for a week, and already Val is laying down the law. "But she's still making him pay for fooling around with someone else."

He rolls his eyes. "Chicks are nuts."

"We are not." I pinch his side in warning. "Oh, and by the way, I decided I'm going to take dance lessons. It's the one thing Jordan does that I'm really envious of. And I know I'm not going to be as good as her with a year's worth of dance lessons, but I still think it would be cool."

"Dad would love that."

Reed pulls me on top of him, and I rub against his deliciously hard body. Our lips meet, softly and sweetly. His hands creep under the fabric of my shorts to press me tighter against him. We kiss until we're breathless and then I roll away, because if we keep this up, we'll be undressing each other in no time. Dinner's soon, and we've all made a conscious effort to start having meals together as a family.

Plus, Gideon's coming tonight and I have a gift for him.

"How're you doing with the whole…?" Reed trails off. As usual, he doesn't mention Steve in anything other than vague terms.

"I'm good," I assure him. "And you shouldn't be afraid to say Steve's name in front of me. Just don't call him my father, because he's not. He never was."

"No," Reed agrees. "He was never your dad. There's not much of him in you."

"I hope not."

Except, as much as I want to deny it, Steve *is* my dad, and that trust fund Reed referenced earlier? It's all of Steve's money that he signed over to me, with Callum serving as the trustee. I've already reduced that trust by about half, but it was for a good cause.

I think Gideon is going to be very, very happy tonight when he finds out about the deal I made with Dinah. In exchange for half of Steve's money, she burned all the blackmail evidence she had against him and Savannah. I know it's gone for good, because I stood at the fireplace with her while she lit the match and torched the USB drive, the printed photos, and the legal papers which she haughtily informed me would never have been filed.

It was the same fireplace where Brooke and her baby died, but I try not to think about that too much. Brooke is gone. So is Callum's unborn child. Nothing is going to bring them back, though, and all we can do now is put the whole tragic ordeal behind us.

I reach out to hold Reed's hand. "Are *you* okay? Are you feeling better about everything?"

"Yeah," he admits. "I'm definitely relieved that I'm not going to prison, but I'm still pissed at your—at Steve. And I'm angry at my mother, too. But…I'm trying to let it go."

I completely understand. "What about Easton? Does he seem weird to you lately?" Easton has been strangely subdued this past week.

"I don't know. I think he might be all twisted up over a girl."

I flip over on my side. "Seriously?"

The side of Reed's mouth quirks up. "Seriously."

"Wow." I shake my head in astonishment. "Hell's frozen over."

"Yup."

Before I have a chance to grill him more, Callum yells from the foyer. "Dinner's ready."

Reed pulls me to my feet. "C'mon, let's go downstairs. The family's waiting."

I love that word, and I love the boy who's taking my hand and leading me out the door so we can join our family.

My family.

STAY CONNECTED

Sign up for the newsletter to be the first to know when more Erin Watt titles are released! We promise to only send an email when it's really important. Stay connected with us by liking Erin Watt's Facebook page for updates and fun teasers!

LIKE US ON FACEBOOK:
https://www.facebook.com/authorerinwatt

FOLLOW US ON GOODREADS:
https://www.goodreads.com/author/show/14902188.Erin_Watt

ABOUT THE AUTHOR

Erin Watt is the brainchild of two bestselling authors linked together through their love of great books and an addiction to writing. They share one creative imagination. Their greatest love (after their families and pets, of course)? Coming up with fun--and sometimes crazy--ideas. Their greatest fear? Breaking up. You can contact them at their shared inbox: authorerinwatt@gmail.com